THE SAND VINES

THE VINE SAGA

BOOK ONE

MICHÈLE CALLARD

ABOUT THE AUTHOR

Michèle Callard grew up in France. A country girl at heart, she swapped her Paris flat for a cottage in rural England where she lives with her Irish husband and the youngest of her 3 sons. She writes novels set in different regions of France bursting with local colour, flavours and history.

1
1870 – NOIRAC – MIDSUMMER'S NIGHT

Flore had waited five years. Five years without news. Tonight, she would have to make her choice. If she was not married by November, her family would lose their house and she would have to go into service.

The sun was sinking behind the oaks that circled the vast clearing, the *airial,* as it was called here on the Grande Lande de Bordeaux, a large area dotted with sparse low-roofed dwellings. In the balmy June dusk, people ambled in small groups towards the bonfire.

Shadows lengthened on the closely cropped grass, and one by one cicadas stopped chirping. Flore closed her eyes. It was Midsummer's Day in Noirac, the feast of Saint Jean, and tonight, anything could happen.

She threw a flowered shawl over her shoulders, tucked the ends into her belt and, a hand over her eyes, scanned the airial that was her world.

Beyond the two cork trees that marked the road, the purple and russet moor stretched all the way to the ocean, a parched vastitude of heather, grass and sky. In winter, it turned into a marsh that could only be crossed on stilts.

These four-foot-high poles tied to one's legs turned into seven league boots, allowing one to power through the watery mush at the speed of a trotting horse.

In the quiet of the evening, stragglers were arriving from Laforge, their stilts clattering on the main road. Children drove home pigs and geese, their high-pitched calls warbling through muffled laughter and the Spanish notes of the local patois.

Trestles and benches awaited visitors under the shade of an ancient oak, long tables dressed with bowls and cups. Delicious aromas of meat floated out of the cottages, and a giant puppet was enthroned atop a huge pyre in the centre of the common.

'Holy Mary, Mother of God, please let me find a good husband . . . I swore to Mama I would never go into service. Please let me find a good man.' Flore was nailing the cross she had fashioned from straw and flowers above the door of her cottage when a gaggle of geese flew out of the forest in a commotion of flaps and quacks. Flore spun around in alert.

Her little sister waddled towards her, struggling for breath, her lips blue from the strain.

'Kesako?' Flore ran to Nanette and hugged her plump body. 'What happened?'

Nanette's gaze went to the forest. 'Boys say bad things to me.'

Flore darted towards the figures retreating in the bushes and shouted, 'Brave of you, huh? Scaring a child! Remember who's feeding you tonight.'

A gangly youth detached himself from a cork oak. Rags hung off his skeletal frame, blackened by charcoal. He stared at his bare feet and muttered, 'Sorry.'

'She has a bad heart.' Flore's voice quivered with anger. 'What has she done to you?'

The youth hesitated. 'It's the new boys. They've never

seen a . . . a . . .' He turned to his friends for support, but they had all bolted away.

Flore's hackles went up. In spite of her condition, Nanette had reached the age of twelve, but her health was fragile. 'A what . . . exactly? She's an angel in disguise, that's what she is.' She shouted to the woods. 'You hear me out there? If anything happens to my sister, your life won't be worth living!'

She put an arm around Nanette. 'Come, I'll help you with the feed.'

Nanette corralled a stray goose. 'I do it.'

'Don't you want to get ready for the party?'

'Big fire!' Nanette pointed to the pyre.

From a cabin at the edge of the forest, the young basket-maker joined them, an anxious eye on the gander.

'F-Flore, w-will you d-dance with me?'

Flore chased in the gander. 'I will dance with everyone.'

As a free man, the basket-maker was a good catch, but would she marry a man who stuttered and was afraid of geese?

'You will jump over the f-hire with me, won't you?' The blacksmith's son vaulted down from his mule and bowed with a flourish. A horse had kicked away his two front teeth.

'*Bensai*, perhaps I will.'

Flore handed her sister a pan filled with mash and grain. 'Here. When you're finished, go in and ask Tanta to help you with your Sunday dress.'

A boisterous mob had gathered in front of the thatched sheepfold where Colin, her brother, was recounting how he and another shepherd, driving a flock across the moor, had come across Empress Eugenie and her ladies trotting from Biarritz in a horse-drawn buggy. The empress had heard of the local shepherds who walked on four-foot stilts tied to their legs. Curious, she had called them over.

Colin caught sight of Flore and signalled to her with a grin. She lowered herself onto the bench with a languid pose and said in a mock Spanish accent, 'Tell me, *pastorel* . . .' Her mouth turned down, she threw a pebble at Colin's feet. 'Is it true that you can pick up this coin without getting down from your stilts?'

Colin trampled on the spot for effect and planted his long stick firmly on the ground. Amidst banter and jokes, he opened out the stilts, drew his knees together, sank down ever lower and, twisting his body to one side, steadily gripped his way down the stick. With a final grimace, he reached out and grabbed the pebble.

The feat was greeted with a cheer.

His face contorted with the effort, Colin hoisted himself back up and held out his trophy to public applause.

Flore pretended to adjust a crinoline and threw another pebble. Once again, the boys jostled at her feet.

A deep voice rose above the din. A soldier in red trousers and blue tunic flicked a volley of copper coins onto the grass. 'Here are a few coins I earned fighting for the emperor.'

A single thud shook Flore's heart, her pulse stuttered, and she forgot to breathe.

Silence enveloped the airial.

The ground tilted. Flore lifted her eyes to the newcomer silhouetted against the flaming sky.

Against the dying sun, figures converged towards the sheepfold, and a murmur echoed around the old oaks, 'Ricar . . . Ricar is back!'

How he had changed. Five years of army had hardened him. His boots dusty from the road, dark stubble covered hollow cheeks, Ricar looked nothing like the boy who, not yet twenty, had swapped his stilts for a bayonet and taken the train to Paris.

His gaze rested on Flore.

She lowered her face, her chest about to burst. When she looked up again, the mood had changed. Father Martial, the young priest, strode out of the little church, caught sight of the soldier and rushed towards him, arms open in welcome. Ricar said something. Under his broad-brimmed hat, the young priest turned crimson, his hands bunching into fists. He thrust them into his pockets and turned away.

A woman in rags pushed her way through the crowd. 'Ricar! My son!'

Ricar held his mother as she sobbed against him, hoisted his haversack and, supporting the old woman, walked away with a backward glance at Flore.

She sank against the warm wall of the sheepfold, wild horses galloping inside her. Ricar was back. He had returned on Midsummer's Day. Oh yes, she would dance with everyone, but there was only one man with whom she would jump over the fire, and at last, at long last, he was home.

2
SPARKS FLY AROUND THE BONFIRE

'I will come back for you, Perloune.' Flore was just fifteen when Ricar had sealed his promise with a kiss. 'I will go to China and bring you a pearl. You'll see.' Flore leaned against the warm bread oven and glanced over at the cottage.

'I don't think Ricar actually went to *China*,' Old Father Anselme had explained, his eyes twinkling under a bushy brow. 'Our emperor—Louis-Napoléon, nephew of the great Napoléon—has conquered many lands, Flore, but not yet China. The colony Ricar is protecting is called Cochinchina. Its capital is Saigon.'

Saigon . . . a name Flore had repeated every night before falling asleep, hugging her sister's solid body.

Ricar was back. Weeks of tension fell from her shoulders. Life could begin again. A new life, a better life. Drunk with anticipation, Flore took a few steps and stopped, doubt puncturing her excitement. Would Ricar still want her? What could a peasant girl who had never been further than Bordeaux offer a man who had seen the wonders of the world?

'*Ola,* Nanette!' Flore waved her sister over. 'Eh, don't you look lovely.'

'Big fire.' Nanette pointed to the pyre, her round face split with a smile. She had been talking of nothing else for days.

'That's right, big fire. You will dance with Colin.'

'Dancing.' Nanette held out her embroidered apron. With her Sunday dress, white bonnet and round face, Nanette looked like a doll.

Aunt Onorina joined them, exuding a scent of goat milk and bacon.

'We were expecting you in the kitchen, and yet I find you here, lost in dreams as ever. Did you get the herbs I asked for?

'Oh yes.' Flore rummaged into the pocket of her apron and held out a bunch of wild thyme.

He aunt breathed in the thyme. 'So Ricar is back.' She grinned. 'Do you think he is going to ask you?'

Flore rolled her eyes. 'Tanta! He's only just arrived.'

Her aunt nudged her. 'Look at you in your Sunday clothes, Perloune. You're the prettiest girl in Noirac. You heard what Colin said. You look like our empress.'

Although it was well-meant, the compliment was barbed. Eugenie might be beautiful, but she was haughty and profligate.

'*Mila Diou,* Tanta! Ricar's been to China. What would he want with a girl like me?'

'He needs a wife. Your skin is flawless; you can count and read. You're a hard worker, and you sing like a nightingale. Who wouldn't want you?'

The clatter of a horse-drawn landau interrupted them. Around the airial, the chatter died down.

A gentleman in a soft hat stepped down and helped his wife before holding out his hand to a girl with straw-coloured hair. About Flore's age, she wore a pale blue bustle dress with a short cape and a hat tilted over a rather plain face.

'That would be the engineer.' Flore's aunt whispered with a meaningful look. 'Our viscount's new best friend.' Her lips tightened. 'They've come to see what us savages do for fun, I shouldn't wonder.'

The girl in blue held on to her mother's arm, darting curious glances at the youths stamping around on stilts.

To impress the new arrivals, several boys unbound one stilt, hopped around on one foot, tilted forward and—for the young lady's benefit—performed a spectacular forward roll before removing the second stilt once they were on the ground.

Flore joined her brother and his friends, her gaze drawn to the old cork oak that stood by the *métayer*'s house, yellow under the rays of the setting sun. The *métayer*, Monsieur Clopin, was the one who carried out the viscount's orders. The one who had ordered Papa to sell his sheep. All two hundred of them.

She tightened her shawl with a shiver.

Colin slipped his arm through hers. 'What's wrong?'

Flore dragged her gaze away from the accursed tree. 'If the engineer is here, it means they're going ahead with draining the moor. They'll extend the forest over our part of the moor.'

Colin's arm tightened against hers. 'The pines are all they care about now. The precious resin that will make them rich.'

Nanette snuggled between them. 'Flore? You sad?'

Flore wiped a stealthy tear and hugged them both very tight.

'Come on, girls.' Colin headed for the tables. 'It's Midsummer's Night, the corn is growing, and Nanette hasn't lost a single goose to the fox. That's something to celebrate. And more importantly,' he chuckled, 'Flore's beau has returned in one piece.' He took his little sister's hand. 'You're dancing with me, Nanette, *oc?*'

Nanette nodded excitedly. Flore trailed behind them, her heart torn between dread and elation. After so many years, who was the Ricar who had returned?

Reed torches were lit and, elbows on the trestle tables, villagers were lifting tankards of cider, slicing off thick chunks of rye bread, holding out their bowls for soup.

In the distance, Ricar was leaving his mother's cabin, his leg dragging slightly.

Light-headed, Flore slipped behind the large thatched sheepfold and waited for him.

'Flore.' His eyes flickered over her face, lighting a trail of sparks inside her.

They stood facing each other, so close she smelled the soap he had used to shave and something else . . . was it pine resin? In Noirac, men smelled of sheep. Wilting under his gaze, Flore struggled to breathe.

'How you've grown.' He caressed her cheek with his thumb, his chiselled face glowing in the torchlight.

She took his fingers in hers and whispered, 'I waited for you.'

'Good girl.' Ricar drew her to him and brought his lips to hers.

Slowly, night fell over the airial. Under the benevolent branches of the centenarian oak, the air echoed with laughter and song while the last of the sheep shuffled inside the sheepfold, their bells clanging softly.

Flore lolled against Ricar's chest, breathing him in, while inside her, great waves of emotions tumbled and crashed.

When all the food was gone, the villagers gathered around the bonfire, leaving the women to clear the table. A pile of bowls in her arms, Flore halted in the darkness.

Time had come for Father Anselme to bless the fire.

Someone handed Ricar a torch. He turned to the engineer and, after a brief exchange, gallantly held the torch out to the young woman in the blue dress. Her graceful silhouette enhanced by a bustle, she leaned forward gingerly, touched the bottom of the pyre and flinched as a jet of sparks shot up towards the canopy of stars, lighting up the monstrous puppet. Ricar rescued the torch, his fingers resting on the girl's fingers a second too long.

Once the tables were cleared, small groups strolled around the pyre. Colin played the first notes of 'Diga Janeta' on his reed-pipe while a couple of charcoal-burners pumped up their bagpipes. First came a choir of altos, underpinned by Father Anselme's steady bass. Gradually, every voice took its place in the harmony. Flore's heart fluttered as the tenors joined in. Ricar's voice had acquired depth and was now a deep bass. Now it was her turn. She took in a deep breath, soared above them with her soprano and sang to the stars.

By and by, more reed-pipes were pulled from pockets, old couples demonstrated a few steps, and the dancing began.

The engineer's daughter remained in the shadows, her eyes never leaving Ricar's face, feral in the firelight. A while later, the Parisians climbed back into their landau and clip-clopped away, their lanterns blinking into the night.

Flore jumped when Ricar took her hand. At the edge of the forest, entwined couples moved stealthily in the dimness, their sighs, murmurs and laughter muffled by the music.

Breathless, she ran her fingers over Ricar's arms, his shoulders, unable to believe he was here. His clothes hung lose over his wiry body, infused with the smell of fire.

'I've been dreaming of this moment for a long time, Perloune. It has kept me alive through nights in the jungle, when it was crawling with tigers and demons.'

'Where there really demons in Saigon?'

Flore had imagined Ricar in a Chinese version of *One*

Thousand and One Nights, at times defending monasteries against armoured attackers who vaulted over walls, at times lying on beds of silk in the arms of women with flowers in their hair.

He pointed towards the ocean. 'They sent us to the Mekong delta, where, from every province of Cochinchina, rebels came to fight us.' He faced her. 'The Chinese tried to rule over them, but they fought them off like wildcats. The Viêts are a fierce race. We take what we can from their land, but we'll never tame them.'

Flore sank into him and circled his neck with her arms.

'I would love to jump over the fire with you, Perloune.' He brushed her lips with his. A bolt of heat shot through her. 'But my jumping days are over. Can't walk on stilts either. We were ambushed one night. A rebel skewered me with a bamboo spear. That's why they sent me home early. Just imagine. I had another two years to serve.'

Flore did not even dare think about what might have happened during those two years.

'You got hurt?'

His eyes burned in the dimness. 'There were six of them. We caught them in the end. Our lieutenant chopped off their heads and lined them up at the entrance of their village.'

Flore bit her lip with a gasp.

'Ah . . .' Ricar took in a long breath of grass-scented air. 'It feels so strange to be back in Noirac, both familiar and . . . foreign.'

They resumed their walk across the airial.At the end of the clearing, moonlight bounced off the yellow cob of the *métayer's* house. They were about to reach the old cork tree when, rigid, Flore held back.

'What's wrong? Old Clopin's getting drunk over there. He won't see us.'

'It's not that, it's—it's the tree.' Ricar had not been told, and now was not the time to go over what had happened there.

'Ah well, if you don't like that tree, there are plenty of others behind which we can hide.' He put his hands on her shoulders. 'So . . . you waited for me.'

'Yes,' Flore exhaled. 'I thought you had died.'

'I'm not the dying sort.' He pushed her against a young oak and pressed his body to hers.

With a whimper, Flore moulded herself to him her heart hammering under his hand.

She opened her mouth to ask another question—there were so many things she wanted to know—but his kiss set her alight, and nothing else mattered.

3

SECRETS OF THE CONFESSIONAL

The last sinner had gone. Martial rested his head against the wooden panel of the confessional with a defeated sigh. He had been here a year, and still the villagers did not trust him. They confessed to Father Anselme, older and of peasant stock.

Why would they trust a curate, the son of the aristocrat who held their life in his hands? Who would be mad enough to confide their sins to the son of the man they feared most? Viscount Boyer, the man who had stolen the common moor and sold it.

From the beginning of time, the moor had belonged to the shepherds until, in 1857, on a whim from a man who called himself emperor, a law was passed. The sheep had been taken away, the moor sold into plots, churned up, drained and planted with pines.

Many shepherds had taken their own lives. Laborde, Flore's father, was not the only one.

Flore . . . Martial closed his eyes. Flore, who came to his church to cry, away from prying eyes. Tall, proud and wild, she asked questions. Generous as Ceres, Flore stood above a cohort of thin shallow-skinned girls in black aprons who never confessed anything worse than missing morning prayers. Flore . . . whose beautiful face tortured him at night and tested his vows of chastity to their very limit.

The door squeaked on its hinges and hit the frame. Martial was startled by the smell of tobacco and gunpowder seeping through the lattice screen.

'Forgive me, *Father,* for I have sinned. *Father,* my last confession was five years ago.'

Ricar? What was he doing here, in his church?

After their acid exchange by the bonfire, a visit was the last thing Martial was expecting.

Delighted to see his old friend return from the army, he had opened his arms in welcome. 'Ricar! You're home! Praise God, you're safe.'

A strange gleam in his eyes, Ricar had stood still, taken in the cassock and sniggered.

'Well, if this isn't Martial Boyer de Pagny. Sorry, I hadn't recognised you in that frock.'

They had been friends once.

Ricar's father had held the position of estate manager for the viscount, and at the time it was assumed that Ricar would follow in his father's footsteps, but fate had intervened.

Ricar and Martial were fifteen when the gate to the bull enclosure was left open. The bull had escaped. Ricar's father had been gored to death. The viscount had removed the widow and her son to a cabin at the edge of the forest, sent Martial to boarding school, and Ricar to work the pines.

The culprit was never found.

Martial clutched the crucifix that hung around his neck.

'Father,' Ricar's insisted on the word.

Taking measured breaths, Martial focussed on prayer. *'Salve Regina, Mater misericordiae, vita dulcedo . . .'*

'Father,' Ricar needled on. 'I have sinned. While in Saigon, I killed, I tortured, I committed sins of the flesh with—'

'You were a soldier.' Martial cut him short. 'Were you not under orders?'

Why confess to me? Why now? Why not consult Father Anselme, who has more experience, or speak with an army chaplain? There were priests in Cochinchina, weren't there? After all, had the French troops not officially been sent there to defend monasteries?

Ricar's voice insinuated itself through the lattice, malevolent, knowing. 'We caught six insurgents in a jungle village, *Father*. I *volunteered* to behead them. I chopped their heads and pushed them onto bamboo sticks at the gates of their own village.' Ricar sniggered. 'They hate the French.'

Ricar had not come to repent.

Bile rose in Martial's throat. 'Do you regret your deeds? Your atonement is crucial for your salvation.'

'Sins of the *flesh, Father*. Did you know that in Saigon, there are whores so skilful, so deliciously gifted, both girls and boys . . .'

His voice very tight, Martial interrupted. 'Ricar, why are you doing this?' He pushed himself forward and faced the lattice. 'I don't know what I did to upset you all those years ago. Perhaps it is I who should seek your forgiveness.'

'Oh, for God's sake, Martial, do you have to be such a damned saint!'

Martial let it go. Until Ricar confessed what was really tormenting him, he would not play his games.

'To show that you truly repent from your deeds,' Martial kept his voice level, 'your penance will be to carry the reliquary of Sainte Elma during the holy procession in September.' He hurriedly drew a sign of the cross in front of the lattice and rushed through the usual formula. *'Dominus noster Jesus Christus te absolvat. In nomine Patris, et Filis et Spiritus Sancti. Amen.'*

He shot out of the box and ran to the vestry, where he leaned against the wall and took several breaths of fusty air, thick with mould and incense. Why had Ricar really come home? He could have stayed away, made his fortune elsewhere, called for his mother to join him.

Had he come back for Flore? Had he? Then why, over the past five years, had he never sent news?

Martial sank into a carved campaign chair. His head in his hands, he conjured up his last memory. Ricar crying in the churchyard the day before he left for the army. They were eighteen then, and Martial was about to enter the seminary. All animosity set aside, he had placed an arm around Ricar, who had clung to him, racked with sobs. They had remained like this for a long time until suddenly Ricar had pushed him away, snarled like a rabid fox and pummelled him to the ground.

What had Ricar wanted to share that day and still could not confess today?

Jaw clamped, Martial got up and paced the small space. His long training as a priest had taught him the power of habits: prayers, rituals and repetitive acts which contained emotions and brought one closer to God.

Today, nothing was working.

Through the dusty window, a movement outside caught his eye. Beyond the low wall, Flore stood near the mound of freshly churned soil that marked her father's grave just outside the churchyard.

Martial pressed his forehead to the warm glass. His heart escaped from its bonds and soared. Sweet torment rampaged through his body, tearing him to shreds.

Flore Laborde. She was beautiful; she had the bearing of a queen, a bright mind, the voice of an angel and was blessed with what, to him, was a supreme quality: she was kind.

A bunch of wildflowers clutched to her chest, she was crying. Martial dug his fingers into the flaking stone, longing to vault over the wall and take her in his arms.

Her father had been a quiet man, a *pastorel,* a shepherd who, when he was not tilling fields or fixing roads, was content to spend his days alone perched on stilts, knitting, huddled in thick sheepskin. The man had known every swamp, every bosk, every mood of the moor where nothing grew but gorse, heather and moor grass . . . until Martial's father, the viscount, had led the race for pines and zealously diverted his source of income from sheep to resin.

When Flore's father was told to take the viscount's two hundred-strong flock to slaughter, it broke him. The next morning, Monsieur Clopin, the squire, had found his *pastorel* staring at him, tongue lolling, from a branch of the oak that stood opposite his house.

Trapped inside his confessional, all Martial could do was listen as lives unravelled around him.

Tortured by emotions he should not be feeling, Martial watched Flore kneel down by the rough grave. Flore, who made him forget his vows. Flore, who was courted by Ricar, a man hardened by years of soldiering, a man so frightened of his own weakness he had beheaded six men just to prove he was strong.

Hands behind his back, Martial tore himself from the vestry window and made his way to the presbytery, repeating with every step, 'Make every effort to supplement your faith with virtue, and virtue with knowledge, and knowledge with self-control . . .'

Flore placed the flowers on her father's grave and wiped her cheeks with a corner of her apron. *Did you not think of us, Papa, before you jumped? So angry at the viscount, did you forget how much we loved you, how much we needed you?*

She sat back on her heels and thought of her mother, buried inside the churchyard on the other side of the wall. 'Look after your father, Perloune,' she had whispered as she lay dying. 'His temper gets him into trouble.' She had added with a sad smile, 'Anger is a monster that takes hold of you.'

'*Oc,* Mama,' Flore had promised, 'I will turn my tongue three times around my mouth, and I will not lash out.'

She crossed herself and scrambled up. That day, Papa had staggered home drunk from the market. In the morning, he was gone.

She joined her hands in prayer. *He was a good man. Lord, if he is still in purgatory, please forgive him. Please don't let a moment's madness condemn him to Hell's eternal fire.*

She looked up. Her whole body tingled as a tall silhouette appeared through her tears.

'Ricar?'

His right leg dragging slightly, he reached her in long strides and leaned over the low churchyard wall. 'What are you doing here?' His gaze darkened as he took in the mound of earth, the flowers and the missing cross.

'Perhaps you have not heard.' Flore's voice dropped to a whisper. 'Papa hanged himself from the oak in front of Monsieur Clopin's house.'

'*Mila Diou,* what drove him to do that?' He scrambled over the wall.

Her answer came out as a whimper. 'He was not the only one. Ten shepherds took their own lives as common land was sold.'

'Oh, Perloune.' Ricar placed a hand on her shoulder.

Flore's insides melted under his liquid brown gaze. She rested her head against his chest, inhaling the strange yet familiar smell of him.

He lowered his face to hers and was just about to kiss her when a movement at the edge of her vision made her freeze. 'Oh no!' Heat rose to her face. 'Father Martial has seen us.'

'Kiss me.' Ricar drew her to him, a hand on her breast. 'He's led too sheltered a life in his seminary.'

'Don't be horrid to the poor man.' Flore giggled. 'Stop it, or I shall have to go to confession.'

He kissed her neck and whispered, 'Meet me on Monday by the river. I'll give you something to confess.'

Flore buried her face against his waistcoat, her senses in turmoil.

'Monday's still washing day, right?' He lifted her chin with a finger.

'Madame Clopin never lets us forget it. It's *in our contract*, so she keeps telling us. You've seen her, huh? She looks like a witch, but her and that old letch are at it like rabbits. Disgusting at their age. Do they think we don't notice their juices on their sheets? We already grow their food, why should we do their washing?'

'Ho ho! Young Flore rebelling against the social order.'

'Is wanting to live my own life rebelling against the social order?'

'And you shall live your own life, Perloune. You shall.'

Flore's heart did a somersault. Was it a promise? Would Ricar help her break the shackles that held her family captive to the viscount?

'Monday. Stay behind. I'll be waiting downstream. Follow the riverbed.' He brushed her lips with his. 'It will lead you to me.'

A warm flush shot through Flore's body, spread around her chest and trickled all the way down, where it raged like wildfire. 'I'll be there when the bell rings for nones,' she whispered in a hoarse voice. 'But, Ricar, please…'

'I know.' His face was serious. 'I won't do anything you don't want me to.'

Flore's memory still rankled from her encounter with the miller's son last Midsummer's Night. Because they had danced together, he had taken it as his right to topple her into a bush and push up her skirt. Colin had arrived just in time and punched him. They now had to ride six miles to have their rye ground.

'You do trust me, don't you?' Ricar tilted his head to one side, his eyes soft and hurt.

Flore kissed his pouting lips. 'We'll see if you can be trusted on Monday, won't we?' With a pirouette, she slipped out of his arms and ran home.

Home was a long, thin cottage that had once housed her parents, aunt and grandparents. Here on the moor, houses, like hermit crab shells, fit the size of the family. If the cottage became too big or too small, Monsieur Clopin, the *métayer* was under orders to move the family to another one. It was what happened here in Les Landes.

For Flore, moving would mean abandoning Papa's vegetable patch, the cornfield, slaughtering Napoleon the pig, leaving the vine her mother had planted by the front door.

Lord only knew how it would affect Nanette. When they had lain Papa down on a trestle in the kitchen, disfigured and cold, Nanette had bellowed all night like a calf. By the end of the week, she had lost all her hair.

On Monday, having hardly slept, Flore hurried to the Clopins' house to collect the washing. She hoisted the bag onto her head and, her large straw hat bobbing against her back, met the other women by the row of planks at the edge of the river.

She bent over the plank with a handful of ash.

'I saw your brother and Arlette together the other day.' The smith's wife plunged a sheet into the freezing water. 'They jumped over the bonfire together. We'll have a wedding soon.'

Flore adjusted her sun hat over her bonnet. What had Colin done? 'A wedding?' She rubbed the ash onto a soiled shirt. 'Colin is not yet eighteen.'

'It's the safest way to avoid being conscripted.' A fluty voice rang above the slapping and sloshing. 'They don't take them into the army if they're married. Seven years away is a long time.'

Ricar's mother had hoped he too would marry and stay home, but Flore was only fifteen at the time. Her mother had refused, saying she was too young.

'I was married at sixteen,' another woman said. 'Didn't do me any harm.'

Conversations humming around her, Flore lathered and pounded the linen. Both her parents were gone now, and her future was bleak. She pushed back her broad hat with the back of a hand and checked the progress of the sun, imagining Ricar's lips on hers, his fingers fluttering over her breasts.

In an agony of excitement and longing, she uttered a whimper when at last the nones bells rang.

'Flore?'

She jumped. 'Huh?'

'We're done here. Are you coming?' In pairs, the women were wringing the last sheets.

'No. I mean, yes. Sorry, I haven't finished.' She had been swishing the same petticoat around for ages. 'You go without me. I'll go straight to the squire's house.'

They picked up their heavy buckets and, sharing the load, filed away down the lane.

Her whole body pounding with excitement, Flore waited for silence. Frantic now, she pushed her sun hat and washing into the bushes, hitched up her skirt, stepped down on the sandy river floor and, light-headed, picked her way downstream, bending and twisting under the jumble of branches, inside a green tunnel sliced by golden rays of sun.

On a small beach, Ricar sat in breeches, bare-chested, his arms across his knees. Flore gripped a low-lying branch and held her breath, afraid that if she blinked he would vanish.

'You came.' He held out a hand.

'I thought they'd never leave.' She clambered out and collapsed into his arms.

His lips on her forehead, Ricar removed her bonnet and ran his fingers through her hair. The world around them dissolved into a green haze.

His lips moved to her neck while his fingers pulled the lace of her chemise. 'I want to see the whole of you,' he whispered. 'And I want you to see the whole of me.'

'I'm not sure that. . .' she gripped her chemise, 'I'm ready for that.'

'It's a scorching day; you've been working all morning. Tell me you're not dying to take a dip.' His lips curved into a wry smile. 'You can't do that with your clothes on.'

Flore's damp clothes clung to her body. When he opened her chemise and removed her petticoat, she blushed, but she did not protest.

At last, they stood together naked in the river under a green shaft of light and splashed about, tickling and giggling, to the delight of a wren flitting from branch to branch.

Ricar helped her onto the bank and laid her down on the soft grass.

'You're shivering, Perloune. Are you cold?'

Flore's teeth were chattering, but it was not from cold.

She ran her fingers along his leg and touched the gash in his thigh. 'Does it still hurt?'

'Sometimes.' Ricar took her hand. 'Let me tell you something, Perloune.' He kissed her fingers. 'In the Orient, I did not just learn how to kill. I also learned how to love. There are many safe ways we can give each other pleasure.'

Flore pulled away from him, dismayed at the thought of him lying with other women, and covered herself with her petticoat, a sick feeling in her stomach. What had the whores taught him? Would she ever be able to compete? Apart from watching pigs mate and the sounds of her parents shuffling about at night, she had no idea of what was expected of her.

'Ricar.' Flore tentatively touched his leg. 'What about, you know, the Church?'

'Ah yes. The Church.' A corner of his mouth lifted in a grin. 'Shall we go and ask Father Martial?'

Her hand shot back as if burned. 'Stop it, Ricar. It's not funny.'

'Pleasure is a gift from God. Love, desire, pleasure are all his gifts. God has given us the means to taste Heaven, and yet we are told it is wrong. It makes no sense at all.' He stretched next to her and whispered in her ear, 'In the Orient, Perloune, love is part of the religion.'

'Really?'

'Absolutely. Let me show you.'

4
SUNDAY LUNCH AT THE MANOR

June gave way to a July so hot, the corn dried on the stalks. Summoned by his father to the manor, Martial stood in the relative coolness of the church, dreading the ride home under a boiling sun.

Clad in their Sunday best, the congregation spilled out of the small church. The men gathered their mules, tied on their stilts or chatted with Father Anselme while the women fanned themselves in the shade of a tall cypress. Noirac counted no more than a handful of dwellings but, situated as it was on the pilgrimage road to Santiago de Compostela, it was a popular halt for believers.

A year ago, a curate fresh out of seminary, Martial knew his uncle the bishop had placed him here as a pawn, with a mission to exhort the populace to let go of their attachment to the fever-ridden moor and embrace the bounties of the newly planted pine God was sending their way. Today, it seemed, he would be held to account.

'*Adishatz,* Father.'

About to lift his foot to the stirrup, he nodded to a gaggle of girls nudging each other as they walked past, and then she appeared. His breath caught in his chest. Statuesque, a head taller than the others, Flore sauntered by, a loving arm around her sister, a strange round-faced child with slanted eyes.

What was it about her that cast an indelible spell on his soul? Perhaps it was her voice, as it soared above others when she sang, bypassed his reason and pierced his heart. Or was it the fervour with which, eyes closed, she parted her lips to receive the host from his fingers?

He followed her graceful figure and, coming to his senses, vaulted atop his mare and galloped away past bonnets, berets and hats. Along the paved road to Marcillac, Blanca's hooves rang in syncopated beat to the clang of clogs and stilts. Bent over her mane, Martial flew over the dizzying nothingness of the moor, filling his lungs with the scent of heather, dust and horse sweat.

Slowing her pace, he lost himself in the vastness that stretched to the horizon, crushed by a huge empty sky.

Here, the moor changed with the seasons. In summer, it was a bottomless immensity where the eye would search for a landmark, a rock or a tree to hold on to, finding nothing but the lonely silhouette of a shepherd perched on his stilts. In a few months' time, the parched desert would be under water, a vast expanse of sky and clouds reflected in the lakes.

For Martial, *la Lande* was a sacred space. His father, however, saw it differently.

As he neared the family seat, Martial reined in his mare to a slow trot. The forest the viscount had planted twenty years earlier wrapped itself around him, dark and lifeless. Grown for their resin, the trees bled into clay pots attached to the trunks.

The scent of turpentine triggered a strong urge to turn back. Where he would ride to, Martial had no idea, but of late dreams of escape had become so vivid they leached into everything.

The mare increased her pace, enticed by the promise of a cool stable and fresh hay, while Martial's heart gradually shut down.

Blanca snickered, prancing with anticipation. A small distance away, snug inside a circle of oaks, the manor appeared, flanked by two pretentious turrets.

Martial's shoulders hunched. His body shrivelled as he clattered into the stable yard.

He handed the reins to a groom.

'Stable her until tomorrow, Iñaki. I'll be leaving after breakfast.'

'Oc, monsieur.'

With a glance at the dour façade, Martial buttoned his cassock down over his breeches and, with a deep breath, ran up the steps before he could change his mind.

Lanky and obsequious, Lambert took his hat and preceded him to the great room.

'Monsieur Martial has arrived, Monsieur le Vicomte.'

'Ah, here you are at last.' Martial's father lifted his gaze from the maps he was studying by the mullion windows.

Martial carefully kissed his father's cheek, avoiding the stiletto moustache copied from the emperor.

The room was furnished like a hunting lodge with leather chairs, thick oak tables and boar heads staring down from the walls. Land maps were rolled out on a sideboard, held down with crystal glasses.

Since Martial's mother's death, the only trace of female presence was her harp tucked in a corner. Today, the smell of cigar overtook the usual scent of beeswax.

A man with a shock of grey hair stood by the maps. Martial had seen him before.

'Monsieur Poirier, you met my son Martial on Midsummer's Day, I believe?'

The engineer held out his hand. 'Indeed. I was there with my wife and daughter. *Enchanté.*'

'Nephew! So glad you could leave your flock.' His uncle set aside his glass and struggled to push himself up. 'I was just telling your father,' He collapsed back into the deep leather seat, 'how sorry I am to have neglected my duties as your mentor. Roads are so damned impassable in your part of the world.'

Martial could tell from the haze in the old man's eyes that he had already sampled the manor's famed Tursan wines.

'Hello, Uncle.' He brushed the large ring with his lips. The bishop's hand smelled of tobacco and incense.

His brother slapped Martial's back with unnecessary vigour.

'Martial! How's life among the savages? I hear you've gone native. Learned to walk on stilts yet?'

'*Bonsoir*, Roderic. Yes, walking on stilts would make my life so much easier, but with the cassock . . . Anyway, how are you, and how's business?'

'All in good time, Martial.' Their father addressed the engineer, 'Monsieur Poirier, shall we proceed to the dining room?'

From all the hand-rubbing and his father's jovial air, it was obvious that some deal was about to be brokered, an investment Martial would be invited to share. The Church had no qualms about men of the cloth augmenting their assets. So much for preaching poverty.

Martial followed them to a richly dressed table, laden with crystal decanters, bread and dainty pastries. His mind escaped to Noirac, where the peasants would be slurping their meagre soup, with the addition of a pig's trotter because it was Sunday.

The bishop had just finished saying Grace when Martial's younger brother, Hugo, breezed into the room with a mumbled apology. He pulled out a chair opposite Martial, his back to the window.

'I hope you're hungry.' Hugo chuckled. 'Marthe has been cooking for *days*. Potage, crayfish in puff pastry, timbales of lark in jelly, boar Saint-Hubert, asparagus, and for desserts . . . hmm.' He kissed the tip of his fingers. 'I shan't disclose any more.'

Martial sipped his potage, wondering when the real subject of the meeting would be broached.

He had to wait until the roast to find out.

'How will game be affected by the extension of the pine forest, Father?' Hugo had shot the boar they were tucking into.

Roderic lifted his glass for Lambert to refill. 'Boars will have the forest to themselves now that sheep are not there to destroy it. Jolly good thing too. We're looking for a way to discourage the Basques from bringing their flocks down from their mountains and destroying our seedlings.'

The Basques had been granted grazing rights by Aliénor and her son Richard the Lionheart.

'How are our farmers going to fertilise their fields,' Martial grumbled, 'without the sheep to provide manure?'

His question was met with knives scraping against china, the sounds of chewing and the ticking of the clock.

'I have just received a letter from the emperor.' His father paused to check the effect of his words. 'Louis-Napoléon has asked me to present him with a plan for draining the rest of the wasteland.' He tapped the table with his knuckles. '*This* is where the future happens, Martial. Of course, your *flock*'— his mouth turned down at the word— 'will mourn the loss of their sheep because that's all they know, but *we* hold the key to the future. All we have to do is convince our peasants.'

Martial kept his voice even. 'Sorry, Father, how is the moor a wasteland? I'd say our family has done rather well out of sheep.'

The scowl his father shot at him pinned him to his seat.

'Sheep are of the past.' Roderic dug a fork into the roast dish and dropped a large slice on his plate.

Bullish like his father, Roderic was the eldest, the one who would put the Boyer de Pagny name on the map of industrialised France. 'America has come out of its civil war. They need pitch for their ships and cannot yet produce their own. Maritime pine,' Roderic's eyes widened with wonder and greed, 'will bring civilisation to Les Landes.' He pointed his fork at each of them in turn. 'The emperor is planning to plant the largest forest *in the world*. We will drain the marshes, put an end to disease, build roads, villages and churches. Our pines will produce resin, turpentine, tar, planks and paper. We will set up stills and sawmills, extract the sandstone and use it for building. We will-' He took in a deep breath, choked with the magnitude of the role he was to play. 'We will show the world how Man can transform Nature.'

Their father took over. 'Vast swathes of heath are going for a song.' His dark gaze rested on Martial.

The boar lay heavy in Martial's stomach. *How can I preach poverty and obedience to my flock while my own family is stealing their common land?*

In a lighter tone, their father added, 'I won't be here forever, boys. The inheritance process will be smoother if each of you has some property of his own.'

Martial counted to three and asked in a measured voice, 'Who's going to dig the ditches, collect the resin and boil the tar? Our peasants are busy growing our food.' He wished he could unhear the sins his parishioners had committed to survive, their despair, mercy killings and infanticides.

'We will import manpower,' the engineer said in a measured voice. 'I have hired a local man as my assistant. Just back from Cochinchina. Made a name for himself in the army.'

Martial's head jerked up.

'Got a medal for bravery, I believe.' The engineer smiled fondly.

Martial growled, 'Or cruelty.'

The engineer carried on. 'The lad knows the moor like the back of his hand. He has saved money and purchased a couple of plots for himself. Clever chap, this Ricar. He knew how to find land on an incline so slight only he could see it, and he was able to drain it. He impressed me, I must admit. His vision has led me to the pumps I mentioned earlier on. They are the solution to our drainage problem.'

'The boy is from good stock. His father was my manager.'

The words were out before Martial had time to think. 'His mother lives in a shack with nothing to eat. Her hands are peeling from pellagra.'

'Bon Dieu, Martial, what is it with you?' His father's face turned crimson. 'What vision of utopia has the seminary been teaching you? If you can't cope with the real world, do us all a favour and enter a monastery!'

Martial put down his fork and grumbled to Hugo, 'Are the teachings of Jesus *utopia*?'

Hugo pointed to the coffered ceiling where bees had been painted over the original fleur-de-lys motif. 'Our family now worships the gods of industry.'

'What on earth . . .'

'Father has met Louis-Napoléon. Very taken with our emperor, is Papa.'

'But . . .'

'Our esteemed emperor,' Hugo explained in a conspiratorial whisper, 'has adopted the industrious bee from his uncle, the first Napoléon. Father and Roderic believe industry will save us all. They see themselves as the instruments of God. Did you notice the pinecone Papa has added to the hall banisters? Pines, Martial! Pines will make our fortune.'

Another course was brought in, another vintage from the viscount's cellar. Lunch dragged on until evening. Lambert shuffled about lighting petrol lamps and refilling glasses while gusts of wind whistled through the old windows. Martial gazed out at the changing patterns of clouds, wishing he could fly away from it all.

By the time Marthe brought in the praline bomb, the conversation had moved on to the challenge posed by the hard layer of rock that made it nearly impossible to drain the moor.

'We brought in convicts, but they were never able to pierce it.' The engineer spoke of the bedrock as of an enemy to be vanquished.

Hugo picked up the word. 'Convicts? I say, I have seen camels on our moor, buffalos brought in from Siam to plough rice, and now we're getting convicted murderers!' He lifted an eyebrow in irony. 'I hear plans are afoot to bring in foreigners to breed with our local girls.'

'Ha. New blood.' Munching on a piece of cheese, their father added, 'Would help with inbreeding.' He was fond of both his peasants and his cattle but could never really distinguish between them.

'Cheaper than sending convicts to Cayenne,' the engineer pointed out. 'But as I explained earlier, we are about to solve the drainage problem. I have located a reliable pump manufacturer in Paris.' He turned to the viscount. 'Perhaps you and your son would be interested in visiting the factory at the end of the month?'

After a glance at Roderic, the viscount carefully dabbed at

his moustache and said that yes, a trip to Paris was indeed agreeable to them. They would take the train.

Marthe came in bearing her *pièce de résistance*, an apple pie made of paper-thin pastry doused with Armagnac produced from their own vines.

'You are staying here tonight, aren't you?' Hugo sidled to Martial in a corner of the room while everyone was discussing the details of the trip.

Martial nodded.

'Good. I'll ride out with you tomorrow. I could do with the exercise.'

Their horses' hooves sank into the moor with great sucking noises. They trotted steadily, shooing horse-flies away.

'You are really contemplating the military, Hugo?' A covey of quails burst from a tuft of heather. Martial kicked his mare, adjusting her gait to Hugo's racy Normand stallion.

'*Oc.* Cavalry, if possible. Make a career of it.'

'Army never appealed to me.'

'Oh, Martial, what does appeal to you? You sounded so angry last night.'

'In choosing the priesthood, I followed my temperament. Ours is a cruel world. I want to make it better.' Martial's voice rose. 'But how can I preach acceptance when my own family is snatching common land? Land that belongs to the peasants? What do I say to them?' He urged his mare again. 'Is my role to stand in the pulpit and say, "Listen, you poor wretches, you are the lucky ones. The more you suffer in life, the more fun you'll have in heaven?" Is that what Uncle expects me to do?'

'Oh dear.' His brother chuckled. 'You care too much. Even

when we were younger, you always used to pick up stray dogs and birds with broken wings.'

'Is that so wrong?'

They reached the airial. In the shade of the common barn, women were threshing wheat to the slow rhythm of a song, hitting the ears over a cloth spread on the ground. Dripping with sweat under the midday sun, two men held winnowing fans at head height, rhythmically shaking the grain against the wind and pouring it at their feet in a steady trickle while the chaff naturally settled a few feet away.

'They never get to eat any of that wheat.' Martial could not keep the bitterness from his voice. 'It just goes to us. They stick to rye.'

Hugo shook his head. 'Father's right. This world is too harsh for the likes of you.'

'You can't have it both ways, Hugo. We talk of the future, and yet here in Les Landes we still have serfs.' He reined in his mare. 'The problem with Father is that he won't stand dissent. If you're not with him, you're against him. He will force me to buy plots of common land, and damn me if I refuse.'

'But why would you refuse? The emperor made the land available by law in 1857, Martial. That was years ago. We're not actually stealing it.'

They led their mounts to the little church set in a far corner of the airial, its thick walls of whitewashed cob and gingerbread stone a refuge.

Flore stepped out of an outbuilding, slender and proud, an oblong basket resting against her hip.

Martial's mouth went dry.

She genuflected and cast them a shy glance from beneath the sun hat she wore over her bonnet.

A shower of stars burst inside Martial's chest.

'*Adishatz,* Father. Would you like some grapes? They are

from our sand vines.' She tore a piece from a cluster and handed it to him.

'Thank you.' He swallowed hard. 'Flore, meet Hugo, my brother.'

Hugo pointed to her basket. 'Your family makes the sacramental wine, am I right?'

She nodded and handed him a bunch of grapes. 'We'll be harvesting soon.'

'I might come around and help.'

Flore blushed, curtsied and walked away, taking Martial's heart with her.

Hugo's gaze remained glued to the basket swaying against her hip. 'The Esmeralda of Noirac. What a beauty! She has more poise than our empress.' His eyes crinkled. 'How do you cope with your vows of chastity?'

'Some days are easier than others,' Martial said honestly. 'Don't get ideas now; the girl is spoken for.'

'I'm sure she is.' Hugo popped a grape into his mouth. 'Who's the lucky fellow?'

'The tallest of the brutes you saw winnowing the wheat. He's the one our engineer is proposing to take as his assistant.' Martial said in a growl, 'I hope he stands by her.'

His brother's laugh rang out in the morning air. 'Uncle is right. It is high time he found you a plush little parish in Bordeaux. We can't have a Boyer de Pagny siding with the serfs, upsetting the system that has served us so well for centuries.'

'But that's just it. We're in 1870. The Revolution eradicated serfdom *eighty years ago,* and yet for some reason we have kept it going! I preach poverty and dine on wild boar and white bread, while those people make do with corn gruel every single day of their miserable lives.' Martial gathered his reins and prepared to dismount. 'I just can't understand why

Uncle doesn't abolish the tithe once and for all. He's a bishop, isn't he? All he has to do is—'

'Ah, Uncle loves *foie gras.* Why would he stop his parishioners from giving him fattened geese?'

'Because—'

'A disciple of Epicurus as well as Lord Jesus, our good uncle loves everything life has to offer. He even has a mistress tucked away in Bordeaux.'

'A mistress!' Mouth open, Martial slid down from his mare in slow motion.

'Oh, Martial.' Hugo chortled. 'What an innocent you are.'

5
THE SAND VINES

Flore pulled the bucket from the well and, water dripping on her feet, poured some into a jug, which she handed to Ricar. He drank thirstily and tipped the rest over his head.

'*Diou biban,* have I just survived savage-infested jungles to work like a mule for the rest of my days?' He grabbed the cloth she handed him and dried his face. 'We're slaving over his lordship's wheat, and for what?' He spat into the wheat and handed her back the cloth, wrapping his fingers over her hand.

A strange heat shot around Flore's body. Tomorrow could not come soon enough. She was to meet him inside a snug hollow in the heart of the dunes: her grandfather's sand vines.

With a wink, Ricar squeezed her hand and walked away, leaving the others to gather the last of the grain, fill wooden barrels and carry them inside the barn, ready to be weighed for tax.

Flore skipped home, honey flowing inside her. She

pressed the cloth to her face and inhaled his smell, imagining his hands . . .

'He seemed very friendly tonight.' Aunt Onorina sat at the table outside the cottage, a basket of root vegetables in front of her.

'Tanta, please, it's not fair.' Flore brushed the chaff from her apron. 'I've hinted, but what can I do? It's not the kind of thing a girl can ask.' She absently reached above her, picked a grape from a bunch growing along their window frame and made a face. Not quite ripe.

'Florette. Sit down and listen to me.' Tanta tapped the bench next to her and placed a couple of knobbly turnips on the table.

Flore steeled herself for a lecture.

'This time last year, your mother was still with us, and your papa—God rest his soul—cared for the viscount's sheep.' Onorina slammed her knife into a turnip and chopped it in two. 'We're running out of time. For a bright girl, you've behaved like a mooncalf since Ricar's been home. You were set on the miller's boy, weren't you? What happened to that? The miller's a free man. Don't know why you turned him down.'

'He tried to rape me!'

'You made eyes at him. He was only taking what he thought was his right.'

Flore's mouth fell open.

'Remember one thing. We only live here because your father looked after the viscount's flock. Now sheep aren't worth a candle, we'll be moved to a shack.' Her left eye confronted Flore.

If not for a right eye too close to her nose, Tanta Onorina would have been a handsome woman. Her disfigurement had kept men away, which meant that the future of the family now rested on Flore's shoulders.

Tanta now attacked a carrot and winced as the knife caught her finger. 'Colin will be of age soon. If he draws a short number, or if some rich layabout pays him to take his place in the army, he'll be gone for *seven* years.' She sucked the blood from her finger. 'Madame Clopin will want you as a maid. Augustine's leaving to get married.'

A band of iron clamped around Flore's chest.

'She can't force me to empty the *pissadou* she keeps under her bed! It's not in our contract.'

'It's very much written between the lines.' Tanta waved her knife. 'We can't refuse.'

'She's a vicious nag, and old Clopin gropes the girls.'

'Yes, well, you should have thought of that when you turned down the miller's son.'

'If I am to work as a maid,' Flore asked in a small voice, 'what will happen to Nanette?'

Her sister was feeding her geese, singing to them in her flat voice.

Aunt Onorina gathered the chopped vegetables and dropped them into a pan. 'If Colin is called up and you're in service, Nanette and I will remain on our own,' Tanta's voice wobbled, 'in some charcoal burner's shack, if we're lucky.'

Still singing, Nanette came in and sat next to Flore. Flore hugged her tightly, breathing in her smell of goose feathers.

They had never spent a night apart.

'Tell you what,' Flore nudged her sister, a huge lump in her throat, 'why don't we have a little game of skittles while dinner's cooking?'

'Kittles!' Nanette clapped her hands.

The die was cast. Whatever Ricar wanted to do with her the next morning, Flore would agree to, but first he would have to promise marriage.

Sleep did not come easy that night. At first light, unable to wait a moment longer, Flore crept out of the tester bed she shared with her sister and crept to the kitchen. Cursing the squeaky door, she halted and tiptoed out, reassured by Tanta's loud snores.

Too nervous to eat, Flore tied on her stilts and flew over the downy mist. The first rays of the sun brushed the moor with touches of gold, the silence pierced by the faint trill of larks and distant sheep bells. Large patches of heather stretched, purple under the morning sky, all the way to the dunes.

The rhythm of her stilts sinking into the moss brought back the tune of 'Se Canta', the lament she had sung during those long five years to guide Ricar home.

A bird sings at my window, calling to you, my love, calling to you.

Flore raced along sheep trails, gorse catching her skirt. The bird had called Ricar home, mountains had rolled away, and he had returned to her.

Her heart knocking against her ribs lest Ricar turned out to have been a dream, she clambered up the dune, plunging her stick into the sand.

Sheltered from the sea winds inside a wattle-and-broom fence, the vines had been allowed to romp. Branches buried like tentacles into the sand, the vines' deep roots anchored the dune against the wind and sprang up, laden with fruit.

Totally out of breath, Flore struggled to the top and gazed in wonder at her lover, lying in the shade of her grandfather's shed, picking at a cluster of grapes. He unfolded his strong body, knelt at her feet, untied her stilts and scooped her up as she lolled into his arms.

Laughing, he kissed her hard and freed her hair from hat and scarf. Around Flore, the world shrank down to the vine snug inside the wattle fence, the feel of the rough jute sacks on her legs, the sound of the surf and the cry of gulls overhead.

She gazed into his brown eyes as he fed her grapes one by one, trying to guess what was in his mind, but when he kissed her and ran his expert hands over her body, all thought of bargaining vanished.

She gripped his shoulders and . . . oh, *Diou biban* . . . how could anything be so good?

'Are you sure this is not wrong?' she asked once she had stopped trembling and returned from her bliss.

'Florette, I told you. Why would God give us a taste of Paradise and make it a sin?'

'Well . . .' She steeled herself and forced out the words. 'We are not yet married.'

There, she had said it. She bit her lip and waited.

He pulled down her skirt and patted her leg.

'Life around here is going to change, Perloune. We are going to transform this moor!'

Though she felt the blow, Flore grasped at the 'we.' She clung to the glow on his face as he imagined their future. 'Just think, two million acres . . . We're going to make it productive!'

'The moor is giving us all we need just as it is,' she protested weakly.

Elbows on his knees, Ricar gazed towards the ocean, silver beyond the wattle fence.

'Our job while I was in Cochinchina was to guard the rubber tree plantations. The locals hated them, but that's where the future lies. We can do the same here with pines. Resin will make us rich.'

His eyes regained their focus. He grinned. 'You know, if we were back in the jungle, we'd be set upon by tigers and crocodiles. They'd smell us.'

Flore noticed the sidestep. Her heart sinking, she went along with him and asked, her throat tight, 'Did you really see tigers?'

'Oh yes, tigers, elephants as big as houses, snakes thicker than my leg and crocodiles that look like a floating branch and leap out of the river when you least expect it.' Ricar ran a hand through his thick hair. 'What a strange country that was. They don't call it Cochinchina. They call it Viêt Nam in their language.'

'What does it sound like, that language?'

Ricar's high-pitched rendition of a Saigon fish wife went some way to dissolve the knot forming inside Flore's stomach. She took in a long breath and shot her last arrow. 'What else did you see? Did you find my pearl?'

The pearl was Ricar's cue. Before he'd left for the army, he had promised to bring back a pearl.

'You want me to tell you all the wondrous things I saw in Saigon?'

Flore gave a weak nod, a bitter taste spreading around her mouth. He had forgotten the pearl.

His gaze returned to the ocean. 'In Saigon, there are places you can go to forget your troubles. Dark rooms where you lie on a bed and inhale opium. It's made from poppies.' He snorted. 'A good trade for France.'

'What is it?'

'It's a drug. A piece as big as a hazelnut will make you happy for hours, but it's dangerous. Soon, you want more, and then you can't live without it.'

Flore inhaled his scent of earth and pine. He was her opium. A kiss from him made her happy for hours, and then she wanted more.

'There are creatures as beautiful as princesses who glide over the ground in red-and-gold gowns. Lithe as reeds, they have alabaster skin and dance like fairies. These enchantresses come from Siam, and for a price,' Ricar's voice wavered, 'you can buy a moment of their time.'

Flore pulled away, disturbed by the yearning on his face.

'And the strange thing is that you never quite know whether these creatures are girls. . . or boys.' Ricar's voice betrayed the spells the Siamese conjurers had cast over him.

Her heart in tatters, Flore lay down as Ricar nuzzled her neck, aroused by his own memories. She tensed up. They were alone here, and now she had allowed him to go so far, he would be within his rights to take her maidenhood.

'But, Ricar,' she whimpered, 'you promised . . .'

'You trust me, don't you?' He gently rolled her over onto her stomach, kissed the nape of her neck and buried his face into her hair. 'Don't you, Perloune?'

Her heart ripped out, Flore pulled down her skirt and sobbed quietly, while against her cheek Ricar's breath deepened. He had not taken her maidenhood, but what she had allowed him to do was much worse. And yet, inside her, the hope that he would marry her refused to die.

Once his soft snores told her he was asleep, Flore pushed herself up and crawled down to the sea to wash away the mess.

6
FLORE GOES TO CONFESSION

Confession was over, and the last penitent left the church. Martial was about to follow when a sigh from a back pew caught his attention.

Diou biban. His heart did a somersault. What was *she* doing here?

'Flore? What happened to you?'

Her face half-hidden under a black mantilla, the girl raised burning eyes to him. It took Martial every ounce of willpower not to scoop her into his arms.

'Shall we go to the confession booth?'

Without the distance created by the lattice, he did not trust himself.

Flore followed him and gingerly wedged herself into the small space.

'Is there anything you want to tell me?'

'Father, I—I'm scared.' Flore's voice cracked.

'Has anyone threatened you?'

'No. No, it's not that.'

'What is the matter, then?' Martial asked, though in his heart he knew.

Her story came out in halting sobs. 'If I am not married soon, I will have to go and work for Madame Clopin and . . . and I can't do that.' She rested her forehead against the lattice, a world of pain contained in her sigh. 'Am I guilty of pride, Father?' She said in a thin voice. 'My mother was in service and she was— She made me promise that I wouldn't . . .' Her words wobbled. 'I promised her on her deathbed.'

From what Martial knew of Madame Clopin, she would mistake the girl's spirit for insurgence and whip it out of her. It would never work.

His hand went to touch Flore's cheek and fell back onto his lap. All that separated them was a thin wooden grid and the cassock he wore, barriers as impassable as steel bars.

'And what of Nanette, Father? What of her? Without me, she—' A sob escaped her. 'She's such a loving child.'

A lump in his throat, Martial ran through his repertoire of priestly platitudes.

'Your troubles will not last, Flore.' Feeling a fraud, he offered her the usual formulas. 'Your challenges are real, but they are a test of strength, and you will come out stronger.'

'I know what Monsieur Clopin will expect me to do as a *servine.* I'm not so innocent.'

Her bitterness made Martial shrink. 'I know how strong you are, Flore, how capable.' *How beautiful, how noble, how kind.*

'What if Colin is called up? What then?'

'Let's try and get him exempted,' Martial proposed, grasping at straws. 'As head of a family, he should be able to avoid the draw.' A clause Ricar could have invoked, but for some reason he hadn't.

'What if he can't? We don't have the money to pay someone to go instead of him.' Flore gently wept against the lattice.

'I will help you write to the authorities.'

He lay a hand on the frame and allowed the warmth of her face to flow into his heart. They remained like this for a long time.

When at last she stirred, Martial cleared his throat and recited the usual words, and together they said, 'Amen.'

Amen. So God wills it. *So God wills it.* Empty of meaning, the words hung in the fusty air of the confessional.

How long, Martial wondered, how long would he be able to go on preaching acceptance to peasants whose fate was so utterly unacceptable?

7

THE GRAPE HARVEST

Autumn was on its way. Flore spent her days plucking poultry, plaiting onion stalks, filling earthenware jars with goose meat and sealing them with fat. Though the buzz of harvest carried her along, her heart was shrivelling. Winter loomed ahead, scary and cold.

Ricar had been busy, and on the rare occasions she caught sight of him, trotting on a new horse, he greeted her with a smile so warm it coiled around her heart and filled it with hope.

Today was the grape harvest in the sand vines. The land had been handed down to her father by a mysterious grandmother who had come from a big Bordeaux family. She had fallen in love with their grandfather, a Basque whale hunter. No one knew how she had acquired the sand vines.

'Come on, Flore!' Colin called from the door of their cottage. 'No dillydallying, you're the one treading the grapes today!'

Flore winced at her brother's jollity, exhausted from a sleepless night. She pulled her sun hat over her bonnet, hitched up her skirt and, resting against a fat oak stump, tied on her stilts.

The blacksmith's son cast her an eager smile as he helped Colin secure a vat onto his cart.

Flore studied the boy. He was strong, easy-going, but when she pictured the toothless mouth on hers, the red pustules grazing her cheeks, her stomach turned.

If she could not marry Ricar, she would not settle for anyone. Flore set off in long strides, overtook the mule and clambered up the dune, her stilts sinking into the sand. Like Tanta, she would be a spinster. She would never work for Clopin.

Papa and Prosper, a beekeeper and wine maker, had coaxed this tiny patch of sand into producing a wine so sweet and so strong that Father Anselme had adopted it as his Communion wine.

'Ah, here you are.' Prosper helped Flore down from her stilts.

Flore hugged him and buried her face into his cloth jacket, which smelled of beeswax and tobacco.

It would be the first grape harvest without Papa.

He lifted her chin, a deep line creasing his brow. 'It's been hard for you, hasn't it? Your father . . .' His eyes were moist. 'I miss him too, you know.'

'Why did Papa leave us, Prosper?' Her chin wobbled. 'What are we to do without him now?'

Prosper answered in a strained voice, 'He couldn't bear it when your mama died. When they took his sheep away, he . . . he just fell apart.' He patted her back and straightened her hat. 'He's watching over us. I know he is. Oh, Florette, he was so proud of you.'

'But he . . .' She returned to the comfort of his arms.

The thick sideburns tickled her forehead. 'Now, now,

don't fret. The Lord knows them that are his. Your papa's in Heaven now. Let's have no nonsense about that.'

Flore clutched at Prosper's words, an anchor in a shifting world.

It took all three men to drag the cart up to the shed at the top of the dune.

While the sun dried the coating of dew on the grapes, women tacked an old sail to the shack's wooden wall to fashion a canopy over a trestle table, under which they buried jugs of water and cider in the cool sand.

When all was ready, Prosper gave the signal and the pickers rushed to the top vines in a joyous tumult. Soon, knives glinted in the sun and plump clusters of grapes vaulted into the *hottes*, the conical wicker baskets strapped to men's backs.

Leaning over the sides of the vat, three women separated the fruit from the stems. Nanette would steal a few grapes and pop them into her mouth, juice dribbling down her chin.

'You'll make yourself sick.' Tanta scooped up the dross and threw it onto a pile of compost. 'Look at you, girl. You're supposed to pick out the leaves, not eat all the grapes.'

Nanette waddled away and went to help the pickers, soon distracted by a cricket on a leaf.

'Flore! Your turn!' Colin called.

Flore shook off her clogs and climbed in to cheers and claps. She hitched her skirt into her belt and lifted her feet rhythmically into the cool mess. In the distance, the ocean rippled, silver all the way to the horizon. Around her, women were singing. These people were her family, her friends. For a moment, the sense of belonging soothed her soul, but when she saw the place where she and Ricar had lain, the idyll shattered into a million pieces and the shards ripped her heart.

Her jaw clamped, she stamped down the mess with a groan. The grapes popped and squelched between her toes as she crushed down her dreams, for dreams were all they had ever been. The bright future her mother had promised her, the hope her father had borne that his children would escape the viscount's shackles, a life with Ricar, crushed . . . crushed . . . crushed. Flore pounded the grapes to a pulp.

'Flore, *hé,* Flore, stop!' Her name filtered through the pain. 'What have those poor grapes done to you? The pressing comes later.' Prosper reached out to her. 'Come down now. You're only to break them open. Come to me.' He opened his arms, and Flore fell into them, sobbing. 'Let's take this vat to the cellar before it gets too warm.'

In the distance, Father Anselme was bouncing up the dune on his mule. Prosper dried Flore's tears and said with a grin, 'Look, here's the good father come to check up on us.'

'I heard that.' The old priest grinned. 'It's the blood of Christ, Prosper, the blood of Christ.'

'Which is why I must get this lot out of the sun before it spoils.' Prosper leaned over the vat and inhaled deeply. 'Smells good, Father. It will colour up nicely in the cellar.' He placed a hand on Colin's shoulder. 'Now you're a man, Colin, you'll help me press it tomorrow, won't you?' Prosper added, his voice tinged with sadness, 'It was your father's job, the pressing.'

'Sure. The tasting was his job too, if I remember,' Colin joked, his voice cracking slightly. 'I'll come with you.' A second cart was brought up, topped with an empty vat.

Prosper turned the mule around and whipped it while Colin pushed the cart to free it from the sand into which it had sunk. Together the two men headed for the coolness of the wine cellar to unload the first batch.

Flore watched them absently. The sand vine was the one

thing her family owned, the one thing the viscount could not take away from them. But it was not enough.

Where on earth could they go to be free?

8

THE FESTIVAL OF SAINTE ELMA

Autumn was the season for thanksgiving, a time for getting together to make preserves for winter. After the grape harvest came the festival of Sainte Elma, when everyone travelled from Noirac to the nearby market town of Marcillac.

A thick blanket of mist covered the ground when, shivering in the crispness of the early morning, Flore fitted the ladder to the chicken coop perched high on a branch of a dead oak and let the hens out. Shivering in the dim dampness, she then fed Napoleon the pig.

The sky was just turning from dark blue to silver when Flore, Nanette and Aunt Onorina left the cottage. Wrapped in thick shawls, they joined the small cluster waiting for the charabanc by the two cork trees.

Old Eulalie, the presbytery maid, limped to Flore and slipped a small bottle into her fingers.

'Take this,' the old woman said. 'Fill it with water from Sainte Elma's fountain for me, will you?' The miraculous spring was reputed to cure rheumatism.

Flore held the old woman's hands in her own. 'I will say a prayer for you, Eulalie. Make sure you rest today.'

In the distance, the charabanc appeared, drawn by two large oxen.

'Ho! Jean! Ho! Martin!' the drover shouted.

The obedient beasts halted in a great clatter of chains, and everyone climbed in. Flore repressed a grin. Hurrying across the airial, hands behind his back, Father Martial was high-stepping towards them like a heron, his cassock billowing around his long legs.

His back to the drover, Martial's gaze trailed over the mist floating upwards in small tendrils, revealing clumps of grass and empty sheep pens. Opposite him, Flore and Nanette looked like dolls in their Sunday black skirts edged in red and flowered shawls.

Nanette slept mouth open, snuggled against her sister. Loved and cared for, the girl had lived far longer than could be hoped for. Her sunny disposition had earned her the status of *mascotte* on the airial, her heart so pure that Martial had no qualms during Sunday mass in giving her the host without confession.

His gaze met Flore's. Her sweet smile shot an arrow of pain into his chest, trickled inside him and dulled into melancholy with each grind of the wheels.

He had not spoken to Ricar since the day he had come to 'confess.' Oh, but he would be here today, pious and repentant, making a great show of carrying out his penance.

Once again, Martial wondered what he had done to provoke such animosity in his erstwhile friend. Unable to come up with an answer, he shifted position and focussed on the heads of the plodding beasts that swung from side to side, immune to the ballet of flies that accompanied them.

A gang of youths galloped by, screaming like Visigoths. The oxen stalled and snorted in a loud rattle of chains.

'Who was that?' someone cried out.

'Colin and the boys from Laforge.' Onorina chuckled. 'They always manage to borrow horses and mules from someone!'

With a few shouts and lashes, the drover convinced his beasts to resume their trek, and by the time the first of the sparse Marcillac houses appeared, Martial knew he was late.

First a low farm appeared, followed by a few cottages, a smithy and, a hundred yards further, the hut of a basket-maker. Unlike the small harbours clustered on rocks like Biarritz and Saint Jean de Luz, space was plentiful on the moor. Market stands sprawled lazily around the church.

People stretched, yawned and chatted excitedly. At last, the charabanc drew to a halt in front of the white church. Martial jumped off and hurried in to meet his uncle.

A few pilgrims hovered around in the light that filtered through coloured glass, some kneeling in prayer, others watching the penitents getting ready.

Imposing in his red robes and lace, the gold of his mitre and cross flashing in the dimness, the bishop lifted his aspergillum and boomed a blessing over the eight penitents.

Martial suppressed a grin as they hoisted up the poles, gritted their teeth and shuffled out, weighed down under the bejewelled reliquary that held three precious bones displayed on velvet: three small toes salvaged from Sainte Elma's body.

Elma, an intrepid shepherdess reputed to have saved Aquitaine when the region was torn between Arabs and Visigoths, had never existed—Martial knew for a fact. She was the creation of Queen Aliénor's troubadours, keen to cement local patriotism. Over the centuries, the legend had spread, the relics had accomplished miracles, and pilgrims flocked to see them. A well-guarded secret the Church was keen to preserve, such were the revenues due to Sainte Elma's miracles.

Flags were hoisted. Drums echoed around the square. Pipes pierced the morning air as the reliquary began its slow trek towards the miraculous spring at the edge of the forest.

At the front of the procession, weighed down by the shaft, Ricar cast Martial a defiant look. An arm around a boy's shoulder, he laughed and said something. The boy blushed.

In step with his uncle, Martial followed the reliquary down a sunken path towards a small pool, where the penitents rested the box atop flat rocks. The bishop blessed the spring with loud invocations while people filled bottles and gourds with the miraculous liquid.

Grimacing, the eight penitents once again shouldered their precious load and made their slow way through the wood, towards the church and salvation.

Hands inside his sleeves, Martial listened to his uncle pontificate in Latin, all the while wondering, *Could I do this? Could I be this man?*

In the old church, all Martial could smell was the air thick with the smell of wool and sweat, thick with want. Arms raised inside a cloud of incense, the bishop spoke in tongues, and at his command the congregation rose and knelt like puppets. Anxious faces beseeched the shards of bone encased in rubies and emeralds to grant them food, health, life. One of them, he knew, was praying for love.

Slowed down by Nanette, Flore and Colin had found a place at the back, right under the statue of archangel Raphael. The prayers in Latin were over. The bishop was now preaching in Occitan, spouting the usual calls for obedience, acceptance and hard work. In front of Flore, a large man shifted his weight, blocking her view of the altar. Her gaze was drawn to the side, to a notice pasted to the wall. A name caught her eye. The words came into focus.

The world shifted. A strange whoosh filled her ears. She gripped the back of a pew as reality came crashing down on her.

'Flore?' Colin took her arm. 'What's wrong?'

She pointed to the note.

Colin read out haltingly, 'Ricar Guyon to marry An-Angèle Poirier in the church of Sainte Elma on the . . . Oh no. The wedding is in two weeks' time!'

Someone turned around with a frown. Colin grabbed Nanette's hand and pulled his sisters outside.

Flore teetered, blinded by the light.

It was over.

'Ricar's a scoundrel, Flore. He really doesn't deserve you.'

'What am I going to do?' Flore twisted her apron in her fingers. 'How are we going to live?'

'What's wrong?' Nanette kissed her sister's hand. 'You hurt?'

'I am not hurt, Ninou. I'm just sad . . . very sad.'

Flore glanced at the church where Ricar was receiving the host, shriven of all his sins. What kind of animal was he, to do what he had done to her, all the while romancing the engineer's daughter?

'Oh, Colin.' She clung to her brother's arm. 'What's to become of us if I can't marry him?'

'You marry Colin.' Solicitous, Nanette slipped her hand inside Flore's.

'I can't marry Colin.' Flore caressed her sister's cheek.

'Why?'

'Because Flore, you and I are already family,' Colin

explained. 'A marriage is when you ask someone new to come into your family.'

'Oh. Then I marry Father Martial.' Nanette beamed. 'He's nice. He can come into our family.'

'Tell you what,' practical, Colin put his arm around Nanette, 'Let's get you a cake before everyone comes out of the church.'

Nanette's eyes popped. 'Cake!'

Dazed, Flore shuffled behind them across the square to a stand where a woman was setting out treats on a green-and-red cloth.

Grief came at her in waves. *That midsummer's night, when the girl stood by the bonfire, Ricar saw his chance and seized it. All that time, he was using me. Of course he was. Who cherishes what comes free?*

How could he have cared so little? Was he already betrothed to that girl when he stood by her father's grave? A realisation struck Flore with a jolt. Was he hoping to return to her? Keep her as his mistress?

One by one the blocks that held Flore's life together crumbled away. A great emptiness opened before her. The market stands around them, the bustle she had so loved, now appeared like the décor of a play in which she had no role. She clutched her sister's hand, adrift in a setting at once familiar and hostile. Not so long ago, Flore had her own stand here with Mama and Papa on market days, selling her father's produce.

Where were they now? Mama had died of swamp fever, then the sheep went, taking Papa with them. Soon, it would be November, and Monsieur Clopin, the viscount's *métayer*, would take stock and claim both their house and the garden that fed them.

Flore leaned against a cattle trough. Father Martial had promised that things would get better. How could things get better? *Boudiou,* he meant well, but how could he understand? He was rich.

For years, Ricar had featured in every single one of her dreams. In the life she had planned, Ricar had built a house. Together they had extended the sand vines; together they had become prosperous.

Ricar had stolen all her dreams and left her with nothing.

Holding on to the rough planks of the charabanc, Martial scanned the purple moor, vivid under the endless sky, so vast it tore him apart.

'How dry the moor is this year,' someone said. 'The new ditches have drained the marshes.'

The wheels of the cart rang across a wooden bridge.

'See how full the river is.'

'It's been a good year for grapes.'

A woman's voice. 'It has been a bad year for maize.'

'They had a fire in Laforge.'

Martial ran his gaze over his flock, lolling in the last of the evening sun, glad of a rare day off. For all his father's talk of a 'bright future,' those peasants faced a life ensnared in the very resin they used to trap larks.

They were singing now, bless them, playing with the harmonies of 'Bela Marion'. Nanette looked like a Russian doll. She sang atrociously. Flore, on the other hand, had the voice of an angel.

Tonight, she looked so sad. The temptation to run away with her had never been so strong, to take her hand . . . and escape. He ached with the need of her, to possess her body and soul, to take away her cares.

When he had taken his vows and pledged himself to a life of chastity, he'd had no idea of the torture it would be.

The mood changed with the next song, the parts sung alternately by men and women, a bawdy dialogue between a *monsieur* from town and a *bergère,* a canny shepherdess whose favours the gentleman was attempting to buy. Flore looked so forlorn as she sang; the ball in Martial's throat nearly choked him.

Within a few weeks, autumn would bring in the traditional changes on the airial. Tithes would be paid, cottages would be swapped, men would be called up to the army. Flore would go into service.

Uncle would find him a well-to-do parish where he would be kept busy baptising fat babies, absolving *messieurs* of their dalliances with maids and placing their bastard children into orphanages. By the next festival of Sainte Elma, Flore would be married to a *résinier,* a man who, like an automaton, would run up a ladder a thousand times a day, scrape a thousand wounds from the pine bark while she poured the resin into buckets. It was what they would do, day after day, after day . . . until they died.

The sheep grass had turned russet under the slanting rays. Beyond the wild moor, dunes bordered the ocean, and beyond the ocean a new world was recovering from its wounds.

There had to be a meaningful life somewhere, a better life, a utopia waiting to be made real. Wherever this meaningful life was, it was not here in Noirac, under the shadow of his father.

9

THE PEARL FROM CHINA

Diou te damne, Ricar Guyon! Flore heaved the heavy fork and stabbed at the soil of her potato patch. *Diou te damne!* A strand of hair escaped from her scarf. She tore off the scarf and used it to wipe her sweat and tears. She had already dug up the potato patch once, but she would not leave the smallest scrap for the next people. A family from the north would take over her house, she had been told. 'Foreigners' come to tend the pines.

In a week's time, Ricar would be married. Would he be thinking of her when he bedded his wife, or would he conjure up the Siamese whores?

Flore knew that she was no match for the engineer's daughter. Ricar had always dreamed big—she had loved that about him. 'All I have, Perloune,' he'd quoted the age-old adage, 'are my shaft and my knife.'

'That and your golden tongue,' she would add, laughing.

Ricar's dreams had never included her; she could see that now. He had not come back for her, nor for Angèle Poirier for that matter. His ambition had taken root when he discovered the treasure in the jungles of Cochinchina: rubber, the magic sap that dripped gold into the cups fastened to its trunk. Excited by resin and its possibilities, he had gambled, cheated and saved to buy up chunks of the moor on which he would grow pines. Resin was his true love, and Angèle was the key to it.

Nanette came out of the coop, chatting with her geese, a cloth bag slung over her back.

'Look! Father Martial give me plums.' Nanette held out the bag. 'I'm going to marry him.'

Flore sighed. Why did the only decent man around have to be a priest?

'Come and give me a hug.' Flore held out her arms.

'I'm a good girl.' Nanette hugged her.

'You are that, Ninou. You're the best.' At night, Flore clung to her sister like a drowning woman to a raft.

She watched her sister walk away behind her flock. Nanette was growing up. Soon, it would not be safe for her to wander the woods on her own anymore. Though under her bonnet Nanette was completely bald, it would not stop a lecherous charcoal-burner.

Flore ran her hands over her face and uttered a choked sound. If she was busy skivvying for Madame Clopin, who would look after her sister?

Voices inside the cottage distracted her. She gathered the gleaned potatoes and went in, surprised to find the *métayer* at the table in front of a glass of her aunt's precious cider. To the side of the chimney, a pan of stew simmered.

'*Adishatz,* Monsieur Clopin.' Flore dropped the basket to the ground and remained by the entrance.

Thickset, his moustache and florid nose hidden under a large beret, Monsieur Clopin came into his own on market days when, overriding the din, he would flaunt the qualities of a draft horse or an ox in a gravelly baritone.

He dealt with humans the same way.

The shutters were closed against heat and mosquitoes.

'Light up a lamp for us, will you?' Tanta said.

'Wine all right this year? Plenty of it? I hear Colin's taken over from your father.'

Flore struck a match and lit the petrol lamp. 'Yes. It was a good harvest.' *It's our wine. It's not part of your tithes. If you want some, you'll have to pay for it.*

He pushed back his beret and studied Flore, his small eyes lingering on her breasts. 'Madame Clopin would be glad to have you as a maid.'

Flore shrank away. 'What about Augustine? She's your maid, I can't—'

'Augustine is betrothed to the miller's son. They will be married at Christmas.'

Flore took the blow. A year younger than her, the girl had seen her chance and grabbed it. Some chance—the miller's son was a violent soak.

'I'm not sure I—I'm better outdoors.' Flore took a few steps inside.

Under the beret, Clopin's eyebrows crawled like caterpillars. 'Working as a maid is a *servine*. It's in the terms of your contract. What else are you going to do with yourself?' He turned to Tanta but, unsure as to which eye to follow, stared down at his cider instead. 'The boy that's just come home from the army.'

'Ricar.' The name sent shivers up Flore's spine.

'Ricar Guyon, that's right. His mother has vacated her maisonette. You will move there, Onorina.'

Tanta blanched.

How dare he call that hovel a maisonette? It's no better than a charcoal-burner's hut!

'Where will our Colin be living?' Flore could not keep the accusatory note from her voice.

'Your brother,' Clopin tilted his chin towards the east,

'will be working in Laforge. The pines there are ready. We need more men to extract the resin.'

So that was how it was done. A simple matter of switching oxen under the yoke. A new Martin, a new Jean. Oxen always bore those two names, and in the man's mind, so did the peasants.

'That brood from the north,' Clopin sucked his moustache, 'will need a big place. There's eight of them with their old folks. This house will do fine.' He cast a glance at the single bedroom, where three tester beds contained a whole family, glad of the warmth in winter. None of the windows had glass.

'What about Nanette? She gets scared easily.' Flore wiped angry tears with her sleeve. For her sister, the change would be traumatic.

The *métayer*'s gaze hovered over his drink as he addressed her aunt. 'The presbytery needs a new housekeeper. The fathers have thought of you, Onorina, and are willing to take in your idiot niece.' He uncovered large teeth in what passed for a smile. 'These children never live long anyway.'

Flore's eyes narrowed. Her hand went to the poker, itching to wipe the self-satisfied smile from the man's face.

Instead, she grabbed her cape and bolted outside, feverishly strapped on her stilts. Hitting the ground with her stick, she clomped towards the forest, casting imprecations into the wind.

I will never let Nanette go. He can't make me work for him. Augustine told me what he's like. He makes her stick her hand inside his trousers while he touches her breasts. Disgusting pig.

A light carriage turned in from the Marcillac road, drawn at a trot by an elegant chestnut gelding. Flore recognised the engineer's horse and stopped, ready to bolt if Ricar was with him. It was not Ricar, but Angèle, wrapped in a plaid.

The carriage slowed down. '*Hola,* mademoiselle!' the engineer called out. 'Do you happen to know if Father Boyer de Pagny is about this morning?'

'Oc.' Flore replied. She steadied herself against the carriage.

A gust of wind lifted the plaid. The girl adjusted it around her shoulders. The sun caught a jewel on her neck.

The ground buckling under her stilts, Flore stepped back in horror.

From a velvet choker on Angèle Poirier's neck hung the pearl Ricar had promised Flore he would bring back from China.

The engineer thanked her, flicked the reins and drove off, leaving Flore teetering on her stilts, dizzy, her gaze burning a hole in the back of Angèle's neck.

A low growl rumbling inside her throat, she clomped across the moor towards Ricar's plots, land he had bought on the sly with money won by cheating at cards—for that was what he did: he cheated, he lied, he betrayed those who loved him. He coupled with whores in unnatural ways, he beheaded people and put their heads on spikes for their mothers to see.

Sobbing, she reached Ricar's pines and slashed the lot of them with her stick, a grimace distorting her face. *Curse you, Ricar!* She hit the saplings. *Curse that pig Clopin, and curse you, Papa*—shaking, she tittered on her stilts and steadied herself with her stick, overcome with grief—*for abandoning us.*

Her anger expanding like steam, she folded over, struck by hurts and betrayals. She wept for her family sacrificed to the pines, the accursed *pines*—Flore sliced a sapling—that sucked all the life from the moor.

'Diou te damne, Ricar Guyon!' she shouted into the wind. Oh yes, he had warned her. He had told her he was devious, told her he was evil, and still she had clung to him.

Something dug into her, something in her front pocket . . . the bundle of matches she had used for the lamp. Before she had time to think, she struck one and dropped it onto a pile of dried grass. The grass crackled. The first pine caught, licked by runaway flames. With raw animal grunts, Flore slashed dry heather and pushed it towards the pyre with her stick.

'Curse you and your precious pines! I hope they're the death of you.'

She stood tall and, numb, followed the trail of fire racing through the new pines. It stopped and hovered at the edge of the heather. She opened her arms wide. 'Monsieur Ricar Guyon, Mademoiselle Angèle Poirier, this . . . is my wedding present.'

She spun around towards the ocean.

The sun was low when Flore reached the dunes and untied her stilts. Her back against the wattle fence, she sat and contemplated the watery vastitude, searching for a way forward. After a very long time, she put her stilts back on and trudged home, circling the old bosks from the north.

Soon, it would be winter, and rain would turn what was left of the moor into marshes. Clouds would blow in, reflected in pools and lakes. Already, the line of the Pyrenees was topped with snow. The first gales would bring the Basque shepherds and their flocks down from their mountains. She would see none of it, trapped inside the Clopins' house, scrubbing floors, churning butter, sleeping alone, her little sister unable to understand why they could not be together anymore.

The wind picked up. Above her, the shrieks of seagulls mingled with the clang of hundreds of sheep bells. From somewhere, bells rang for vespers . . . and did not stop. Flore sniffed the air. Was it smoke? Another tocsin joined the first bells, low and threatening.

She shook herself and hurried home. Nanette . . . *Oh Diou,* what had she done?

The airial was teeming with people running to and fro, shouting orders, gathering buckets and filling containers. A human chain ran from the pendulum-pump well to the forest. Smoke billowed in eddies above the old trees. Someone rushed to the stables and let out the mules, their eyes wild with fear.

Where was her sister? Fingers shaking, Flore collapsed against a stump and was unlacing her stilts when several geese flapped in, honking, from the undergrowth. A strong gust shrouded the airial with smoke.

'Nanette!' A raw animal cry came out of Flore's throat as she tumbled down from her stilts. Imploring the Virgin, she ran into the woods, met by a line of men beating down flames that licked the ground. She spun around, back to the airial.

No, no, no. Nanette is safe. She has to be safe. Flore's mind refused to consider the alternative. Nanette was safe. She must be. There was no alternative. Flore started bargaining with God, she begged until, in the cold light of day, she knew what she had done.

A small group had gathered around the bread oven. They lifted their face to her and parted without a word.

Nanette lay on the ground like a rag doll, her skirt a faded blue, her limbs at an awkward angle. Her bald head nestled on a clump of dried grass, free of her bonnet. Flore's soul shrivelled, and she sank to her knees. She lovingly replaced the bonnet and took her sister's small hand. It was already cold.

'Nanette!'

'We were too late,' a friend of Colin's whispered. 'We normally keep an eye on her, you know, make sure she's all right, but we were sent to collect resin on a new plot today.

She must have fallen asleep—overcome by smoke.' His chin wobbled as he said, 'She didn't suffer, Flore.'

With an inhuman howl, Flore collapsed on her sister's body.

A long time later, she scrambled up and, shredded from the inside, clawed at her chest to rip out her heart. She zig-zagged crazily out of the airial, oblivious to where she was going. Her mother had warned her about anger, the madness that takes hold of you and robs you of your senses, and she had not listened. Nanette was a blessing, an angel from Heaven, and Flore had killed her.

Sucking in great gulps of air, Flore stopped by the cork tree and stared up at the branch from which her father had ended his life. The darkness was inside her too. Soon, everyone would know. The priests would turn Tanta away. Colin would be shunned, and it would be her fault.

Flore ran. She ran with no purpose. She ran to dull her mind. Her lungs burning, she caught sight of the wooden bridge. She stopped, a hand to her side, and sucked in a painful breath. A few more steps took her to the bridge. The wind whipped strands of hair over her face. She leaned over the parapet. Below, brown waters were churning.

She had destroyed all her options, both in life and in death. She had killed her sister. Now, Heaven was barred. Damned for eternity, she would never meet her mother or Nanette again.

Flore dug her fingers into the wide wooden parapet and clambered onto it. Her cape flapping around her, she scanned the moor for the very last time. Shreds of smoke twisted up into the darkening skies.

At her feet, the river beckoned, dark and wild. A cruel emptiness touched her core. If she stayed, her sin would ruin Colin and Tanta's life. There was nothing left for her.

The tocsin stopped. From the distant mountains came the muted sound of a thousand sheep bells.

Her father's face beckoned in the eddies below. He was waiting for her.

'Papa!' Flore toppled forward.

10

THE BRIDGE

Martial leaned forward in the saddle against the bitter wind blowing down from the Pyrenees. He lifted his face, distracted by the unmistakable tinkle of bells, a sound that filled his heart with joy. Great swathes of sheep would be pouring from Biarritz along the shore, heading towards the fertile plains that lay north of Bordeaux.

Thank God Father and Roderic were in Paris. Obsessed with their precious pines, the two of them had declared war on the Basques and their thousand-strong flocks. Roderic had spent the previous week scowling by the mullion windows, knocking back Armagnac and plotting their demise.

As Martial neared the bridge, the mare flared her nostrils. In the twilight, dark swirls of smoke rose from the airial and church bells clung erratically. The church! His mouth went dry. He kicked Blanca to a canter.

Down by the river, a black shape stood on the parapet, a woman, he could tell by the white bonnet and the cape lifted by the wind. *Diou biban,* what was she doing? A cold shiver ran through him. The shape swayed. He cried out a warning, snapped away by the wind.

'Wait! No!'

The woman wavered and, arms open, lurched into the dark waters.

Martial kicked his mare. She shot forward, gravel sparking under her hoofs.

He vaulted off, threw the reins over a post rail and scrabbled down the side of the bridge, clutching at grasses and rocks. In the brown waters, the woman was thrashing about, one of her legs trapped in a mess of branches. Martial tore off his hat, shoes, cape and cassock and jumped in. Sucked by the current, he floundered, carried downstream towards the mill. He fought his way across, grabbed a branch and, inch by inch, hauled himself to the other bank. By the time he reached her, the woman had stopped struggling. She was floating face down, her hair spread out like seaweed. Martial steadied himself on a rock and gently lifted her head out of the water.

A raw cry escaped his throat.

No, please, God, no! He untied Flore's heavy cape and tried to pull her to the bank.

Flore coughed, flailed and uttered a scream when he tugged at her leg. Instinct kicked in. She gulped for air, gripped his shoulders and pushed him under. His lungs bursting, Martial freed himself from her death grip. Again, he tried to dislodge her foot. He yanked at the branches. Muttering prayers, he dragged her towards the shore and hoisted himself up the steep bank, his breath rasping.

'Come on, Flore, I've got you. Give me . . . your hand.' He reached out, but she was unconscious. With his last ounce of strength, he pulled her up by her wrists, lay her on her side, made sure she was breathing and, teeth chattering, darted across the bridge to gather his clothes and his horse.

'Flore? Can you hear me? I'm taking you home.'

With a whimper, Flore crawled away and rolled towards the water.

He grabbed her sodden skirt and yanked her back. 'My home. Everyone's away in Paris. No one will know you're there.'

Martial untied her muddy apron, hurled it into the current and wrapped her in his cape. His fingers numb with cold, he struggled into his cassock, wondering how he would reach the manor, still several leagues away.

'Listen.' He crouched next to her. 'I will not let you die. I just won't, you hear? I have to get you onto this horse before we both catch cold. Do you think you can do that?'

Flore pushed herself up and collapsed again. '*Aïe!* My ankle!'

A cold realisation hit Martial. Was this Ricar's doing? What else could have led her to this?

He carried her to the mare, hoisted himself into the saddle, hauled her up and wrapped his arms around her, amazed at her softness. Her head lolled back on his shoulder as she slid to one side, heavy and lifeless. Holding her tightly, he urged the mare onto the road and plodded home, teeth chattering, imploring the Virgin Mary all the way.

It was night when they reached the manor. Martial rode to the kitchen door, relieved to catch the glimpse of a candle through a window. He dismounted and laid Flore down on the grass.

'Marthe.' He knocked and whispered loudly. 'Open up, it's me, Martial.'

'Oh! *Mila Diou!* Monsieur Martial, whatever happened to you?'

'Is Hugo here?' Martial glanced back. Flore was not moving.

'Yes, he is. What . . . Oh!' Marthe grabbed an old coat by the door and threw it over Flore.

'She's just fainted. I'll be right back.' His legs weak from the effort, Martial staggered up the stairs, shouting his brother's name.

He found him in the parlour, reading an almanac by the fire. 'Hugo, come quick, I need help.'

Hugo leapt out, carried Flore in and laid her down in front of the fireplace while Marthe busied herself wrapping fire bricks with rags and preparing a tisane.

'Monsieur Martial, you'd better get changed into something dry while I help this poor girl.' Marthe shooed both men out of the parlour.

'Do you know who she is?' In the warm kitchen, Hugo found a dry towel and handed it to him.

Martial nodded. 'She's the girl you met the other day.'

'The pearl of Noirac? Oh no! Did she mean to drown?'

Martial shrugged. What girl would be fishing alone on a cold night? Suicide was a cardinal sin so, until he knew more, he would assume it was an accident, though Hugo was no fool.

'How long are father and Roderic away exactly?' Martial rubbed his hair and warmed his hands over the range.

'They're away for the week. The engineer has gone with them; so has Lurking Lambert. The girl will be safe here for a few days. Don't worry.' Hugo patted his shoulder. 'I won't say a word.' He went upstairs and brought back a motley assortment of clothing. 'Here. These are the warmest things I could find. Now, let's see if Roderic has left us some Armagnac.'

'Armagnac is all very well.' Marthe bustled into the kitchen. 'Have you had supper, Monsieur Martial?' She took out two bowls, set them on a tray and ladled soup out of the pan simmering over the tiled *'potager,'* as the warming shelf was called in these parts.

'The girl won't tell me her name,' Marthe confided once Hugo had left the kitchen. 'She's adamant she's not with child. Now, that is a relief. Here you are, dear. Carry this in for me, will you? I must find some ointment for her ankle.'

Martial held on to the tray. With child? Yesu, why had he not thought of that?

Flore lay back in a velvet chair, a blue tinge to her face. Marthe had combed her dark hair, which reached down to her waist. Wrapped in an old woollen robe, she remained motionless, eyes closed, her foot on a small stool, swollen and bruised.

It was too soon to ask questions, so Martial picked up a bowl of soup and offered it to her. Flore ignored him.

'I'm not sure she can hear you,' Hugo said when he got back. 'Why don't you have your soup, a shot of Armagnac and I'll help you put her to bed.'

'I'll just go and warm the bed in the yellow room.' Marthe bustled about. 'I'll come down when it's ready. I will put her to bed myself.'

'I will get the wood.' Hugo rushed out.

Once they were alone, Flore's large brown eyes rested on Martial.

'Don't be so kind to me, Father. When you know what I've done, you'll soon cast me out.'

The tolling bell and smoke over Noirac told their own story, so he asked instead, 'When was the last meal you had?'

She did not answer.

He pushed his chair closer and tried to spoon a little soup into her mouth. 'I will hear your confession in the morning. Things can look very bleak on an empty stomach.'

Flore kept her lips clamped.

'When your hair is dry, Marthe will bind your ankle and we'll carry you up.'

She pushed herself up. 'No . . . no . . .'

'My family are in Paris for a week. No one need know you're here. Tomorrow, when I have heard your confession, we'll discuss the best course of action.' Martial's chest was bursting from the need to take her in his arms, angry that life could do that, push a beautiful soul to the limit.

'You are a good person, Flore. I know you are.'

'No!' She hid her face in her hands. 'Don't say that!'

'We are human. We struggle, we fail, we fall, we pay the price, and we get up again, humbler, stronger. That is what life is about. Right now, you see no way out, but God is merciful and will help you on your journey. Please don't give up.' *Not for a cad like Ricar.* Martial handed her the bowl and spoon. 'Now, let's eat our soup, or Marthe will despair.'

11
RICAR'S DEVIOUS PLOTS

The terce bells were ringing when Martial set off under thick clouds rushing in from the ocean. As he approached Noirac, he was joined by villagers from Laforge, some on stilts, some on mules, who had come to help in any way they could. He stabled his mare in the presbytery and pushed through the crowd gathered outside the church.

'Ah, there you are!' Out of breath after his bell-ringing exercise, Father Anselme wiped his face with a large handkerchief. 'I was expecting you last night.'

'I was held up.' Martial followed the old priest to the vestry. 'We prayed around a sick child. The mother insisted I stay for *souper*. It got dark, so I spent the night at my father's. Tell me, I smelled smoke on the way down. What happened?'

'Oh dear, Martial, I have terrible news. Yesterday—'

A voice rose outside. Martial tensed up.

Ricar had joined the crowd. 'You all heard the Basques and their sheep rattle by yesterday. Every year, about this time, they come down from their mountains and graze their animals on our moor. Their goats bark our trees; their cattle trample our saplings.'

The *our* did not escape Martial. The rights of pasture had been granted seven hundred years ago by Queen Aliénor, when the moor was common land, available to all.

Flore's brother cried out, 'What are you talking about, Ricar? The Basques are welcome here. We need their sheep's manure to grow our food.'

'Pines don't need manure. The future lies in resin. The Basques know that. Last night, they set our plots on fire.'

Ha. The gall of the man! Last night, the Basques were miles away. Martial checked the faces around him. *Is Ricar trying to turn the fire to his advantage?*

An angry murmur rose from the crowd, and in an instant the Basques, who for centuries had been welcome, fêted and invited into local homes, had become the enemy.

Ricar was not finished. 'The fire came so close to our village; it took the lives of two of our girls. Nanette and her sister, Flore.'

The truth hit Martial in the chest. Nanette had died in the fire . . . He pushed his way to Flore's brother. Sizzling with anger, the boy lifted a fist to Ricar. 'What are you saying, Guyon? We all know who caused Flore's death, you scumbag!'

Martial gripped Colin's arm and said in a low voice, 'Now is not the time, Colin. Please fetch your aunt and meet me in your house.' He tightened his grip. 'Don't say *another word* until we have spoken.'

Colin shook himself free and glared at him. Martial held his gaze.

The boy pulled his sobbing aunt from the arms of the blacksmith's wife.

'Be strong, Onorina,' the woman said. 'I will come to help you later with your little one.'

In the old cottage, the kitchen was dark and cold. Dull light seeped through chinks in the shutters. In the hearth, the fire had not been lit. Nanette's small body lay on a trestle of planks, waiting for her coffin to be made, her hands arranged around a cross.

Martial removed his hat, crossed himself and prayed by the body until Onorina's sobs stopped and Colin's rage died down. He pointed to the benches around the table, took a seat and cleared his throat.

'I confess that I am struggling to see where the truth lies, but I have news for you.'

Elbows on the table, Colin stared at him, ready to bolt. The aunt's straight eye bore into him.

'Please hear me out and promise you will not repeat anything I tell you.'

The aunt nodded with fervour. Colin snarled.

'Colin?'

'Oc.' Sullen, the boy crossed his arms.

'Flore is alive. She did not drown.'

'Diou biban!' Onorina's hand flew to her mouth. 'But—but the miller found her clothes in his pond! Her apron and her . . .'

'I got to her just in time.' Martial shivered at the memory.

'Where is she?'

'She is safe, but she has sprained her ankle. Until we know her state of mind, it is best if we agree to say nothing.' Martial hesitated. 'I believe that Flore is the one who set Ricar's plot on fire.'

Her brother uttered a growl. 'Ha! If she hadn't, I would have. That scumbag strung her along—'

'No! Flore is a good girl,' Onorina cried out. 'She would never do that! The Basques did it!'

'She told me.' Martial met their gazes squarely.

The aunt glanced over at the body of her little niece and slumped over the table with a whimper.

After a long time, Colin said, 'But why is Ricar saying that the Basques . . .' He stopped to think. 'Do you think he knows?'

'I think he does. The fire started on his plots. But what advantage would there be to the truth? Flore would go to prison, but first she would expose their relationship. Even if his fiancée stands by him, Ricar would lose her father's trust.' Martial ran a hand through his hair. 'The engineer holds Ricar's future in his hand.'

'So the Basques didn't set our forest on fire?' The aunt's face creased in confusion.

'Why would they? They are just passing through. The plots are not *ours*, Onorina. The pines belong to Ricar.' Martial rubbed his face. 'In the end, it has all worked in his favour. Flore gone from his life, he can get married without fuss.' *When had Ricar become so manipulative?*

'How about the Basques?' Colin too was struggling to process Ricar's reaction.

'The Basques have already moved on, unaware of any problem. Next spring, all the plot owners will remember the fire and vote new laws against the shepherds. Next autumn, the Basque flocks will be barred from grazing our moor.'

'If Flore comes home, will she go to prison?' Now that he had calmed down, Colin was asking pertinent questions.

'It's best if she doesn't come home just yet. I will tell her that she is in your prayers and keep you informed. Don't worry, with a sprained ankle,' Martial smiled at Onorina, 'she won't be going very far.'

Flore would never go home. Unspoken, the sentence hovered over them.

Martial went to Nanette, so small on her trestle. 'Such a

good soul. Just think, she's already in Heaven, playing with the angels.'

'She wanted to marry you.' Colin's voice caught. 'So you could be in our family.'

A rush of emotion brought tears to Martial's eyes. He made the sign of the cross over the child and commended her soul to God. *Put in a good word for me up there, Nanette. The Lord is merciful, but I am going to need all the help I can get.*

12

FLORE HIDES AT THE MANOR

Flore lay in a half-tester bed, her foot on a cushion. She had been at the manor for three days, or perhaps four, she wasn't sure, terrified of being caught by the viscount when he returned from Paris.

A sharp rap at the door and Marthe walked in with a jug of water, a pile of almanacs and a cheerful greeting. She pulled open the drapes.

The light bore into Flore's skull.

'Monsieur Hugo asked me to give you these.' Marthe placed the magazines on the bedside table. 'Oh, and one of the boys will be around later with a pair of crutches.'

'Thank you,' Flore whispered.

'Let me arrange your bed.'

While the housekeeper straightened her sheets, Flore leaned forward over a large pillow. The smell of goose feathers reminded her so much of Nanette that she burst into tears.

'Poor child.' Marthe ran a hand over Flore's hair. 'You've never slept on your own, have you?'

The touch of Marthe's hand opened a raw wound.

Clawing at the pillow, Flore shook with racking sobs, gazing into an abyss so deep, so dark, her heart was begging not to feel any more.

Marthe sat at the edge of the bed and hugged her. 'There, there, child. You've a lot to cry about. Don't think I don't know that.' She pulled a handkerchief out of her apron and handed it to Flore. 'You have reached the end of your strength.'

'I d-don't deserve your k-kindness,' Flore hiccupped.

'Monsieur Martial vouches for you. That is enough for me. Now, tell me, the viscount will be home in three days. Is there anyone that could take you in?'

Flore shook her head. Felizia, a cousin in the south, had married a Basque, but they had sailed to America. Some distant cousins worked the pines, but they lived in huts with broods of children.

Marthe brushed and plaited Flore's hair. She rebandaged her foot and tucked her in.

On her way out, she picked up the enamel soil pail.

Heat rose to Flore's face. Thank God it had a lid. 'You shouldn't have to do that.'

'Bah, I've been doing it for most of my life.' Marthe said with a proud smile, 'I brought up those three boys, you know.'

Flore held the pillow against her chest. 'Our *métayer* wanted me as a maid, but I didn't . . . I couldn't.'

'Why on earth not?'

'Mama was in service in a big house when she was young. She . . . she was . . . She never said, but she made me swear I would never be a servant. The *métayer* sold off all our sheep and broke my father's heart.'

'The *métayer* is a serf like us, a beast of burden. Top dog he may be, but he too works for the viscount. Everyone does around here. There are worse jobs than being a servant.'

'Perhaps there's something wrong with me, some kind of wilderness.' Flore's cheeks burned with shame.

'You're not bad, child. You just lost your way.' The housekeeper went to close the door. 'When Monsieur Martial is better, he'll come and sit with you. You can talk to him then.'

'He is ill? What's the matter with him?'

'He has developed a bad cold. You know how men are with these things.'

'Oh no!' Flore's face dissolved again. 'It's my fault. He jumped into freezing water to rescue me.'

'Listen, dear, you *are* being tested.' Marthe waved away her concerns. 'Your heart needs silence and kindness to heal. There is a long, sad road ahead of you, but you *will* get better. I know it for a fact. You are a strong girl, with much to offer the world.'

'Thank you.' Overwhelmed by Marthe's compassion, Flore fell back on her pillow, tears flowing freely.

The room was stuffy. Glass panes on the windows turned it into an oven. She hobbled out of bed, threw the window open and, from her vantage point, gazed out at the world which had once been hers.

It was a clear, crisp day. In the distance, an army of tiny people, heads covered in white bonnets and dark berets, were gathering manure, throwing it into oxcarts.

Les Landes. The moor was her world. Made of water and sand, five days long and three days wide, edged by dunes and ocean, in winter it was an infinity of sky reflected into lakes. The moor had made her who she was, and wherever she went, she would always carry it inside her.

After a long time, Flore picked up a couple of large almanacs. She flipped through pictures of crinolines, bustles, hats and articles about Paris, but nothing spoke to her.

As a girl, she had sat with Father Anselme on the benches of the old church when he taught the Noirac children the basics of reading, counting and catechism. Her young mind like a sponge, she had done well, though French, with its silent letters, was a challenge. Mama could speak French, Flore spoke it sometimes when selling socks on the market.

She turned the stiff pages filled with pictures of carriages, hats, models wearing corsets and bustles without really looking at them until the word *Saigon* jumped out. Flore was not sure she wanted to probe into the landscapes that populated Ricar's mind. In the end, curiosity won over.

It truly was another world. The emperor of Cochinchina and his dignitaries stood proud in bejewelled robes, but instead of uniform and medals like the French emperor, they wore comical headgear with flaps that stuck out like ears. Flore lost herself in the daguerreotypes of osier huts build on stilts 'to stop tigers from clawing through the walls,' women planting rice, knee-deep in water, hidden under large cone hats, and rubber plantations. She wondered what it would be like to travel. Had she been born a man, she would be tempted to leave.

A sigh escaped her. Stuck in this old manor with a sprained foot, what options did she have left? Another sob rose through her chest. She couldn't even die.

That night, the cassoulet Marthe brought on a tray tempted her to eat.

Flore fell into an uneasy sleep, caught in a magic lantern horror show where her father's face appeared, bloated with a lolling tongue, Nanette's body dumped like a rag doll and Madame Clopin whipping her with a stick. The small hours of the night echoed with her mother's sobs as she lay dying, Nanette bellowing like a calf when Papa was brought home . . . and Ricar's groans of sinful pleasure.

Flore woke up in tears, wondering where she was.

Marthe was wrong. There was no hope, nowhere to

escape to, either in this life or the next. Wherever she went, her sins would always haunt her.

A knock at the door woke her up. Flore looked around, surprised to find a bowl of milk by her bed. It was still hot.

Father Martial stuck his head around the doorframe.

'May I come in?' His eyes were red-rimmed and his voice thick with cold.

Flore pulled up the sheet to her neck, self-conscious in the hemp nightdress Marthe had given her.

The father did not look well.

'How are you feeling?' He added a log to the fire and pushed the window closed.

Flore winced. Back home, the bedroom was never heated. In winter, they would simply pull the drapes tightly around the bed and hug each other under a thick eiderdown.

'Did you find anything interesting in the almanacs? My mother had a whole collection of them.'

Apart from Saigon, an article had caught Flore's eye. Pictures of Basques, easily recognisable from their wide berets, herding sheep from horseback in a country that sounded Spanish.

She pointed to the open almanac under the window.

'Nevada.' He pulled it to him. 'Yes, quite a few Basques are making their way there, from South America mostly. Nevada is famed for its gold and silver mines. The Basques reckoned those miners needed feeding and went over with their sheep. They call it "mining the miners."' The father glanced towards the ocean and added so quietly Flore thought she had imagined it, 'I sometimes think of doing the same myself.'

They sat in silence, taking in the crunching of wheels carried up by the breeze, the lowing of oxen and cries of, 'Ho, Jean! Ho, Martin!'

Outside, life carried on, while inside it had stopped.

Father Martial's chair creaked. 'I have told your aunt and

Colin that you are here. They send their fondest thoughts. Father Anselme will keep your secret. Your aunt has agreed to look after him at the presbytery. You can rest easy.' He smiled. 'Old Eulalie will go to live with her daughter.'

'My brother . . .' Flore croaked. If word spread of her madness, Colin's chances of finding a wife would be ruined.

'Colin will be sharing a cabin in Laforge. He will be trained to collect resin.'

Flore wanted to ask about Nanette's geese, but her throat was too tight.

'Flore,' the priest leaned forward, 'I know it is too soon, but you are going to have to make a decision. My father will be back in two days' time and . . .' His Adam's apple bobbed up and down above his dog collar. 'I think you should know that you are officially . . . ahem . . . deceased.'

Flore hid her face in her hands with a strangled moan.

'I am sorry, but Father Anselme thought it was for the best. He conducted your funeral together with Nanette's.'

The nothingness set in Flore's chest like mortar.

'What do you want to do? Shall I have a quiet word with my uncle and see if he can find you a position in Bordeaux?'

'Nani!' Her *no* shot out like the wail of a trapped lamb.

Father Martial gave an almighty sneeze.

'Sorry.' He blew his nose. 'Marthe tells me you have no family to take you in.'

Unable to think or feel anymore, Flore just closed her eyes.

'Marthe is a good woman. We both want the best for you.' He sneezed again. 'I think she may have found a solution. We are working on it.' He went to the door and, before leaving, added, 'I won't tell you more until we're sure, but I can promise you that it does not involve you being a maid.'

Moments later, he returned with crutches he left against

the foot of the bed. 'In the meantime, you've got a couple of days to learn how to use these.'

Flore pointed to the almanac. 'Father, how far is Nevada?'

He ran a hand over his stubble. 'Let me see . . . Nevada. You would have to make your way to the Bordeaux docks and board a steamer. The ship would first stop in Dakar—that is in Africa—then sail across to Brazil and bob down the coast of South America all the way to Argentina. There are quite a few Basques there, Spanish Basques, that is. Then down and around Cape Horn and up the other side. It would probably stop in Chile and then . . . yes, sail up the west coast of America to San Francisco.' Lost in some dream of his own, the father's gaze had drifted towards the ocean.

Having no concept of these places, Flore interrupted him. 'I was just wondering how long it would take to get there.'

'Well, if you sail from Bordeaux, you'll be on that ship for a month and a half at least.'

'A month and a half to get to Nevada?'

'Well, more like two months, all told. Or less, if you sail from Le Havre straight to New York and take a train. Yes, from Le Havre, it would only be a matter of weeks.'

'Oh.' Crushed, Flore fell back onto her pillows, thinking of Cousin Felizia, awed by the courage of the Basques who had made it so far. 'I'd better practice on those crutches, then.'

13

THE DEATH OF A RÉSINIER

Acutely aware of Flore's presence in the room next door, Martial was having breakfast, a newspaper on his lap, but he was not reading. In spite of the wretched circumstances that had brought them together, this was the happiest he had been for as long as he could remember. Free from his father's sermons, Roderic's sneer and their valet's ominous presence for the first time since his mother's death, the manor was somehow filled with warmth, with purpose.

What had led him to Flore that night as she stood on the parapet? Why had their lives collided at that precise moment? Was God responsible for this miracle, Martial wondered, or were his vows being tested to the limit?

Separated as they were by class and religion, he just could not shake off the feeling that fate had led him to Flore, that in some way they were connected.

What a strange spell that girl had cast on him. Her resilience, her strength, her raw energy delighted him, the way she danced through life . . . until Ricar had snuffed out her light like a candle.

A rustle caught his attention, hesitant steps in the next

room, the sound of crutches on the parquet floor. So she did want to live. Martial smiled, mellow and sad.

Tomorrow would be her last day here. Marthe had found a place where Flore could wait for her ankle to heal.

He returned to the newspaper on his lap, his attention drawn by a picture. A single cast-iron Godin stove would, an advertisement claimed, heat a room a whole fifty percent more efficiently than an open fire. He had heard of the stoves, manufactured in the north by a utopian community. Profits were shared between the factory workers, and the owner, Godin, an unconventional inventor, lived in one of the comfortable apartments of a 'social palace' he had built next to his foundry.

On a whim, Martial grabbed a piece of paper, a request to Monsieur Godin forming inside his mind. Instead, he found himself drawing the silhouette of Flore walking past a pendulum-pump well, a basket on her head.

He ran down to the kitchen for a piece of charcoal to complete his sketch. A knock on the door made him freeze. He jumped into the pantry.

'Sorry, Monsieur Martial,' Marthe said with a look of concern. 'There's a young man from Laforge outside. I told him you were unwell, but he insisted. Said they need a priest urgently.' She opened her hands. 'An accident.'

'Thank you, Marthe. Get Iñaki to saddle Blanca. I might not be back for lunch.'

Donning a winter cape and a fur travelling hat, Martial gathered what he needed and hurried to the stables.

'It's my brother.' Perched on stilts, the young man stepped on the spot. 'He's a *résinier,* fell onto his *hapchot* and sliced his leg.' Tears ran freely on his tanned face.

Martial translated the information to himself. Day in, day out, a *résinier* ran like a monkey up a notched stick from pine to pine and scraped the bark ever higher with a *hapchot,* a tool with a very, very sharp blade.

'Did you send for a doctor?' Martial put a foot into the stirrup and gripped his saddle.

The young man's voice broke. 'We can't afford it, Father. If you hurry, you'll be just in time to give him the last rites.'

Martial kept his horse to a trot and, once they reached the main road, kicked his mare into a canter, the youth clanking close behind him.

Since the advent of resin, Laforge had grown into a hamlet, its dwellings much closer together than in Noirac. Outside a cabin at the edge of the green, a woman was waiting for them.

Martial dismounted, bowed his head under the low doorframe and stepped into the tiny cottage. Around a pallet hastily arranged in the kitchen, women were crying softly.

His thigh wrapped in dirty bandages, the *résinier* had lost a lot of blood. His face was so pale Martial wasted no time. He whipped out his holy oil.

The finality of his gesture drew out loud sobs.

Wan, vacant, topped with dark curls, the handsome face on the pillow still carried traces of childhood. The man could not have been much older than twenty. With a heavy heart, Martial gave him the extreme unction and whispered, 'Would you like me to hear your confession?'

The young man gave a weak nod.

Martial turned to the women, indicating that they should leave. By the time they had filed out of the room, the *résinier* was dead.

A wail rose from a cot in the corner. Martial ran a hand over his face. The child was a newborn. He stood by the corpse, drew the sign of the cross and intoned the prayer for the dead, *'Requiem, aeternam dona . . .'*

The story was always the same. There would be no

money for the funeral. The young man would be lowered into the common grave. The young widow would starve, and the baby would die.

Martial comforted the family as best he could and rode away, ashamed and tired to the bottom of his soul. His father had the means to employ a doctor to look after his workmen. The loss of the young *résinier*'s life need not have happened.

Father Anselme, Martial found digging manure into his potato patch, saw things differently: he was from farming stock. His position as a priest gave him status and guaranteed an income, but when food was scarce, he too had to tighten his belt.

'Father Martial!' The old man wiped his hands on a rag and limped to the gate. 'Are you better?'

'Yes. My cold was nothing compared to the fate of the young man to whom I have just given the last rites.'

'Oh dear, their instruments are far too sharp. One false move and . . .'

'I will ask my father to set up a fund for his widow and orphan. After all, the man died working for him.'

His eyebrows arched ever so slightly, the old priest held Martial's gaze. His silence spoke volumes.

'Well, well . . .' He looked away and wiped his hands on a handkerchief. 'Here is the postman.'

A man in a blue uniform and képi was striding towards them on stilts, a satchel slung over his shoulder.

'A letter for you, Father Anselme, from your sister. And one for Père Martial Boyer de Pagny.' The moustachioed postman delivered the letter with a flourish. 'From the bishopric.'

Martial grabbed the letter and headed for his room, intrigued by noises coming from the kitchen.

'Is Onorina still making sausages?' he asked over his shoulder.

'Ah.' Father Anselme grinned. 'You will find it very warm in there. She is pressing honey. Prosper is helping her. A man of many talents, our *vigneron*. He is not only a hemp weaver, but a beekeeper too.'

A wave of heat greeted Martial. A fire was raging in the cooker. Upturned skeps were lined on the table, their contents waiting to be pressed. Surrounded with buckets filled with honey and wax, Flore's aunt and the beekeeper were slicing out chunks of comb and dropping them into the cloth that lined the press, a process they seemed to find hilarious. With a giggle, Onorina ran a sticky finger over a stray lock and tucked it back into her bonnet.

Seen from her good side, she was not bad-looking.

Martial greeted them and hurried to his room.

If the letter contained what he presumed it would, the timing was bad. Or was it? He picked up a silver letter opener stamped with his family crest and gently tapped his lips with the handle as he read,

Dear Nephew,

I hope this letter finds you well and that your father and Roderic returned from Paris in good health.

I have given thought to what we discussed when we last met and feel you are indeed ready to progress to a larger parish. One has just become available in the vicinity of Bordeaux, for which you are eminently suitable.

I would be grateful if you could make arrangements to visit me at the bishopric on Monday.

I shall be expecting you for lunch.

Please give my regards to your father and brothers.

Yours affectionately,

Amédée Boyer de Pagny. Evêque de Bordeaux.

Back in the kitchen, the two beekeepers were now grimacing as they reached the last turn of the handle.

'There is some soup warming on the *potager* for you,

Father. I will serve it in the dining room.' Onorina's face was flushed.

'Thank you, but I'm not hungry. I think I'd better get back to the manor.'

'Let me prepare a tisane of mint and honey,' she insisted. 'It won't take a moment, and it will keep you warm.'

'Thank you.'

While Martial drank his tisane, it came to him to ask Prosper if he could spare a few hours helping with the presbytery garden. Father Anselme was getting old, and his back gave him trouble.

Before he left, he went to the church and spent some time in prayer, the bishop's letter weighing heavy on his mind.

His thoughts of leaving Noirac suddenly seeming cowardly. A parish in Bordeaux did not appeal to him, but what else could a man do with all that Latin?

Still deep in thought, he dragged a reluctant Blanca from her stable and cantered back to the manor in a cold driving rain.

'Flore?'

He peeped through her half-open door.

'I have nowhere to go.' Flore cast her clutches aside and sank to the edge of her bed. 'What is to become of me?' She lifted her face to him. 'Father . . .'

Father. There was the chasm that stood between them. *Father.* He was only four years older than her. In Flore's eyes, he was a priest, a gelding and, what was worse, the son of the viscount who had caused her father's death. By rights, she should hate him.

He stepped inside and sat by the window.

'Do not despair. Marthe has found a place for you to stay until your ankle has healed. Her sister is a nun in a convent. You can spend some time convalescing there.'

14
BORDEAUX – THE BISHOP'S PALACE

Dwarfed by the architecture of the episcopal building, Martial reminded himself that awe was exactly the sentiment the palace's grand columns and pediments were meant to inspire.

He threw back his shoulders and saisdto the groom, 'Come back for me around three o'clock, Iñaki.'

Tightening his coat against the draughts that sliced through the open corridors, Martial hurried behind a servant through an enfilade of rooms. Persian rugs muffled their steps, the spoils—Martial found himself beset by cynical thoughts—of wars waged to save the souls of heathens.

The servant knocked on a thick door and announced him.

The bishop's lair was a sober mix of deep green and blood red with touches of gold that bounced off mirrors, chandeliers and crystal vases. The place reeked of lucre. Just one of the marquetry cigar boxes would have been enough to save the life Martial had consigned to God yesterday.

'Martial, welcome!' In a black habit, a wide belt around

his ample waist, Uncle sat behind his desk, grey sideburns adding a touch of bonhomie to his dour features.

The prelate's only luxury items today, apart from the solid gold chain and cross of office, were gold-rimmed spectacles and, of course, the ring he held out for Martial to kiss.

'You're just in time for lunch. Cook has promised me a jugged hare, an absolute delight.' The bishop rubbed his hands in anticipation.

Martial followed him to a private dining room overlooking a neatly clipped lawn hemmed by oleander bushes. A small fire glowed in the hearth.

'Let us drink to your health, Martial, and to your new position.'

Already? Martial wondered if an unsuspecting priest had been demoted to make room for him. He opened his mouth to ask and thought better of it.

A valet standing to attention by the sideboard served them a glass of Floc as an aperitif.

'So how are you? I heard there was a fire in Noirac. They are a dangerous breed, those Basques, not to be trusted.'

Martial choked on his Floc. How had gossip reached Bordeaux? Had Ricar already served it to 'foreign investors,' neatly packaged to serve their interests? Why not? A couple of words in the right ear, a few francs in the right pocket and his reputation would be safe.

They chatted between courses, drifting from the delicious hare to the subject of gifts in kind. Emboldened by the wine, Martial asked the question that weighed most on his mind.

'Uncle, how do you reconcile the wealth of the Church, the message of Jesus and the fact that our peasants are starving?'

'I am glad you are asking me that, Nephew.' His uncle leaned forward. 'As a young man, these things troubled me too, but you are asking the wrong question. *Starving* is too strong a word. There has not been a famine in Les Landes for over a hundred years. There is disease and want, but thanks to the office I hold, an office to which you too can aspire, I am able to do something about it.' The bishop dipped a chunk of bread into his sauce and sucked it, his eyes closed in rapture.

Martial searched his memory for signs of the bishop's generosity, but apart from a new altar cloth in Noirac church, he could not recall any.

'It will never matter how much or how little money they earn, there will always be poor people. The poor will always drink, gamble, fight and beget children they are not able to support. Your father, on the other hand, invests for the future, drains the marshes to stop the spread of swamp fever . . .' Uncle held out his glass for a refill. Impassive, the valet poured wine and retreated to the side.

The episcopal ring glinted in the oblique sunlight to make a point. 'Education is the way out of poverty.' Uncle tapped the table with his forefinger. 'Now we have planted pines, resin will attract workers, hamlets will flourish, and schools will follow.'

Martial struggled to stop the cynicism from curling his lips. In all his years as a bishop, his uncle had never built a single school.

'Resin is all very well, Uncle, but yesterday I gave the last rites to a *résinier*, a young father who died for want of a doctor. His wife told me that they simply could not afford it.'

'Bah!' The whiskers shook. 'They don't trust doctors! They prefer healers who will give them potions concocted from bats' wings and hedgehogs' tongues.' Uncle brushed away the topic with a benign smile. 'You will like the new parish I have in mind for you, I promise.' A bushy brow arched suggestively above his eyeglasses. 'Make a career of it. The job does have its rewards.'

So I heard. Martial squirmed, wishing Hugo had not told him.

Dessert was brought in, an Armagnac-soaked sponge floating in custard.

Coffee was served in a small library lined with leather-bound tomes of the lives of saints. An ornate cast-iron Godin stove snored gently in a corner. Under a window, incongruous in such a temple of pious learning, was a velvet chaise of the palest blue.

Martial cleared his throat and, before he could change his mind, blurted out what had been weighing on his mind.

'Uncle, I have been thinking. I really don't think I am suited to the life of a priest.'

'Oh dear, your father will be so disappointed.'

How curious, Martial sat back in wonder, *that this should be Uncle's first reaction. Leaving the priesthood is a terrible step, not punishable by prison, thank God, but oh, the shame, the opprobrium . . .*

'Maxime has fathered three sons: a future viscount, a general and a bishop. He has it all planned, you know. None of you can desist.' The bishop's dark eyes narrowed behind the glasses. 'Your father is a proud man, Martial. Whatever scheme you have, he will not take kindly to. I assured him I would find you a parish in Bordeaux, and I have done so. Please do not disappointed me.'

Martial swilled the Armagnac at the bottom of his coffee cup. 'We can't all lead our lives bullied by Father.'

'When you left the seminary, I advised him to let me place you in Dax, but he was of the opinion that it would do you good to confront the real world.' His uncle's face softened. 'I named you after Martial, the patron saint of Bordeaux because, somehow, I always hoped you would follow in my steps.'

Martial swallowed hard. 'In truth, the root of my struggle comes down to . . .'

'Is it the vow of chastity?' The old man gave a benevolent nod. 'It can be a problem, especially for one so young and full of vitality, but it is no *cardinal* sin to . . . how shall I say, once in a while . . . We are human after all, and as long as you are discreet, and confess.'

'No!' Martial jerked back. 'It's not that at all!'

Or was it? He was attracted to Flore, but the attraction was not just physical, there was a mystical dimension to it. Flore might be the catalyst for his qualms, but she was not their cause. He gripped the arms of his chair. 'I want to lead a useful life. I hoped I could do so within the constraints of the Church, but those very constraints—receiving food from peasants who don't have enough to eat, watching them struggle to make ends meet while I . . . while we . . .'

'You want to join the House of Saint Vincent de Paul and live in poverty? Is that what you want?'

It had crossed Martial's mind.

'Lofty ideals are the prerogative of youth. It is a fine thing to want to help the poor, but if you leave the priesthood, I warn you. You *will* join their rank.' The bishop's voice rose. 'Can you not see that even if you were to feed *all* the poor, there would always be more. One million people are not getting enough to eat in Paris, but strangely most of that million is getting enough to *drink*.' He removed his glasses and declared, 'That is how God wills it.'

Martial's eyes widened. 'What do you mean?'

'God ordains your station in life. You are one of the chosen few, Martial.' His uncle's eyes drooped sadly. 'You are a very confused young man, Nephew. If you throw away your privilege, yours will be a very hard life.'

'So what would you have me do?' Martial had run out of arguments.

'You will see things differently once you are installed in your new parish. In the meantime, by all means set up a benevolent fund for the *résiniers.* I am a great advocate of charity.'

'And what do I say to the poor soul who sobs in my confessional, her skin peeling away with pellagra because she has nothing but corn gruel to sup on?'

With a sigh of irritation, his uncle spoke as to a dim child. 'Tell her that the first quality the poor must acquire is *patience*. Remind her that however hard her suffering, it will never equal that of our Lord Jesus Christ who died on the cross for our sins. The *duty* of the poor is to offer their suffering to God, and God will reward them.'

A knock on the door saved Martial from protesting. A valet whispered something into the bishop's ear.

'Yes, of course, let the lady in! Tell her she is welcome.'

In her late thirties, a petite woman in a layered black-and-white crinoline stepped in shyly, her perfume mingling with the smell of coffee and Armagnac. Her plump cheeks glowed from the cold, and under a mass of chestnut hair, striking blue eyes twinkled.

She genuflected to the bishop and kissed his ring. 'Monseigneur.' The flesh on display beneath the cape made Martial's face burn.

'Madame Villeroy, this is my nephew Father Martial, priest of the parish of Noirac. We were just discussing your good works.'

Glued to his chair, Martial realised his mouth was open and snapped it shut.

The lady's flush deepened. She apparently had not expected the bishop to have company.

'Madame Villeroy is the widow of a sea captain,' the bishop explained, unruffled. 'As such, the lady organises charity events and takes collections for the widows of sailors in Bordeaux.' He pointed to the blue chaise. *'Asseyez-vous, madame, je vous en prie.'*

The woman winced when the chaise squeaked. She spent some time arranging her crinoline and cape, casting covert glances at the bishop.

No cardinal sin indeed. Martial realised that for his uncle, charity clearly began at home.

He shot to his feet. 'You have given me sound advice, Uncle. Thank you for listening to me. I must leave, I'm afraid. I have an appointment with my lawyer.' He bowed to the widow. 'Madame, I am delighted to have met you.'

His uncle rang a bell.

While Martial waited in the corridor for the servant to return with his coat, inside the room the chaise squeaked as his uncle gathered the 'rewards of office' and the pretty widow carried out her charitable works.

'I'm due at my lawyer's, Iñaki,' he said to the groom. 'His office is straight down rue Sainte Catherine.'

'It would be quicker to go around rue de la Merci, monsieur. With all its bakers and butchers and that omnibus stopping every few paces, we'll never get through Sainte Catherine.'

Bypassing the hubbub of the big city, they reached the lawyer's rooms in no time.

Plump, with an oval face and skin as smooth as a woman's, Clodomir Mercier reminded Martial of a eunuch. He had attended the seminary at the same time as Martial and, dismissed for inappropriate behaviour with another boy, had found his calling as a lawyer.

'The good news,' Clodomir confirmed to Martial, 'is that your income is managed by a trust, and even if Monsieur your father disapproves of your actions, he is not in a position to cut you off.' He crossed elegant fingers. 'I suppose this is what you wanted to know?'

'Are there restrictions?'

'No.' The lawyer met Martial's gaze, expecting an explanation. When none came, he added, 'You might, if you so wished,' Clodomir added, 'sign a power of attorney and appoint a member of his family to manage your income.'

'Why would I do that?' Martial frowned.

'Should you wish to withdraw from life and become a monk, for instance.' The glint in his erstwhile friend's eyes reminded Martial of the reputation he'd once had. 'We all admired your Spartan leanings.'

'I may have changed, Clodomir.'

'Ah, we all do.' The lawyer said pensively as he accompanied Martial to the door. 'We all do.'

Back on rue Sainte Catherine, Martial said to his groom, 'Come, Iñaki, let's go and dream a little.' He pointed to the Gironde River visible between tall buildings. 'Take us to the docks.'

It was high tide. From the cabriolet, they watched the noisy throngs that always haunted the quays, bringing in the day's catch, loading and unloading barrels and bales. Redolent of seaweed and fish, the air was thick with the cries of seagulls and the calls of dockers scurrying around the tangle of cranes.

Beyond the loading bays, three deep and sometimes more, was a forest of boats with their yards, poles and rigging, a large leafless forest in the centre of town, clinking and clanking in the wind.

The tide high enough for steamers to dock, the shape of a steamer from the Messageries Impériales loomed in the distance.

Iñaki drew up to the barrier that separated the curious from the dockers employed to feed the monstrous ogre its cargo of coal, grain, wine, sheep and enough poultry required for it to reach the end of the world.

Martial pointed further down to a ship displaying a yellow flag, waiting to disgorge its passengers. Porters and relatives waited excitedly on the quay, waving to people on deck.

'See that yellow flag?' Martial said. 'The captain has to check that no one on board carries any infectious disease. If there is an outbreak of cholera or yellow fever, not a soul will be allowed to disembark. Imagine! They have been at sea for over a month.'

'Where have they come from?' Iñaki's eyes shone with excitement.

'This one is called *Amazone*. Just sailed in from South America. You will find many of your Basque countrymen there.'

'One of my cousins went to Chile,' Iñaki said pensively. 'We never heard from him again.'

'Can he write?'

'No.'

'Perhaps it has something to do with it.'

Martial loved the harbour. He used to come here with his uncle as a child, always seized with an unbearable yearning to travel to the lands of fairy tales. The yearning was still there, buried inside his heart.

He hopped down from the carriage and walked past tugs and fishing boats, dominated by the bulk of the steamer. Majestic with both masts and funnels, the ship was a self-contained island that held the promise of a new life, a life free from his father's tyranny and a hypocritical Church that preached humility while acting with ostentation.

As he strolled along the quay, Martial's heart raced at the realisation that somewhere there was another life waiting for him.

15
TO THE NUNNERY

Flore had never been so far away from home. They had left before dawn, hours ago, and ridden north, though where to, she had no clear idea. Huddled between the father and Marthe inside the brougham, she abandoned herself to fate.

At last, the horses slowed down. Steam rising from their flanks, they drew up alongside a tall forbidding stone wall.

'Here we are, dear. The Benedictine convent of Saint-Sauveur.' Marthe pulled a bag from under the seat. 'I salvaged what I could from your underclothes. You will be given a novice's habit. My sister is a nun here, but she won't be able to talk to you. You are allowed to pray and sing, but you will have to walk and eat in silence. Come, Monsieur Martial will help you down and take you to meet Mother Superior.'

Flore fell into the priest's arms, surprised at his warmth and comfortable scent of cotton and soap. Self-conscious, she picked up her crutches and hobbled away.

He cleared his throat. 'Marthe, you'll want to go to the parlour to meet your sister. I'll see you there after I have spoken with Mother Superior.'

A tall nun was flapping towards them down the cloister, a raven in full flight.

Flore shrank and sidled to the priest. Why had he brought her here, really?

'So this is my young charge. Welcome to Saint-Sauveur.' The nun took Flore's hands in hers, nervy and strong. 'I am Mère Marie-Emmanuel.' She turned to the priest. 'Have you explained our rules to your ward?'

'Yes, Flore understands. I am sure silence will help her heal. She has lost most of her family in a short time and is in need of rest.' He pointed to the crutches. 'There was an accident. We assumed Flore's ankle was sprained.'

'We will take you to the infirmary, Flore. The nurse will have a look, but first let us drop your bag in your cell.'

The word *cell* hit Flore like an arrow. She was being sent to prison. Casting a fearful glance at the silent ghosts gliding around the cloister, hands hidden inside their sleeves, Flore grabbed her clutches and started towards the gates.

Father Martial placed a soft hand on her shoulder. '*Cell* is what they call their bedroom. You will stay here until your foot and your heart have healed.' His gaze softened when he added, 'Longer, if that is what you wish.'

Flore held back. What if he was lying? What if they had decided to leave her here for the rest of her life?

She took in a long breath and asked in a strangled voice, 'Will you come back for me?'

'Yes, of course. I'm not plotting to have you committed here. When you are able to walk, I will come and fetch you . . . if that is what you want.'

'Father, I—' Flore gripped his sleeve.

'Goodbye, Father Boyer. I will keep you informed, and thank you.' Businesslike, Mother Marie-Emmanuel pocketed the fat envelope he had given her, called out to a sister and handed her Flore's bag.

Too choked to speak, Flore let go of Father Martial's arm. His dark eyes bore into her soul.

She picked up her crutches and started down the cloister. Halfway down, she stopped and cast a glance over her shoulder.

He had not moved at all.

Slow step after slow step, Flore followed the sister to a narrow cell furnished with a bed, a small table and a prie-dieu. Under the bed was a chamber pot and above it a crucifix. A small rectangle above the door let in some light.

The door was free from bolts. The ball inside her throat loosened a little.

Mother Marie-Emmanuel came to the door. 'Sorry, dear, but I do need to ask this. Are you with child?'

With child? Flore cast a fearful glance around her. What kind of place was this?

She shook her head forcefully.

Once the sisters had gone, she breathed out all the air she had been holding and collapsed on the bed. Since Father Martial had pulled her out of the river, she had tried to bear Marthe's jolliness, forced down her soup, read Hugo's almanacs and endured the priest's silent pleas to get better, when all she really wanted to do was lie still, neither moving nor thinking for fear of waking up the pain.

Flore picked up her bag, surprised to find it full. When she pulled out the goose feather pillow Marthe had the forethought to pack, the pain broke free.

Nanette . . . An inexhaustible torrent poured out of Flore's battered heart. Nanette . . . Wave after wave of tears fuelled by guilt and despair until, at last, she fell asleep.

A soft knock on the door woke her up. An old nun came in, her face withered and kind inside the black wimple. She slowly led the way to the chapel, where, for an hour, the sisters sang and prayed. Curious glances slid in

Flore's direction and, when they met her eyes, turned to smiles.

Flore bowed her head. These women would not welcome her so readily in their midst if they knew what she had done.

After the service, Flore was taken to the infirmary, where the rule of silence did not apply. Four beds lined the room, scented with soap and aromatic herbs. A shape slept in one of the beds.

Sister Gervaise sat in front of Flore and prodded her foot. 'What happened?' she asked in French, her voice soft and warm.

Heat flooded Flore's cheeks. 'An accident. I tripped on my stilts and fell awkwardly,' she answered in French, aware of her southern accent.

'You have damaged one of the ligaments quite badly. It will heal, but it will take time.'

Flore winced. She had skinned enough rabbits to know about ligaments.

'I will make a poultice of comfrey.' The sister disappeared into a cupboard.

'Psst!' A voice came from the bed. A young girl, who also spoke French. 'What's your name? I'm Joseta.'

Reluctant to leave the safety of her silent bubble, Flore did not reply.

'Why are *you* here?' The girl pointed to her round belly. 'Me, I got in trouble. My papa cast me out. The sister's nice and I get fed, but not being able to talk's driving me witless.'

Flore hesitated. 'I'm not sure I'm allowed to talk.'

'But you aren't a real nun, are you?'

Joseta's chatter chipped the flimsy scab over Flore's raw wound. Tears rising dangerously close to the surface, she lifted her eyes to the heavens and made a big show of crossing herself.

The girl's parents don't even care if she dies. Flore felt for Joseta, but she could not find the strength to care for a soul other than her own, and yet it could so easily have been her in that bed.

Choked with emotion, Flore took the girl's hand in hers. Her chin wobbled as she muttered, 'I will pray for you, Joseta.'

Her foot tightly bandaged, she took her crutches and limped past an open door. She tottered in, eyes wide in wonder. The room was lined with books from floor to ceiling. Small desks and wooden chairs were dotted around a cylindrical stove next to a basket of logs. Arched windows overlooked a knot garden asleep under a film of frost.

Scouring the shelves, Flore uncovered a treasure trove of illustrated parables. She pulled a chair next to the window and set about tracing each word with a finger, relieved to find that, thanks to Mama's teachings and Father Anselme's rudimentary catechism, she could read French and make sense of the story.

Now, she had a purpose. She would use the time here to learn to read properly.

One morning, as she sat by the fire, engrossed in the story of Abraham, about to plunge a knife into his young son's heart, a bloodcurdling scream made her jump, a scream followed at regular intervals by a series of groans, wails and sobs.

The steps of Mother Superior rushed past to the infirmary.

'Her time has come.' The nurse's voice.

'I will send word to the parents.' Mother Superior darted away.

Flore closed her book with a prayer of relief. Joseta's parents had relented. They were coming to take her and their little grandchild home.

The moans carried on for most of the day. Unable to concentrate on the story, Flore winced with every grunt. As the day wore on, one by one, the sisters joined her to read under pools of yellow light cast by petrol lamps, indifferent to the ruckus next door, which Flore found strange.

At last, the wail of an infant rose in the stillness. The sisters exchanged a glance.

No one smiled.

Night fell over the cloister, lit by dim lanterns. Flore was hovering on her crutches outside the infirmary when a sleek carriage drew up outside the gates.

She flattened herself against the cold wall. Who could it be in such a carriage at this time of night? Were Joseta's parents not simple farmers?

She drew back into the shadows. An elegant couple in city clothes stepped into the cloister.

Mother Superior greeted them and led them to the infirmary. Her voice rose, clear and authoritative. 'This is the mother. As you can see, she is healthy. And here is your little boy.'

'He is beautiful.' The lady's voice.

'God is merciful,' Mother Marie-Emmanuel replied. 'He is yours now. Make sure he is baptised promptly.'

'Thank you.' The man added, 'I will have the alms delivered to you within the week.'

Flore recoiled further into an alcove. *Diou biban, is that what they do here? Sell babies?*

The new parents left with the newborn wrapped in a blanket, the lights of their carriage soon swallowed up by the night.

Inside the infirmary, that still smelled of the day's travail, Joseta was sobbing quietly, her nightgown pulled down to her waist, Sister Gervaise bandaging her breasts.

When the nurse was finished, Flore took Joseta in her arms and let her tears mingle with hers.

16
JOSETA GOES TO PARIS

Two weeks after the birth of the baby, Flore was limping around the frosty cloister with a stick when the clatter of a carriage broke her reverie. She'd known the day would come, but so soon?

Joseta was being sent to Paris to work in service. She stood by the gates, tiny in a light blue cape, a basket at her feet. Flore hobbled closer and with a heavy heart, hugged the weeping girl. Her despair crept into Flore's heart, ripped open its fragile scars and she sobbed with her, unable to let go.

'Come, dear.' Sister Gervaise gently pulled them apart. 'It's time.'

Joseta wiped her face with her sleeve, pulled a folded piece of paper from her pocket and held it out to Flore.

'This is where I will be. If you ever come to Paris, I'll sure be glad to see you.'

Though she doubted she would ever go to Paris, Flore took the address written in Mother Superior's florid hand and held it to her heart, unable to stop her tears. Poor Joseta.

With her neatly parted hair, wide-set eyes and heart-shaped mouth, she exuded the very air of innocence that stirred stir men's instincts. Paris was a dangerous place.

'Don't worry, I'll find you,' Flore promised in a shaky voice.

'We will all pray for you, dear.' Sister Gervaise helped Joseta into the open carriage.

The gate clanged shut. Her fingers clutching the cold metal, Flore watched the blue cape through her tears until it was nothing but a shimmering dot in the snowy landscape.

Life on the moor may be hard, but it had its own rules. Here, Flore had learned to read, but she had also learned that babies could be sold like puppies, girls cast out of their homes by their own parents and that from one moment to the next, life could shift like a sand dune, leaving nothing behind.

As winter dragged on, Flore's world shrank to the draughty cloister between the refectory, the chapel and the library. In the golden candlelight of the chapel, she found solace, human warmth, and when she sang, her soprano pitch reached out to the heavens, begging for atonement.

When the three gongs announced mealtimes, a flutter of hands would summon her to the refectory and pass on broth, ham, bread and cheese, which the nuns ate mindfully.

Searching for a new challenge, Flore carefully clambered on a chair, drawn to a book from a top shelf. The cover bore the picture of a man in a dark habit, his love reflected in the radiant face of a young girl.

Her pulse racing, Flore hobbled back to her desk, clutching the book. A love story? Here in Saint-Sauveur? Intrigued, she checked the title. *Abélard et Héloïse.*

From then on, Flore would creep into the library and while away the hours with Héloïse who, Flore was surprised to discover, had been a gifted scholar who lived around 1130. From a very young age, the girl was so bright her name had spread around learned circles. Her rich uncle hired a tutor, a famous professor called Pierre Abélard. Their love scandalised the society they lived in, they were separated, and Héloïse became an abbess.

Astonished that seven hundred years ago girls were considered to be worth educating, Flore read with renewed interest. Muttering the words on the page, she followed their story until a sentence from Héloïse shook her to the core. *It is not the deed, but the intention of the doer,* wrote the abbess from her distant century, *which makes the sin.*

It is not the deed . . . Flore buried her face in her hands and sobbed with gratitude. Her *intention* had been to burn Ricar's pines. It was a sin, of course, but saplings could be replaced. Her *intention,* however, had never been to kill Nanette.

Eaten alive by guilt, Flore had never found the strength to confess her crime to the visiting priest. Shriven at last, she clung to the hope that in death she might see Nanette again.

Additional vigils and prayers kept Flore away from the library during the Christmas celebrations, and when she returned to the lovers, she felt as if she was meeting old friends.

With our lessons as a pretext,' breathless, Flore deciphered Abélard's candid confession, *we abandoned ourselves entirely to love. Her studies allowed us to withdraw in private, as love desired, with our books open before us, more words of love than of our reading passed between us, and more kissing than teaching. My hands strayed more often over the curves of her body than to the pages; love drew our eyes to look on each other more than reading kept them on our texts.*

Flushed, Flore stared into the flames of the stove. She had loved Ricar for so long she simply did not know how to stop.

For five years, he had reigned over her thoughts, and when he had returned, so desperate was she for his love she had allowed him to use her. At night, alone in her cell, her memories filled her with shame, her body yearning for the pleasures he had taught her.

Héloïse too had known the torments of desire, the craving for a man that inflamed your body and never ever dulled.

Please, God, free me of this, Flore prayed. *The price we pay for love is too high.*

After marrying her teacher in secret, Héloïse gave birth to a boy she named Astrolab, but Abélard had pledged his life to God and, incensed at what they saw as treason, his colleagues crept upon him and castrated him. Héloïse's uncle locked her up in a convent. Astrolab was taken away.

The price of love was terrifying, Flore could see it now.

As for poor Joseta, she had fallen for a handsome carpenter who had promised marriage, all the while planning a four-year tour de France as an apprentice. By the time she found out she was pregnant, he was gone.

Love was dangerous. Love was a poison, a sweet poison, perhaps, but it killed all the same.

In the chapel, Flore cast furtive glances around her. What had led these women to choose a life away from men, a life without love or families, a life without words? What were they running away from?

If I ever give my heart away to anyone, first I will be settled. I might work in a shop or run a market stall. Perhaps Father Martial can help me find such a position. Whatever happens, I will earn my own keep and never depend on a man.

How she would achieve that, Flore had no idea. Unreachable as it was—when did girls ever get to do what they wanted?—it was her ambition.

Glances were exchanged in the chapel as Flore's voice soared above all others, fuelled with vigour and purpose.

When, a couple of weeks later, a scrawny waif arrived—pregnant and not yet fifteen—Flore told Mother Marie-Emanuel that she was ready to return to the world.

17

IÑAKI GOES TO CHILE

As the brougham reached Bordeaux station, Martial jumped out and went to his groom.

'Thank you. Iñaki, I would appreciate if you didn't tell anyone where you were today. I will write to my father when I arrive, but if he asks you questions, tell him—'

The young Basque shrugged. 'Don't worry, sir. I won't be at the manor long enough to answer questions. I'm leaving tomorrow.'

'Leaving? Have you found a better position?' The boy had been with the family for as long as Martial could remember.

'No, sir. The trip we took to the harbour last month got me thinking. Remember the cousin I have in Chile?'

Martial nodded.

'I'm taking a steamer and joining him in Valparaiso.'

Martial stared at his groom. 'He has contacted you?'

'Yes. He got someone to write a letter, inviting me over.'

Martial slowly closed his mouth and pulled a large gold coin from his top pocket.

'Take this. I hear they only feed you oats and dry biscuits on those ships. Make sure you get out at every port to buy yourself some fruit, or your teeth will fall out. I wish you luck, Iñaki. You're a braver man than I am.'

With a tinge of envy, Martial watched the carriage pull away, soon swallowed by the throngs.

'Fancy him going to Chile.' He turned to Flore, self-conscious in her presence.

What had possessed him to invite her to follow him to Paris, he wasn't sure. There they stood, he in his cassock, Flore in her novice's habit, for the simple reason that she did not have any clothes.

'Did he say he was leaving on a *steamer*?'

'Yes. Lucky him.'

Had he known Iñaki was leaving, would he have joined him? Perhaps. Then again, another plan had taken form while Flore was away, a plan in which she could join him in all propriety.

'Is it very far?'

'Paris?'

'No, Valpa—where your coachman is going, is it very far?'

Martial pushed his way onto the concourse and replied over his shoulder, 'Over a month away.'

Flore limped behind him. 'What is he going to find there?'

'His cousin, hopefully. Stay close to me.'

Though Martial was not escaping to Valparaiso, he too was absconding. After weeks of indecision and soul-searching conversations with Father Anselme that went deep into the night, he had come to terms with the fact that the priesthood was not for him. A brief stop in Paris would give him time to think about the next step and decide on Flore's future.

All he had told her on the coach was that they were going to Paris to stop by at his cousin's for a few days.

Like a frightened doe, Flore tripped against his bag every time a locomotive belched out a cloud of steam.

'Why don't you carry your own bag? Here, it weighs hardly anything. Look, our train's just over there.' Martial grabbed her hand and headed for the far platform. His palm tingled.

Giddy with sensations that swirled inside him like sugar syrup, he was sweating by the time they reached the train a mere fifty yards away.

He located the second-class carriage, found seats, tossed their luggage into the nets and fanned himself with his hat. Opposite him, the plucky peasant girl who used to swing her hips across the airial was gone, replaced by a virginal novice in black habit and white wimple.

'I can't believe we're going to *Paris*.' Flore's eyes sparkled. 'How long will it take us to reach it?'

'Five hundred kilometres? When I was a boy, by stage-coach it took us *well* over ten days to get there. We used to spend the whole summer in Paris. I dreaded the journey.'

'Ten days!'

'Yes. Now it only takes ten hours.' A shiver of anticipation ran through Martial at the prospect of a whole day spent cocooned with Flore inside the great caterpillar.

A strident whistle blotted out Flore's next question. Doors slammed. The locomotive hooted and pulled away with great asthmatic puffs.

They stared out of the window at the tall ships moored along the Garonne, hoping to catch a glimpse of the steamer that would take Iñaki to Valparaiso.

Once the estuary was out of sight, Flore asked, 'Father? What are we going to do in Paris?'

Martial bristled at the word *Father*, but how could he object when he wore a cassock and Flore a habit?

'My brother Roderic was smitten with the modern Paris. I am very keen to see it. Apparently, Louis-Napoléon and his architect have transformed the city from top to bottom.'

'*É bé*, if you look at the mess he's made of our moor just to please himself, it doesn't bode well, does it?'

'We'll spend three days there and do whatever takes our fancy. How is your ankle, by the way?'

'Much better, thank you. Sister Gervaise made me promise I'd be careful.' Flore hesitated. 'Do you know where I'll be staying?'

Her question pricked Martial's conscience. Of course she was worried.

He cleared his throat. 'Not too far from my cousin's.'

Jules and his parents lived in a grand mansion Parisians called *hôtel particulier*, where it would be unseemly for Martial to roll up with a comely nun. A man of the world, Jules had understood. 'My cousin suggested a pension for young ladies situated on rue Bergère. Rather fitting for a shepherdess, don't you think?'

Flore shrank into her seat. 'Oh.'

'Don't worry, I have no intention of abandoning you. Tomorrow, we'll go and visit the Jardin d'Acclimatation. There are all kinds of animals there. Zebras, camels, even elephants. We'll take a carriage. You won't have to walk far.'

Flore kept her gaze on the countryside gliding by. Father Martial was kind, but there she was again, whisked about like straw in the wind. She only had herself to blame. Although he had asked her what she wanted to do, she had never been able to give him an answer, aware that, had she asked him to find her a position as a market-stall holder, he would not have known where to start. She still had no clear idea of where they would be going after Paris, if anywhere.

The train crossed a lush patchwork of fields in various shades of green, acre after acre of wheat and nascent beans interspersed by thick forests and the promise of turnips and beets. If that was what France looked like to the French, no wonder they balked at their scraggly moor.

After a while, she pulled out her book.

'What are you reading?'

She held it out to him.

'Abélard and Héloïse?' With a strange look, the father pushed the book back into her hands as if it burned his fingers and rose to pull down the window.

'Mother Marie-Emmanuel gave it to me as a parting present.'

'Did she?' he said distractedly. 'It's a famous love story,' he fanned himself with his hat, 'between a young girl and a . . . a monk.'

Flore shrugged. 'I know.'

A blast of coal dust blew in. He coughed and slammed the window shut.

Why could he not sit still?

Flore clutched the tome to her chest. 'There is something in here, something Héloïse said, which touched my heart.'

'There is?' Father Martial leaned forward, suddenly keen.

Flore's voice cracked with emotion as she read, '"'Tis not the deed that matters, but the intention." You see, Héloïse is speaking to me through time, helping me find forgiveness for what I did to Nanette.'

'Oh. Yes. I see. Absolutely.'

Flore lowered her face. 'You said that to me too, but I couldn't understand at the time. I was . . . I was in a bad place. I was angry with you for pulling me out of the river.' She turned away. 'The nuns, the silence, the hymns . . . were just what I needed.' She lifted her eyes to his. 'How did you know?'

Father Martial thought about it for a long time. 'Silence. Compassion. Not being judged. We all need that at some time in our life.' When she did not respond, he carried on.

'Flore, I have a confession to make. My father does not know where I am. Neither does my uncle, the bishop. Father Anselme will spread the word that I have retired to a Benedictine monastery. It's something they will find easy to believe.'

'Is that what you want to do?' Flore was doubtful. 'Become a monk?'

'You see,' Martial leaned forward, 'my father accuses me of yearning for utopia. There are many of us out there ready to map out a new world, and I want to join them.'

'And you will work as a priest in this utopia in Paris?' Flore cast her question at random, hoping his purpose would eventually become clear.

'Paris is just a stopgap. I am thinking of giving up the priesthood.'

'But you can't do that!'

A flame danced inside his dark eyes. 'There will be no more pretending.'

Her hand jumped to her lips. 'You . . . you're pledged to God.' She stared out of the window for a long time before asking in a small voice. 'Will you go to prison?'

'No. There is nothing illegal about it. If anyone found out, they would strongly disapprove, but I joined the Church to help the poor, and wherever I turn I find myself having to help the rich. It's not a step I am taking likely. So yes, I have offered my services to a utopian society, where I am hoping to learn how men and women can live together without greed or social division.' He added, a little breathless, 'You can join me if you want.'

Flore slowly nodded, wondering what she was letting herself in for. Then again, did she have a choice?

Back at the manor, she had heard him use the word *utopia* enough to know what it meant. Utopia was something that did not exist, though from what she could tell, it certainly did exist inside this man's head.

As the landscape rolled past, Flore's thoughts hopped about like frogs on a rainy day. *What if the father is wrong and he is arrested? What will become of me? I can't believe I am going to Paris . . . I'll surprise Joseta. I hope we can hire a dress or find one in a pawnshop. Father Martial is deluded if he imagines he can stop being a priest. One look at him and people will know, even without the cassock. Is my dream of being independent my own utopia?*

'Father, this garden we are going to visit tomorrow . . .' To quieten her mind, Flore directed the conversation to a more mundane topic. 'What is it called again?'

'Le Jardin d'Acclimatation. It's in the Bois de Boulogne. It's not a garden, it's more of a park and a zoo.'

'What does *climatation* mean?'

'*Acclimatation?* Well, because explorers and diplomats bring our emperor offerings of all sorts of plants and animals from foreign climates . . .' Hands dancing as they did whenever he stood behind the pulpit, Father Martial described all the animals they would see before finally explaining the word. 'Paris being much colder—or warmer, I suppose, in the case of polar bears—the new arrivals are sent there to *acclimatise*, to get used to the new climate.'

Thoughtful, Flore met his gaze. 'It will be a fitting place for us, then, won't it? To climatise to our new selves.'

18
PARIS

Flore pinched herself the next morning, riding down the Champs Elysées. Trees were just coming into leaf along the avenue that led to a majestic stone arch that rose in the distance, built, Father Martial explained, in the style of Roman triumphal arches. She had nodded gravely. Around them, carriages jostled for space, young boys darted between horses' legs to scrape the manure carpeting the road, while along the pavements ladies charged through the throngs, umbrellas at the ready.

Next to her, gone was the country priest. Fully acclimatised to Paris, Martial—as she had to think of him now—wore long trousers and a short jacket. Thank God he had drawn the line at the ridiculous top hat everyone favoured and settled for a beige soft hat.

For Flore, getting dressed had been an ordeal. Back home, all she had to do at the start of a day was braid her hair and, after a perfunctory wash, slip on an additional chemise and skirt. Then, apron, bonnet, clogs, soft shoes if she took the stilts, and she was ready to go.

Paris was a battlefield and, as such, required battledress.

Flore's hired hat pulled at her tortured hair, a rigid corset was strapped like armour around her middle, and the bunched-up bustle—a sort of pliable basket—dug into her back. The woman from the hire shop had recommended it as 'most comfortable.' *Boudiou,* if this was comfortable, how did the real ladies manage? As for her feet, they had just been shod by the most modern shoemaker in France: Monsieur Pinet.

'Monsieur Pinet has made a name for himself,' Father Martial shouted over the clatter of hoofs and the barrage of insults flying about. 'He did his tour de France as a shoemaker's apprentice and patented a new heel and sole made of one piece. The sole is made of latex.'

'Latex comes from Cochinchina,' Flore shouted back. Ricar had told her how latex made men rich. The prospect of money was what had excited him, she could see that now. Angèle Poirier may be plain, but all Ricar would have to do to service his wife was to think of her bank account.

'Monsieur Pinet is a pioneer of social justice.' Father Martial's face glowed with fervour. 'His employees work reasonable hours.' He opened his hands to emphasise his point. 'He even puts money aside for their retirement pension!'

Her protector was a good man, Flore could see that, a man set on making the world a better place, but what a dreamer he was. The father may admire businessmen like Monsieur Pinet, but he would struggle to rule an industrial empire. He was simply too nice.

She thought back to the fun he'd had that morning choosing garments for her in the hire shop, searching for the dress that would turn her into a Parisienne. Keen to atone for his privilege, he had found a worthy cause in her.

A jolt put a stop to Flore's musings. The horses stalled, eyes rolling in fear when a man shot past on a contraption made of two flimsy wheels, powered by nothing more, it seemed, than his feet.

'Father!' she cried out. 'Over there! Look! Isn't that clever. No need for horses fouling the street.'

'Flore, look at me.'

'Oc?' Oh dear, what had she said?

'You can't call me Father anymore.'

'Sorry . . . Martial.' His name stuck in her throat.

The traffic around the Arc de Triomphe was at a standstill, but thanks to a few chosen expletives, their driver got them through to avenue de l'Impératrice and on to the Bois de Boulogne.

After the cotton-wool atmosphere of the convent, Flore's ears were ringing, and she breathed a sigh of relief when they reached the relative quiet of the Jardin d'Acclimatation.

The zoo was an assault on the senses of a different kind. The feral smell of big cats mingled with the sweat and cheap cologne of the crowd pressed around them. Bouncing on Monsieur Pinet's patented latex soles, Flore gripped Martial's sleeve past llamas and antelopes, marvelling at an ostrich strapped to a cart in which you could sit to have your portrait taken.

The animals were fascinating, but what intrigued her the most were the humans gathered there. Every region of France was represented by starched lace coifs, smocks and striped trousers. Scraps of the familiar Occitan cut through various shades of garbled patois.

She had never seen so many sailors, zouaves in pantaloons and képis, and soldiers jostling with maids pushing children around in wheeled contraptions. Young girls paraded in pairs, and old men stood to attention, their war medals on display.

Flore had dreamt of travelling, and here she was, in the

midst of the great zoo of life. She hooked her arm inside the father's and abandoned herself to the experience.

Flore's fingers dug into Martial's sleeve as they came face-to-face with two huge elephants. He cast her a glance, unable to believe that she was with him at last. Spending the morning dressing her had been unlike anything Martial had ever experienced.

'They are called Castor and Pollux.' His heart melted at the expression on her face. 'They're still young and will get twice as large. Look, a camel! Do you remember when some were brought over to our moor from Algeria?'

'*Oc!* Colin and I covered quite a few leagues on our stilts to see them.'

'They died of cold in winter.'

'That's because no one bothered to climatise them.'

Her remark was so sweet, Martial's face melted.

'What?' She frowned. 'Did I say it wrong?'

Struggling to contain the rush of treacle inside him, Martial shook his head. 'Not at all. It's just . . . good to see you're better, that's all.' He pointed to a gaily painted green-and-white pavilion. 'Come, let's have some lunch.'

Flore ordered soup. He chose beef and vegetables and observed her covertly, amazed at her transformation. Poised, elegant, she looked like a born Parisienne.

Sadly, once the soup arrived, the way she grabbed her spoon and hunched over her plate somewhat destroyed the impression. She didn't quite slurp, but it was clear that she could not be taken to a restaurant. Not with cousin Jules anyway.

'How are the new shoes?' Martial enquired while they were waiting for coffee. 'And how is your ankle?'

'Fine. But Sister Gervaise was right. I will have to be careful. Still, it's much better.' Flore's face fell. 'I'm sorry. I don't know how to thank you for everything you're doing for me. It all feels like a dream.'

'I'm glad. Once we've had our coffee, we'll go for a spin around the lake before I take you back to your pension.'

Their coffees arrived. Flore took a tentative sip. Martial burst out laughing as she spat it out.

'I take it you're not keen on coffee, then?'

'Yuck! Why do people drink that sauce?'

'You have to get used to it, like everything in Paris, I suppose.'

He noticed how she would take a breath, lean forward, about to speak, and slump back on her seat, somewhat defeated.

'What is it?'

'Fath—Martial,' Flore twisted her napkin, 'where are we going after Paris?'

He berated himself. Of course she would want to know. What had he been thinking?

'You saw Monsieur Pinet's shop this morning, right?'

Flore's nod was followed by another deep breath.

Martial ploughed on. 'I have read of an inventor who has set up a utopian village, and I would like to pay him a visit.'

'You think I might find a job there?' Flore's voice wobbled.

Martial read the hope in her eyes. So this was what she wanted to know. Chastened, he realised that he may have dragged the girl out of serfdom but had not yet ascertained how she could contribute to the nineteenth century without being crushed in the process.

'I think so. After Paris, we will pay him a visit and see if he can find a position for the both of us.' He called the waiter and paid. 'Come on, let's go and gape at the human zoo.'

'Boudiou.' Flore shook her head. 'We've been doing nothing else all morning!'

'Ah, the best is yet to come.'

They hailed a small gig from which they could admire the great lake circled by courtesans, cavaliers and velocipedes.

'Where are all these people going?'

'They're not going anywhere. Their only purpose is to be seen.' A magnificent landau trotted past them. 'See this lady?'

Swathed in yellow silk, a dark-haired beauty cast languorous smiles and waved a bejewelled gloved hand to the crowds.

'Oh!' Flore gasped. 'Is that the empress?' She turned around and stared at the woman unashamedly.

'She is richer than the empress. Her name is La Païva. She is one of the most influential women in Paris, a courtesan. One of many. We call them *les grandes horizontales*.'

Her eyes widened. 'Richer than Eugenie? And she's a . . .'

'She's the mistress of a Russian millionaire. Her only duty, apart from keeping him entertained, is to spend his money in the most ostenta—in the showiest way. According to Jules, La Païva once invited a hundred guests to a dinner in a room decorated with chandeliers, candelabras, fabulous tables and velvet drapes.' Flore was gazing at him wide-eyed, her adorable mouth in the shape of an O. 'At the end of the meal, the drapes fell away and the guests realised they had been dining in a stable with La Païva's seventeen magnificent horses around them.'

'Why?'

'One thing *les grandes cocottes* have in common is that they are all born poor and illegitimate. They are shunned by polite society and, because they are prostitutes, will never be presented at court, so they take their revenge by being richer, more beautiful and so much more interesting than their aristocratic counterparts, confined to prayers and needlepoint.'

'Martial! *Par ici!*' A fair-haired moustachioed cavalier cantered alongside them.

'Jules?' What was his cousin doing here? 'I was not expecting you until tonight.'

'My appointment fell through.' Jules cast a surreptitious glance at Flore.

Martial felt the colour rise to his face. 'Actually, we were just about to turn back.'

Flore dragged her gaze away from the crowds and studied the newcomer.

Martial had no choice but to introduce them. 'Flore, this is Jules, my cousin, with whom I am staying at the moment. Jules, this is Flore, from the parish of Noirac, where I used to officiate.'

Flore felt the heat rise to her cheeks. Relatively comfortable as she felt with the father, she was not ready to be foisted upon his family. Suddenly aware of her lowly status, she wished she could become invisible. She had not forgotten Joseta and had been about to ask if they could visit her, when Jules's arrival had disturbed her plan.

Since they were in Paris for a week, there was still time to find her.

'Messieurs, I've had a lovely time,' Flore said in a French she hoped was not too accented. 'I'm a little tired now. Could you please tell the driver to take me back to rue Bergère? I won't need a chaperone.'

After a hurried conversation and a discreet transfer of coins, the men took their leave and Flore remained in the carriage.

After a few seconds of terror at the idea of being alone in Paris, Flore arranged her bustle—the cage folded away accordion fashion—and reclined on the seat, wondering what it would feel like to *be* La Païva. The monstrous selfishness, the lies, the hunger that nothing could slate . . . Flore shuddered. The poor, poor woman, having to wear so much yellow just to prove that she mattered.

Paris was a strange place. For all its elegance, it stank. It stank of coal fires and sewers. It stank of poverty. The elegant apartment blocks, the gay shop fronts, the elegant tableau of frockcoats and crinolines bloomed out of a squalid muck of workshops, hovels, rag-and-bone-men and beggar children for whom every day may be their last.

The carriage stopped just outside the arch of Cité Bergère. Exhausted, Flore limped past the concierge's booth and into the paved courtyard.

A girl stood at the bottom of the stairs. Flore had met her last night. She lived in the room below hers.

'Adieu!' Flore greeted her in Occitan, desperate to pull off her corset and new shoes. Her ankle had swollen, and the shoes pinched.

The girl chuckled. 'Did you just say goodbye?'

Flore stopped. A little shorter than her, the girl had a pointy chin, the green eyes of a cat and brown hair dressed in a bun atop her head. She tightened her worn satin robe and pointed to Flore's dress. 'You were a nun when you arrived last night.'

'*Adieu* means both hello and goodbye where I come from.'

Her green eyes twinkling, the girl held out a hand. *'Adieu,* I'm Minnie.'

'Flore.'

'Tell you what, Flore, you look done in. Why don't you come up to my room? I'll make us some coffee.'

'Oh. I—I'm not sure.'

'First time in Paris?'

Flore gave a slight nod, wilting under Minnie's gaze.

The girl tilted her head. 'Did you hire this dress?'

'Yes. I don't think I've made the right choice. I can hardly breathe.'

'Come, let's see what we can do.'

Moments later, Flore was sitting in Minnie's room, her foot in a basin of cold water. Shawls draped over the bed and chairs gave the place an glamorous look. Larger than her own garret, the room was on the fourth floor overlooking the busy rue Bergère.

'Coffee?'

Flore made a face. 'I don't really like it.'

'I can't afford it, but it was a present.' Minnie's brow creased. 'What's your accent? I can't quite place it.'

'You're the one with an accent.' Flore chortled.

'I'm American. Are you Spanish?'

'Not quite, but I come from that part of the world.'

Was Minnie alone, or did she have a protector? How did an American girl on her own fare in Paris?

'What made you decide to come to Paris?'

'A man, what else? That's why you came to Paris too, isn't it?'

Flore bit her lip.

'I'm a dancer,' Minnie volunteered.

'A dancer?'

'I was lucky. I found a job just after he left me.' She shrugged. 'I've been doing it for about a year. A large store just round the corner had just expanded into a theatre.'

Flore's eyes widened. 'What kind of store?'

'It started off as a mattress shop. Then they added a building to the side and called it Les Folies.'

'A mattress shop?' Having slept on a straw-filled *paillasse* most of her life, Flore struggled with the concept. As for the theatre . . . One thing, however, puzzled her even more. 'You live here on your own?'

Minnie sat in the armchair, facing her. 'I sure do.' She stretched her legs. 'No one to tell me what to do.'

Flore's mind reeled at the possibilities, both elated and terrified.

'Don't you get lonely?'

'I spend most of my time at the Folies. We're a strange bunch, for sure, but we look out for each other.'

A small door was opening inside Flore's mind. What if being alone was not the ultimate punishment?

'Tell you what,' Minnie tapped a finger against her lips, 'what are you doing tomorrow?'

After promising he would never leave her alone, Martial had remembered he had banks to visit, lawyers to see, 'visits to clubs' with Jules. They would go down the Seine the following day on the famous *bateaux mouches*.

'I'm free tomorrow. I'm not sure I'm ready to spend another day in a corset. *Boudiou,* I don't know how you can stand it.'

'Come here.' Minnie helped Flore out of her dress. 'Hmm. Your corset is too tight. Have you never worn one before?'

Flore's miserable expression convinced Minnie not to ask any more questions, perhaps assuming that Flore had escaped from a convent.

'Try this.' Minnie handed her a black skirt and a waisted jacket.

Flore put them on and twirled. Yes, this was more her style and so much more comfortable.

'Très midinette,' Minnie approved. 'Listen, I'm working out a tour of Paris for my fellow Americans. A sort of ghoulish tour. How would you like to try it?'

'What kind of ghoulish—'

A church bell rang six times.

Minnie jumped up, untied her robe and stood in chemise and petticoats. 'Six o'clock. I have to go to work. I'll knock on your door noontime tomorrow. We'll spend the day together. It'll be fun.'

Minnie piled shoes, bustle dress, skirt and jacket into Flore's arms and sent her on her way. She headed up to her room, one step at a time, new concepts popping up in her mind like bubbles in muddy marsh water.

She unlocked her door and smiled. Now she had a friend, Paris did not seem so daunting.

19
MINNIE'S GHOULISH TOUR

Flore returned to the hire shop and swapped them for a more comfortable skirt, blouse and jacket combination similar to Minnie's. She pocketed the difference and headed for a bakery she had noticed on the corner of the street and bought a slice of brioche.

Eyes half-closed, she inhaled its sweet smell, hurled back to the past, to the day of the Sainte Elma festival in Marcillac . . . The first bite left a bitter taste in her mouth. Minnie was right, it was always the same old story.

Her gaze was drawn to a child wrapped in a shawl hovering outside a café, her matted hair and tattered clothes a common sight in the capital. Back home, people were poor, but unless they were charcoal-burners or vagrants travelling from place to place, they took care of their appearance.

'*Petite*, have this,' Flore held out her brioche, surprised to see the girl lift her nose, searching for the smell, empty eyes lifted to the sky.

Flore took her hand and pushed the pastry into it. '*Pour toi, une brioche*.'

A look of fear passed on the child's face. Her nose twitched. She lifted the pastry to her lips and smiled.

Flore walked away. Paris was an ogre that devoured people, belching coal fumes that coated the inside of your nose. The buildings were so high you had to crook your neck to glimpse the sky. For the weak, it was pitiless, but the opportunities it offered were many. Perhaps with Minnie's help, she would find work, though the scant skills she possessed were useless here. With salaries as low as they were, could she find anything that would keep her alive without having to sell herself?

Minnie knocked on the door a little after the noon bells.

'Let's start with lunch.' Flore trailed behind Minnie through the cobbled courtyard. 'I know a cheap *bouillon* in the Latin Quarter. It's like a canteen, but it's magnificent. This way. Boulevard de Sébastopol. We'll find an omnibus that goes south.'

The day was crisp and clear, and wearing the same clothes as Minnie, Flore felt inconspicuous amongst the girls pouring out of milliners' and sewing workshops.

Minnie nudged her. *'Les midinettes.'* She pointed to benches where flocks of girls perched, chattering like sparrows. 'At noon, *midi,* they come out to have their lunch in the nearby squares.' Minnie pronounced it the French way, *skwar*.

Flore focussed on the girls. Did they all live alone? Could she too sit for ten hours, glued to the same chair, sewing or making hats? A long sigh escaped her.

Striking out on her own was terrifying.

Minnie nudged her. 'Ho ho, here comes the pack of wolves.'

Hands in their pockets, a gang of men in blue smocks and caps mooched out of a carpenter's courtyard and circled the square, eyeing the girls, who made a great show of ignoring them.

While they waited for the omnibus, Flore observed a different game. A milliner perched at the edge of a bench, nibbling at her lunch; at the other end, a portly gentleman—whose florid complexion, top hat and gold watch indicated a love of pleasure and the ability to pay for it—engaged her in conversation.

'Paris may be the city of pleasure, but for the poor, pleasure is either stolen or sold,' Minnie declaimed, her voice thick with the weight of experience.

The clang of the approaching carriage put an end to their study. 'You sure you want to pay for the both of us?'

'*Oc*. Where are we going again?' Flore clung to Minnie's arm.

'Saint Michel.' Minnie found seats. 'What was that word you said?'

Flore bit her lip. '*Oc*. It means *oui*. How do you say it in English?'

'We say *yes*. I'll teach you some more if you want. How long will you be in Paris?'

'I'm not sure. A week, I think.'

'And after that?'

Flore simply shrugged. Minnie meant well, but *boudiou*, how she missed the unquestioning silence of the convent.

The traffic was such that it took them nearly an hour to get to the Seine.

'*Eh bé*, I can't imagine how anyone got anywhere *before* the emperor had the streets widened.' Churned up and chaotic, the capital was still in the throes of its rebirth.

By the time they had reached the *bouillon* in a Left Bank side street, Flore's stomach was growling. They shared a table with a group of rowdy students.

The dining hall was palatial. Dappled light bounced from a painted glass ceiling onto tall gilded mirrors. Surprisingly opulent, Flore thought, for a working-class eatery.

Minnie pointed to the menu on a board. 'I'll have the mutton and vegetables. What do you fancy?'

Flore ran through the simple choices. 'I think I'll start with soup.'

Minnie stuck her fork into a carrot and stopped, her gaze glued to Flore's spoon.

'Hey, slow down.'

'Huh?' Flore wiped her mouth with the back of a hand. Thick with bacon and beans, her soup was delicious.

'All right.' Minnie put down her fork. 'Did they not teach you how to eat in that convent?'

'It was a silent order.' Shame burned Flore's cheeks.

Minnie blinked as the information sank in. She cleared her throat. 'Listen. Your young man might—'

Flore sighed. 'He's not my young man.'

'Sure. He takes you out, he gives you money, but he's not your young man.' Minnie waited for an explanation. Flore returned to her soup.

'Anyway,' Minnie said softly, 'he might not take you to a fancy brasserie if you eat like that.' She reached for Flore's hand. 'I really like you. You're interesting, but you'll never get anywhere if . . .' She demonstrated. 'Look. Scoop up like this.'

Flore's gaze darted sideways, relieved that the students had gone, replaced by two old men too busy discussing politics to pay any attention to her.

She tried to imitate Minnie, but the bones of the jacket compressed her stomach.

'Sit straight and lift the food to your lips.' Minnie nodded with approval as Flore managed the soup without spilling any onto her borrowed clothes.

'Great. Now let's order you some meat and make sure you hold your knife and fork correctly.' She lifted a hand.

The moustachioed waiter added the price of the dish to the list he'd scribbled on the paper table covering.

'Finger forward on the handle . . . There you are.' Minnie smiled once the lesson was over. 'Very elegant.'

'Thank you.' Flore cringed at what the silent nuns must have thought of her eating habits. To dispel her embarrassment, she asked, 'Tell me, how much would a *midinette* earn per day?'

'Somewhere around two francs fifty for a ten-hour day. No wonder they supplement their earnings, hey?' Minnie waved the waiter over.

'Did you—' Flore blushed. 'Have you ever had to supplement yours?'

'I've had plenty of offers, but I've learned my lesson. He was going to show me the lights—you know, the usual lies.'

'I do.' Minnie's admission relieved Flore of the guilt she still carried, of having fallen for Ricar's tricks.

Minnie pointed to the numbers scribbled next to her plate. 'That's how much it is. Thank you. I appreciate it.'

Flore discreetly slipped a hand inside the pocket sewn at the bottom of her petticoat and felt around for the coins Martial had given her.

'That's for the both of us,' she said to the waiter.

'Give him a tip,' Minnie whispered. 'No less than two sous, or he'll make fun of you.'

As Flore searched for the extra coins, she found Joseta's address. Hopefully, they would have time to meet up with her tomorrow after the boat trip.

'Right, now we begin our tour.' Minnie hooked her arm in Flore's.

They were about to cross the Seine when Flore noticed wooden boxes affixed to the quay side.

'Minnie, look!'

'Bouquinistes,' Minnie said, impatient to carry on. 'Second-hand books for students.'

A familiar picture caught Flore's eye on a cover, the story of a hunchback bell-ringer and a beautiful Gipsy. It was called Notre Dame de Paris.

She remembered her grandfather the sea captain, acting out the part where Quasimodo, the hunchback, won a prize for making funny faces. How Colin had laughed and made faces. Excited, Flore negotiated a price and caught up with her guide.

'Oh! The cathedral!' She gasped. 'It's gigantic!'

Renovated and polished to pristine whiteness by one of the emperor's magicians, the stone lacework glowed in the afternoon sun. Flore stepped in, crushed by a sense of awe. Mouth open, she spun on her heels on the black-and-white marble floor. 'Oh, Minnie,' she exclaimed as they toured the building, 'I never thought I would actually *see* Notre Dame!'

Tears welling in her eyes, she lit a candle for Mama's, Nanette's and Papa's souls, hoping they could see her from where they were.

I am here in Paris, Mama. If Nanette is with you, please . . . Sobs escaped her. *Oh, Mama, I am so, so sorry for what I did. I pray for you every day.*

Unable to stop, she fell into Minnie's arms. Minnie caressed her shoulders, murmuring soothing words in English.

When it was over, Minnie led her to a tiny staircase.

'Feeling strong enough to attack four hundred steps?'

Flore nodded and puffed all the way to the gargoyle gallery, where a zoo of fabulous beasts stood guard over

Paris: chimeras, griffins, lion-men, snakes with teeth, wild boars, bulls and even a three-headed dog.

'Look, Minnie. Look at this elephant!' Flore said to dispel the mood. 'I saw his brothers yesterday.'

'You went to the Bois?'

Flore bit her lower lip. 'Yes, I—he . . . Have you not been yet?'

Minnie's mouth turned down. 'Like I told you, the rat scarpered after three days. Left me high and dry with just one day to get out of the room.' She ran her fingers over the pocked fur of a stone lion-man. 'Men have all these beasts lurking inside them.'

With a shiver, Flore chased Ricar from her mind. 'I saw La Païva yesterday. I hear she eats men for breakfast.'

'You *saw* her?' Minnie's eyes widened. 'Really? What was she wearing?'

'She sat like a queen in a fluff of yellow and white.'

'Was she stunningly beautiful?'

'I don't know.' Flore shrugged. 'She just looked like an omelette.'

Minnie giggled behind her hand. 'What do you mean?'

'All I could see was her sadness.'

'How can you be sad with so much money?'

'There's got to be something wrong with her if she needs *seventeen* horses,' Flore said as she attacked the last set of stairs.

Out of breath, she crept towards the delicate parapet and gazed at Paris spread at her feet.

Just below her, corseted inside brand-new quays, the wide ribbon of the Seine flowed west, carrying trains of barges. Snug inside its wall, an stylish elegant Paris was rising from scaffolding and rubble. It was not at all what Flore had expected. No wonder Martial's brother had fallen in love with it. He had money. Paris was a courtesan, a *grande cocotte,* fun only for those who could afford her. Beguiling, expensive, the elegant Paris put on airs, while at her heart lurked a core of poverty and shame.

Flore imagined herself, as La Païva had done at the end of her famous dinner, pulling the cord that held up the elegant chalky façades to reveal the dark truth concealed behind them.

She let her eyes roam over the panorama. Shut inside the convent, she had missed the immensity of her native skies. Could she make a life here? Could she?

After a long time, she turned to Minnie. 'What is it like where you come from?'

Minnie did not answer at first, focussed on a large expanse of green to the right of the river. 'See those two grand buildings down there? They are the Louvre and the Tuileries Palace, where the emperor lives. A lot of people hate him. They want a republic, as we have in America. He won't last much longer.' Serious, her gaze now bore into Flore. 'Let me tell you something. When he goes, I won't want to be around.' Her chin in her hands, she leaned against the parapet. 'I come from New York. It's just like Paris. How about you?'

'My country is marshy and wild, but to me it has everything, woods, rivers, the ocean.' Flore's voice trailed. Would she ever see it again? 'They're planting pines all over it now. Soon it will be the biggest forest in the world.'

'What's wrong with pines?'

'You can't eat them.'

Minnie pointed south. 'Over there is the entrance to the catacombs, the first stop in my ghoulish tour of Paris. Underground caves full of bones and skulls. You visit them by candlelight. Americans love it.'

'Bones?'

'Uh-huh. You can also visit the sewers, ride over them in a

little cart. It's a bit smelly, but it's fun.' She hugged herself. 'Brrr, it's windy up here. Come on, let's go down.'

Skulls? Sewers? Flore wondered as she crossed the wide space where Quasimodo had yearned for Esmeralda. *Fun?*

She caught up with Minnie at the bottom of the steps. 'The catacombs, is that where you're taking me?'

'Not today. Our next stop's right here.' Minnie halted in front of an imposing stone building just behind the cathedral. 'We're in luck—there's no queue today. You would not *believe* the queues normally. They go on for *miles*.'

They joined a line of working women in aprons and bourgeoises in crinolines herding their broods into a wide corridor and shuffled forward, following the sound of water. An aquarium! They were all the rage. Flore had seen them in almanacs and could not wait to see the fish.

Step by step, they chatted until they came to a large marble space with a floor-to-ceiling expanse of glass to one side. Flore halted, suddenly very cold. This was no aquarium.

Displayed on black marble slabs, rivulets running at their feet, a dozen naked corpses lay, their modesty protected by a strip of leather.

Her hand went to Minnie's sleeve. She cried out, '*Diou biban!* What's going on in here?'

'It's the new morgue. Tourists love it. It's going to be the best part of my tour.'

Skeletal bodies covered in sores were decaying in shades of grey and white.

'How did these poor people end up here?'

Minnie shrugged. 'Found in dark alleyways, parks, pulled out of the river. No one knows who they are. When someone goes missing in Paris, this is the first place you look. See that poor little boy, how peaceful he looks.' She pointed to a child who did look asleep.

A skeleton of a man, his face hidden inside a wild grey

beard, bore a great gash to his side and a multitude of scars. The rags he had worn hung behind him, complete with war medals.

'No one will be claiming that one,' Minnie said with a sigh.

The queue shuffled forward past another derelict, another child.

Flore's blood turned to ice. Right in front of her, on a black marble block, bloated, greenish-white, her matted blond hair snaking over her breasts, was the body of a young woman. She did not look peaceful. She did not look asleep. She looked glaringly, obscenely dead.

The tall window warped. Flore saw her own swollen body on the slab, snakes of dark hair coiled around her neck and a bruised purple foot. She pressed her hands against the cold glass. A sour taste filled her mouth. That girl could have been her. *Mila Diou,* her stomach heaved. *If Martial had not rescued me, this is what Colin and Tanta would have found.* She gripped Minnie's arm and dug her fingers into her sleeve. The queue pressed her forward. Someone tried to push them out of the way.

'Ouch, you're hurting me!' Minnie prised Flore's fingers from her arm. 'Flore? Flore, talk to me! Hey, you're not going to faint, are you? Come, let's get you outside.'

'No, wait.' Something compelled Flore to look closer. That girl . . . she knew her. The shock sent her reeling. *I got here too late.* Her shoulders slumped. 'Sorry,' she muttered and shuffled away with a backwards glance at the cape that hung behind the girl, sky blue and covered in mud.

'What happened just now?' Minnie grumbled once they were outside.

Overcome with nausea, Flore struggled to speak.

After a long time, she said in a broken voice, 'Minnie . . . that dead girl in there, I—I know who she was.'

20
FATHER MARTIAL AND SISTER FLORE UNCOVER THE TRUTH

Cloaked in the habit and wimple she had hoped never to wear again, Flore slipped out of the pension. Under the city walls, the last market gardens were being razed, replaced by large white stone buildings in an unwavering push for modernisation.

She reached Saint Eugène Church, the place she had selected as a landmark to meet Martial, relieved to see his cassocked figure weaving his way around workers and handcarts.

The father crossed the street, slightly out of breath. 'Ah, here you are. I received your message, but why are we wearing our habits?'

Flore twisted her hands. 'It's about Joseta, the girl I met at the convent.'

'Yes, you mentioned the girl. You were hoping to visit her. Why, has something happened?'

Shock, revulsion and incomprehension spread on his face as Flore described the morgue and the naked bodies.

'I was hoping you would accompany me to the place where those Durocs live. That is the name of the people for whom she worked as a live-in maid. Perhaps we'll discover how she died before . . .' Flore's chin wobbled. 'Before they throw her into the common grave.'

They walked into the stone building. Father Martial removed his hat and, about to cross himself, his mouth dropped open. Flore too gasped. The church was a vision. Barley-twist metal columns supported a yellow canopy studded with stars. Rainbows dripped through stained glass and melted into gold and brass fittings. Martial ferreted out a potted history of the church, amazed that the bland stone façade they had seen from the outside concealed yet another of the emperor's visions.

'Who would have thought . . .' the father scanned the star-studded ceiling. 'This must be another one of the emperor's creations.'

Flore, once again, found herself revising her presumptions. Could the magician who had dreamt up this enchanted space be totally bad? Her opinion of Louis-Napoléon softened. Maybe the emperor had a heart after all.

Hands behind his back, Martial allowed himself a moment of wonder before he pulled a chair next to hers.

'Have you informed the morgue authorities of Joseta's identity?'

'Not yet. I wanted to see where she worked before I did anything.' She leaned forward, tears pricking her eyes. 'I want to see who they are. I want to know what they did to her. Joseta was in such a state when she left the convent; it wouldn't have taken much to push her over the edge.'

'Yes, yes, I see. Oh, the poor girl.' Martial's brow crinkled. 'Is your plan simply to rattle them? I know you thought well of her, but perhaps she *was* dismissed.'

'That is what I hope you'll help me find out.' Flore handed him Joseta's address.

'Rue des Amandiers. I think it is a little way east, near the Père Lachaise Cemetery. How is your ankle?'

'Pretty good, thank you. I could probably walk one league.'

'Four kilometres, huh?' Martial chided her. 'The metric system has been in place for several decades.'

'Metric, is it?' Flore grinned. 'Well, it never reached us in Noirac.'

'Indeed. Civilisation bypassed us.'

They set off, avoiding carts, mud and piles of cobblestones. The Duroc family lived in one of Haussmann's elegant blocks, halfway up rue des Amandiers.

Martial knocked on a polished oak door set under a deep entrance porch, beyond which the usual inner courtyard was littered with wood chips, planks and stacks of beams. A din of hammering and sawing came from a workshop.

A maid opened the door, a whippet-thin girl with a pockmarked complexion and a missing tooth at the front.

'Bonjour,' Father Martial began. 'Does Joseta Mercier work here?'

The maid's hand flew to her mouth. 'Have you found her?'

'Alberte, who is it?' A woman's voice.

'A priest and a sister, madame, asking about Joseta.'

As Alberte stepped back, Flore took in a large hall cluttered with gilded consoles, chandeliers and all manner of mirrors and paintings. She had never seen such a display of wealth. A middle-aged woman in a moiré bustle dress glided to the door.

'*Mes respects, madame.* I am Père Boyer. My niece met your maid Joseta at the Saint-Sauveur convent. We are in Paris for a few days and wondered if Joseta would like to join us for mass this Sunday, if you saw no inconvenience to it, of course.'

The woman stood rock still. A stocky youth in waistcoat and check trousers joined her. His thick greasy hair was parted in the middle, and his face was covered in spots.

'Have they caught her, then?' He slipped his thumbs into his waistcoat pockets.

Just one look at him and Flore knew. She knew from the pouty lips, the stubborn brow of a boy who had never been denied pleasure. It took all she had not to hurl herself at him and claw his eyes out.

Father Martial kept his composure. 'What do you mean? Is Joseta not with you anymore?'

'No.' The woman's face was stern. 'I'm afraid she left without warning three days ago. We are not at all happy about it. Sorry, but your visit has been in vain.' She closed the door in their faces.

Martial and Flore stood rooted to the spot. Inside, an argument erupted.

They crossed the street. After a few paces, Flore pulled Martial behind some scaffolding.

'Wait,' she whispered. 'The maid, Alberte, she knew something.'

Moments later, the maid hurried towards them, glancing over her shoulder.

'Have you seen her?' There was hope in her voice. 'Do you know where she is?'

Flore's heart went out to the girl. She let Martial explain. He was a priest after all, and familiar with difficult situations.

'Were you friends with Joseta?' he asked, his voice full of compassion.

'What happened to her?' Alberte twisted her apron in her fingers, glancing from Martial to Flore. '*Mon Dieu,* you know what happened to her, don't you?'

Flore answered with a sad nod.

'Oh, the poor thing. How did she . . .?'

'She was found in the Seine. God rest her soul.'

Alberte's face dissolved. 'Oh, why could he not leave that one alone?' She buried her face in her hands. After a while, she said in a cracked voice, 'You saw him, didn't you? Ugly beggar. He's Madame's son. He was besotted with her from the start.' She cast another glance over her shoulder. 'Joseta tried to fight him off. I heard them. My room's next to hers in their attic.' She hung her head. 'I know about the baby too. She took it real hard. She wanted to keep it.'

'Joseta is with God now,' Martial murmured.

Alberte crossed herself. 'Do you . . . do you think so?'

'The Lord is merciful. Listen, it might be best if you didn't say anything just yet. Someone will come along tomorrow and inform Madame Duroc officially.'

'Poor girl. She was so lovely. She was my friend. It isn't fair, is it?' The maid wiped her cheeks with her sleeve and said to Flore, 'You're lucky you're a sister. Being pretty makes for a hard life in Paris.'

'How do you fare with the son?' Flore asked.

'Oh, he won't bother me.' The girl pointed to her pock-marked skin with a sour grin. 'I got the groom to tell him I had the pox.' She shrugged. 'Got to defend yourself with the weapons you have. Anyway, he won't be here much longer. He's off to the army soon, away for seven years, and good riddance. He thought he could do the dirty and get away with it, didn't he?' She cast a glance at the house. 'He won't let his mother buy his way out of the army. She wants to send someone in his place, but he won't let her.' Her face a grimace of contempt, she added, 'Says he wants to show 'em what he's made of.' She concluded with a sorrowful sigh. 'Poor Joseta. She was too good for this world.'

This is what happens when you work as a maid. The whole concept of surrendering herself to another person filled

Flore with terror. Whatever work she found had to afford her a measure of independence, or she would go mad.

A last glance at the building told her that the Durocs were rich enough for Joseta's death never to be questioned. It would be as if the poor girl had never existed.

A great emptiness gaping inside her, Flore followed Martial's tall figure through the muddy streets. In a way, she too was dead. Soon in Noirac, apart from Tanta and Colin, no one would remember her.

The street broadened. A high wall ran along an avenue, topped with a froth of new leaves.

'Where are we?'

'This is the Père Lachaise cemetery.' Martial's features softened. 'You found the Bois de Boulogne too crowded, so I thought you might like this better, although today may not be the best day for you to see it.'

Touched by the look on his face, Flore said, 'I could do with a moment's quiet.'

As soon as they were through the gate, they stepped into a world of reflection and silence. Beyond the tall wall, the roar of the city had dimmed to a soft hum.

'What will they do with Joseta's body?' Flore rubbed her arms.

'Her employers will arrange for a discreet funeral, I imagine.'

'I think we should go back to that house and tell them we want to attend her funeral. I'm sorry. You didn't know her, but her family disowned her through no fault of her own. They cast out their own daughter, not caring if she died. I can't imagine . . . I must at least try.'

Martial greeted her statement with a soft look. 'Of course. I will go with you tomorrow, and we will suggest that.'

Along shady alleyways, statues, porticos and grandiose

mausoleums rose between headstones. Here in Paris, even in death, there was a need to impress.

Wordlessly, Martial led the way to a thin Gothic spire soaring above the delicate bones of a chapel, around which the ground was littered with petals. Bunches of fresh flowers were tucked into the railings.

'Your two favourite people.'

'Quasimodo and Esmeralda?' Flore guessed before she'd had time to see the effigies lying rigidly side by side.

Martial shook his head. 'Try again.'

'Victor Hugo and his wife?'

He smiled. 'Hugo is alive and well in Guernsey with both his wife and his mistress, waiting for the emperor to be deposed so that he can return to Paris.'

Flore bit her lip. 'I give up. Who is it?'

'This is the grave of Abélard and Héloïse, separated in life, together for eternity. Their remains are buried together in one grave.' He pointed to the flowers. 'Lovers who can't be together leave flowers and messages for each other. They pray to Héloïse and ask her to help them be reunited.'

Disturbed by the intensity in Martial's gaze, Flore leaned on the metal railing and studied the face of her heroine, sweet and round inside her wimple, in contrast to a very gaunt Abélard.

The realisation that Héloïse was there, just under that stone, made Flore dizzy.

Martial walked away, his hands behind his back, his steps crunching the gravel.

Flore imagined Héloïse hovering above Paris, looking down on her with benevolence. She put her hands together and addressed a fervent prayer of gratitude to the abbess who had reached out to her through the centuries.

Her future a blank canvas, Flore asked for advice for her life ahead.

Men are strong, an ethereal voice floated inside her head, *but remember, you are stronger.*

Flore glanced around. She was alone. Nothing disturbed the silence. Even the blackbirds were quiet. After a moment, the voice rose again, fainter this time, edged with mirth. *Though it is wise never to let men know our strength.*

'Women are stronger,' Flore repeated under her breath. Hands clutched to her heart, she begged the abbess to ensure Joseta's soul was not barred from Heaven for taking her own life.

Martial's steps brought her back to reality and, light-headed, she followed him past chapels, stone angels and grieving muses, distilling the wisdom she had just received.

'Thank you for bringing me here,' she murmured just before they reached the gate. 'I heard her voice, you know. Héloïse. She spoke to me.'

Father Martial met her gaze. He waited for her to say more and, when she didn't, walked away ahead of her.

Outside the walls, Paris was noisy with hammering, sawing and whistling. A cacophony of hooves, clangs and insults rang both at street level and above their heads.

A mouth-watering scent drew them to a small restaurant, where they stopped for a lunch of beef and mash, Flore carefully copying Martial's every move as they ate.

They had to walk all the way to Place du Prince Eugène to hail a cab. Still awed by the miracle of Héloïse's words, Flore walked inside a cloud, attempting to decipher the message she had received.

While Martial paid for the cab, she ran her eyes along the line of expectant visitors snaking all the way from the river's edge at the back of the cathedral to the morgue. A notorious murderer had been guillotined that morning, and his remains were on display.

Flore pointed to a small office situated to the side of the

viewing gallery and let Martial go in to explain. His French was much clearer than hers, and anyway, priests carried more authority.

She waited in the sun while thousands queued to see the corpse. A memory surfaced, her father when they'd brought him home and placed him on two planks, the noose still around his neck, his face like a gargoyle. Nanette bawling like a calf. Flore pushed the memory away and focussed on the cathedral.

Built right at the end of the island, Notre Dame resembled a great ship in dry dock her seafaring grandfather had once taken her to see, the buttresses like so many oars about to dip into the Seine.

Lost in thought, she jumped at Martial's touch. Haggard, he opened his lips, but no sounds came out.

'What is it?' Flore's face crumpled. 'What did they say?'

'She . . . she wasn't there. Joseta—she was gone.'

'What?'

'They said her brother came and . . . and took her away.'

'But she doesn't have a brother!'

'Oh, Flore, I'm so sorry. We got here too late.'

21

LE BATEAU-MOUCHE

Joseta's funeral took most of the morning, a simple affair Martial knew would never have taken place had Flore not insisted. The only people present, apart from himself and Flore, were the maid they had spoken to, her sobs echoing around the church, a coachman and Madame Duroc, who did her best to ignore them. They were not invited to follow the coffin.

After a quick lunch taken in reflective silence, Martial sat next to Flore on a Bateau-Mouche they had boarded near Notre Dame, the boats yet another of the emperor's schemes to improve circulation through his beloved Paris. It was a blustery day, but inside the space was warm.

'May I ask you a question?' Flore asked as the Bateau-Mouche steamed towards a medieval edifice of blackened stone and slate.

'Of course.' A smile lifted the corner of his lips. The elegant Parisienne he had tried to create had obviously been a step too far. With money he had lent her, Flore had purchased ready-made garments that suited both her country accent and simple manners much better.

'What kind of work do you think I could to do in . . . Utopia? I mean, I can stuff a goose and skin a rabbit, but these aren't exactly skills that are useful in a town, though I'm quite good at counting money. What kind of place is it?'

'I'm not quite sure, but it really is vast, and I imagine, well, yes, there should definitely be . . . opportunities.' *Diou biban,* what could he say?

The boat veered to one side, narrowly avoiding a huge coal barge. Angry hoots covered Flore's reply. Something about a shop.

Martial settled deeper into his seat with a sigh of content and breathed in a long draft of river air. 'Look over there, the Louvre is coming up.'

'What if there isn't any work for me in—what's the name of the place again?'

'Guise,' Martial answered, marvelling at the Louvre the emperor had turned into a museum. 'Would you like to visit a museum? If so, we should get off at the next stop. Is it something you would like to do?'

'Yes.' Flore gave a serious nod.

'Then we should get off here.' Martial pushed himself up and held out a hand.

'Huh? I thought we were going all the way to the Champs Elysées?'

'You just told me that you wanted to visit the Louvre Museum.'

Flore gave him a puzzled look.

Had they been talking at cross purposes? Did Flore even understand the concept of a museum? Martial sat down again, about to explain, when Flore spoke, following her own train of thought. 'If I can't find a position, what will I do then, all alone in the north?'

'But you won't be alone. I'll be there. Don't worry. I'm sure that Monsieur Godin will—'

'But what if he doesn't? I really think it's best for me to stay in Paris.'

'Stay in Paris?' Suddenly, the river lost all its appeal. The flatboats slipping by, the sprawling Tuileries, the huge horses pulling barges along the banks vanished from Martial's field of vision, reduced to one person, calmly proposing to disappear from his life.

'Minnie will find me something.'

'Minnie?'

'The American dancer who lives in the room below mine,' Flore insisted. 'I mentioned her to you. She knows people, both in her theatre and in the mattress shop next to it. Rue Trévise, perhaps you've heard of it. It's called—'

'Wait.' Martial swallowed hard, his carefully laid plans tumbling around him like a house of cards. This simply could not be. He could not let her go. It would mean losing his Émile, the female counterpart to Rousseau's guileless pupil. She was so bright, and with just a little guidance, she could achieve so much. Without Flore, the whole utopian experiment would make no sense. Life would make no sense. His hands hovered next to her. Unable to touch her, he took off his hat and kneaded the rim. 'Listen, Paris is a dangerous place for a girl on her own. If anything happened to you, I would never forgive myself.' He stared at his hat and replaced it on his head.

Flore turned away, her gaze on the columns of the Palais Bourbon. Although they had reached their stop, neither of them moved. Martial's heart slowed down to the heavy chug of the wheel. Lost in a strange fog, he found himself praying to the very God he had forsaken, praying for his turmoil to end.

'This is what we will do,' he said in a tired voice. 'If Monsieur Godin cannot find you a position, I will personally bring you back to Paris.'

A slow smile lit up Flore's features.

'I simply could not bear to leave you in limbo.' Martial added, 'Not with what happened to poor Joseta.'

'Thank you.' Something still troubled Flore. 'Monsieur Godin does not know your previous . . . You have not told him that you are . . . were a priest?'

'It didn't seem relevant.'

'Is it, is it not hard for you to . . . It must be like shedding your skin, I imagine. Will you not miss it?'

How perceptive she was. Also blessed with empathy, energy and, most of all, something he envied: a conviction of her self-worth that came from having been loved as a child and not, as he had been, called to his father's study and whipped for the slightest misdemeanour.

'But, Father, what about God?' Flore insisted. 'What do you say to him when you pray?'

Martial let the *father* go. Yes, he still prayed, out of habit mostly. His conversations with God had not ceased, quite the opposite.

'I ask for guidance, of course. I have not lost my faith, not totally. What I am losing is my faith in man. It is not so much God but the Church with whom I am severing my ties. Its theatrics and hypocrisy are not what I pledged my life to.'

'In Noirac, you helped Papa when Mama died; you helped us when Papa took his life. You collected alms for Ricar's mother. These were not theatrics, were they?'

How could he explain the ambiguity of a Church that glossed over men's 'peccadillos' and condemned 'fallen women' for selling their bodies just because they were hungry and then sold their children?

Jules had taken him to political meetings in café back rooms where orators thundered against industrialists and bankers. Tired of the misery he saw in his hospital, Jules too was looking for a solution.

What could Martial say to Flore, who saw him, like the mayor or the viscount, as a figure of authority?

'Confessing the dying and helping the living are privileges given to very few. It was what I lived for, but I was to be transferred to a new parish where most of my parishioners would have been like the Durocs.'

'Oh no!'

Hopefully, time would help her see him for what he was, a good man searching for his place in the world, much in need of a woman like her to help him out of his confusion.

'So what will you tell Monsieur Godin, then?'

'Ah. Well, I will tell him that I have come to learn from him, that, as the son of a Bordeaux family, I wish to expand my family assets along utopian principles such as his.'

'Your family assets?'

'Yes, our vines, our pines, our flock of resin workers, which is what I *would do* if I were the eldest born. A minor extension of the truth. My father and Roderic, unfortunately, see things quite differently.'

The smile that softened Flore's face reassured him that he was on the right path.

A vast empty field appeared to their right. The Champs de Mars. A biting wind greeted them on the bank, pulling at their hats. They decided to return to rue Bergère by cab.

As he caught sight of a ragged urchin sheltering inside an alleyway, the bishop's words returned to Martial. *Poverty is endemic. In Paris, there are a hundred thousand indigents, and if you were to feed them, another hundred thousand would come.*

Flore's hand went to her heart. 'So many poor children . . . in such a rich city.'

The boy's bare legs bore the red welts of a whip.

'Living in dire conditions breeds cruelty,' Martial murmured. 'Here, give him this coin, though if his father finds it, he will probably spend it on drink.'

He closed his hand over Flore's.

Her humid eyes met his. 'When are you thinking of leaving Paris?'

'I still have a few things to sort out with Jules. Shall we say the day after tomorrow at dawn? I will be with you at six.'

He watched her call the urchin to one side and take him by the hand towards the *crèmerie*. The fearful glance the boy cast into the café told a desperate tale.

22
BEHIND THE SCENE AT LES FOLIES

Barefoot, wrapped in her old pink robe and the smell of coffee, Minnie peeked out of her door, relieved when she saw see Flore.

'Ah, c'est toi, entre.' She cast a glance down the stairs. 'I was worried it might be the concierge. I'm a bit late with the rent this month.'

'I brought you a milky bun.' Flore handed her the pastry. 'I wasn't sure how hungry you'd be, having just woken up.'

'Mmm, *un petit pain*. Thank you! This is a treat. I normally drag myself to the café around the corner and have the *soupe du jour.*' Minnie ran her fingers through her tousled hair. 'Oh *zut,* I have to work this afternoon. We're rehearsing a new show.' Sleepily, she ground a handful of coffee, holding the grinder between her knee, shook it into the top of an enamel pot and poured boiling water over it.

'Can I come and watch you? Would anyone mind?'

'Oh dear. Have you been abandoned again?'

'Not really. We're leaving tomorrow. That's what I came to tell you.'

'You can't leave! I'd planned for us to go out to dance the can-can!'

'I'm sorry.'

'Just tell your friend that you need to stay for another day.' Minnie opened her hands. 'How can you visit Paris without dancing the can-can? I was going to take you to the Bal Bullier. It's wild. You'd love it there.'

When Flore did not answer, Minnie narrowed her eyes. 'You *are* a nun. That's it, isn't it? You won't dance the can-can for fear of going to Hell.'

'I'm not a nun, Minnie, and I do want to go dancing. Of course I do. It's just that I'm sad. We buried Joseta yesterday, the girl we found in the morgue. I'm sad to have to go. I like doing things with you.'

Minnie poured her coffee, added milk and dipped her bun into her cup. 'Want some coffee?'

Flore shook her head. 'What kind of show is it at the Folies?'

'Oh, a bit of everything.' Minnie brushed the crumbs from her robe and, without warning, dropped into a front split. 'I was doing my exercises when you came in.' She leaned over her foot and embraced her knee.

'How long have you been rehearsing the new show?'

'Ages,' came the muffled answer. 'Why don't you come with me? You can meet all my friends.'

Though she had not said so to Martial, Flore had not completely abandoned the idea of looking for work in Paris.

Moments later, she grabbed her shawl and followed Minnie into the street, her fingers tingling from the biting wind.

'Minnie,' Flore pointed to the café on the street corner, 'I saw a blind girl there the other day. Does she live around here?'

'Not sure. They're street singers. They roam around Paris.'

Ahead of them, a large flat building lined the street, a huge establishment topped with the name Aux Colonnes d'Hercule, a modern two-story affair supported by several columns.

Minnie took her arm. 'Come, let's go in and have a peek. It's huge.'

The cavernous space was topped with a long glass roof supported by curved struts. It was filled with row upon row of elegant sofas and beds, the likes of which Flore had never seen. Not even in Martial's manor.

She stood in awe, wondering how much they all cost. Back in Les Landes, furniture was inherited or, if broken, repaired by the same carpenter who would fashion your coffin. If you needed new clothes, you would first grow the flax or spin the wool. At best, buy a length of cotton. Here, if you had the money, you could buy everything ready-made.

A sleek young man came towards them. When he saw their attire, his smile melted into a supercilious sneer. 'Mesdemoiselles?'

'Bonjour.' Minnie chuckled. 'We've come to check out your famous bouncy mattresses.' *Le sommier élastique* was the shop's nickname, an allusion, she had explained, to the waitresses at the Folies selling their favours.

His gaze settled on Minnie's chest. 'Well, if you ladies are free later . . .'

Giggling, she pushed Flore towards the door. 'Pah! Did he really think he was in with a chance?'

Around the corner was a small door. The side entrance to the Folies. A dirty corridor carpeted with trodden-on straw and scraps of paper opened into a large space cluttered with planks, crates and coils of rope, crisscrossed by boys rushing to and fro, bent under ladders or piles of tulle. Somehow inside, the air was more glacial than it was outside and smelled of sweat and wood shavings.

Voices rose from the stage, a duo of shrill grievances met with a baritone rebuke.

'The conjoined sisters.' Minnie rolled her eyes. 'They're always arguing.'

A man walked past them on his hands, followed by a poodle toddling along on his front paws.

'Ah! Minnie, there you are.' He righted himself with a pirouette and bowed to Flore. 'Mademoiselle, Valentin at your service.' He turned to Minnie. '*Vite!* Get into your costume. Your girls are to line up in five minutes.'

Rubbing the goose bumps on her arms, Flore took tentative steps towards the heavy curtain. All she knew about theatre were the ambulant players who would stop by in Marcillac during cattle fairs. A rig, a painted curtain and their décor was set.

Here, rope ladders, wheels and weights dangled from the ceiling. Fascinated, Flore checked out the pulleys and was pushed out of the way by a woman who rushed past her, her Oriental costume held together at the back by various pegs and pins.

'Who removed the blankets from my boxes? Who was stupid enough to do that? If my pythons catch cold, that's the end of my act!'

'Put your snakes in my office.' A man's voice. 'I've got a fire on. They'll be toasty in no time.'

'*Ben voyons,* wake them up so they can strangle me on stage, no thanks.'

'Thérèse, take this!' Minnie held out her shawl. 'Use this for now.' She stepped out of the changing room in a skimpy top and knee-length skirt.

'Brrr. Are you not freezing?' Flore tightened her shawl.

''Course I am, but not for long. Come on, girls.' She

turned to her dancers, corralled out of the changing room by Valentin. 'We'll all catch our death if we don't start moving. Look out for the chalk marks on the stage.'

A portly man dressed as a boxer rushed in, his face gleaming with sweat.

'Where is that kangaroo?' He turned to Flore. 'Have you seen the kangaroo? It was supposed to be here hours ago.'

Flore made her way through the chaos down to the café area and took a seat at a table, awed by the size of the place. The ground floor was a café, crowded with tables and chairs; above it ran a two-tiered U-shaped gallery where people could drink and view the show from the balconies.

So this was Minnie's life. *Could I work here? Would all these people accept me?* Flore watched the shivering girls line up while the pianist ploughed through his melody. *Is there even a job I could do?*

Paris was exciting, and although—with her new clothes—she looked like any local girl, Flore felt like a zoo animal plucked out of its familiar setting. Getting acclimatised would take her a long time.

While the stage was being cleared for the evening show, Minnie came to sit next to her, warm and out of breath. 'So what did you think of our dancing?'

'Oh, Minnie, it was wonderful. Did you . . . Is it all your idea?'

'Yes, I choregraphed all the moves. I'm thinking of including a can-can for our next show.'

'I didn't realise you were so talented. You're the star of the Folies, I bet.'

'Not really. People may come to see us because we show our legs, but the true star is Thérèse—Mamouna—our snake charmer. I wish I had her gift.' Minnie fluffed up her skirt and relaxed against Flore, gazing at the boxer coaxing a scared kangaroo with a carrot.

Minnie placed a hand over Flore's. 'Will you be coming back to Paris?'

'Oh, I hope so. I will see you again, that's for sure. I am not sure when, but I will. You have been such a friend. I feel like I've known you forever.'

'Promise me that when you do come back, we'll dance the can-can at the Bal Bullier. It's fantastic fun.'

'I promise. I'll write to you.'

She kissed Minnie goodbye and turned away, leaving Minnie to her strange tribe. Remembering her early start, Flore called her back. 'I've to get up at five tomorrow morning. Martial won't be allowed to come up, and I won't sleep a wink from worrying. What can I do?'

Minnie placed both hands on her shoulders. 'Don't worry. I'll arrange for a waker-upper to hit my window. I'll tell the concierge.'

'A waker—what??'

'She'll have a pea-shooter and shoot at your window—well, my window in this case; yours is too high and on the wrong side. I'll fetch you. Five, you said? Here, give me a *sou* for her. Trust me. She'll be there.' Minnie hugged her one last time.

The sun was setting over Paris. Here, the bar would soon open, the costumes would sparkle, and once again the Folies would sprinkle their magic over the Parisians' drab life.

Flore trudged home, through the many inner courtyards at the heart of the new Parisian blocks. The voice of an angel soared into the evening sky. The child sang a ballad. Her father, a thatch of hair escaping from his cap, turned the handle of a hurdy-gurdy and pressed its wooden keys while tapping with his clog.

Flore leaned against the porch, her heart in tatters. When the song was over, coins rained from the windows above. Ghostly, wrapped in a thick beige shawl, the girl stood motionless while her father scrabbled for the money, obviously relieved when people had the forethought to wrap the coins in white paper, bright in the dimness and the dust.

Flore searched in her petticoat pocket for a franc and pushed it into the girl's hand—half a day's salary for some—sure that Martial would not mind. 'For you, little nightingale. You light up the darkness.'

The voice followed Flore her to her room, where she spread all her belongings on the bed and shook out the contents of her pockets. She still had enough money for a few slices of quiche at the nearby *crèmerie*. If she hurried, it would still be open.

Night was falling to the sounds of lamplighters' ladders clanking against metal. One by one, the streetlights flickered, hissed and cast an orange glow on the tired faces of workers going home. The wind died, and on the hill, the Montmartre windmills slowed and stood still against the dark blue sky. Tomorrow, Flore knew, Paris would carry on just as it was, without her.

23

MONSIEUR GODIN'S UTOPIA

Martial and Flore's train chugged out of Gare du Nord in loud gusts of grease and smoke. A chilly rising sun briefly caught the hovels, wooden fences and shacks of Montmartre. One last windmill, and Paris was gone.

Flore carefully pulled out two packets wrapped in paper and handed Martial one.

'What is it?'

'It is called *quiche*. It has cream, eggs and bacon in it. It's delicious.' Flore took a bite and made sure her mouth was empty before asking, 'How far is this place?'

They spoke Occitan. Eyebrows were raised in their direction, so they kept their voices low.

'It's two or three hundred kilometres from Paris. The place we're going to is called Guise. I was told that we should say it Gouise, like Louise.'

'Tell me more about this Monsieur Godin,' Flore said before taking another bite.

'You were asking me about my faith the other day.' He leaned forward. 'You and I are going to a place where, though the man in charge does not believe in God, God's principles are still put into practice.'

Flore nodded vigorously. Lost in the sensuous creaminess of her quiche, she was not really paying attention.

'Monsieur Godin started life as a *locksmith*, Flore. At the end of his tour de France, he worked for his father who, as well as locks, made tin stoves. Godin took the idea further and created beautiful cast-iron stoves.' Martial noticed her staring at the package unopened on his lap. 'Here, have mine. I had quite a good breakfast.' He returned to his theme. 'Remembering how he'd had to work twelve hours a day as an apprentice, Godin vowed to improve the condition of the working man.' Martial opened his hands. 'According to him, all workers should be paid a salary that actually allows them to live.'

Flore nodded again.

Martial sat back. Eyes burning with anticipation, he waved his hands. 'You and I, Flore, are going to experience Monsieur Godin's utopian fantasy.' In his enthusiasm, he dislodged the hat of the man sitting next to him. 'Oops. Pardon, monsieur.'

Flore brushed the crumbs from her new skirt and said in Occitan, 'Monsieur your father, does he know where you are?'

Martial cast a side glance at the elderly bourgeois couple. 'I am as much a runaway as you are, Flore.' He lowered his voice further. 'I informed my uncle the bishop that I wished to become a monk in a silent order. Father Anselme is the only one who knows where I am. In due time, I shall write to Hugo, my younger brother, to inform him of my whereabouts . . . with the caveat that he will not divulge them to anyone.'

'Why?'

'Because Father is trying to force me to purchase plots of

common land and invest in pines, because I could never steal what belongs to my parishioners and stand in the pulpit preaching poverty when I am profiting from that theft.'

'That's because you're a good person.' Flore licked her fingers. 'You know, our moor is not the only place where peasants are pushed out. Minnie told me the same thing happened to her family in Scotland.' Her eyes narrowed at the unfairness of it all. 'The masters just took the peasants' land and threw them out of their houses!'

Martial nodded. 'Indeed, the Highland clearances were a dreadful business. It happened in England too. Peasants flocked to towns in search of work or, as Minnie's ancestors, looked for new pastures in America.'

'Father—' Flore's hand jumped to her lips. 'Oops, sorry, Martial. About this new way of living, what will we say to Monsieur Godin about me? He won't be expecting me, will he?'

'Ah.' Martial rested his elbows on his knees. 'Now would be a good time to put our heads together. It grieves me to dally with the truth, but our situation is unnecessarily complicated.' He took out his fob watch. 'We have three hours to get our story straight.'

Guise did not have a station. The closest train stop was in a town called Laon, where, on the concourse, Martial overheard a couple discussed returning to the Familistère. He proposed they share a cab, relieved when they accepted. He wanted to know more about the place.

A strong breeze chased clouds across the sun, painting moving patches of light and dark over forest and fields. As the carriage slowed at the top of a hill to allow the horses to catch their breath, their fellow passenger pointed to a massive block of pink bricks.

'There! Can you see it?' the man cried out. 'Inside that river loop. That is our Familistère. On the other side of the road is our factory.'

Martial noted the pride in his voice. 'Heavens. I didn't realise the stove factory would be quite so big.' He had imagined one or two large buildings—a foundry was bound to be sizable—but never would he have expected the sheer expanse of roofs that spread beyond the river loop.

'We don't just make stoves. Monsieur Godin's inventiveness knows no bounds. He designed the building from the cellar to the rafters. You'll see.'

'There are nine hundred of us living in those flats. We call it the Beehive.' The woman's face lit up. 'Monsieur Godin has a flat of his own on the ground floor.' She thinned her lips. 'Madame Godin doesn't approve, mind. She lives in a grand mansion at the edge of Guise.' She added in a lower tone, 'She was the one with the money, you see.'

They followed carts heading for the factory, but while the utilitarian vehicles turned right into the paved front yard, their cab made a sharp left.

As they clip-clopped over a bridge, a ray of sun flooded a palatial building of pink-orange bricks surrounded by a park and well-tended gardens.

'Indeed . . . the Versailles of the North.' Emotion welled up inside Martial as the horses clattered into the yard.

It had been a long road, and at last he had reached utopia. His heart bursting with hope, relief, excitement and other feelings he dared not put a name to, Martial drank in the park and the elegant four-storey building. His hand jumped to Flore's and stopped just in time. How easy it would be to shatter her trust.

He helped her down—his princess in sabots—and

together they stepped inside the Beehive, a vast space covered with glass, surrounded by walkways that led to dozens of doors on three levels.

A lightness of being lifted Martial's soul. The shackles imposed by being a de Pagny fell away, and a world of possibilities opened. This was the product of one mind, the vision of a man who had started life as a locksmith. Elated, he yearned to take Flore in his arms and polka around the yard.

A young man in jacket and sharp trousers stood before them.

'Monsieur Godin will receive you. He's sorry, but he won't have much time.' He took their bags, tucked them inside a small office and, at a pace, led them past buildings Martial had not noticed before. Offices? Stables, perhaps?

'I understand Monsieur Godin is a very busy man,' Martial said as they reached a bridge. He looked over his shoulder. From the outbuildings he had mistaken for offices, a woman came out with a basket of vegetables.

'Our shops.' The young man noticed his interest. 'Should you want to buy food, coal or even material, you don't have to go into town.'

Below them, gardeners were scything the grass on the riverbanks in broad, regular strokes.

A few steps behind them, Flore was taking long gulps of grassy air. Martial smiled with relief. She would like it here; there was enough vegetation to compensate for having to work indoors.

'Here is our laundry.' A small building was reached by a footbridge. 'The hot water comes directly from the factory across the road. We also have hot water piped to each floor of the apartment block. There is no waste. Monsieur Godin is planning to build baths next year. A swimming pool. Won't that be wonderful?'

His mind in a whirl, Martial followed the employee

across the main road towards the immense factory, its chimneys belching smoke scooped up by the wind.

'Here we are.' The young man pushed open a heavy door.

The smell of coal and metal was overpowering. 'This is the office of Mademoiselle Moret. And next to it is Monsieur—'

Just at that moment, a portly gentleman in frock coat and cream trousers came out of the secretary's office. In his early fifties, his dark hair resting on his shoulders, Godin would not have been out of place in a Bluebeard story. Though his thick beard and dour frown were intimidating, the illusion evaporated as soon as he smiled.

'Monsieur Boyer de Pagny! Did you have a pleasant journey? Did you arrive straight from Bordeaux?'

'Enchanté.' Martial held out a hand. 'No, we were in Paris this morning. Boyer will suffice.'

'Ah, bien, très bien.' Monsieur Godin's gaze went to Flore, who bobbed a curtsy.

'May I introduce Mademoiselle Flore Laborde. I mentioned her to you in . . .' Martial hesitated, unsure of the protocol.

'Why don't we take this young lady to Mademoiselle Marie-Adèle, hmm?' Godin suggested. 'She will look after her. Remind me, how long were you planning to stay with us?'

Martial gave the explanation he thought Monsieur Godin would find easiest to understand. 'As I explained to you in my letter, I am keen to experience your principles in the hope of applying them myself. Would two or three months be agreeable to you?'

'I don't see why not. We'll certainly find something for you to do.' Monsieur Godin turned to Flore. 'Come, let me introduce you to Mademoiselle Moret.' He opened his secretary's door and ushered Flore in with, 'Marie-Adèle is my assistant. She looks after the laundry, the schools, the shops and the library.'

Once inside his office, Godin took a seat behind a large cluttered desk, invited Martial to a leather chair and made a bridge with his fingers. 'So what were you doing in Bordeaux? You told me you received your education in a seminary.'

Martial recited the brief he had been practicing. 'I am the middle son of a land owner in la Grande Lande de Bordeaux, where my father has acquired plots. The emperor has plans to turn the region into the biggest man-made forest in Europe. We will be employing a large workforce, and I am interested in social progress.'

'Quite, quite. How about your lady friend, where does she fit in?'

'Mademoiselle Laborde's circumstances are a delicate matter.' Martial cleared his throat and hoped that Flore, on the other side of the door, was telling the same story.

'She was employed as a chambermaid in a relative's household and,' they had adopted poor Joseta's tragedy as their narrative, 'the son's attentions had become unbearable. As I was leaving, she begged me to chaperone her to Paris. I would have left her there, but with her country ways . . .' Martial paused. 'I thought a few months of adaptation in a safe environment . . .'

'You won't be living together, then.' Godin casually sifted through a pile of papers.

'What? No! Oh no.' Martial's mind was reeling. Had he arrived in the Land of Plenty?

Godin lifted a hand. 'That's all I need to know. Bourgeois morals are not something I hold in high regard. Women, especially of the serving classes, do not have an easy time.' He pulled out a sketch. 'I have just finished designing a coffee roaster I am about to patent. The patenting process demands great attention to detail and takes far too much of my time. It is something you could help me with. Let me take you to our design bureau. They will explain everything. It won't be the most exciting occupation in the world, but time is of the essence and we are behind schedule. Your arrival is timely, Monsieur Boyer.'

A smile tugging at the corners of his mouth, Martial followed his new boss into a large office. Bathed in sunlight that dripped from roof lights, the place buzzed with industry. The beehive was a fitting emblem. Men in white smocks stood over trestle tables while others scratched their heads over articles as diverse as petrol lamps, waffle irons, stoves—Godin's trademark—and other objects Martial struggled to identify.

The inventor deputised one of the designers to take over from him.

'Monsieur Klein will show you around and take you to your apartment later on.' Godin exchanged a few words with a white-haired man, went to stand over the desk of a designer, chatted, pointed to sketches and returned to his office.

Martial's first stop was the foundry, where Klein, in slow Germanic French, explained how cast iron was cast into sand moulds.

Sheltered as he had been in a seminary steeped in ink and parchment, Martial watched, wide-eyed, the smiths of Vulcan in black smocks as they mixed coal dust, sand and water into moulds and casually poured liquid fire from giant cauldrons.

The place was sweltering. He took out a handkerchief and wiped his brow.

'This looks like dangerous work. Do you have many accidents?'

'A couple of months ago, a man ignored the rules. He was scorched to death.'

With a backwards glance at the cauldrons, Martial followed his guide across workshops where spare parts were polished, screwed together and packed. By the time they returned to the apartment block, Martial's admiration for Monsieur Godin had turned to awe.

The first person Martial saw inside the small shop by the entrance was Flore, chatting with a small woman in a black dress and white apron. As fair as Flore was dark, the woman wore her blond hair gathered up in the popular brioche style. A gangly man of about their age was detailing packets, tins and jars lined up on the shelves.

'Your friend will be sharing Madame Berthelot's apartment.' Klein lowered his voice. 'She is recently widowed.' He canted his chin towards the factory. 'Her husband was the one who died there. They had a young child. Monsieur Godin gave the widow a position in the shop so she would not be totally without means.'

A bitter memory surged inside Martial's mind. Their estate manager staggering down the path, holding his guts in his hands. By the end of the week, his wife had been relegated to a shack, and their son, Ricar, grew up in anger. It could have been so different . . .

Monsieur Klein stood by the door, consulting his notes.

In the shop, the somewhat myopic chap pulled a pair of spectacles from his top pocket to check a ticket and lifted his face to Flore. The studious frown melted into a smile that hit Martial like an arrow.

As he was planning the trip to Guise, he had assumed that the Familistère would remove the social difference between himself and Flore. Not for a moment had he considered that she might slip away from him.

Yesu, how many unmarried men were there in this place?

'What do you say to that?' Klein stood at ease, hands in his pockets.

'Pardon?'

'Would you like to join us for lunch?'

'Oh.' For a mad moment, Martial worried about Flore's table manners.

Klein followed his gaze. 'Madame Berthelot will take your ward to the laundry and make sure she has lunch.'

'The laundry?'

'Yes. That is where she'll be working. Shall we go up to your apartment?'

The die was cast. Martial would join the men in white smocks and Flore the battalions in aprons.

He cursed himself. Why the big hurry to come here? Why had he not spent a few more days alone with her in Paris? Had he really imagined that because Monsieur Godin lived in the same building as his workers, social classes would be erased?

In the little shop, Flore stood silhouetted against the light of the large entrance doors, her hat perched over a tumble of dark curls. The accountant took both her hands in his and said something. She threw her head back and laughed.

A discombobulated Martial traipsed up a broad curved staircase where, every few yards, posters reminded the Familisterians how to behave, how to work and how to live. 'No running on walkways', 'No clogs on the stairs', 'No singing after 10:00 p.m.', 'Do not block the toilets.' Community living, it seemed, did not come naturally.

Martial leaned over the rail of the third-floor walkway, looked down at the glass-roofed inner yard now crisscrossed by workers going home for their lunch and wished himself back under the arches of the Palais Royal, giggling with Flore at the thought of a night of can-can after a good dinner at the Closerie des Lilas.

Klein unlocked the door to the airy flat which was to be Martial's home for the next few months. A night of can-can indeed. Martial glanced around the elegant space. Who was he deluding? Six years of the seminary had killed any spontaneity he might have possessed.

Coming here to record patents was probably the wildest thing he would ever do.

24
LIFE IN THE BEEHIVE

Two weeks into her Familistère adventure, Flore was getting used to the bustle and the rush. The place was vast! Yesu, was it vast. Bless Martial for buying her comfortable shoes. She covered several leagues a day, from Adeline Berthelot's flat to the laundry, to the nursery to fetch her baby son, Georges, and, three evenings a week, to the library, where she met Alfred Lecomte for lessons in accountancy.

Alfred had explained that, as an apprentice working a twelve-hour day, Monsieur Godin had missed having time to study. As soon as he could, he had reduced the working hours from twelve to ten and set up a library for his staff.

Tonight, Flore twirled across the yard, her mind unfurling like a flower after a drought, buoyed by a confidence she had never felt before.

After washing up—she never ceased to marvel at the gift of warm water on tap at the end of the corridor—Flore sat down with the shop's accounts.

'Sure you don't mind doing this?' Dark circles under her eyes, Adeline was spooning mash into the baby's mouth, determined he should sleep through the night. 'I'm not very good at counting. Not as good as you.'

Flore grinned. 'I used to sell knitted wares with my parents on the market. You got to be quick. People will always try to diddle you. I was ten when Papa first let me hold his stall.' She was dying to work in Adeline's shop. Though laundry work was made bearable by hot water, it was not teaching her anything.

'Are you seeing Lecomte tomorrow?' Adeline asked a little too casually.

'Yes. I could show you what I'm learning. It would help you.'

Adeline fed Georges the last scoop. 'Bah, I'm so tired I'm not sure I'd remember.' She pushed herself up and rested a hand on Flore's chair. 'He fancies you, you know.'

'Who?' Flore stopped the pen over her tally.

'Alfred, silly. Have you not noticed how he blushes whenever he speaks with you?'

Flore puckered her lips, wondering what to do with the information. Alfred was kind, he was not bad-looking, and his explanations were clear, but a life with him would be like the flat plains of France once glimpsed from the train, empty of surprises or challenges.

Counting bags of sugar in the *économat* would be a first step to some sort of career. She was itching to do so much more.

'Alfred is very patient with me.'

'He follows you like a puppy, Flore. I can't believe you haven't noticed.'

'Thank you for telling me. I must make sure I don't encourage him.'

'Yes, that is probably wise.'

There was a hint of relief in Adeline's voice. Hmm . . . did she fancy him for herself? Her husband hardly in the grave, she could not show her feelings.

Adeline put a hand to her head. 'Headache coming on. I get them sometimes. Bright light makes me feel sick. I'll go and lie down in the dark. *Gott im Himmel,* I don't know how I'm going to cope with the shop tomorrow.'

Flore picked Georges up and bounced him in her arms around the tiny flat, singing 'Se Canta'. She tucked him in his cot, an unusual design of Monsieur Godin's creation: a cradle filled with bran above which the baby slept unswaddled and free to kick about.

Back in the sitting room, she dimmed the oil lamp and gently placed a hand on Adeline's shoulder.

'I'll run down to Mademoiselle Moret in the morning and ask if I can take over from you. I won't be missed at the laundry. Plenty of us there.'

'Really?'

'We'll work something out. Just get Georges ready in the morning. I'll take him to the nursery.'

Adeline pushed herself from her chair and said in a faint voice, 'Thank you. I don't know what I'd do without you,' and teetered to her room. Moments later, Flore heard the sound of retching.

Far from their village and family, the Familistère women had to rebuild the support network they had left behind, but Adeline had not yet had time to do that. She came from Alsace. Like Monsieur Klein and Alfred, she spoke slowly, her French peppered with strange German expressions.

The Familistère was a Babel Tower. The Alsatian people garbled in German, the Bretons spoke their mysterious Sabir, and in all that clamour, all Flore understood was French and Provençal, which, like Occitan, was the language of the south.

Alfred thought her southern accent 'adorable'.

She put away her accounts and carried the lamp to the sewing machine, a marvellous invention she was keen to practice on. In the shop across the forecourt, she had purchased a length of light blue material and set out to copy one of Adeline's dresses. In only a week's time, on the 5th of June, *la fête du travail* would take place, the Familistère's very own celebration of work. The whole Beehive was buzzing with excitement.

From the inner yard rose the voices and laughter of women and children making paper garlands under gaslight. Across the walkway, the gardeners were hammering hoes, rakes and spades fan-fashion onto a plank, an oversized heraldic badge of their trade. Hands behind his back, Martial was watching them, asking questions.

How aristocratic he looked from up here. As hard as he tried to mingle with the workers, his blend of confidence and aloofness would always keep him apart from the men in smocks. Did he plan to stay? Flore did not know. Monsieur Godin was keen to bring him onto his team, according to Alfred. She hardly saw Martial now, their paths slowly diverging.

More retching came from Adeline's room. Flore felt powerless to help. Uprooted from her moor, there was nowhere for her to gather the herbs that would alleviate the pain. Towns were so sterile. How could anyone stand it?

In Paris, she had briefly enjoyed the sense of *dépaysement,* that thrill of being 'elsewhere' when every smell, every sound assaulted your senses with its newness, but three days had sufficed. Her moor might have seemed bleak to outsiders, but to her it was generous. In Paris, without Martial's money, she would not have lasted one day.

Flore folded the dress. There would be time before the party to hem it, add buttons and sew on the belt. She returned to the walkway and glanced down at the inner yard, lit up by gaslight. The gardeners' coat of arms was finished, the tools displayed like weapons. Below, piles of trestles and benches awaited guests, and a dais had been erected at one end where Monsieur Godin, Mademoiselle Moret and the mayor of Guise would sit under swoops of tricolour flags.

Shunned by the local aristocracy for living in sin with Mademoiselle Marie-Adèle—his niece and soul mate—and being pally with his workers, Monsieur Godin had set out to create what Alfred called 'his own aristocracy of merit'.

The whole idea, he had explained, was to ennoble man through work and reward the most deserving workers with palms and medals. Sometimes, Flore wondered what the Lord made of these men who tried to upturn the world order. On Sundays, she escaped to town and attended mass just to reconnect with God and pray for the souls of Nanette and her parents.

She leaned over the railing and, chin in her fists, watched the last of the gardeners polish their badge, helped by Martial, who had clearly never handled a hoe.

A grin spread to her face. Together with Adeline, Flore had an important mission. After all the knighting, speeches and feasting, the party would begin in earnest, and the two of them would teach Martial to dance.

He had unwittingly set the challenge by swearing it would *never* happen.

Flore stretched, yawned and turned in. Every night before she went to sleep, she knelt by her little bed in a corner of the lounge and thanked God for giving her the chance to meet men like Monsieur Godin, Father Anselme and Father Martial, good men God had placed along her way in spite of the terrible sins she had committed. Tonight, she added Alfred Lecomte to her list. In teaching her bookkeeping, Alfred had given her skills a name and opened a door she had never known was there.

She crossed herself and ran her eyes around Adeline's flat, the solid oak furniture and plush armchairs, the flowered paper on the walls. While her husband was still alive, Adeline had had the leisure to crochet enough doilies to cover every surface.

Flore snuggled down and closed her eyes. *If Tanta and Colin could see me . . .* Tomorrow, she would write to Father Anselme and ask him to forward her adventures to them. As her mind drifted into the nonsense of dreams, her thoughts wandered to the airial, to her cottage and to the churchyard, where a grave had her name on it.

The following morning, her heart thudding, Flore received the key to Adeline's kingdom of household articles, alcohol, sugar, spices and preserves. It was small, but it was hers for the day, the first step to her dream.

After all, had Monsieur Godin not risen from being a lowly locksmith to a man who made speeches from a dais fit for an emperor? Had the owner of the Bon Marché not begun as a barrow boy? It was 1870, and if you wanted it badly enough, anything was possible.

Today, however, as Flore surveyed her tiny empire, the dream seemed as unreachable as the moon.

Her first customer was Alfred Lecomte, who rushed in when he caught sight of her taking delivery of large crowns of bread from the town baker. A line of children had formed, holding out their coins before darting back up the stairs with their families' breakfasts.

'Flore? What are you doing here?'

'Putting your lessons into practice, dear Alfred. I am very grateful. Did you say I had to enter everything I sell into a ledger?'

A teenage boy pushed past Alfred and asked for a pound of roasted coffee beans.

'Hmm.' Alfred smiled. 'Perhaps I will come by at lunchtime and go over the ledger with you.'

Oh no, he does look hopeful. Yesu, what do I do now?

Martial's tall suited silhouette detached itself from a cluster of burly men in smocks.

'Flore? Is something wrong with Adeline?'

'Yes. She has a terrible headache and will not let me open her curtains.' Flore took coins from small hands and distributed loaves.

'A migraine? How awful.'

'Back home, I could have made a tisane, but where do I find St John's wort here?' She hauled up a basket of fragrant bread and set it behind the counter.

'I have to go, Flore. I'll pop by later.' Alfred followed the black smocks out of the building.

Leaning on the end of the small counter, Martial followed the accountant's progress. The man's easy manner had obviously seduced Flore, who spent most of her evenings with him.

'What did he mean, he will pop by later?' Alfred seemed far too friendly.

'I am learning bookkeeping. Debits, credits, you know.' Flore's eyes shone with excitement.

Martial suddenly realised where he had gone wrong. Gone was the half-wild peasant he had dragged out of the river. Flore had blossomed into a confident woman with a mind of her own. A slanting ray caught the basket of bread, revealing Flore as the Ceres she was, beatific, generous, surrounded by the smiles of children reaching out to her.

Could she ever be his? Martial cringed with shame at how

easily he had allowed her to be relegated to the laundry, assuming she would be grateful.

The accountant might be shortsighted, but he had seen Flore for who she was and found the key to unlock her heart's desire.

If I lose her now, Martial dug his nails into his palms, *I will only have myself to blame.*

He straightened up. He had waited too long to be beaten by a feeble pen pusher. Suddenly, he knew exactly what to do. There was a lady in town who, with a little persuasion of the financial kind, would teach him all he needed to know to make Flore see him as a man instead of a gelding.

25

PLANS ARE AFOOT TO GET MARTIAL TO DANCE

It was Midsummer's Day. The days were lengthening, and, Georges asleep, Flore and Adeline sat by the open window. Beyond the vast lawns where children shouted and called to each other, the river Oise glowed copper in the setting sun. A bee buzzed into the room.

'Leave it,' Flore said. 'It will soon find its way home.'

'Who taught you to knit?' Adeline pointed to the small garment Flore was knitting for Georges.

'My father did.' Flore winced, ready for the questions that were bound to follow. She had been evading them for too long. *Stick to the narrative. Never add nor deviate.*

'Your father? How come?'

'He was a shepherd. He died while watching his sheep—of apoplexy. They found him on the moor three days later.' There, that wasn't so hard.

'Is that why you left?'

Flore took in a deep breath and spun out the tale of the big house and the lecherous son. 'Martial was visiting. I overheard him say he was going to Paris. I knew him from my village and begged him to take me with him. He was kind enough to listen. I am so grateful. I feel safe here.'

A tune rose from the inner yard through the open kitchen window. The newly formed Familistère orchestra was rehearsing a waltz. Flore held up the section of the tiny jacket she was knitting and thought of her father, threading the wool through his thick fingers, casting on. She buried her nose into the ball of wool and breathed in the smell of home, her heart aching with memories of how life had been only a year ago.

Martial had received news from his brother Hugo. Tanta was housekeeper at the presbytery and had married Prosper, the *vigneron*. A new curate had been appointed to replace Martial, a young man from Biarritz who knew more about fishing than he did about mass. Father Anselme excused him by quoting that Jesus himself had been a fisherman. Colin was collecting resin in Laforge while he waited to hear from the army.

Ricar and the engineer were buying up plots like they were going out of fashion. In May, the Basque shepherds had been ordered to keep to the coast when returning home. The whole of the moor would soon be a forest, Hugo said. The engineer's daughter was expecting. Martial's elder brother, Roderic, was making a foray into politics.

Adeline picked up her crochet. 'We had fun at the *fête du travail,* didn't we? What a party that was. I do love it so when we all eat together. And the acrobats afterwards!' Tittering, she put down her crochet. 'Why on earth did Martial pretend he couldn't dance?'

'Yes. He really had us foxed!' Flore laughed. 'He could dance better than any of us, couldn't he? Polka, schottische, waltz, he knew them all.' Impressed, Flore had discovered another side to her country curate and wondered what else he would pull out of the bag to surprise her.

'I was wondering . . .' Adeline frowned. 'Do you think he took lessons?'

'Nah. He's from a good family. They all have dance masters, don't they? He was just shy.' Keen to change the subject, lest Adeline should want to know more about Martial's family, Flore moved on to the plan she had been hatching.

'Poor Alfred lives in Guise and has to walk quite a way after my lessons,' she lowered her voice, 'alone and hungry in the dark. It would be nice if we cooked him a meal, you know, to repay him for his generosity. What do you think?'

Adeline was a great cook, but in order for her to find her way to Alfred's stomach—and ultimately to his heart—they first had to lure him in.

Flore added, 'I'm not as good as you. I can only cook garbure. You know, that soup I always make.'

Adeline mulled over the plan. 'He comes from my corner of France. I could bake a *flammekueche.*'

'Fla-me-kush? Which one's that?'

'The quiche I make with bacon and cream.'

'Quiche?' Flore's hands jumped to her heart. 'Oh yes, he will love that! Wednesday's your free afternoon. You'll have time to make it, won't you?'

They had convinced Mademoiselle Moret to let them to share the responsibility for the shop. Flore still worked part-time in the laundry and received a full salary for both, while Adeline made up the difference with the rent Flore paid her.

'You look so much better now that you're not working such long hours. I was worried about you.' Adeline's cheeks had regained some colour.

'Yes, I was just so exhausted all the time. I'm feeling much better.'

Flore realised that the Familistère was home now. She had friends, was in no hurry to leave and, since Martial had

Monsieur Godin's ear, a position in one of the small shops across the yard might be a possibility.

The news Martial brought with him the following day changed all that.

It was midmorning. The shop was empty. Flore was filling pound bags of coffee from a freshly roasted batch. Eyes closed, she breathed in the smell before folding down the top of the paper. Coffee . . . she had even begun to like it.

'Flore?'

'Martial? What are you doing here at this time?'

He checked they would not be overheard. 'Monsieur Godin just told me such surprising news that I had to come straight to you.' His breath was short. There was strain around his eyes.

Several scenarios fired inside Flore's mind. Someone had died. She had been found out. He had lost his position. Whatever it was, it looked serious.

'Monsieur Godin assumes I have been instrumental in convincing my father to order two dozen wood-burning stoves.' He ran a hand through his hair. 'Two dozen stoves!'

Flore read the concern on his face when he added, 'Father is sending someone from Marcillac to have a look at the stoves. What do you make of it?'

While inside her, the world was unravelling, Flore calmly sealed the bag and placed it on a shelf. She gazed up at Martial. 'Does your father have twenty-four rooms to heat?'

'No, of course not, and even if he did, why would he send anyone *here*? The order is big enough for it to be delivered to Godin's offices in Bordeaux. Do you think he's tracked me down?'

'Could your brother have said something?'

'No! Hugo knows how much I have to lose. As far as everyone's concerned, I'm a monk in a Benedictine monastery. Even Marthe doesn't know where I am holed up.'

'Where do you send your letters?'

'Just as I told you, I send them to my lawyer. Hugo fetches them from Bordeaux once a month. Father Anselme hands your letters to your aunt. He would never betray us.'

'Well then, there's nothing to worry about. Godin stoves are popular all over the country. Perhaps your father got together with the engineer and Monsieur Poirier is the one coming to visit the premises. We're only a few hours away from Paris.'

'You might be right. I just don't know how to play this.' Martial ran a finger through a spill of ground coffee. His eyes met Flore's. 'It's just that Monsieur Godin doesn't know that I'm estranged from my family. I don't want a scene.'

'Did he give you a date?'

'Ha, if it were that easy, I would most certainly be ill that day or called away on some urgent business.'

A woman came in for a bottle of wine. While she was making her selection, Flore measured out a kilo of flour and bagged it up. Martial pretended to be interested in beer. The woman paid and left.

Flore cupped her chin in her hand. 'This is not good news. You'll be in trouble with your father for sure.' She lowered her voice to a whisper. 'And God help me if anyone discovers I'm still alive.' Her throat tightened. 'Do you think it's time for us to leave?'

Her gaze darted around the shop, *her* shop. How could she leave it when she had only just begun? It was her world, her domain, the bud of her ambition. Would she never find peace? Had she condemned them both to be fugitives for the rest of their lives? Perhaps it was time for her to return home and face the consequences of her actions. Martial had done nothing wrong. Leaving the priesthood was no crime, not punishable by law anyway. Surely, his father would be glad to know he was interested in furthering the family business.

An old man limped in to buy the last loaf and a couple of beers. With little else to do, he settled for a chat with Flore.

'Lunchbreak,' Martial mouthed over the man's head, 'meet me by the bridge.'

Flore wistfully watched his retreating back.

Life always had a way of catching up with you.

They walked along the river, Martial keeping his hands in his pockets, unable to decide whether it was appropriate to take Flore's arm. In the pleasure gardens, the air was balmy and smelled of cut grass. Red poppies, blue corn flowers and daisies, the three flowers of France, swayed in the gentle breeze that played with Flore's hair, loosely tucked under a straw hat.

They turned onto a gravel path. 'Where did you see us going after this?' Flore's face creased in concern.

'I've been asking myself that question.' Martial linked his hands behind his back, relieved to hear she had said *us*. For a while, he had worried that, to protect his reputation, she would dissociate herself from his life. 'I have learned much from Monsieur Godin. He is a genius, a philosopher and a leader.' His hands moved of their own accord. 'He has the creativity and energy of several men. The problem is I don't yet know what to do with my new knowledge.'

Flore faced him. 'We come from the moor, you and I. Its soil is in our blood. We rose from the marshes of Les Landes and know nothing of industry. You would be better suited to agriculture; that is what you know.'

There it was again, that *you and I*. A small shiver of pleasure ran through Martial at the way she lumped them together.

'Sadly,' he pointed out, 'there will soon not be any agriculture left where you and I come from, only maritime pines . . . and resin.'

'You would make a better leader than your elder brother.'

'That may be so, but first I would have to overthrow my father. Like Brutus, I would have to kill Cesar.'

'*Diou Biban!* Do they own pines as well?'

Martial's chest filled with syrup, and he dug his hands deep into his pockets to stop himself from reaching out to her. 'What I admire most in Monsieur Godin is the way he sticks to his ideals. Like him, I hate what he calls 'society's posturing, hostility, injustice and alienation'.

'Is that what he says? It's a good word, *posturing.* There's a lot of it about.'

'The other industrialists hate him for overpaying his workers, but he doesn't care.'

'Ha! *Overpaid,* are we?' Flore bristled. 'We get just enough to live on.'

Martial placed a hand on her arm. 'I know, Flore. I know. That's just the point. If workers were simply paid *enough* to live on, there would be no need for all the debates, philosophising and revolutions!' His hands fluttered away. 'Why all the greed? I just don't understand. These people go to church every Sunday! What do they do there?'

'Posturing?' Flore quipped before returning to her topic. 'Has anyone ever tried out utopia in the countryside?'

'Oh yes! Monsieur Godin supported a group in America —in Texas, I believe—and I read about an interesting experiment in California.'

'Minnie wrote to me last week.' Flore skipped over a pile of cut grass and twirled to face him. 'She's thinking of leaving Paris and going back to New York.'

Martial's heart melted. She looked so pretty as she twirled. He hooked his fingers behind his back and casually kicked a stone. 'Is she now?'

'Is New York anywhere near Cali-frounia?'

'Not really. California is about three thousand kilometres from New York. Before the advent of the railway, it would have taken settlers six months to get there. Now the train has cut it down to less than a week.'

'Oh. America is very big, then?'

Martial marvelled at Flore's blend of perspicacity and innocence. The female version of Émile, she bloomed, just as Rousseau had imagined his pupil would, given the right tuition, and he loved her for it.

Similarly inspired by Rousseau, Monsieur Godin had named his own son Émile. Ironically the boy had rebelled and sided with his mother, a woman who, untroubled by greed, lived in unabashed luxury on the other side of the river.

'Do they all speak English in America?'

'Well, yes, officially, but it's a nation of immigrants, so everyone speaks their own language.'

'Like us?' Flore chuckled.

'Like us.'

Martial loosened his collar. Did she not realise the effect she was having on him? The torture and bliss of the recent *fête du travail* came back to him. The delicious agony to have her so close, relaxed, laughing and gorgeous in the dress she had made for the occasion. The embarrassing dancing lessons he had taken in Guise had paid for themselves, if only for the look on her face when he had invited her to waltz—that and the satisfaction of dragging her out of Lecomte's sweaty paws.

'How are your accountancy lessons coming along?' Martial threw in, casually studying a heron on the opposite bank.

'Oh, Martial, it is *so* interesting. I understand how Monsieur Godin buys in bulk at a certain cost, makes a profit and pours that profit *back* into the nursery and the school Mademoiselle Moret has set up. Just think, all that money could go into buying a stable in which she could trick all her friends to dine with her horses!'

Martial burst out laughing. 'La Païva's really got to you, hasn't she?'

'I can't stop thinking about the waste when so many are in need.' Flore's face became serious. 'I have learned that buying in bulk makes everything cheaper and that roasting coffee bumps up the price for very little effort. Monsieur Godin charges his workers a fair price for his goods, and then the money they earn goes back to him, so it is a double win.' She spun on her toes. 'Alfred told me what that's called.'

'Did he now? And what is it called?'

'It is a *virtuous* circle.'

'Well, Monsieur Godin is indeed virtuous.'

'Not according to some. Mademoiselle Marie-Adèle is his niece and his cocu-conco . . . He sleeps with her, you know.'

'They are soul mates.'

'Exactly.' She added, her eyes sparkling with excitement, 'One day I might have bigger fish to fry, who knows. I could offer my services to the Bazar Napoléon in Paris and buy spittoons for them in their thousands.'

'So Monsieur Lecomte is a good teacher?'

She nudged his elbow and whispered with a grin, 'I'll tell you a secret, but you must promise *not* to repeat it.'

Martial's heart plummeted. Had the wretched man proposed? His breath caught in his throat. Why had he not declared himself that night as they waltzed?

'Adeline is in love with him.'

'Is she?' Relief coursed through Martial like a fresh spring shower. He had to stop himself from pirouetting on the grass.

'He will return her favours soon, if I have anything to do

with it.' Her chin jutting with determination, Flore set out her plan.

Unable to help himself, Martial grabbed her and danced a polka, loosening the straightjacket the six years of seminary had woven around him. How would she respond?

'*Oh là là!* What was that for?' Flore adjusted her hat and stumbled away from him, giggling.

'Nothing. I am in awe of your plans as a matchmaker.' He stiffened up. She had not responded to the test.

'Is there anyone *you* fancy?' Flore touched his arm and said, mischievous, 'I could try and set you up.'

He studied her face. No. She really had no idea. A thick grey cloud obscuring his thoughts, he turned to the river, pretending to search for small fry by the bank. When at last he spoke, his mood had changed.

'What are we going to do when my father's envoy arrives? Monsieur Godin is bound to bring us together. You will be the first person they set eyes upon as they push through the door.'

'Perhaps it's time for us to return to Paris. Our three months are nearly up anyway.' Flore kicked a stone into the water. 'Heartbreaking really. I was getting to like this place.' She heaved a long, sad sigh. 'And I *love* baby Georges.'

'I'll write to Jules in Paris. See if he can come up with a suggestion.'

'Let's sleep on it,' Flore said as they parted. 'Night brings its own counsel.'

The very next day, the viscount's envoy vaulted off his horse and strode right into Flore's shop.

26
THE VISCOUNT'S MESSENGER

Flore froze. The bag of coffee she had been filling dropped onto the counter and spilled over.

Ricar stood by the door, emotions flickering over his face.

'You . . . you can't be here!' Flore stumbled back into a sack of flour and only just managed to steady herself.

'I could say the same to you, Perloune.' He took a step forward. 'We buried you not so long ago.'

Flore's hand clutched at her heart to stop it from jumping out of her chest. 'What do you want?' She checked the door, desperate to run, but, having recovered from the shock of finding her here, Ricar blocked the exit.

A sob of relief escaped Flore's lips when her next-door neighbour, Madame Duchêne, shuffled in to buy some bread.

Ricar turned away to study the labels on the bottles of wine.

Flore wrapped a loaf in a sheet of paper, tore a strip from it, quickly scribbled a note of warning to Martial and pushed the slip deep into her apron pocket.

Coming to her senses, she called after the woman as she

walked away. 'Madame Duchêne! Something has come up. Could you ask Adeline to run down and stand in for me for an hour? Please?'

The woman muttered, 'Hmpf. I'll see if she's in.'

'So this is the Versailles of the people.' Ricar grinned, his smile two shades from evil. 'For someone who's dead, it sure looks like you've landed with your arse in butter.'

Flore shuddered. Her head in a spin, she watched him trawl around the shop, picking up each item, commenting on it. She answered with short words, just to fill the silence, and wiped her damp hands on her apron, willing Adeline to hurry.

The sound of her friend's shoes tapping on the tiled floor reached her through a mist.

'Sorry, Adeline, an acquaintance has arrived from,' Flore tried to remember what she had told her, 'from my home village. He is here to buy stoves. I must take him to meet Monsieur Godin. I'll be back as soon as I can.'

Adeline took in the scene and wordlessly removed her smock from its hook.

Flore went as far as the entrance hall, Ricar in tow, and remembering she was still wearing her apron, ran back to the shop.

'Adeline.' With a backward glance, she pushed the strip of paper into her friend's hand. 'Make sure this reaches Martial as soon as possible. Whoever you send, do it discreetly.' She threw her apron on the hook and ran outside.

'Ricar,' Flore asked once she could breathe again, 'why are you *really* here?'

Once over the bridge, she veered towards a bench in the pleasure gardens that bordered the river, hoping the diversion would give Adeline time to find a messenger. She added in a tight voice, 'Tell me the truth for once.'

He faced her, imposing with his dark beard and well-cut jacket, and pointed to a bench.

'I need influence, you see. Just as your saintly Monsieur Godin rules over his little kingdom, I too want to rise to the top. My father-in-law has detected skills I did not know I had and allowed me to marry his daughter.'

'A step in the right direction.' Flore's head inside the lion's mouth, now was not the time for recriminations. 'And yet you need more.'

'We discovered that Martial was hiding.' He lifted an eyebrow. 'And that he was no monk. In fact, quite the opposite.'

'What? No! You're wrong.'

He lifted a hand. 'Wrong, am I?' When no answer came, he carried on, 'Anyway, let me reassure you that I had nothing to do with it. Neither had Hugo. Martial writes to him, doesn't he?'

Flore did not move a muscle.

'Hugo has left the manor and enrolled in a cavalry regiment.' Ricar patted his top pocket with a smirk. 'If Martial does our bidding, I'll even give him the name of the regiment. You see, I am here with a proposal. Of course, knowing Martial, he will refuse.' He leaned forward, his dark eyes boring into her soul. 'You will help him see sense.'

Fear churned inside Flore's stomach. 'W-what do you mean?'

'I promised the viscount that I would come back with rather more than twenty-four stoves, you see. I need Martial's signature on a piece of paper. A simple little signature that will allow monsieur his father to buy pines in his name. The more land they have, the easier it is for them. If I return with the prize, they will support me and my father-in-law's endeavours. If I don't . . .'

Flore jutted her chin forward. 'You're blackmailing me.'

Ricar casually rested an arm on the back of the bench and studied her from under his brow. 'We are poor peasants, you and I, Florette. Mud shufflers. I am beholden to that scavenging de Pagny family. They are vultures, but what can I do? We have to use the cards we've been dealt. You use your charms; I use my devious mind.'

'You are wrong! I never . . .'

Ricar gave her pitying look. 'Bah, just because your silly curate has tied himself up in knots doesn't mean he's not gagging for it.' He leaned forward and whispered, 'And you would roll over if he asked, because you have no choice.'

'No, I wouldn't!'

'Oh, you may despise my ambition, but one day you will look into your own heart and see the same fire, the same need to claw your way out of the pit where they've tried to keep us. In their mind, we *deserve* to be poor. It's *ordained* by God that we should be poor. The more we suffer, the better our eternal life, right? Ha!' His voice rose. 'There *is* no eternal life.'

Flore jumped as he slapped the bench.

'Here is where it happens!' He was nearly shouting. 'We are worth ten of them, you and I.'

Emotion distorted Ricar's features. Hatred or humiliation, Flore was not sure, but she understood why he had married Angèle Poirier, and why for courtesans like La Païva, nothing would ever be *enough*. Beautiful, clever, proud, but humiliated to death, they scrabbled at everything that came their way just to dull the hurt.

Ricar was wrong if he thought they were the same. She too was ambitious, but she had been spared the need to prove anything to a world that, frankly, did not care. Mama had always told her she was loved, that she was clever, and for Flore it was enough. Whatever she had to prove now was only to herself, not to anyone else.

She shuffled forward a fraction and placed a hand over Ricar's. 'You're right, Ricar. I do want to better myself, but not at any cost. And whatever I say won't change Martial's mind. Why should it?'

He slapped his hand over hers. She pulled back in fear, but he held her down, his dark gaze threatening.

'Your aunt has settled in the presbytery.' After an ominous silence, he added, 'Did you know that your brother has found a girl to his liking?' He narrowed his eyes. 'When it is known that *in a fit of madness* his sister once set the forest on fire, no one will ever want to marry him.' He added with a wolfish smile. 'Think on it.'

'You have no proof.'

'Don't I? There is a grave in Noirac with your name on it, and yet here you are, alive and well.' He tightened his hold. 'Would you care to come back with me and explain that?'

Flore rubbed her hand as if burned. 'I ran away to avoid working for the *métayer*, a dirty old man who molests the girls who—'

'Ha! He's the *métayer*. Using the maids is his prerogative, his *droit de cuissage* and all that.' A snarl distorted his features. 'Just count yourself lucky it's not Roderic you have to serve.'

Ricar's tone now soft, almost loving, he concluded, 'I know you started that fire, and if I need proof, I will find it.' He pushed himself up and rubbed his wounded thigh. 'Come on, Perloune. Show me that paradise of yours.'

'Why is your soul so dark?' Flore murmured. 'Martial is not your enemy.'

Ricar turned away and gazed at the river for a long time, taking in long thoughtful breaths. His eyes were haunted and his words heavy when he said, 'No. No, he isn't, but I'm afraid it's him or me right now.' He walked back to her and placed both hands on her shoulders. 'What would you have me do?'

She shrugged him away. 'Why sink so low, Ricar Guyon? Whatever it is you need so badly, you're going about the wrong way to find it. I feel sorry for you.'

27
WHAT DOES RICAR REALLY WANT?

Martial ran every scenario through his mind as he read Flore's note, her childish letters dancing before his eyes. Why had Ricar travelled all the way here? Was he sent by his father? Had he come of his own accord, the stoves nothing but a pretext? More importantly, how had Ricar known where to find him?

Martial crumpled Flore's note into a tight ball, dropped it into his paper basket and positioned himself by the entrance.

As he caught sight of Ricar through the glazed doors, he took a few hesitant steps and acted surprised.

'Ricar? What a surprise!' Unsure of Ricar's motives, Martial kept to the sentences he had rehearsed. 'I must say, when Monsieur Godin mentioned a visitor, I was expecting the engineer. Good to see you.' He held out a hand.

Ricar's handshake was firm and his smile genuine. The old connection was so strong, Ricar's embrace so warm, Martial hoped they would be friends again.

How that boy had changed. The cream trousers, dark waistcoat and jacket were those of a bourgeois. Gone was the pomaded hair parted in the middle and the roguish moustache. Ricar's thick curls were cut short, and a neatly trimmed beard gave him an air of authority.

'Is my father well?'

'Never better.' The old cockiness was back. 'Getting ready for winter, blocking up draughty fireplaces. Looking to the future.'

'Twenty-four stoves is a large order. Are they for the manor, or are you setting up a shop?'

Ricar laughed. 'I was tempted, I must admit. No, I wanted to see the factory for myself.'

How did he know where I am? Swallowing his doubts, Martial indicated the double doors.

'Come. Monsieur Godin has asked me to guide you around our factory.' The sword of Damocles would fall soon enough. 'Let's start with the foundry.'

'It all got too much for you, then, the Church?' Ricar glanced at Martial's white smock.

'You could say that.' Martial wondered what Ricar really thought of his decision. 'And you've thrown in your lot with my father. He doesn't tolerate dissent; you do know that, don't you?'

Ricar snorted. 'Indeed. The viscount is very good at letting people know their place.'

The noise of the foundry preventing any further conversation, Martial tried to puzzle out the deal his father and Ricar had made, and to what purpose. His mind reeling with suppositions, Martial explained how the iron was cast and pointed to the myriad household objects manufactured here, from umbrella stands to free-range cookers.

Ricar's eyes widened at the sheer vastness of the foundry, men in black smocks running like ants around giant cogs, pouring out rivers of fire with total precision.

'Godin is a titan!' Martial shouted above the din. 'Few of us will ever achieve so much in our lifetime.' He could not keep the fervour from his voice. 'Just think: the man started life as a locksmith.'

'Indeed.' Ricar wiped his brow with a handkerchief. 'He is to be admired.'

By the time they reached the assembly rooms, Martial had had enough.

'Out with it. Why are you here?'

Ricar acknowledged the question with a grin. 'Poirier and I have purchased a few plots, as you know. Our pines will bring returns in about fifteen years or so . . . if we don't have any more forest fires, that is.' He waited for a reaction. Receiving none, he carried on, 'In the meantime, we are draining swamps, boring into the layer of alios, pumping out water. It's a huge investment. We're not the only ones doing that. The moor has attracted all manners of competitors who bring in bands of men and steam machinery. The viscount's patronage gives us an edge. Your father has many friends.'

'My father does not have a single friend, and you know it. Only greedy associates. Why has he sent you here?'

They moved on to the cool packing rooms, where heavy stoves and cooking ranges were waiting to be packed in straw. Busy with their lunch, men cast them indifferent glances.

'In order to be competitive, the viscount needs to acquire more land than anyone else. For tax reasons and reasons of his own, he needs you to buy up plots.'

'I liked the moor just as it was.' Martial hoped this would put an end to the conversation.

'Draining the moor has led to a healthier environment. We're fighting swamp fever. The marshes have gone.'

'So have the sheep and the peasants. Anyway, what exactly does my father want from me?'

'You don't need to do anything. Just give him power of attorney.'

'Power of attorney? Put my name to his schemes? Why should I go along with this madness? I have a reputation to keep.'

'A reputation? Really?' A dangerous edge crept into Ricar's voice. 'Do you want to be remembered as a defrocked priest who ran away with a mad peasant suspected of arson and murder?'

Martial crossed his arms. 'Is that all you can come up with? However disappointed my father may be with me, I doubt he will allow you to spread rumours that discredit our family.' He studied Ricar's face. 'I wonder what he has over you.'

'He doesn't have anything *over me*. It's much simpler than that.' Ricar picked up a petrol lamp and worked its mechanism.

Interesting. Though he was acting casually, he had coloured slightly. So Ricar had secrets too . . .

'I want to go into politics, and your father has offered to support me.'

Martial burst out laughing. 'Politics! Then you *have* sold your soul to the devil. He'll have your hands tied behind your back.' He slapped his forehead with the palm of a hand. 'Christ, for someone clever, you've done something remarkably foolish. My father is a staunch imperialist. Siding with the emperor at this point in time is suicide. The French Empire is dead. Republican wolves are howling at the door, and Bismarck is itching for a war.' Martial punched a packing box to make his point. 'For heaven's sake, Ricar, stick to digging ditches. Even with dynamite, it's safer.'

He studied his erstwhile friend and, once again, caught a glimpse of vulnerability. The toughness had gone, replaced by something like . . . longing. What was that about?

They walked back to the offices. 'Tell you what, Ricar, now you've come all this way, take a moment to watch and learn how one can be a leader of men without trampling them down. Look beyond the placards, the banners and all the utopian tenets. Just follow the money. See how the profits are ploughed back into the factory to ensure our workforce is educated, healthy and *productive*.' He encompassed the facilities with a tilt of the chin. 'The restaurant, the shops are not just practical. The workers' salaries are poured right back into the capital.'

Ricar was listening.

'Monsieur Godin keeps at the forefront of progress; he's always *ahead* of the pack. If you side with my father, you'll be dragged back to the past. He rules by fear, no better than a slave-owner. Will you cast out your men when they're wounded, condemn their families to starvation, as he did you and your mother?' He uttered a long sigh. 'You know my father's ways.'

'Need is my teacher.' Ricar shrugged. 'I don't have the leisure to be broad-minded.'

'How about common sense? How can workers function when they're exhausted from a twelve-hour day and weak from meagre rations? Why rule by fear over a rabble of starving wretches who hate you when you can both grow your profits *and* make the world a better place?'

'Ah, Martial, you will never change, will you?' Ricar said fondly.

'Tell me,' Martial opened his hands, as he did from the pulpit, 'once you've drained the whole moor and are sitting on a pile of resin, what will you do with your money?'

'We'll build machines.' Ricar's face softened. The years fell away, and Martial's heart ached as he saw the boys they had once been, dreaming of a golden future.

Martial rolled his eyes. 'Machines, huh? Like Jules Verne's American millionaire? We both read *From the Earth to the Moon*, didn't we? Ah yes,' he grinned, 'I can just see it. Ricar

Guyon, the French Impey Barbicane, the industrialist who has nothing better to do with his dollars than waste them on building a *spaceship*.' He lifted a hand to his head. 'What in the name of sweet Jesus is the point of a spaceship?'

'Actually, you're not far wrong there.' Ricar laughed. 'Poirier is investing in hot-air balloons.'

'But you can do that *and* pay your workers a living wage!'

'You've made an interesting point,' Ricar admitted. 'I'm dying to see the inventions of Monsieur Godin's emporium of wonders. But before that . . .' He pulled a folded document from his pocket.

'I am *not* buying plots,' Martial growled. 'I'm not signing anything. Especially not a power of attorney!'

'If you don't buy plots, someone else will. Most of the moor has gone. It will save on your inheritance tax. All you need to do is sign on the dotted line. See? Three little signatures. Your revenues will be invested for you and bring returns. Shall we go and find a pen?'

'You're wasting your time.'

'Even if I blackmail you?' The affectionate look remained. 'I see your paramour is here, the girl who set my pines on fire, destroyed the ancient Noirac oaks and murdered her own sister, tired of having to look after a retar—'

'Stop! Please don't do that. You're better than that. Ricar, I'm your friend, but I won't play your games.' Tired of being manipulated, Martial cut short the discussion. 'I'll be leaving here soon. You won't know where I've gone.'

'I found you this time. I can find you again.' Ricar faced him, his gaze intense, yearning. 'Martial, I will always know where you are. Always.'

'Come,' Martial said to break the spell. 'Let me show you around our design office.'

After a second's hesitation, Ricar pocketed the documents

and followed him. He took in the men in white smocks, the trestle tables, desks and shelves crammed with various objects. 'I say, what a hive of creativity, but tell me, what does a man who spent six years in a seminary know of machinery?'

'I asked myself that question at the start, but all I do is check patent forms, make sure they bear the right dimensions and numbers and sign off the designs before Monsieur Godin puts his name to them.'

'He doesn't just make stoves, huh?' Ricar whistled as he scanned the shelves, impressed by the spittoons, door handles and waffle irons on display. 'You make all these here?'

'Yes, over there is a coffee roaster, for instance.'

'A coffee roaster? We have one at home. Clanky old thing burns my coffee. How does it work?'

Martial left his desk to demonstrate the smooth workings of a sphere mounted above a tripod and a small box containing charcoal.

'Excellent! I'll have one of those too. Angèle will be delighted.' Ricar pointed to a large contraption on the floor, which Martial had to study before he could remember what it was. Laundry equipment. For warming several flat irons at the same time.

'When I build my spaceship, I shall be sure to come here for assistance.' Once again, Ricar was the boy he had known. 'And I'll point out to monsieur your father that his stoves were built by happy workers.'

What a strange visit, Martial pondered after Ricar had left. He may have threatened to expose him, but would he really go as far as causing a scandal, or was it just bluff? Whatever it was, they were in danger.

Martial's stomach churned with fraught emotions. He had thought himself safe here. Once again, they would have to leave, return to Paris, perhaps, or visit another utopia: Monsieur Godin had mentioned a community in the Jura.

Would there never be an end to the running, to the lying? The whole point of leaving the Church had been to live a purer life, a life consistent with his ideals. Why was it so hard?

Lost in thought, Martial rummaged around his desk for an application he had wanted to send with the afternoon post, a patent for the enamel coating of a spittoon. What had he done with it? He was always so careful with papers. He ran a hand through his hair. It could not have gone very far. *Corne tonnerre.* He had only signed it that morning. Where was it?

He pulled out his chair and frowned. The scrap of paper Flore had used to warn him of Ricar's visit lay uncrumpled on the seat. He definitely remembered throwing it in the bin.

On the other side of her hastily scribbled message were the words *Régiment de Cavalerie de la Garde Impériale.*

28
LE TEMPS DES CERISES

The following Wednesday, Flore set out a lunch of salad, pâté and cheese on the table, to the babble of voices rising up from the park through the open window.

She looked around the flat. Warm and cosy, it was the loveliest place she had ever lived, designed by a man whose mission was to make the world a better place.

Could the world ever be better as long as there were people like Ricar in it? She shuddered. Ruthless, he held her life—and the life of those around her—in his hands. What would Adeline think if she learned that she was sharing her flat with a woman who was both an arsonist and a murderer?

Adeline was just returning from the pump at the end of the gangway. 'I can't believe it. The Old Owl is out again, snooping on everyone.' She dropped the bucket with a clang. 'Since we've been inviting Alfred, she waits outside the waste chute like a fat spider, just so she can get a glimpse of him. *Ach*. I bet she thinks I'm a *midinette* for having a man around so soon after my bereavement.' Adeline had received stern glances from several women when she swapped her widow's weeds for dark blue. In many French regions, widows wore black for the rest of their lives. 'She's so nosy, that Madame Duchêne.' She took a loaf of bread, plonked it on a cutting board and attacked it with a knife.

'Adeline . . .' A lump in her throat, Flore interrupted the flow. 'Listen, I have some good news, and I have some bad news.' Without giving Adeline time to choose, she said, 'Let me start with the good news.'

Adeline slowly lowered her knife, her face tense.

'I won't be here tonight. You'll be having dinner with Alfred on your own.'

'But I can't!'

'I said it was the good news, didn't I? Just think. You will have him all to yourself.' Flore breathed in the meaty scent pervading the flat. 'Mmmm, not mutton, not chicken . . . beef, right? Boeuf bourguignon!'

'Well, I—'

'And for dessert?'

Adeline gave a modest shrug. 'It's still cherry season, so I made a cherry flan.'

Flore brought both hands to her heart. 'A creamy flan. He will love it!'

'Why can't you be here?'

'Now for the bad news.' Flore's voice wobbled. 'I'm so sorry, Adeline but . . . I have to leave.'

'What do you mean, leave?'

'Leave the Familistère.'

'Oh, oh no!' Adeline's face dissolved. 'Why? When?'

Tired of pretending, Flore searched around for a simple explanation but couldn't think of one.

'Is it to do with the man who came the other day?'

Flore nodded and dabbed her tears with a tea towel.

'Are you going with him?'

Flore shook her head. 'No. I wish I didn't have to go. I really do.'

'You're not leaving tonight, though, are you? That would be too cruel.'

'No, tonight Martial and I are going to Guise to discuss our next move without all the Familistère's eyes and ears trained on us.'

'Martial is leaving too?'

Flore simply nodded.

'Autsch . . . Mein Gott!' Adeline twisted her hands. 'What do I tell Alfred?'

'I'll tell him myself when I cancel our lesson. He will arrive here a little earlier.'

Adeline cast a worried glance around her pristine flat. She pulled out a chair and sat at the table, laden with all manners of delicacies neither of them felt like eating anymore.

'Flore?'

'Hmm?' Flore pulled out a chair opposite her.

'Do you think I have a chance with him? Be honest, it's you Alfred fancies. What if he laughs at me?'

'Oh, Adeline, why would he not love you? You're pretty, kind and such a great cook. He loves baby Georges, doesn't he? He will help you with the accounts, and who knows, one day you two could even open your own shop.'

'So you think I have a chance?'

'Well, it depends.' Flore bit her lip. 'Women are not really allowed to run their own business, are they?'

'I meant with Alfred.'

'Oh yes! Of course you do. Alfred and I would never work. He's nice, but I want to see the world. I need to be outdoors, beholden to no one.' Flore pinched her lips. 'I blame my Gipsy grandmother.' There was no Gipsy grandmother, but she hoped the lovesick accountant would balk at that detail when Adeline told him.

Guilt gnawed at Flore's conscience. Adeline would have

to return to her ten-hour day job and, until she married Alfred, care for Georges on her own.

Damn you, Ricar. Why could you not leave us alone? I'm not ready to go. I still have so much to learn.

After lunch, Flore trudged to the laundry, the one place she would not miss, especially at this time of year, when it was sweltering outside. Her afternoon dragged on, scrubbing recalcitrant stains with lye. Over and over, dripping with steam and sweat, Flore plunged in a dolly, pounded sheets in boiling water, pulled them out with a stick, rinsed them, dumped them into the huge circular spinner and, with the help of another woman, set it in motion, cursing under her breath.

As soon as the bell rang, she rushed home to change and halted on the gangway.

Madame Duchêne was waiting by the gaslight to exchange news with the lamplighter. Mumbling to herself, she leaned over the balustrade, spying on the comings and goings inside the Beehive.

With its long rectangular shape and gangways facing each other, the Familistère might be stylish and warm, it might be hygienic, and it certainly was convenient, but it was noisy, and one could not help but feel confined somehow.

On an impulse, Flore went to the end of the corridor where the utilities were hidden in a corner. It smelled of refuse and gas.

'Madame Duchêne, I am so glad I could catch you. Remember the person in my shop the other day? A man with a beard?' Flore took on a sad mien and clutched at her heart. 'My cousin. A death in the family. I must go home.'

The gossipmonger's face drooped, mirroring her own. 'I'm sorry to hear that.'

'Tell me,' Flore cast a conspiratorial glance towards the

door of her flat and asked with genuine concern, 'did Adeline's husband . . . was he rough with her?'

'Well, I'm not one to gossip.' The woman twiddled a corner of her dirty apron. 'He would shout at her when he came back from Guise on Saturday nights—the worse for wear, you know. I could hear her crying, poor girl.'

Flore did not have to pretend when she said, 'Ah, I thought as much. So brave, so loyal. She won't speak ill of him. Listen, I know it's not long since he's gone, but she's too young to be alone.' Flore checked the gangway and took a step closer. 'I've been doing some matchmaking with an accountant. A lovely young man. Madame, you are a wise woman. I will need your help.'

The round face lit up. 'The poor thing. She's very young indeed.'

'I knew you'd understand. If you could make sure no word gets out until, you know.'

Madame Duchêne beamed, delighted with her mission.

Casting off her damp clothes, Flore changed into a thick skirt and shirt. She picked up a shawl and, her heart breaking, ran her gaze over the flat. Dressed with a white cloth, the square table was set for two. Adeline was singing to Georges, and from the kitchen the meaty aroma of boeuf bourguignon mingled with sweet cherry notes.

Bathed in golden sunlight, how could the cosy setting not tempt the bachelor into family life?

Flore hid by the chute until Alfred arrived. Soon, his steps echoed on the gangway. She peeped out. He adjusted his jacket before knocking on their door, the customary box of candied fruit in his hand.

Alfred was kind, but he was not for her. Ironically, leaving might be the best thing Flore could do for Adeline.

Once the accountant had gone in, she galloped down the stairs and caught up with Martial's tall silhouette by the school. She slowly spun around, and, walking backwards, her heart swelled as she cast a long look at the bulk of the Familistère, orange in the evening light. The building was enormous, and yet Monsieur Godin had plans to extend it—to add baths, a pool and even a theatre. Yes, the man was greedy, but his was a greed for life, driven by an incredible energy and the dream of a fairer world.

The experience had been an inspiration, something granted to very few, and she would have loved to stay longer.

'Flore.' Martial took her arm. 'Runaways once again.'

'If I were to leave, would Ricar still hold power over you?'

'Oh yes,' Martial said with feeling.

'You could let me go. You don't have to pay for my crime.'

'Ricar has known me long enough to predict that I will not abandon you . . . and that I will remain loyal to him, in spite of everything.'

Martial's jollity was forced when he glanced over at her. 'You're shackled with me, I'm afraid. Together we'll face the stormy seas.'

Unsure of how to feel after his admission, Flore responded in the same vein. 'So where to now, Captain?'

His arm tight against hers, they swerved towards town. 'First, *moussaillon,* we must consult our charts.'

Flore chuckled at his use of *cabin boy,* more grateful than she had ever been to have Martial in her life, ready to rescue her once again.

'Let us set sail for Guise.' He took a strong captain's voice. 'Dock Chez Dédé for a parley.'

Dédé's was full that night. What the devil was going on? Around the bar, clusters of men were talking loudly with animated gestures. From a quiet table in a corner, Flore watched Martial join the men at the bar. He towered over the caps, his stance betraying his aristocratic roots. He listened, asked a few questions and whispered something to the *patron,* pointing to their table.

'What's happening?' From the raised voices, Flore could tell that the matter was of national importance. 'Has the emperor died?'

Martial's mien changed. 'You must have heard of the recent troubles over the throne of Spain.'

'Oh, that. Alfred tried to explain it to us, but Georges was teething. Something to do with the Spanish queen stepping down.'

'The next in line to the Spanish throne is a German prince.'

That was all well and good, but how did this affect French men in a northern café?

'Does it have anything to do with Eugenie? She's Spanish.' The woman was a liability.

'It does involve her, actually. She's horrified at the idea of a Hohenzollern prince in charge of her country. So our emperor has asked the German prince to withdraw.'

'Just like that, *hé*? And has he?'

'Yes.'

'Well, that's good, then, isn't it? I still don't see why everyone's making such a fuss about it here in Guise.' Flore wished Dédé would hurry. Her stomach was growling and her interest in politics limited. 'So what are we eating tonight?'

Martial's eyes twinkled. 'Dédé's brother caught a batch of trout. He's fried them in butter.'

'Oh my! *Truite au beurre noir.* Oh, how long is it since I've had trout.'

Flore's mind travelled back to the days she had spent fishing with Colin . . . in the very river where she had tried to end her life.

Martial had pushed the cutlery to one side and sketched something on a piece of paper torn from the table covering.

'Do you know what France looks like?' He turned the sketch towards her. It bore a six-sided shape, long squiggles and a few dots.

'I only saw snatches from the train.' Eyes half-closed, Flore searched her memory. 'There's an ocean near us, just over the dunes. The Pyrenees are to the south of course, Spain on the other side. Hmm, a vast flat plain in the centre, where wheat grows without much trouble. Let's see. One large river called . . . the Loire? Paris is on the Seine and . . . yes, it's quite hilly around here. What does that have to do with the Spanish queen?'

Martial tapped his sketch. 'This is a map of France. If you were high in the sky, this is what you would see. Our moor and Bordeaux are down here, near Spain. Guise is all the way up here, eight hundred kilometres north. Paris, the capital, is just there, see? Inside those wriggles of the Seine.'

Flore had seen maps plastered on the Marcillac town hall but had never understood their purpose. She put her brain into gear, eager to find out more.

'Down here is Nice. It's French now. The Italians just gave it to the emperor as a reward for helping them against the pope. Up here, along a river called the Rhine, is the place where Monsieur Klein and Adeline come from. It is called . . .' He gave her time to answer.

'Alsace!'

'Alsace has always sat between two chairs, half-German and half-French, but the Rhine flows alongside, and Monsieur Bismarck wants it all for himself.'

By the time their fish arrived, Flore had absorbed the geography of France, still none the wiser as to the animation at the bar.

She waited for Martial to start with his trout and carefully copied the way he lifted the flesh from the bone with his knife, pretty much as she would have done, though how he managed to lift the whole bone and head without once using his fingers was a skill that would take a lifetime to acquire.

Dédé's potatoes were sautéed to perfection. Discovering new foods had been one of the perks of travelling on a gentleman's coattails. She glanced at Martial, intent on his fish, and wondered about Ricar's comment. Would she give herself to him if he asked?

No. She was too proud, and he would never ask. Not that he would even think about it. Why would he want her? She was an ignorant peasant, part of his father's chattel, and anyway, he was still a priest at heart.

'All right,' she said once they had finished. 'I understand that France would be inside German claws if the prince took the Spanish throne, but he hasn't. So Spain will have a Spanish king, and we can have our dessert.' She signalled to Dédé. 'I hope it's cherry flan.'

'How did you guess?' Martial folded away his sketch while Dédé set out slices of the flan.

'It's cherry season.' Flore hummed the tune of the popular song, 'Le Temps des Cerises'.

'Did you want coffee?' the jovial chef asked.

Martial nodded. Flore shook her head. She only drank it in the morning, with plenty of milk.

'Sorry, Flore. I've not quite finished.' Martial unfolded his map again.

'I thought we'd come here to discuss our next move, and here we are talking about politics in Spain.'

'The thing is, when he answered Louis-Napoléon's request, the terms of Bismarck's telegram were so rude they angered our emperor, or rather our empress, according to the gossip around the bar.' Martial met Flore's gaze. 'There is talk of war.'

'War?' Flore's eyes popped.

Martial returned to his sketch. 'As you can see from this map, Guise is not very far from the German border. When the Prussian army charges towards Paris, the Familistère and all its food and *metal* supplies will be on their route. So what I suggest is that we wait until we get our wages at the end of next week and leave the next day.'

Flore forgot her dessert. 'Where to?'

'That is our problem. Paris at first, of course. I have business to sort out. Then, who knows? I was aiming for a utopian settlement in the Jura, but . . .' He tapped a spot just below Alsace.

'It's close to Germany.' Flore stared at the map, her head in her hands. 'And the Prussians will be marching right through it.'

'Exactly. Oh. Talking about armies . . .' Martial reached into his top pocket and pulled out the strip he had found on his chair. 'What do you make of this?'

Flore stared at the word CAVALERIE written in bold letters on the back of her hastily scribbled warning. The blood drained from her face. Her fingers were unsteady as she handed the note back.

'Your brother has gone into the army. That is the name of his regiment.' She closed her eyes, suddenly very tired. 'Ricar said he would tell me if you gave him what he wanted.'

'But I never . . . I didn't . . .' Martial protested. 'He asked me to sign a power of attorney over to my father. Of course, I refused. Anyway, what does it have to do with Hugo?'

'Your letters to Hugo won't reach him now. He's left home. Has he not told you?'

'Well, no, I've not heard from Hugo. I was worried. What did Ricar—'

She tapped the paper. 'That is where you should write to Hugo now.'

'How can I write to him when I don't know his regi—oh.'

His brow puckered, he grabbed the note and traced the word CAVALERIE.

'Ricar said he would tell us if you gave him what he wanted . . .' Flore's last words trailed off.

When reality hit, Martial slumped against his chair. *The missing document . . . it had my signature on it. How easy it will be for him to forge it and pretend to Father that I agreed.*

'Never mind the Prussians.' Flore uttered a long sigh. 'How do we defeat *him*?'

29

FRANCE DECLARES WAR AGAINST PRUSSIA

Their last week flew by, the parting all the sadder for the threat of war.

Monsieur Godin held out his hand to Martial. 'I could do with more men like you, Boyer. Men who share my vision and are not afraid of responsibilities. Do you know what you're going to do next?'

'I would like to see a little more of the world. Actually, I was fascinated by the Icarian agricultural experiment you supported in Texas.'

Monsieur Godin's brow darkened. 'Ah yes, I had such hopes. Funded it for years, but launching a utopia in a new land on a wing and a prayer is asking for trouble. The climate in Texas, both political and natural, was not propitious. Even if they had been able to grow produce, whom would they have sold them to in Dallas, with a population of only four hundred? Should you be tempted to follow their example, I strongly advise you to do your research first.' Godin accompanied Martial to the door of his office. 'I commend you for wanting to see the world. Should be compulsory for every young man. Everything I know I learned during my tour of France.' He held the door open. 'Lecomte will give you your salary. Do write and let me know how you fare.'

Martial took a step and halted, a question troubling him. 'Sorry, monsieur, but what do you make of the emperor's declaration of war?'

'Bah, the emperor is a buffoon of the first order. The wording of Bismarck's telegram was designed to anger him, and predictably, he fell into the trap without a care for the thousands of lives that will be lost.' Godin's brow darkened. 'Guise is right in Bismarck's path. My foundry will certainly be of interest to him.'

His words troubled Martial as he made his way to accounts, feeling like a deserter. There was a monastic atmosphere in the large space Alfred shared with another twelve clerks. Bent over ledgers, they reminded Martial of copyists in a medieval scriptorium.

Alfred looked up from his desk, pulled an envelope from a drawer and accompanied Martial out of earshot.

'I wish you didn't have to go, old man.' He handed him the envelope containing his salary. 'Are you going back to Bordeaux?'

'First we will be spending a couple of days in Paris.'

'Flore said she was going home to sort out family business.' Alfred hesitated. 'Are you two related somehow?'

'With war on the horizon, we are the first rats to be deserting this ship, I'm afraid. We're so glad you are here to look after Adeline. She has become a dear friend.' He held out a hand. 'I wish you all the best.'

Martial left before Alfred had time to ask any more and found Flore outside Mademoiselle Marie-Adèle's office. She was clutching a letter to her heart, her eyes still damp with parting from Adeline, back in the main building.

'Did Mademoiselle Moret give you a good reference?'

'Oh yes! It might help me find a job in a Paris department store.'

'I thought you didn't fancy living in Paris.'

'*Eh bé?* Where else would I go?' She threaded her arm through his. 'So, Monsieur Boyer de Pagny, can you see yourself at the head of a resin empire built along Monsieur Godin's principles?'

A delicious shiver ran through him at her touch. 'Hmm.' He tried to remain casual. 'I somehow don't think Father and Roderic would stand for it, though it would be to their advantage—if only they could see it.' He pointed to the gigantic factory across the way. A tinge of nostalgia crept into his voice. 'This place will stand for a long time yet, a model of justice and equality. It was a privilege to be part of it.'

Flore turned to him, her eyes shining. 'I'll never be able to thank you enough for bringing me here. Never.'

Her face was like a magnet, pulling him to her. Unable to resist, Martial leaned forward, prevented from kissing her by the clatter of the carriage.

'*Aïe!*' he cried out as he hefted Flore's bag. 'What on earth have you got in there?'

'I'm a woman of means now.'

She took a seat and looked away as the driver flicked the reins, her eyes glued to the Familistère, its bricks purple under leaden clouds.

A sorrowful sigh escaped Martial. 'How do you feel, now we're leaving?'

'One eye is smiling and one eye is weeping, as my mother used to say. I shall miss Adeline and little Georges terribly.'

Martial was about to ask whether she would miss Alfred when the driver swore, pointing to the main road.

'*Sacrebleu!* Will you look at that! I've never seen the like of it.'

'Mila Diou!' Flore leaned forward. 'What's going on?'

A herd of cattle was blocking the road to Saint-Quentin, a long file of barrows, carts and mules trailing behind it. An ox-drawn cart filled with a tottering pile of mattresses and bags caught Martial's gaze. Sitting on top was a grandmother holding a canary cage. It was as if the whole world was on the move.

A fiercely moustachioed aristocrat in white breeches was cantering up and down the fields shouting to his peasants, 'Go home, for goodness' sake. The Hun yet has to cross our borders! Go back to your village and protect your property. Listen to me, *corne tonnerre*! I speak the truth! Go to my manor and you will see that I have not moved a single candelabrum nor chair.' He pulled the reins of his bay horse and accosted their landau. 'All I did was ask my man to move my cows to a lower pasture, and those boors took it as a signal that the uhlan is at our door. Where are they running to, for heaven's sake? They've nowhere to go!'

Martial read fear in the faces around them, fear of the pointed helmets and the horrors the Huns were purported to commit. According to Madame Duchêne and her informant, the lamplighter, it was known that Prussians ate babies for breakfast.

Wielding his whip, the aristocrat exhorted the fugitives to go home, his imprecations falling on deaf ears. With a final string of *'diantre'* and *'sacrebleu'*, he cut a path through the exodus and galloped back to his chateau, his chairs and his candelabra.

By the time they reached the station, the train to Paris had long gone.

'That was a waste of time,' the driver grumbled as he took out their bags. 'Our factory should really have its own station. Monsieur Godin spent years requesting a track, but it's always been denied.'

'Why do you think that is?' Flore asked Martial as they queued for a ticket.

'Godin's a pariah. Well-to-do society regards him as a dangerous man, afraid of his methods, afraid they will have to increase their own workers' salaries to match his thirty percent bonus.' He added with an encouraging smile, 'He will get his station in the end simply because it makes economic sense. Every year, he keeps re-applying. I know, I filled in the papers. Helping your fellow man is not always easy, as Jesus found out.'

'So you still believe in Jesus?' Flore whispered as they sat on a platform bench. 'You haven't lost your faith?'

'Charity is a universal message, and yes, I still want to put it into practice.'

'How?'

It was a pertinent question, one Martial had been asking himself for a long time. He was spared having to answer by the whistle of a locomotive approaching the station.

It was a hot and muggy summer day. In the train, all the windows were open and hurriedly snapped shut before each tunnel to prevent embers from blowing back into the carriage.

Already, the fear of invasion had reached Laon. The train was overflowing. People sat in corridors, between seats, on bags, baskets and bundles. Some of them had spilled into first class. There were objections, of course, but the numbers were such that nothing could be done.

Unable to find a seat, Flore and Martial stood facing a window, hoping fresh air would dilute the stink of bodies and cigar smoke. Such scenes as they had witnessed on the road were repeated along the way: possessions piled on carts, men, children and women wrapped in shawls trudging along roads that led nowhere, desperate to put some distance between themselves and the monstrous shadow-puppet of the Hun, still hundreds of kilometres away.

Pressed against Flore, Martial inhaled her scent of lavender, drinking in her closeness, wishing the trip would never end. Her hat tickled his chin. He kept a hand on the window frame to stop his body from moulding to hers, excruciatingly aware of how close he was to experiencing an inappropriate response. She was studying the geography rolling by, occasionally pointing to a slag heap, a river or a cathedral, asking its name. When she did, he caught a glimpse of her cheek, soft as a peach.

All too soon, the new suburb of Saint-Denis rushed by. Plumb north of Paris, with its blend of fields, factories and windmills, the town had been selected by the emperor to take the heavy industry out of his sophisticated capital.

'See those new houses over there?' Martial whispered into Flore's delicate ear. 'They are for factory workers. Twenty years ago, just out of prison, when he was a hopeful politician looking for votes, our emperor vowed to harness industry and help the common man.'

'You can't mean that,' Flore objected. 'He *tramples* over the common man!' She glared up at him. A sudden jerk brought them together. Martial swallowed hard and leaned into the man behind him, whose smell of sweat, garlic and tobacco dampened his arousal.

'Still, before he was emperor,' though they spoke Occitan, Martial kept his voice down, aware of the glances around them, 'he was elected on the promise he would "regulate a saturnine industry that ate its children and only lived from their deaths".'

Flore snorted. '*Eh bé,* that was some mouthful. He was lying, though, wasn't he? Once he was elected, it didn't take him long to turn into a dictator. Don't tell me he hadn't been plotting that from the start, him and Eugenie with all her waltzing in Biarritz.' Her pouting lips were so inviting Martial viciously dug his nails into his palms to stop himself from kissing her.

'The problem is that none of his ideas would have come to fruition without the influence of industrialists and bankers.' Martial congratulated himself on having managed another complete sentence, his mind adrift in thoughts he could not control.

'Diou Biban!' Flore rolled her eyes. 'You sound like you feel sorry for the man.'

'Don't judge a man until you've walked a mile in his shoes,' was the only thing he could think of now, his lips wondering how a kiss would taste.

As sweet as it was, Flore's closeness was torture. He was relieved when they reached the Gare du Nord. They fought their way out of the station, caught inside a strange ebb and flow of Parisians desperate to flee and refugees from nearby villages looking for shelter within the walls.

After a long search, they found a cab willing to take them west of Paris to his cousin Jules, who lived near the elegant Parc Monceau.

The city had changed in the few months they had been away. Plane trees were in full leaf, people dawdled on the boulevards, and the mood was effervescent, both joyous and belligerent. Red, white and blue flags floated above buildings, and the tune of 'La Marseillaise', which had not been heard for some time, rose from every street corner.

Baron Haussmann, the driver explained, had turned Paris upside down. Below their feet, two thousand kilometres of sewers were being dug. The mess was colossal.

'And you can visit them on little trolleys!' Flore nudged Martial. 'How about we do that tomorrow, eh? Would you like to visit the sewers?'

'Heavens above, why would I do that?'

Flore burst out laughing. 'You got to live a little.' She patted his knee. 'Remember, we promised Minnie we'd dance the can-can with her.'

'*You* promised. I'm not sure it's quite my thing.'

She faced him squarely. 'Come on, look at me and tell me you didn't enjoy the Familistère festival.' As her large brown eyes rested on him, Martial realised that if he wanted to keep this girl, he would have to overcome some of his reticence. 'I confess. I did enjoy it.'

Flore settled back against the seat, a huge grin spreading on her face. 'Ha! I can't wait to tell Minnie!'

The cab turned into the long rue de la Bienfaisance and stopped in front of a green coach door. While Martial was paying the driver, Flore gazed up at the windows reflecting the last rays of the sun. She had written to Minnie to expect her in the early afternoon. They were *hours* late.

Martial held out a hand. 'Are you coming in?'

Startled by the offer, Flore hesitated. 'I don't think so. I'm late as it is. Minnie will have left for work, and I won't be able to get into her room.'

'Why don't we ask the driver to drop your bag with her concierge? I will write a note. Why don't you come in and have dinner with us? Jules's coachman will drive you home afterwards.' He went into the house in search of ink and paper.

'Don't worry, dear.' The driver grinned. 'I won't be stealing your petticoats.'

Martial's cousin, Jules d'Alembert, came towards her and leaned against the cab. 'Ah, Flore, *bonsoir*. Lovely to see you again. We're just about to have dinner. You will join us, won't you?'

During their previous stay, Martial had been reluctant for her to meet his cousin. 'Thank you,' she said, wishing Martial would hurry back, 'but I have made other arrangements.'

Jules insisted. 'My parents have left for the country to avoid this dreadful mess. I am a surgeon in a hospital and, with a few friends, have hunkered down here with a couple of servants. Do come in and join us. We'll make sure you reach your destination later on. Where does your friend work?'

'She's a dancer at the Folies Bergère.' Flore met his gaze. If Jules's lips so much as quivered, she would remain in the cab.

He drew out his watch and flicked it open. 'Hmm, what time does she have to be there? You've probably missed her.'

'Ah, here you are!' Martial ran out with a message and instructions for the driver.

'But . . .' Flore gripped the side.

'Tell you what.' Jules knocked the matter on the head. 'We'll all go over to the Folies after dinner. I've always fancied a visit.'

'Oh, all right, then.' Flore told the driver the name of the concierge and followed the men in. Determined not to gape at the luxurious décor, she kept her lips firmly closed but could not stop her eyes from widening in wonder.

The last time she had seen a hall of such magnificence had been at the Durocs', Joseta's employers. A wave of guilt overcame her. Here she was in Paris, a guest in this fabulous house, while Joseta's wretched life had been cut short before it had a chance to begin.

Elegant consoles exuded a smell of beeswax. In the panelled dining room, chandeliers were reflected in mahogany furniture and crystal twinkled in the gaslight. In comparison, Martial's family manor was squat and rustic.

The table was set for a crowd. As hungry as she was,

Flore's stomach clenched at the sheer number of plates, stem glasses and eating implements laid out for each guest.

How much easier it would be to grab a bowl of soup in a small eatery.

'You'll be fine,' Martial whispered. 'Just do as I do.'

'Who else is coming?' she whispered back.

Jules's valet led in several characters wearing day clothes. Flore relaxed until, as they were about to sit down, a young woman bustled in, in a flurry of lace, lily-of-the-valley scent and golden curls.

'Bonsoir! Oh, charmante compagnie ce soir. What fun we are having while the cats are away!'

'Violette d'Alembert, my cousin,' Jules said, a note of apology to his voice. 'Our parents have bolted to the country and left us to man the fort. Heaven knows how they will find it on their return.' He then introduced Arthur, a dishevelled civil servant from the local town hall, and a dandy called Gontran.

'Do you study medicine too?' Violette asked Flore with a chuckle.

Flore glanced at Martial. Was the girl goading her?

'Jules's friend does,' Violette said with a knowing grin. 'She's *American*. The first woman to study at the Sorbonne.' She whispered for effect, 'Well, she looks like a woman, but she has a man's . . . brain.'

Jules uttered an exasperated sigh. 'Mary is caring and competent. We need more women like her.' He turned to Martial. 'She works in the Anglo-American ambulance service.'

'Ambulance?' Martial was given a seat opposite Flore.

'Field hospitals. The British and the Americans are sending money and staff to help us treat the wounded. Some have already trickled in from the eastern front.'

The valet led in a woman whose easy manner and simple dress contrasted with Violette's efforts.

'This is Mary, Mary Putnam.' Jules blushed slightly.

Mary took a seat next to him and greeted everyone with a move of the head.

Flore studied the new arrival. Dark hair framed a round face, and a thick brow gave her a studious look. She was visibly at ease in the company of men, unlike Violette, who simpered and giggled at anything Arthur said.

'Bonsoir tout le monde.' Mary ran an appreciative gaze over the company and asked Martial, 'Are you bringing news?'

While Martial described the scenes they had witnessed out of Guise, Flore studied the American covertly. *How has this girl found the confidence to come from America to Paris on her own and learn enough French to study medicine?* Flore found herself thinking back to Héloïse, who, seven hundred years ago, had studied with men, to Mademoiselle Moret who implemented her own ideas on education in defiance of society. How did these women manage, Flore wondered, when the mere thought of having to get through this dinner filled her with dread?

She sipped her broth without mishap and, unaware that there would be another six courses, helped herself to a substantial portion of *saumon en croute,* horrified when roasted pheasants were brought in, followed by *soufflé* potatoes, cheeses and a mountain of desserts which made her queasy. At the other end of the table, Violette held court, picking at everything with practiced indifference.

'Of *course* there should be a war!' The girl's ringlets shook with indignation. 'The words of Chancellor Bismarck's telegram were *unspeakably* rude.' She added in a strangled voice, 'How *dare* Kaiser Wilhelm send *an adjutant* to tell our ambassador he *refused* to see him?'

'The whole thing was a ploy.' Jules lifted his glass for more wine. A servant rushed forward. 'Bismarck was German ambassador in Paris.' He tapped the table with a finger. 'He was here for years. As a diplomat, he knew exactly what he was doing when he *invented* that adjutant. He was simply waving a red rag to a bull, or rather, a heifer. Eugenie stamped her little foot and *olé*! Thousands of Frenchmen will be despatched to teach the chancellor some manners, and I mean *despatched*. The Prussians are trained and they are ruthless. What we have seen is nothing.' He concluded gloomily, 'It will be a bloodbath.'

'I disagree.' Mary's voice rose, confident and strong. 'Empress Eugenie is not the fool most people think she is. If it were not for her, I wouldn't be here.'

Violette snorted. 'How so?'

'She supported my application to study medicine, and thanks to her, Elisabeth Garret-Anderson, the English girl, has just received her degree in medicine.'

Violette scanned the room, searching for someone supporting her own views, but found none, not even Arthur.

'Your emperor is far too ill to embark on a war.' Mary checked that the servant had left and whispered in a sombre tone. 'We have met with his physician. I would get in trouble if this got out of this room, but Louis-Napoléon is too weak to fight.'

'Our army is ready *to the last gaiter button*!' Violette made a fine figurehead at the end of the table parroting opinions Flore had heard bandied around in the train. She pouted. 'Bismarck will eat his words.'

Martial nudged her and whispered in her ear, *'Piota.'*

Flore nearly choked on the grape she had popped into her mouth. The girl did gabble on like a turkey.

The conversation turned to medical matters and the superiority of the American field hospital where, in spite of her qualifications, Mary had struggled to get a position of nurse.

Exhausted, Flore yearned to reach Minnie's room and collapse into bed. Letting the conversations roll over her, she focussed on the hiss of the gaslights, the scraping of knives and the buzz of a bug trapped inside the lace curtains.

Mary said something to her.

'Pardon?'

'Flore, *c'est ça?*

'*Oui.* Flore.'

'I hear you came across people fleeing their homes?'

'Yes. We were working at Monsieur Godin's factory. Have you heard of him?'

'Oh yes. Such an interesting concept.' Mary's brown eyes lit up. 'What did you do there?'

'I was an apprentice in a shop and . . .' Flore searched for the simplest explanation. 'I was learning the basics of accountancy.'

'Is that what you're interested in?'

'Yes. I'm good with numbers.' A blush crept to Flore's cheeks. 'You're a doctor, aren't you? How did you . . . Were you able to . . .'

'Stand my ground in a world of men?'

Flore nodded, her cheeks now aflame.

'As you heard, I still have a way to go, but I would say this: When you were a child and you were unwell, who tended to you?'

'Hmm . . . my grandmother knew plants.' Flore's gaze slid around the table, relieved that no one was paying them attention.

'Your grandmother gave you concoctions, herbs and tisanes to make you better. Your grandmother was in charge of the family's health. Did people raise an eyebrow when you told them you wanted to study accounts?'

'Well, I . . . I only told Mademoiselle Moret. She's Monsieur Godin's . . .'

'Monsieur Godin's assistant.' Martial came to her rescue. 'She was very supportive, but I see what you mean, Mary. There were no women in the accounts department.'

'Exactly. In the home, women also hold the purse strings and yet,' Mary turned to Violette, 'it is clear that women have always been in charge of their family's health and finances, but strangely, there are some who think that in order to be a doctor or an accountant, a woman needs the brain of a man.'

Violette's china doll complexion turned a dark beetroot hue.

'The only thing women do *not* do,' the American stressed, 'is fight useless wars.'

Gontran, the banker, lifted an elegant hand. 'Louis-Napoléon, who started with the best intentions of applying social reform, is completely at the mercy of financiers. I'm afraid the rumour in financial circles was that a short war would boost a falling stock exchange. The bankers, not his wife, talked him into declaring war to Germany.'

Mary's hand jumped to her high collar. 'Oh no! How dreadful!'

'How Mammon rules the world,' Martial commented in a funereal voice.

Flore was about to ask who Mammon was when Jules clapped his hands. 'Right. Now we've put the world to rights, who's coming to the Folies Bergère with us later on?'

Flore whispered to Martial in Occitan, 'I don't mind, as long as the *piota* doesn't come along.'

Unfortunately, the *piota* thought it a grand idea.

After dinner, they moved to the yellow salon while waiting for Violette to change into what she called her '*midinette* outfit'.

A striped summer skirt showing off petticoats, a fringed

shawl and a round hat were Violette's idea of a working-class girl. In a merry mood, they all piled into Jules's largest carriage.

With his imposing moustache, bobble nose and shaggy fair hair, Bernard, the coachman who drove it, reminded Flore of a Pyrenean sheepdog.

As they trotted past Gare Saint-Lazare, people were settling down for the night. Uprooted from their suburbs, they had come to Paris looking for refuge inside the impregnable walls while the emperor's army defeated the Hun, convinced—just as Violette was—that it would only be a matter of weeks.

30

LES FOLIES BERGÈRE

During her first stay in Paris, Flore had only visited the Folies' backstage rooms—an indescribable chaos—and wondered how a well-run show could ever emerge from the jumble of costumes and props that stank of tallow and sweat.

Entering the Folies through the grand entrance was like stepping into a palace. Dripping with gold and red velvet, the hall was filled with ladies gliding along polished floors and gentlemen in dinner suits. Gaping at the fabulous décor that glittered under gaslight, Flore made her way up a grand staircase. Pushing past crinolines and bustles reflected in the famous curved mirror of the first-floor gallery, she led the way to the bar while, with a frisson of excitement, Violette was casting fearful glances, worried about pickpockets. She slipped her arm through Jules's and cooed, '*Mon Dieu,* I can hardly *believe* we are here in the Folies Bergère! You will look after me, cousin, won't you?'

Flore rolled her eyes. Tonight was probably the girl's first foray into 'real life,' thrilled to have stepped into a bawdy den that would have scandalised the nuns.

While the men ordered drinks, Flore propped her elbows on the balustrade and studied the efforts of the contortionist on the stage below. What was his name again? He had a soft spot for Minnie and often walked her home at night. Valentin—yes, that was it—unknotted himself, bent backwards into a perfect circle, drawing gasps from the crowd as he slowly hooked his large pointy shoes around his ears, and walked away on his hands.

Mary, Flore could tell, was fascinated by the conjoined sisters. As the two of them bantered, the student doctor tilted her head this way and that, no doubt imagining where to wield the scalpel to free them from each other.

The clapping died down. A languorous tune filled the space. Men jostled for position at the balcony, and a voluptuous Amazon in bolero, fringes and sheer organza skirt sashayed in, rotating her hips, two huge pythons draped around her naked shoulders. The serpents, a natural extension of her limbs, slithered around her waist, coiling and uncoiling in fabulous patterns to gasps from the crowd.

During the day, Thérèse looked ordinary, but at night, she became 'Samira the snake charmer,' a mythical being who talked to snakes.

In a corner of the balcony, Jules and his friends were waving their cigars and champagne glasses, cheering Samira on. Those men belonged to Martial's milieu, his natural environment, so different from the Familistère. Martial, Jules and his posse took it for granted that outside Bernard the coachman would be waiting for them to call him to heel.

Perhaps Flore too had taken Martial for granted. Tonight, aware of the abyss that divided them, she longed for Minnie's easy presence.

Perhaps it was time for their ways to part.

The orchestra struck a military tune. A line of dancing girls in striped red, white and blue skirts marched across the stage, a hand to their képis. To catcalls and whoops, the képis flew about and the stage exploded in an athletic display of patriotic fervour.

'Which one is your friend?' Violette enveloped Flore in her lily-of-the-valley scent.

Uncomfortable at her closeness, Flore pointed to Minnie dropping into a front split and tried to disengage herself from Violette.

'Oh, how thrilling!' Violette tightened her hold. 'I say, don't you wear corsets?'

Flore stiffened. 'In this heat?'

The girl's hand lingered on her body with the deliberate slowness of a python. 'Flore, what an interesting girl you are. You never told us what you do.' She pushed a strand of hair behind Flore's ear.

Overwhelmed by the cloying scent, Flore struggled to find an answer, all the stories once concocted with Martial now irrelevant.

'Oh, chérie,' Violette said with a knowing look. 'Where did Martial find you?'

'In a swamp, where else?' Flore replied in a weary voice. 'You know where we come from.'

'Girls.' Jules dropped his paws on their shoulders, 'we're thinking of going to the Bal Mabille on the Champs Elysées. Flore, do you think your friend would like to join us?'

'Oh, we'll both be too tired tonight, thank you. Another day, perhaps?'

She slipped out of Violette's tentacles and took Martial's arm. 'I hear you're going dancing?' She narrowed her eyes at him. 'You left me in the *piota*'s clutches. She thinks I'm your mistress.'

'Poor Jules, having to look after her.' Martial looked away. 'Paris is no place for a girl like that. He should send her home.'

The music stopped. A man's voice rose from the stage.

'*Messieurs-dames,* I am sorry to announce that Les Folies will be closing for the foreseeable future, but our shop, le Magasin des Colonnes d'Hercule, will remain open. These are uncertain times, and many lack a roof over their head. If ever you find yourselves with unexpected guests, don't forget . . . we sell beds and mattresses.'

A ripple of uneasy laughter met his announcement. The ringmaster wished everyone good night, his last words lost amidst a rousing 'Marseillaise'. Acrobats, conjoined sisters, snake charmer, actors and dancers filed back onto the stage for a final rendition of the rousing anthem.

Minnie looked up. Her face brightened when she caught sight of Flore.

31

LE BOIS DE BOULOGNE

A week days later, Flore woke up on the rug of Minnie's bedroom, disorientated. The night had been so warm they had kept the window open.

'Nanette?' She pushed herself up. She had rolled off a mattress rescued from Les Colonnes d'Hercule—her dream so vivid she was convinced she was home.

She sat up in her chemise and scratched her tangled curls. Where did the bleating and sheep bells come from?

Yawning, she stepped out onto Minnie's narrow wrought-iron balcony, peered down and rubbed her eyes to dispel the vision. A torrent of sheep was gushing below her feet.

The familiar smell of wool brought tears to her eyes.

'What's going on?' Minnie's hair, wrapped in *papillotes*, surfaced from the sheets.

Too choked to speak, Flore just pointed down, and together they watched the flock—which had presumably been driven through Porte de Pantin—make its way west on streets parallel to boulevard Hausmann.

'Come on, let's follow them!' Minnie grabbed her clothes

and halted, thinking better of it. 'Bah, we'll do that later. With the Folies closing, I'm free as a bird now. They gave us a week's wages, but I won't find another job.'

An hour later, washed, combed and dressed, the two girls sat in the sun outside their favourite *crèmerie*. Further down the street, a few shopkeepers were nailing boards over their shop fronts.

'How long are you staying in Paris?' Minnie said when she had finished her omelette. 'Are you still tagging on to your beau's coattails?'

'His name is Martial.'

'Martial, huh? And when are you going to introduce us?'

'I'm not sure you'd like his friends. His cousin Jules is all right, but—'

'Why don't we try and get them to take us to the Closerie tonight? You promised we'd go there, didn't you? Dance that famous can-can before the world ends. What do you say?' Minnie sipped her coffee, her green eyes never leaving Flore.

Flore stared into her warm milk, unable to make a decision. She found the banker intimidating and Violette's attitude an embarrassment.

'You promised.' Minnie would not let the matter rest. 'Where does that Jules live, then?'

'Somewhere near the Parc Monceau.'

'Parc Monceau is only about two miles away.' Minnie grinned. 'Three kilometres, right? We'll stop by on the way to the Bois.'

The Bois de Boulogne, Minnie explained, had been turned into a holding pen for livestock in preparation for an eventual siege, and she was very keen to see it.

Now that war had been declared, the atmosphere was defiant along the boulevards. Every other man carried a rifle. As they reached the Champs Elysées, a National Guard regiment made up of local men was marching and counter-marching, cheered on by the crowd.

At a street corner, a man wearing a képi lifted his rifle and declaimed, a hand over his heart, 'Parisiens! Let us form a barrage from our chests and let the people rise, loyal and quivering, willing to give their life for a worthy fight. God bless our weapons!'

'Can you hear them?' Minnie said, a bitter twist to her mouth. 'That's how it starts. With big words.' Her eyes dull, she spoke as if to herself. 'Next thing you know, they're dumping cartloads of dead men and asking you to pick out your own.'

Flore shivered. 'Do you understand what this war is about? I'm not sure I do.'

'It's about men and their pride, what else?'

Rue de la Bienfaisance was blocked by a troop shuffling outside the large green doors to Jules's courtyard. Bearded and rough, the men all wore blue smocks, clogs and round hats. A mounted officer was haranguing them in a foreign language.

'What's going on?' Minnie frowned.

'Ah, Flore! There you are.' Jules lifted a hand. 'Let me sort out these men. They've just arrived from Brittany. Martial is out gathering supplies. It is him you wanted to see, I assume.' He acknowledged Minnie with a brief smile.

'Yes. We're on our way to the Bois.'

'To the Bois? Really? There's not much left to see there. The zoo is closed, I hear.'

The coachman came out, wiping his hands on a rag. 'They're filling the park with cattle, monsieur. If you don't mind, I was going to have a look myself, see if I could get us some logs.' He turned to Flore and Minnie. 'Tell you what, I'll just go and hitch up the horse. You can hop on the cart. I'll drop you there.' To Jules, he said, 'Mademoiselle Violette said to tell you that she's gone to visit the Comtesse de la Boissière. I'm to pick her up tonight at ten.'

'Diou Biban!' Flore cried out as they reached the Bois de Boulogne. Gone were the dandies and duchesses riding around to be seen.

Minnie was right. It really was the end of the world.

A siege was looking more and more likely, Bernard had explained on the way. Animals brought in to be slaughtered were waiting, shuffling over the hay that was supposed to feed them. Ancient trees were being chopped and metal gates ripped to be melted into cannons.

Still reeling from her dream, Flore became acutely aware that she had nowhere to go. What would she do, trapped between these walls? A weight settled on her chest. Could she return to the convent? What if Mère Marie-Emmanuel did not want her? What if there was no room there? Paris was shutting down. Soon, there would be no escape. Minnie would leave, and France would be at war. Jules might take her in, but what did she have in common with those people? Could she work as Violette's maid? Teetering at the edge of the void, Flore's heart stuttered. She struggled to breathe.

'Flore? Flore! What's the matter?' Minnie put an arm around her and helped her to a large log. 'What is it?'

'I—I'm scared.' Eyes wide, Flore opened her mouth, but her lungs had closed up. Her breathing became shallower. Around her was nothing but the mournful bawls of cattle and axes felling trees. Soon, the gates would close and they would all starve. The vise tightened around Flore's ribs. An edge of darkness gathered around her vision.

'Come on, breathe with me.' Minnie helped her sit

straight. 'Slowly. Breathe in through your nose . . . then out. Breathe in . . . That's it, and again.'

With her last ounce of willpower, Flore travelled to the moor, scrambled up her dune and faced the ocean. A soft breeze caressed her face. She sat down inside her vines, the slanted sun shining through translucent leaves above her. The darkness subsided.

'Come, let's go over there.' Minnie pointed to a bench at the edge of the lake which, only a month ago, had been the mirror in which *la société* had contemplated its own reflection.

When she spoke again a long time later, Minnie's voice had changed. 'I told you I came from New York, didn't I? That's because everyone's heard of it, but I'm from Atlanta, nine hundred miles south. I'm not sure how far that is in kilometres, or leagues for that matter. It's a long way.' Her eyes dull, she gazed into the grey waters as if they were a portal into the past. 'It was the summer of '64. I'd just turned seventeen when the Yankees arrived . . . six years ago, now.' Minnie's eyes were half-closed. 'Every day, they shelled our town. Every night, we hid in the cellar. Eventually, my aunts and cousins left. But we stayed. We couldn't leave, you see; our house was all we had, and Mom was expecting. Five weeks we were under siege.' She rested her elbows on her knees. 'My baby sister was born in that cellar.' She jumped as a great oak was felled behind them. 'I remember how boring it was, being housed up, missing my cousins, my friends. Sundays were the worst; we couldn't even go to church. All I did was sew, knit and nurse my brother and baby sister.'

'Did your house get hit?' Flore too had lost her home, but it had been more insidious.

'No, but when the Yankees came in after the siege, they took our hog, so we only had bread to eat. Then they set the whole town on fire. We saved our house. Over and over, we doused it with water. We were lucky.'

'Yesu.' Flore rested her head on Minnie's shoulder. 'I can't imagine . . .'

'They came in and looted everything.' A guilty grin spread over Minnie's face. 'So us kids went about looting too. Got us over the worst.'

'And you think it will happen here?'

Minnie pointed to the scene of devastation around them. 'For sure. The way the Parisians are going on about their wall and their Chassepot rifles. They won't protect them. Not like they think they will anyway.'

'What do you mean?'

'They'll be trapped. Right now, they're all fired up with "we'll build ramparts from our chests". Pshaw, the French sure have a way with words, but while they're talking big in cafés, the Prussians are training their battalions. Our boss, Monsieur Montrouge, reads out the news to us every day. American papers tell a different story, so I know what's really going on. Whatever their boasts, it's clear to me that the French will never win.'

Another wave of panic rose inside Flore's stomach. 'When are you leaving?'

'I was waiting for you to come back, and for my last paycheck, of course.' Minnie faced Flore. 'What we went through in Atlanta was a civil war, and I can't help thinking that it will happen here. So many people wanting to get rid of that emperor, and they all have guns. You saw them, didn't you? It's going to be a mess, mark my words.'

'Hmm. There *is* talk of a republic. The aristocrats won't like that.'

'Ha. You French have had enough revolutions to know. Listen, I'll be taking a train to Le Havre. I hope I can find a place on a steamer. There is no time to lose.' Minnie's gaze was intense. 'Look at it this way: the French aren't going to win this war. Come with me. I'll lend you the money.'

'C-come with you?' The words stuck in Flore's throat. She knew she had to leave but . . . America? What about Martial? He had been by her side every step of the way, guiding her, shielding her. Would he be coming with them?

'We'll see what Martial has to say.' Minnie read her thoughts. 'We'll talk to him on our way back.'

Everywhere, troops of men in regional costume were marching up and down the boulevards. Most workshops had closed and their workers enrolled in the National Guard, given a gun and paid thirty *sous* a day.

On rue de la Bienfaisance, a handful of Bretons stood chatting in the courtyard. Some had swapped their round hats for képis. Jules waved the girls in and carried on talking to the officer.

A valet led them to the yellow salon.

Mary was writing at a small desk. She put down her pen and greeted them with a smile.

Martial glanced over his newspaper.

'I wanted you to meet Minnie.'

He stood and took Minnie's hand. '*Enchanté*. I admired your talents last night. How did you learn to dance so . . . acrobatically?'

'I shared a room with a dancer in New York. She taught me.'

Martial invited them to sit on the settee facing his, its spindly legs looking far too thin to support a person's weight. He burst out laughing at Flore's hesitation. 'It won't break, don't worry.'

Flore lowered herself opposite him, her hands tucked demurely between her knees, while Minnie remained by the window.

He tilted his head to one side. 'I'm glad you two stopped

by. As you see, we are overrun with guards from Brittany.' Martial addressed Minnie. 'Jules, who is a kind soul, took your boss at his word and sent for twenty mattresses to lay in the ballroom. The problem we have now is that apart from their priest, not one of those fellows speaks French.'

'Law sakes alive!' Minnie scoured the elegant assortment of rosewood consoles and chaises in the salon. 'You mean they'll be living here?'

'Well,' Martial suppressed a giggle, 'I'm not sure Violette will allow them in her boudoir.'

'Did I hear my name?'

Flore's heart sank as the girl floated into the room in a corolla of turquoise silk, with blond ringlets cascading fetchingly over bare shoulders. A gauze scarf showed off her alabaster skin, and a glimpse of ginger underarm hair hinted at further delights.

Had *la piota* chosen her outfit to impress Martial, Flore wondered, or was her aim to cast a spell over the dandy banker?

When the Prussians sprang their trap and the wounded were carted in by the hundreds, would Violette still be trailing around Paris dressed like this? Mary, on the other hand, wore a practical shirt and skirt.

'Martial,' Flore went straight to the point, 'we came to tell you that we don't think it is safe for us to stay in Paris.'

'Huh? Where else would you go? The Prussians are spilling all over the country!'

'You see, Minnie lived through a siege when she was a girl.' Flore cast a glance at Mary. 'She told me of it, and well, I don't fancy sleeping in a cellar with nothing to eat.'

'Really? You were in a siege?' Over Violette's fan, the blue eyes widened with excitement.

'Yes, mademoiselle.' Minnie stepped away from the console topped with fragile vases and crystal decanters.

'During our civil war, and I don't want to live through it again.' The threat in her voice was real when she added, 'Even if the Prussians don't rape and kill us, there'll be hunger; there'll be fighting in the streets.'

Violette slammed her fan shut. 'The Prussians will not come *near* Paris! Why, the whole of France is united behind the emperor. Can you not tell?' She waved her fan towards the courtyard, where the Bretons were shuffling out of the ballroom to the whine of a bagpipe. 'These men have come all the way from Brittany to defend Paris. Many more are pouring in from all our regions.' She faced Martial. 'Your friends obviously don't understand the situation.'

'Flore's feelings are totally patriotic, I can assure you,' Martial said with a grin. 'As for Minnie, it seems that she is speaking from experience. You have to face the facts, Violette. The emperor might not survive this conflict, and we may once again revert to a republican government. There will be protests.'

'A *republic?*' Violette shivered. '*Mon Dieu,* do the third estate really think they can govern themselves? It has failed every time.'

'Republics worked in Rome and Athens, Violette, and the system is working in America now.' Martial's gaze slid to Mary for support.

'We choose our government.' The American's voice was accented but steady. 'Elections are the fairest way. There is a lot to be said for an aristocracy of merit.'

Violette lifted her small round nose. 'How can those . . . those *people* be equal to us in the eyes of God? Tell me, Martial, without the character bestowed on aristocrats, how can *anyone* presume to rule a country?'

Flore swallowed hard. *Those people?*

Martial stated blandly. 'You believe that social order is preordained by God.'

'Is there any doubt?'

In a corner of the room, the two Americans had closed ranks. Minnie and Mary studied Violette with a mixture of curiosity and contempt. Flore gripped the edges of the sofa, dying to scratch the girl's eyes out.

From their picture frames, the ancestors snarled and sucked all the air out of the room. That rag doll's conceit was beyond belief. Hot, compressed fury exploded inside Flore, and it took all she had not to smash a decanter over Violette's empty head. If this was Martial's world, she wanted none of it.

She stood up and went to the door. 'Sorry, Martial. We have to go. We only came in to tell you that Minnie and I will be taking a steamer to New York. We'll be leaving very soon.'

Martial's face turned ashen. He blinked and shook his head, as if dislodging a mosquito. When he moved his lips, no sound came out.

'Oh? Please don't leave.' Violette coloured slightly. 'I would so love to hear your opinion.'

'We understood you, mademoiselle,' Minnie said. 'Now, we have to pack.'

Violette took Martial's arm. 'Martial, do tell them to stay a while. We could discuss abstract ideas. Flore, I hoped we could be friends, so rarely do I have the chance to talk to people from another class. Let me ring for some tea . . . or chocolate if you prefer.' She went to pull a bell.

Minnie's green gaze was scorching when she warned in approximate French, 'They have just armed the Parisians, mademoiselle. If I were you, I'd keep my *abstract* ideas to myself, or those rifles will be pointing at your pretty dress.'

32
THE CAN-CAN

Martial's original plan was, after leaving Monsieur Godin's factory, to follow Flore's advice and spend some time in an agricultural utopia situated in the Jura. Unfortunately, the Jura was the very region Bismarck was invading.

Jules had been confident that he could find Flore a position in one of the shops he patronised around the Parc Monceau, but as the week wore on, businesses were closing down, rue de la Bienfaisance now a depressing succession of boarded-up shop fronts, cobbled courtyards and doorways piled with straw, filled with evacuees from the suburbs flocking to take refuge inside Paris's impregnable walls.

'I'm going home.' Minnie had made up her mind. 'It's not my war.'

She was right, of course. Remaining in Paris made no sense. Flore was reluctant to abandon Martial, but, unable as she was to contribute to Jules's household, her presence would weigh him down.

The atmosphere had changed. The Paris streets did not

feel safe. Armed drunken men whistled and stared at her in the most embarrassing way.

New York stirred the sense of adventure she now knew she possessed. Martial too was looking to escape. Would he join them? Would he abandon his cousin and his friends?

On their way to Montparnasse for a night of fun, ensconced next to Minnie inside Jules's carriage, Flore was searching her heart. Her conversation with Violette still rankled, but the girl was right. They belonged to different worlds.

Determined to have fun, Minnie had somehow convinced Jules and Martial to celebrate their last moments of freedom in style at the Bal Bullier. They had invited Mary, but she was on shift, and dancing the can-can was not to her liking.

Flore sighed. Yes, she had learned a lot since Martial had dragged her out of the river, but was she ready to pit herself against the New World? Would she be able to step into the unknown without Martial's presence, his contacts and his endless supply of money?

She shook herself. Minnie would be with her. She would not be alone. After all, had she not wished for independence? Had she not decided that she wanted to be her own woman?

Unable to come to a decision, she pushed aside the coach curtain and shook off her mood. Tonight, Paris was festive and defiant. Restaurant terraces spilled out onto brightly lit pavements where Parisians gathered to discuss the war. In the dimness of the carriage, Jules and Martial chatted quietly, their faces taking on an eerie orange tinge whenever they passed under a gaslight. The mood in the streets was patriotic. Flags hung limp. Clouds of cigar spiralled up to the gaslights and laughter rang in the tepid air.

Street singers grinded their hurdy-gurdies to the nostalgic 'Le Temps des Cerises'.

'I tell you, they won't know what's hit them, those

Parisians, when they slam the gates shut,' Minnie had predicted that morning while brushing Flore's hair. 'Look at them. They've no idea, the poor souls.'

In a display of bullishness, the Parisians were having fun. Outside la Closerie des Lilas, small groups gathered. The smell of pomade mingled with that of horses as cab after cab dropped clusters of partygoers by the dance hall to the left of the restaurant. Heat rose from the cobblestones and rippled along the long wall of the Bal Bullier.

'When will you need fetching, monsieur?' Jules's coachman cleared his throat. 'It's just that Mademoiselle Violette will need me around one and,' his eyes crinkled in an affectionate grin, 'you know how she is. She's not always on time.'

'Why don't you take her home first and then come back for us?' Jules reassured the man. 'We'll be fine.'

'Your coachman seems devoted to Violette,' Martial noticed.

Minnie bristled. 'And what is *she* still doing in Paris? Don't her parents care about her?'

Jules found seats under a plane tree at the edge of the square and looked around for a waiter. 'Her family seat is in Normandy, but my cousin refuses to go home, convinced, she says, that her mother is plotting to marry her off to a decrepit old marquis.' He chuckled. 'The man is all of thirty-five.'

'Seems to me she's rather enjoying the preparations for the siege.' Martial frowned. 'She has swallowed General Trochu's tales and believes the Prussians will be licked in a matter of weeks.'

'My cousin is a foolish girl. She was "educated" by nuns who taught her lace-making and that God favours aristocrats.' Jules snorted. 'She has a lot to learn.'

'Can you not send her home while there is still time?' Flore insisted. 'Tell her she could be raped and killed?'

'*Bon Dieu,* I've tried, but she's dug her little heels in. Bernard assures us he will keep her safe. Saint Bernard, we call him. He does look like one of those dogs, doesn't he?' Jules followed his retreating carriage with an affectionate smile. 'God help the Prussian who dares touch a hair on her head if our coachman is around.' He leaned forward and confided in a stage whisper, 'Violette has set her sights on the Duc de Montmorency, a star of the salon she is attending tonight.'

'Montmorency?' Martial lifted an eyebrow. 'Doesn't he run on steam and sail?'

Jules opened his hands. 'And so does my uncle, but Violette doesn't know that.'

'Wow, you mean her father is . . .' Minnie lifted a limp wrist, tickled by the revelation.

How could they talk of this so casually? Flore wondered if she had misheard. Back in Marcillac, men who loved men were vilified. How could they just *joke* about Violette's father?

Paris was indeed a strange place. Perhaps she would never have fitted in.

Martial glanced at the menu, his gaze straying to Flore, sophisticated in a hired green taffeta dress, the temptation to run away with her almost too much to bear. Dread pulsed inside his throat and fogged his brain. They had been together for the best part of the year, her presence a constant balm, but she talked of leaving. As for him, he was needed in Paris. Jules had asked him to join his hospital. Already, casualties were trickling in from the eastern front and more hands were needed.

Martial would never be able to live with himself if he deserted his country in its time of need. Although he would not fight, there was much he could do: organise supplies, find lodgings for the refugees . . . the list was endless.

When the food arrived, Flore breathed in the smell of the sea and, enraptured, tweaked her *fruits-de-mer* out with a needle, showing Minnie how to do it.

Martial's gaze caressed her thick curls, her soft olive skin and naked shoulders. He craved her presence like some men craved drink. She was his 'green fairy', his absinthe, so addictive it allowed men to glimpse perfect beauty and drove them to madness.

Soon, she would be gone.

Perhaps it would always have come to this. Violette might be silly, but she had put her finger on it. They simply did not belong to the same world. Keeping Flore as a mistress in a *petite maison*, as his uncle the bishop had suggested, would never have been be an option.

Society did not take kindly to men who married beneath them. By the time Monsieur Godin had taken Marie-Adèle as his concubine, he had already established his empire, and together they lived on their own terms.

Martial slipped a hand into his pocket and patted the tickets, the second-class tickets he had just purchased, unable to bear the thought of the girls packed in third class like cattle.

'Not hungry?' Jules pointed to Martial's untouched *goujons*.

Martial said the first thing that came to him. 'I don't know how everyone can remain so cheerful with the Prussian threat hanging over us.'

'That's because we've convinced ourselves that we're invincible.' Jules lowered his voice. 'We are losing battles, our army is untrained, our emperor so ill he's doing all he can to get himself shot,' his gaze darted to the next table, 'and he can't even manage that.' He put a finger to his lips. 'If anyone heard me, I would be hanged as a traitor from the nearest lamppost. You have heard what happened to the newspaper that published news of the Metz debacle, haven't you?'

'No, what happened?' Minnie looked up from the lobster she was dismembering. She had ordered the most expensive items on the menu, eating as if it were her last meal. It made sense, Martial realised, if she faced surviving for a week and a half on stale ship biscuits and cabbage.

'The newspaper was torn from stands and burned, its offices and print room trashed by irate patriots.'

'Eh bé, what will happen if the emperor is taken prisoner?' Flore whispered back.

'The empress would be regent, but not for long. Rumour has it that she roams around the Tuileries, terrified of ending like Marie-Antoinette.'

'Who's she?' Flore asked, loosening an oyster from its shell.

Martial was submerged by the impulse to take her in his arms and never let her go. When would he again explain the world to her, his Flore, his very own Émile, his adorable shepherdess?

'Was she not a queen?' Minnie waved a lobster claw. 'She was beheaded, right?'

'Exactly.' Jules explained, 'She too lived in the Tuileries. When the first revolution happened eighty years ago, she escaped but was caught and sent to prison. One of her ladies-in-waiting,' Jules confided with a grimace, 'the Princesse de Lamballe, was murdered there and then, her breasts sliced off and her head paraded on a stick.' He added in a funereal voice, 'Rumour has it that a butcher cut off her labia and used them as a moustache.'

'No!' Flore choked on her oyster.

'The mob is a wild animal.' Minnie shivered.

'Are you two not worried about staying here?' Flore's gaze went from Jules to Martial.

'I've a job to do.' Jules shrugged. 'Paris is short of doctors. Wounded soldiers are already being shipped down the Seine on the *bateaux-mouches*. Our hospital's filling up fast.'

Minnie engaged him in conversation, giving Martial a chance to talk to Flore.

'I took a vow not to bear arms, but there's still plenty I can do.' Martial picked up a *goujon* and brought it to his lips. It was cold. 'I can bring comfort to the dying.'

Flore met his gaze. 'You still feel the call of the priesthood?'

Her comment touched a raw nerve in the dark Sturm und Drang that had been plaguing him since they had left the moor.

'Yes, these are dark times, and it is a call I cannot remain deaf to.'

'Come on, folks, it's our last night in Paris!' Minnie rinsed her fingers in a bowl, dried them and slapped her napkin on the table. 'Let's go over to Bullier and have some fun!'

'Back in Guise, my friend Adeline and I convinced Martial to dance,' Flore confided to Jules as they followed the wall to the arched entrance. 'He's a surprisingly good dancer.' She nudged Martial with a grin. 'Aren't you?'

Jules burst out laughing.

Once a priest, always a priest . . . She would never see him as anything else. Hands in his pockets, Martial managed a smile. Inside, he was dying.

The dance hall was larger than anything Flore had imagined, the covered space so vast, it reminded her of Monsieur Godin's factory. Come to think of it, with its ornate columns, arches and exotic gardens strung with Chinese lanterns, the Bal Bullier *was* a factory, a fun-factory.

They edged their way along the dance floor, avoiding the kicks of a gentleman in a top hat lifting his feet like a string puppet, and bumped into couples hopping to a polka.

Jules ordered champagne, lemonade and biscuits from a distracted waiter.

First was a quadrille. They all joined in, Minnie and Jules parading and spinning with practiced confidence while Flore and Martial attempted to memorise the sequence.

A drumroll announced a mazurka. Flore's eyes popped as all hell broke loose and the dance floor erupted in a confusion of boots, clogs, képis, top hats, uniforms and medals glinting under the gaslights. Satin skirts swayed to the violins, petticoats frothed, the whole place burst with bright fabrics and the sheer thrill of being alive.

After the drums, violins led the way. As Martial drew Flore into a waltz, she realised that she had never thanked him. 'Thank you,' she said as they twirled amidst the dizzying swirls of colour. 'Thank you for everything.'

He met her gaze. 'What do you mean?'

'Thank you for saving my life. I hated you for doing that, so I never thanked you,' she said, unable to stop tears that sprang from nowhere. 'I'm glad you did.'

Martial's arm tightened around her waist. He looked so melancholy; she leaned against him.

A schottische slowed the chaos down to a flow and they glided steadily by, forward and back, forward and back, like the basket of a hot air balloon, only to jump again at a clash of cymbals that lifted Flore's heart and filled her with hope.

After a glass of champagne, she felt ready to take on America. Paris could look after itself.

'Why don't you come with us, Martial?' Minnie flopped on a chair next to him. 'Leave Paris. Start a new life in New York.'

Flore already knew his answer.

'What would I do there? My English is dreadful. I will be needed here if Paris comes under fire. The local priest has already put me in charge of supplies and soup kitchens. In the Parc Monceau, hundreds of people are sleeping in the open. We're busy knocking on doors, searching out Parisians willing to host them, requisitioning empty houses. How can I desert my country when so much is at stake?'

Jules picked up his glass. 'Come on, everyone, it is too hot in here. Let's sit outside.'

In the garden, dimmed voices filled the air, and lanterns cast strange shadows over the lilacs and rosebushes.

'We could be in Arabia.' Jules stretched his legs and lifted his gaze to the stars. 'Let's enjoy the time we have left before the world ends.'

'Martial?' Flore touched his arm. 'I wish you didn't look so sad.'

'Just trying to hold on to our last moments of sanity.'

In the still air, heavy beetles bumped around the lanterns. To Flore, the evening felt surreal, suspended as it was between past and future.

She made light of his mood. 'Wine is making you melancholy. My grandmother was like that. Give her a drop of Armagnac and she was a sobbing wreck.'

He did not smile.

It wasn't the wine, she knew that. He had to put his

utopian dream on hold. Also, they had, over several months, built a friendship based on mutual respect, beyond the confines of class. However artificial it had been, it mattered to him, and now it was over.

Should she stay? Suddenly conscious of what she was about to give up, Flore came to her senses. She would remain here, join the war effort . . . But Violette's insidious smile came back to her, the feel of her hand around her waist. No. She would be trapped with that girl while Martial and Jules were away. At best, she would be relegated with the servants.

Flore made up her mind. Leaving was the only option.

Jules had just ordered another round of lemonade and biscuits when the first ponderous notes of Offenbach's 'Galop Infernal' rose from the dance hall.

'Oooh, hmpf!' Minnie spat out her drink. 'The can-can! Come on, folks, we can't miss that!' She rushed in, Flore in tow.

Jules pulled at Martial's sleeve just outside the door and gave him a hard stare. '*Bon Dieu,* Martial, for all we know, we'll both be dead in a month's time. Life happens *now*, my friend.'

'Easy for you to say. I . . .' Martial did not have the leisure to finish his sentence. Around him, women were lifting their legs in the air as far as decency would allow. Gone was the restraint of the quadrille. In the middle of a circle, men flung their arms and legs about like puppets held by a madman, crawled like worms, stood on their heads and twisted their bodies in impossible positions. As a response, girls twirled their ankles every which way in a froth of petticoats. The whole room erupted in a buzz of explosive defiance.

'Women want to do their own thing,' Jules shouted. 'Cast

away their shackles. A revolution which begins with showing the world that they too have legs, and that they own what's in between.'

'Is that what this is about?'

'Your sylvan princess is not running *away* from you.' Jules put a hand over Martial's shoulder and took a few steps into the garden. 'She's running *towards* herself. You've helped her out of whatever predicament she was in . . .' He waited for an explanation. When none came, he carried on, 'And she's off now to find out what she's capable of.'

Martial's brow darkened. 'Life is dangerous for unmarried women.'

Jules laughed. 'As a doctor, I know how dangerous it is for *married* women.' He gave Martial a friendly nudge. 'You've always wanted to be someone's knight in shining armour; that's your problem.'

'She's got to me, Jules.' Martial could not hide the truth anymore. 'I just can't bear to let her go.'

'Then tell her.'

Weighed down by a truth he could not fight, Martial cried out, 'She's not ready to hear it!' His pain was drowned by the whoops and shouts from the dance floor, where Minnie was showing off in the middle of the circle, dropping into splits and making cartwheels.

When it was over at last, the two girls staggered back to their table, arm in arm.

'This dance was exhausting, Minnie!' Flore panted. 'I don't know how you can keep it up!'

'It's my job.' Minnie grinned. 'I can teach you.'

'Phew!' Flore blew hair from her brow and beamed at Martial. 'We did it! We actually danced the can-can in Paris.' She grabbed a glass, exchanged a toast with Minnie, 'New York! Here we come!' and knocked back her drink. 'Oops, that wasn't lemonade.'

This is what it must feel like to have a limb removed. Not trusting himself to look at Flore, Martial watched the chafers knocking into lanterns. *Tomorrow, she will be amputated from my life, and I will have to go on living.*

Torn between pleasure and pain, Martial wished the night would never end. He danced the polka with Minnie, lithe and muscular, and he waltzed with Flore, solid and languorous in his arms. Close, warm, yet unattainable, her nearness enhanced every sensation. The touch of her skin, her scent, the tendrils of hair that tickled his cheek wove an indelible spell.

In turn relaxed and thoughtful, Flore touched his arm, patted his knee, at times familiar, at times formal. Every fibre of his being was pulled towards her. His skin screamed for hers, and yet she did not know.

When a waiter came to tell them that their carriage had arrived, Martial teetered out of the ball, cold and disoriented. Outside, the air stank of sweat, cold tobacco and horse manure. It smelled of garrison.

Beyond the square, the Paris wall rose, tall and threatening. Martial tried, and failed, to build a wall around his heart.

It was two o'clock by the time they reached the girls' pension.

'Good night, girls. I hope you get some sleep. Bernard will be with you at five thirty.'

'Thank you, Jules. Thank you for the most wonderful night.' Minnie hugged them both very tightly. 'I will hold you two and Paris in my heart until the day I die.'

'*Ouf*, I had such a good time!' Flore leaned into Martial's arms. 'So, Monsieur Boyer de Pagny. We got you dancing in the end. Who knows what else you will have tried when I see you again?'

He held her in his arms and smiled, though his heart was

breaking. 'I will have tried to sleep. Bernard and I will see you off tomorrow.'

'Oh, Martial, you don't have to do that!'

'Oh yes,' he replied with all his soul, 'I do.'

Flore skipped away from him, arm in arm with Minnie.

He watched her go, wishing he had kissed her.

33
AU REVOIR, PARIS

The next morning, dizzy and nauseous, Flore crammed her possessions into her bag and, floating inside a strange vacuum, climbed into the carriage.

'I'm not looking forward to a week and a half in steerage,' Minnie said as they clip-clopped through empty streets. 'My fancy man brought me over in first class, but I saw how it was for them down there. It stank like a midden, and the rations were dreadful. Let's make sure we stock up in Le Havre.'

'I might be able to help.' Martial had not said much since they had left the pension. He pulled out an envelope and handed it to Minnie. 'Here, two second-class tickets. You will be given decent food, I hope.'

'Oh, Martial, you are so kind!' Minnie threw herself across and hugged him. 'Oh my! Oh, you cannot know how much it means. Thank you!' She grinned. 'We'll look after you when you come to New York, won't we, Flore?'

Flore's stomach was churning too much for her to reply. Last night's excitement had dimmed, and tiredness painted everything grey. Had she been rash? After all, the idea had only been seeded by Minnie less than a week ago.

Lamplighters were returning the streets to drabness. The last drunks were staggering home. Just before dawn, Paris belonged to cats and dogs.

They reached Saint Lazare. In spite of the early hour, the station was full of people trying to leave. Shapes slumbered along walls. National guards in képis and rags sat slumped next to their rifles, having spent their wages on absinthe. In the distance, hay and coal were being unloaded from trains and piled onto carts.

Leaving the girls to thank Bernard, Martial wordlessly grabbed their bags and went to find their train. On the platform, a crowd was waiting amidst piles of baskets, bundles and cages.

A locomotive puffed in with a grinding of brakes, disgorging refugees who swelled the ranks of those searching for shelter in the capital while the carriages were stormed by those desperate to leave.

Minnie elbowed her way towards the middle of the train and clambered in. 'Flore, hurry up!' she shouted through an open window. 'I've found us seats!'

A guard was arguing with a woman, sobbing over her trunk. 'We can't take any more luggage, madame. There's no room. This has to remain here.'

Rooted to the spot, Flore stopped, teetering, as she once had, at the edge of the void. This time, Martial would not be catching her. She turned to him and looked into his eyes, surprised to see them damp.

'Oh, Flore.' He pulled her into his arms. 'How am I going to manage without you?'

Startled, she lifted her face. He drew back, but it was too late. The truth had touched her heart. The noise, the shouts, the hissing steam dimmed. They were alone on the platform. His heart stopped. He had betrayed himself.

Suspended in time, he waited, terrified.

She stared back, her face frozen, and just when he thought he would die, she flung herself at him. Their lips met. Breathless, they tore away, only a few inches, the first of the thousand leagues gaping between them, and kissed more fiercely than before.

Flore's lips, soft and fragrant, invited him to kiss her deeper. She moulded herself to him with a moan. His hands caressed her face and slipped to her yielding waist.

A strident whistle brought Martial back to the present.

'Flore! Come on! You'll miss the train!' Frantic, Minnie was banging on the window.

Flore's hand gripped his shoulders, her eyes wide, pooling with tears. She turned away with a sob. He drew her back for a final savage kiss. 'God in heaven, Flore, do you have any idea how much I love you?'

'Oh, Martial, what have I done?'

'You've done what you needed to do. You have done the right thing, but when this is all over, I will find you, *amor,* wherever you are.'

The locomotive belched a huge cloud of steam. The guard went along shutting doors one by one.

'Flore!' Minnie screeched.

Martial let her go.

The guard slammed the door behind Flore and blew his whistle. Her forehead resting on the glass, she kept her gaze on him, willing him to hear the words she'd had no time to say.

The train moved away. Standing amidst the discarded baggage, Martial lifted a hand, both dazed and filled with awe. His battered heart gave a tentative beat, and another.

The train got smaller and smaller, and then it disappeared. He smiled sadly, confident that he had done the right thing.

Letting her go was the only way to keep her.

34

FLORE AND MINNIE MAKE PLANS

The steamer had been chugging along for two days. In the dim dining room, waiters were clearing the plates of those who had been brave enough to risk supper.

Inured to the pitch and yaw of the ship, Minnie propped her elbows on the table and rested her eyes on Flore. 'Talk to me. We've been gone two whole days, and you've hardly said a word. Look,' she swept the room with a hand, 'we're the only two from our cabin who aren't seasick, and yet you look half-dead.' She crossed over to Flore's bench and hugged her. 'Why don't you tell auntie Minnie all about it?'

She reached out for Flore's wineglass, cleverly held in place by a grid of planks fixed to the table. 'You haven't even touched your drink.'

Flore shrugged.

Minnie swallowed a large glug and handed the glass to a passing waiter. 'If you love him so much, how come you never told him?'

'I didn't *know* I loved him!'

Minnie let out an exasperated sigh. 'That's what I don't

understand. When a man takes my fancy, I know it straightaway, and so does he. How long had you been together?'

'We weren't *together*.'

'Sorry. I keep forgetting. You ran away together, you worked together, you more or less lived together, but you weren't *together*. I got that.' She tilted her chin towards the end of the room where an olive-skinned youth was balancing several plates along his arm. 'See that waiter over there?'

Flore lifted tired eyes. 'Hmm?'

'Well, we've never exchanged a word, but I know I like him and . . . see how he looks at me? He likes me too.' She opened her hands. 'It's that simple.'

'You don't understand.'

'That's right, I don't. That's why you're going to explain it to me.' Minnie crossed her arms. 'Let's start with why you ran away from home.'

'Minnie,' Flore said, suddenly animated. 'We'll be at sea for another week. Why don't you teach me some more English?'

'I will. As soon as you've answered my questions. I like you, Flore, but I don't even know who you are.'

Realising she could not escape her friend's probing any longer, Flore took in a deep breath.

'Back in my village,' she said in a soft voice, 'there was a man . . .'

'There always is.' Minnie leaned back, an I've-got-all-the-time-in-the-world expression on her face.

'We were promised to each other, but all the while he was planning to marry someone else.' Memories gushed inside Flore's mind, the Sainte Elma festival, the pearl around Angèle Poirier's neck, the flight on stilts through the moor, the rage, the elation when the flames took hold, the growing terror as smoke engulfed the forest, Nanette's body on the ground and the final descent into a darkness that still plagued her soul.

Minnie placed a hand over hers, compassion softening her face. 'Go on.'

'He married her because she had money and he wanted to buy more pines. I'd set his pines on fire, you see. I only meant to burn the saplings he'd just planted, but the fire spread. It had been so dry. The flames got out of hand. I—I—' Flore moved her lips, but no words came out. She hugged herself and rocked. Eventually, she said in a whisper, 'That's when Martial found me.'

Minnie kissed her cheek and gently helped her up. 'Come, let's go outside for a bit of fresh air.' Wrapped in shawls, they stepped onto the deck, squeezed between two lifeboats and leaned against the rail, the wind blowing stray hair around their faces.

The sun had sunk beneath the horizon, silver-plating the waves.

Flore took in a deep breath of sea air.

'Did you live near the ocean?' Minnie asked softly.

'We did. My grandfather was a whale hunter in his youth. Later, he collected oysters. Our village was just inland from the dunes.' Flore brushed a strand of hair from her cheek, damp with tears and spray. 'We lived on a moor. You would call it a swamp, I suppose, but it had everything we needed: forests, game, lakes, fish, sandy soil that was easy to till.' A sharp pain stabbed at her heart. 'I will never see it again.'

'You never know what life—'

'Yes, but you see, even if I went back, it won't ever be the same. It will soon be a forest.'

Minnie nodded absently. 'When you say that Martial found you . . . I know he took you to the stove factory.' She faced Flore. 'But what was *he* running away from?'

How could Flore explain Martial's fight for social justice?

How could she explain that he had not fully decided to leave the priesthood? She compromised with, 'He didn't get on with his father.'

'There's something else I don't understand.' Minnie tightened her shawl. 'Martial's dying of love for you. I could see it, Jules could see it, even that goose Violette could see it, which is why she was so rude to us. I think she fancied him for herself. And you're telling me that, in all the time you were with him—even though you weren't—you never once wondered why he was looking at you with those big puppy eyes?'

Flore could not help but giggle at Minnie's comical expression.

'Then, at the very last moment, three minutes before the train leaves, pft!' Minnie hit her forehead. 'You suddenly realise he's the man of your dreams! What the devil did you *see* when you looked at him before? A tree? A bear? A monk?'

'A priest,' Flore muttered.

'A what?'

'He was, he still is, a Catholic priest. He was our parish priest. That's how I know him. When I got in trouble, he was about to be moved to a new parish. He felt—oh, I don't know.' Flore leaned on the rail and stared at the grey clouds over the pewter sea. 'I saw him as a priest.' She lifted her gaze to Minnie. 'I'd waited five years for the rotter who jilted me to come out of the army. I was angry. I hated men, all men. Martial felt safe *because* he was a priest.'

'My folks are Methodists. Our ministers are allowed to take a wife. It's so much simpler.'

'Really?' Flore's eyebrows shot up. 'Your priests can marry?'

'Sure.' Minnie burst out laughing. 'Where have you been that you don't know that?'

'Just told you.' Flore glowered. 'Crawled out of a swamp.'

'Hey, I'm sorry.' Minnie nudged Flore's elbow. 'Cheer up. I'll teach you some English. Shall we start with numbers, or shall I go straight to the naughty words?'

Their lesson was interrupted by the whine of a hurdy-gurdy from the upper deck. The steerage passengers, whose cramped quarters stank as much as the pigpens, had come out, and tonight they were singing the nostalgic 'Le Temps des Cerises'.

Tears streaming down her face, Flore warbled along with them, her heart in tatters. She too had held love in the palm of her hand, and she too had allowed it to slip away. 'Don't cry. You'll see him again,' Minnie murmured. 'I know you will. Before you even have time to miss him, he'll be turning up at Castle Gardens and saying to the immigration officer, '*Bonjour,* monsieur, I've come to claim my fiancée.'

On the upper deck, the mood turned raucous. A fiddle was playing a *bourrée* to much clog thumping, cheering and hand clapping.

Flore stared back at the froth churned by the ship. 'Oh, Minnie, how could I have been so stupid to abandon him in the middle of a war?'

'Paris was never our city to defend. We've no reason to hate the Prussians, you and me. Come on, let's take a walk.' Minnie hooked her arm in Flore's, and together they ambled along the deck, hit in turns by bursts of spray in between lifeboats, animal smells and emanations from the hold. 'If we'd stayed at his cousin's, we'd only have been two more mouths to feed.' Her arm tightened against Flore's. 'Me, if I had been the general in charge of Paris, I'd have sent Violette home, and anyone who wasn't a soldier, marched the national guards up and down the grand boulevards until their feet were sore instead of letting them waste their wages on absinthe and got sappers to dig secret tunnels to make sure information got in and out. That's what I would have done if I was General Crochet.'

'Trochu,' Flore corrected. 'What if Martial is wounded?' She wrung her hands. 'Oh, what is it with me? I spent five years worrying about that rotter, and now I'm worried about Martial. Is waiting for a man going to be my destiny?'

Minnie placed both hands on Flore's shoulders. 'You won't spend your life *waiting* for a man. We'll be our *own* women, you and me. So. Tell me. What do you want to do once you reach New York?'

Flore exhaled a loud breath. *That question again. 'Bon,* I will try to tell you. I like the idea of being my own woman. So first, I want to learn English. Then—I'm not sure what I can hope for, but I would quite like to work in a shop, but I need fresh air, trees . . . the noise of the ocean.'

'Well, you'll be in the right place. Plenty of water around Manhattan. We'll try and set you up with a little booth on Coney Island where you can sell whatever you like on the beach.' Minnie beamed, relieved to have found something for Flore to latch on to.

'How will I know if he is unable to come?'

Minnie's grin widened. 'Jules and I got friendly.' She rolled her eyes. 'No, not *that* friendly,' she corrected when she saw the look on Flore's face. 'I told him where to telegraph us if ever he needed to contact you in a hurry.'

'Telegraph?'

'Sure. There's a telegraph cable running all the way under the ocean from France to America.'

'Oh, Minnie, you are a good friend.' Flore kissed her. 'I shall sleep much better tonight.'

'I hope they've stopped being sick in there.' Minnie wriggled her nose when they reached their cabin. 'After two days, they can't have anything left to throw up.' A middle-aged woman and a nun slept on the lower bunks of their four-berth cabin.

Flore shivered. 'I can't imagine how we would have fared in steerage, eating bad food, unable to wash for a week and a half.'

'Just think.' Minnie made a funny face. 'By the time Martial arrives, you'll be fluent in English.'

'Yes,' Flore said. 'I'd better start learning in earnest. How do I say *bonne nuit*?'

'Good night.'

'Good night, Minnie. Thank you.'

Flore quickly changed, clambered to the top bunk and pulled the curtain that provided some manner of privacy. It did not, sadly, deaden the snores of the woman on the bunk below hers. She tuned into the distant sounds of the accordion and the rhythm of clogs thumping in time to the ship's great engine. Having poured out her soul, she soon fell asleep, lulled by the rocking and the country music that carried her home.

She woke early and crept out of the cabin. Her shawl wrapped tightly around her, she looked out to sea, her skirt flapping against her legs, her book held against her chest. A memory struck her. In the Père Lachaise cemetery, Martial had known exactly where to find the lovers' shrine. Her head swam. Of course, the young girl and the older priest! Yesu. How long had he been in love with her? Never had he given her any clue that she had been anything more than a rescue mission. Then again, racked with shame and grief as she was, would she even have noticed?

Eventually, Flore opened her book, and in the warmth of the salon, Héloïse rose from the spirit world, feminine, immortal and wise. Castrated for his sins, Abélard had become dour and ponderous; while unrepentant, Héloïse had always stood by her love for him, open about lust and the torments of female desire.

It is the last violence to our nature to extinguish the memory of pleasures which, by a sweet habit, have gained absolute possession in our minds. I, who have experienced so many pleasures in loving you, feel, in spite of myself that I cannot repent of them, nor forbear enjoying them over again as much as possible, by recollecting them in my memory.

Flore repeated the sentence to herself, dreaming of the letters she would write, if only she could write properly, letters that would bring her closer to Martial.

Cursing her poor schooling, Flore read on. *During the still night, when my heart ought to be quiet in the midst of sleep, which suspends the greatest disturbances, I cannot avoid this illusion my heart entertains. I think I am still with my dear Abélard. I see him, I speak to him and hear him answer.* Eyes closed, Flore imagined Martial in Jules's yellow salon, reading her letter.

'*Bonjour.*' A plump lady wrapped in a woollen coat studied the room. 'We are both larks, I see.' She assessed the oval tables and plush red benches, deciding where to sit. 'I believe we share a cabin, but you may not have seen me. My name is Lafarge, Léonie Lafarge.'

'Madame. My name is Flore Laborde.' *I may not have not seen you, lady, but I have certainly heard you.*

'Flore? What a delightful name. I am not a good sailor, I'm afraid. I have been feeling so sick I preferred not to move. Do you suffer from seasickness?'

'No. I love the sea.'

'You are lucky. I feel much better today and hope to enjoy what is left of the voyage. Sorry. I am disturbing you. You were reading.'

Flore hid the book under her shawl. 'I don't mind.'

'You are with the other young lady. Is she English?'

'American. We are going to New York together.'

'Excellent idea. France is not a good place at the moment. Declaring war on Prussia was very foolish, so I will be spending time with my daughter. She has married a doctor in Boston.' Madame Lafarge settled herself on the upholstered banquette, both hands resting over a large bag from which knitting needles stuck out. 'Steamers make such a difference. We are not at the mercy of winds anymore. We know when we are leaving and when we will be arriving.' She added with a broad grin, 'To think America was once at the other end of the earth! Now it is only a week away.'

'Will you be returning to France?'

'Oh yes. As soon as this ill-advised war is over.'

'How about your husband?'

'My husband was killed in the Crimean war in '55. I have been a widow for fifteen years.' She added, 'I worked as a governess in Paris, but the family have moved to safety in their country manor in the Auvergne.'

'A governess? You teach reading and writing?'

'I do. Why do you ask, dear?'

Flore blushed. 'I struggle to write French.'

'Ha! French grammar, it fools the cleverest of men.'

Madame Lafarge took out her knitting. They chatted about their lives, Flore carefully stepping through the labyrinth of her past until she felt comfortable enough to ask, 'I would like to write a letter. Could you help me?'

'Of course, dear. Tell me what you want to write, and we will call for ink.'

35

EMPRESS EUGENIE ESCAPES

A week later, Martial took Flore's letter out of his pocket, his chest pulsing with the usual confusion of amazement, hope, despair and ecstasy. It had arrived at the beginning of September, hours before the Paris gates were locked.

Defeated at Sedan, seventy miles east of Monsieur Godin's factory, the emperor had been deposed and imprisoned in one of Bismarck's castles. As for the empress, no one knew where she was.

Paris had been under siege for a month. Martial could not remember a time when life was normal, when dinner was something one looked forward to and mail was delivered by a cheerful postman. Food and news were scarce and the efforts to acquire them all-consuming.

The letter Martial held was a tenuous thread to the life of which he had once dreamt. How Flore, whose smattering of education had been gleaned at the back of the Noirac church, had managed to write so fluently was a mystery.

He sat on his bed and read in the last of the afternoon light,

Mon très cher Martial,

I am writing to thank you for allowing us to travel in comfort. We are very grateful. We share our cabin with two other ladies, one a governess from Paris. She is very kind. The other is a nun, so seasick she has not yet been able to go on deck.

Minnie and I have 'le pied marin'. *Some of Minnie's Scottish ancestors were whale hunters, like mine.*

I am writing to you in the salon of the steamer. I want to post this letter as soon as we arrive so that it can return to France with this ship . . .

Martial ran through Flore's strangely stilted description of life on board, musical entertainment provided by the steerage passengers and even a burial at sea. With a frisson, he hurried to the last paragraph, written in a different pen—three lines he knew by heart.

During the still nights, when my heart ought to be quiet, listening to the sound of the steem and the waves, I think I am still with my dear Martial. I see you, I speak with you, and I hear you answer.

Amused by her spelling of *steem*, he pressed the letter to his heart, a poultice over the agonies he witnessed day after day as he consigned the lives of young men to a God who did not care. Some nights, when he was drowning, all that kept him sane was the memory of Flore's kiss on the platform. The tears in her eyes. How tightly she had held him . . .

He tucked the letter back into its envelope and returned to the daguerreotype his brother had sent from the barracks. Hugo cut a fine figure in polished breast plate, shiny helmet and red trousers. Red, a beacon for sharpshooters. Red, to hide the blood.

Hugo's regiment had been part of the shameful battle of Sedan, ordered to charge by unprepared generals who, without any clear idea of where the Prussians were, had sent their troops into the mess of wires used to support hops.

The Ardennes were famous for their beer.

Hugo had been lucky. Not so the general, pilloried and exiled.

Berating himself for not having had a daguerreotype made of Flore, Martial ran his own stereopticon of their time together: the way she used to skip across the airial, a basket on her head, her face so close to his behind the lattice of the confessional that he could feel her breath, her body moulded to his while they danced, her thick black hair, the feel of her lips on his . . .

He picked up a pencil and tried to capture her face, the folds of her flowered scarf, the curves of her body. Flore, his Ceres . . .

She was escaping him.

He opened his inkwell and wrote,

Dearest, dearest Flore,

You will never know how grateful I am to have received your letter. The gates of Paris are locked tight. I work alongside Jules at la Salpêtrière, where I confess the men and comfort the dying. My role is not just spiritual. I often find myself holding bedpans and basins. Casualties are brought in after every 'sortie' over the Paris wall. Women and children are dying of typhus, consumption and hunger. We are working to save Paris and France, and I am privileged to have met many brave men.

Some of them not so brave: Duroc, Joseta's employer, was on my ward. Blinded and bleeding, he did not recognise me. When the end came, he did confess his sins and begged for absolution. Poor Joseta was not the only one! God will look into his heart and see whether he was crying for himself or for the girls whose lives he had destroyed.

Did you receive my last letter? Weighing the mandatory four grams, it accompanied Gambetta on his epic hot air balloon flight out of Paris over a month ago.

The aerostat had safely landed a few leagues north of

Paris. Whether the letters it contained had arrived at their destination, no one knew.

Voices downstairs drew him to the yellow salon, where he found Jules and Mary poring over medical journals Mary was translating into French, advocating ventilation in wards.

A hand in his pocket, Gontran stood by the window, consulting his watch. In a corner, Arthur was grumbling over a newspaper spread over a table, his fingers dug into his thatch of hair.

Martial cast an affectionate glance at his cousin. Jules had a terrible crush on Mary but, intimidated by her achievements, had not declared his interest. Often tempted to whisper 'carpe diem,' as Jules had done at the Bal Bullier, Martial kept his counsel.

When the gates of Paris were locked in September 1870, many foreigners opted to remain in Paris. There were quite a few Germans, some British citizens . . . and there was Evans, the dentist.

Appalled at the lack of hygiene in all the Parisian hospitals and the make-shift facilities sprouting in restaurants and theatres, Evans had donated material rescued from the American Civil War and set up a modern field hospital under canvas on avenue de l'Impératrice, near the Bois de Boulogne, the very place where Mary had eventually been accepted by going straight to the top and befriending Evans.

The field hospital was so popular that French officers often carried a card in their pocket asking to be taken there in case they were shot. In their warm well-ventilated tents, most of the wounded survived. Jules's hospital lost over half of them.

'Ventilation? Ha! Ha! Is our hospital not draughty enough?' Jules imitated the voice of his superiors. 'Mary, what can I do? My colleagues don't believe in germs.' He stood up and rubbed his eyes.

'We must keep our faith, Jules,' Mary said primly. 'Soon, the old guard will die. It will be up to us to lead the world out of darkness.'

Gontran waved his cigar towards Martial in greeting and said to Mary, 'I hear Kanzler Bismarck is slipping your Mr Washburne money to ensure his compatriots don't starve. What is that all about?'

Martial paid attention. Washburne was the American ambassador.

Jules stretched. 'Bah. Who knows? Washburne's a diplomat. Bismarck was ambassador in Paris. Together they played cards with the emperor.'

Lowering himself onto the edge of the empire sofa, Martial cursed the flimsy seat where one could only perch, when after a hard day spent listening to men confessing their sins or tracking down the last few turnips inside a damp Paris cellar, all he wanted to do was knock back a glass of Armagnac and slump into oblivion.

Mary cleared her throat. 'Nothing would surprise me, coming from those wily foxes.' A knowing grin slowly spread over her face. 'I have gossip of a juicier kind, Gontran. However, it would be best if it did not leave this room.'

All eyes turned to the door.

'Violette has gone to a concert with her friend Léontine.' Jules rolled his eyes. The hardships of the siege yet had to affect his cousin. 'Gossip away, *ma chère*. Our lips are sealed.'

Martial poured himself a shot of whisky and ran the glass under his nose with a grimace. Gontran, a seasoned traveller, had told him that New York was awash with the stuff, imported in great vats from Scotland. In an attempt at mithridatism, Martial forced down a finger of the poison every night, hoping he would eventually tolerate it.

He held up the bottle to Gontran, who nodded. Lanky, clean-shaven, with an equine face and dark slicked-back hair, the banker—who never had to be anywhere in particular—was forever consulting his gold watch, looped with a fancy chain to the top pocket of his silk waistcoat. He had settled himself in a Louis chair, his long legs stretched before him.

'Do you mind if I call for tea?' Mary pulled the bell cordon.

Jules asked his valet for tea and madeleines.

'Madeleines? Is that not a little extravagant?' Since the start of the siege, Arthur, a clerk at the town hall of the 8th arrondissement, had been advocating rationing.

'Those madeleines were baked before the siege,' Gontran said in a puff of smoke. 'They are a little dry, but dipped in coffee or Armagnac, they will be perfectly fine.'

Jules filled his glass with Armagnac and lifted it to Mary. 'We're all ears.'

'We owe our field hospital to the esteemed Doctor Evans—'

'Ah, Evans. The emperor's dentist,' Martial interrupted.

'Indeed. A popular man, famous for his table.' Mary allowed a pause for effect. 'We all heard how, after the emperor was taken, Empress Eugenie was running around the Louvre like the ghost of Marie-Antoinette.'

'I heard she has escaped,' Gontran dropped casually.

'Huh?' Arthur's eyebrows shot up. 'How has she managed that?'

There was a glint in Mary's eyes. 'Well, it appears that I was only a few feet away from her when she did.'

'Oh, Mary, you are teasing us.' Jules grinned. 'Do tell.'

Mary waited until the valet deposited the tray.

They listened for his steps fading into the corridor. Arthur poured the tea. Mary resumed her tale.

'A few days ago, Evans had invited a few people for dinner. I was one of his guests. It was a good evening and our dentist a charming host. We chatted and sang around the piano, you know the sort of thing.'

The three men nodded, reluctant to break the thread.

'After dinner, I excused myself and went in search of the facilities. Evans's *hôtel particulier*—you may know it, at the corner of avenue de l'Impératrice and Malakoff—is *vast*. I lost my way, and as I passed the library, I heard two women's voices.' Mary met their gazes in turn. 'They were speaking Spanish.'

A stunned silence met her revelation.

'You mean to say that Empress Eugenie left Paris with her . . . dentist?' Arthur spilled tea on his jacket. 'How?'

'No one knows,' Mary said with a mysterious smile. 'Doctor Evans has not returned.'

'Saperlipopette.' Arthur whistled between his teeth. 'How did she end up with *Evans*?'

'No one else would help her.' Gontran straightened himself in his chair. 'She'd first knocked on a friend's door.' The banker's smirk implied that he, once again, knew the juicy details. 'He was out that night. His *maid* sent her packing, it you can believe it.' Gontran took a long draft of cigar smoke and blew it out with an amused smile. '"Do you know who I am?" Eugenie insisted. "Oh, I know who you are, madame," the maid retorted, "but we don't want you 'ere."' Gontran narrowed his eyes. 'And the girl had the gall to add, "Just think yourself lucky I'll keep me mouth shut."' He picked up a madeleine and crinkled his brow. 'The worm will turn.'

Martial went to stand by the window, imagining the caped empress and her lady-in-waiting rushing around the Louvre, trying on bourgeois clothes, huddling inside a carriage, perhaps. Had they got through the Paris gates? Were they hiding in someone's *hôtel particulier* or languishing in a Prussian prison?

And where was Evans?

Outside in the courtyard, the Bretons were chatting and cleaning their guns, waiting for their evening meal of donkey fat and God knew what else. The melancholy whine of a bagpipe rose into the cold air. Sitting on a step, arms around each other, two young men were crying. In the centre, a dozen grizzled soldiers held hands and, facing out in a circle, shuffled around to 'An Hini Gozh'.

The melody wrapped itself around Martial's soul.

'How did today go?' He turned to his cousin. Busy with finding supplies for both the Bretons and the soup kitchen, Martial had not been to the hospital.

'Two legs, one hand and two arms.' Jules rubbed his face. 'Right arm, just below the shoulder.'

Jules had lost a lot of weight. His trousers hung lose. He ran nimble fingers along his moustache and addressed Mary with a bitter smile. 'I did a good job. You would be proud of me. Those chaps might just live long enough to go begging on church steps . . . if there are any churches left by the time this *foutu* siege is over, that is.'

'But they will survive,' Martial pointed out. 'Which they might not have had you not followed Mary's rules on modern hygiene.'

'Bah. Whatever I suggest is met with: "Americans do things their way, but this is how we do things in Paris."'

'But Lister is British!' Mary objected. 'Just remind them that he's simply following in Pasteur's footsteps. Pasteur was French. That should count for something.'

'I know, I know!' Jules's exasperation was palpable. 'Lister's theory of germs? I'm told that nurses have better things to do than wash their hands between patients. As for the nuns, they would rather save souls than full-blooded men.'

He cast a longing glance at the whisky bottle. 'Why would

they listen to a junior doctor and an American *woman* with a fetish for carbolic soap?'

His gaze went to Martial. 'Why are you still wearing that cassock? Don't you realise that is a red rag to some very dangerous bulls? The mood has turned, Martial. Priests are a prime target.'

'Men may challenge the priests, but when they reach the end, confession brings them comfort. They all hope to meet their mother again in Heaven.' Martial forced down a sip of whisky. It was like drinking formaldehyde.

'This war will bring shame on all of us.' The gloom in Arthur's voice summed up the ambient mood.

'Remember how I told you about the falling stock exchange?' Gontran unknotted his long legs and put on a gruff voice. 'Six weeks at the most.' Oh yes, the bankers' verdict was clear. "We'll lick Bismarck. We might lose around fifty thousand lives, but it will be worth it. Stocks will shoot right back up."'

'Did they really say that?' Jules cried out. 'Fifty thousand lives, but it will be worth it?' The words caught in his throat. *'Just to save the stock exchange?'*

'The best-laid plans . . .' Gontran opened his hands.

Jules ran a hand through his thinning hair. '*Bon Dieu*, if I hadn't amputated half the life out of five men today, I'd say the whole thing was a farce.' He refilled his glass.

'Careful with that stuff, old man,' Martial warned. 'You don't want your hand to shake when you handle that saw tomorrow.'

With a sheepish glance at Mary, Jules poured himself some tea.

'I don't know about you,' with a yawn, Gontran checked his gold watch again, 'but this siege bores me. Now that my bank's ingots have been secreted away, I have a mind to join them. For a mere two thousand Francs, I have secured a passage on an aerostat. I shall be leaving very soon.'

Four pairs of eyes turned to him.

'But, Gontran,' Martial exclaimed when he could speak again, 'it's downright dangerous! You never know where you're going to land and . . . you'll freeze!'

'Just think, you lily-livered naysayers.' Gontran stabbed his cigar into an ashtray. 'How exciting it will be! As for the cold, I have furs. The heat from the flames must count for something.' Gontran waved an elegant hand. 'This siege is so dreary. I am more than ready for an adventure.'

36

NEW YORK

The smell of burned toast woke Flore. In the bed next to hers, Minnie was snoring lightly, mumbling indistinct words. The ceiling shook with heavy steps as the girl in the room above theirs was getting ready for work. Someone galloped down the stairs. A door slammed. A volley of 'Good morning!' rang in the cold air. The rattle of spoons rose from the dining room.

Flore pulled the thin blanket over her ears, willing herself to go back to sleep. It was no use. Once again, yesterday's news was taking shape in her mind. Although French newspapers such as *Le Courrier des États-Unis* announced victories over the Prussians, the American bulletins Minnie translated to her told a very different reality.

Paris had been under siege for three months now, and Bismarck was winning on all fronts. He was pulling his cannons to the last stronghold. Soon, Paris would be under fire.

How was Martial coping? Was he too eating rats, or could Jules afford meat? Not knowing was the worst. Hot air balloons did leave the capital every week, but so far she had not received any letters.

On the front page of every paper was news of Empress Eugenie's flight from France. She had escaped from besieged Paris—with her American dentist, of all people! A man called Evans. In disguise, armed with English permits, they had been allowed out of Paris, made their way to the coast and paid a British yacht owner to sail with them to England at midnight.

Martial would never abscond. For him, it would be desertion. He would not think of it.

Oh God, how could she have been so blind? How had she not read the love in Martial's eyes that day at Monsieur Godin's ball? Undeterred by her country ways, Martial had never seen her as a 'savage', as the Parisians called her people when they visited the moor. For this, she would forever love him. What he had seen in her, she simply could not fathom.

She had been so self-obsessed, so lost in guilt. Would she ever be able to make it up to him?

A draft seeped up the frigid stairs as someone opened the front door. Flore pulled down her nightcap.

The front door slammed one last time, and finally there was silence. Minnie turned over with a yawn. 'They gone?'

'I think so.'

Her hair twisted around rag curls, Minnie dragged her sleepy body behind the screen, sat on the *pissadou* and snuggled back into bed.

Flore returned to her reveries of Martial, wandering around the ruins of Paris in search of souls to save.

Flore went mad with worry at the thought of Martial under fire. Hardly rebuilt, Paris would soon crumble to dust, and none of Jules's money would help them if his house was hit.

Unable to sleep for worry, Flore got dressed. By the time

she got downstairs, the breakfast had been put away and all the girls had gone.

Outside, snowflakes fluttered in the icy wind that sliced through her cape. She thought back to the piles of logs in the Bois de Boulogne. In Paris, it was said, no trees were left at all. Every morning, frozen bodies were found in gutters.

The street where they lived was a mix of ramshackle houses that had seen better days and five-storey buildings forming solid walls that shut out the sun. It stretched out from a central avenue wider than any Paris boulevard. To one side were the tenements, thick blocks in which people were packed in their hundreds with only one tap and four toilet cubicles at ground level. For Flore, who had grown up in the unbroken emptiness of the moor, such a concept was inhuman.

'Monsieur Godin is not the only one who wants to improve the world,' Martial used to tell her. 'There are men everywhere who are building model villages, setting up agricultural communities where profits are shared.' His eyes shining, he would tell her of the new world just waiting to unfold. A new world they could be a part of. After living in the comfort of Monsieur Godin's Familistère, Flore stared at the tenements where the two Irish girls who served behind the bar lived with their parents, ten to a room, and wondered how those responsible for these monstrosities could live with themselves.

She made her way to the main avenue where carts offered all manner of vegetables and fruit in spite of the cold weather. Towering, the five-storey brownstone buildings made her feel insignificant. Back in her village, she had known everyone. Here, apart from Minnie, she knew no one. Not one of the faces was familiar. She followed the crowds milling on the pavements. Purposeful, focussed, they rushed forward without seeing her. She touched their sleeves, she smiled at children, but they could not see her.

Caught in the bustle of people hurrying to and fro, Flore felt like a ghost. *Is this what it is like to be dead?* She shivered. *To walk by unseen through others' lives, condemned to eternal loneliness? Is this my punishment?*

37

RATS BELOW, HOT AIR BALLOONS ABOVE

Martial, Jules and Mary were walking home from the soup kitchen, keeping people alive for another day. *Diou biban,* how *long* could this siege go on? A freezing fog fuzzed the harsh edges of the Parisian winter. Inside the cotton wool cloud, sporadic noises intensified, ghostly figures moved about in the greyness, but what Martial noticed was not so much what he could hear, as the sounds that had gone: the clatter of hoofs, the shouts of drivers, oaths, creaking wheels, cries of hawkers and the hurdy-gurdies of street singers.

Paris was silent. All that remained were the shuffle of clogs, the pointless marching of national guards, and the clippety-clop of the last horses, spared for pulling hearses.

A street urchin popped in front of him. 'Father Martial?'

'Jojo!' Martial's face broke into a grin. '*Bon sang,* you gave me a fright. Where did you spring from?' He remembered the boy. A regular attendee of the soup kitchen he patronised, Jojo was famous for his quips and irreverent songs.

'I'm doing fine, Father. Really well, in fact.' Jojo threw Mary a side glance and winked. 'She the doctor's girlfriend?'

'The lady is a doctor too. An American doctor.'

Jojo let out a slow whistle of admiration. After a few seconds, he said with a grin, 'Want to see where I live?'

'You found a place to stay?' Martial's question remained unanswered. Jojo had disappeared.

Mary's and Jules's gazes ran up the tall white façades, only their wrought-iron balconies visible in the mist.

'*Par ici!*' A hirsute head popped up, level with the pavement.

'*Saperlipopette, mais qu'est ce que tu fais là?*' Jules pulled up his nankeen trousers and peered down.

'Come, Father, Monsieur Jules. I'll show you.' The boy hesitated. 'Not sure about having a lady down there.' He grinned, uncovering a missing tooth. 'Mind you, before the siege, ladies did pay a fair few *sous* to visit the sewers. Over the water they trundled . . . in a little train pulled by a horse. The King of *Protudal* even went down there!'

'The King of Portugal indeed?' Martial smiled at Jojo, King of the Sewers. 'Doesn't it get smelly down there?'

Jules peered down.

'Come and have a sniff, monsieur.'

Jules's grey hat disappeared below the pavement. Mary tucked up her skirt and followed him down the ladder.

Holding his cassock, Martial stepped down carefully and stood mouth open.

'*Bienvenue chez moi!*'

A vast dome glimmered in the strange light that filtered from the grilles along the walls, reflecting a tidy canal. Fourteen feet high and very wide, the space radiated calm, only disturbed by the odd plop. The fetid air was warmer than outside, and in a corner, Jojo had decorated his living quarters with an artistic installation of scavenged objects. Milk churns mostly.

Scrabbles and squeaks rose from one of them. Mary took a step, peered into it and shot back. 'Gee whillikers! Rats!'

'*Eh oui,* madame.' Jojo pulled the plank that leaned against the churn.

'*Corne tonnerre,* boy, do you catch them to sell?' Jules cautiously glanced into the tall metal receptacle and called Martial over.

Rats were scrabbling on top of each other, covered in a shiny substance. Using the bodies of the weaker ones as launching pads, the stronger ones jumped but never reached the top.

'I catch them with sugar.' Jojo beamed. 'We've a shortage of everything, but Paris has enough sugar and booze to last a whole year. Rats smell it, run up this plank and—' A lid swivelled around a piece of doweling. 'Plop! The lid tilts and they fall in. All I have to do is skin 'em, thread 'em onto a stick and sell 'em as brochettes.'

'Yes,' Martial said weakly. 'I saw them at the butcher's.'

'I can deliver a few to your house tomorrow if you want. I'm sold out at the moment.'

'Thank you, Jojo,' Martial replied diplomatically. 'I'm sure you'll find customers who will appreciate them more than we might.'

'For sure. The gentlemen from the 'cademy did a blindfold test, you know, between rat, cat, dog and bird, and they all said rat was the best meat. I *preficted* the method to catch 'em, and I'm taking orders. The other day, I even sold some to a cook from a *big* restaurant. Made them into a terrine with *spitachio,* he said, and champagne. I peeped inside that place when I was delivering. Very grand. Gold everywhere. He gave me some bread. White bread too, and us three months into the siege.'

'Can't say I even remember the taste of white bread,' Jules muttered.

Mary returned to the ladder, took a couple of rungs and held out a hand. 'Listen.'

'What's the matter?'

She came down again. 'I think I heard shots.'

'Bah.' Jojo shrugged philosophically. 'Drunken national guards taking potshots at Prussians. Hankering after that *grande sortie.* Talking big. Poor chaps dream of getting out, but they got as much chance as my rats.'

Martial went up the ladder first and helped Mary out. She peered cautiously into the street, and as she hauled herself over the edge, a smile spread over her face as Jojo lowered his voice and said to Jules, 'Glad to see you got yourself a nice lady friend.'

The wistfulness in Jules's voice went straight to Martial's heart. 'We live in hope, Jojo. We live in hope.'

'Allez, bonne chance, monsieur.'

Along the avenue, the stumps of centenary trees poked through the mist, chopped down to help Parisians survive one of the coldest winters in living memory.

Gone were the elegant silhouettes of ladies who had once walked their dogs towards the Arc de Triomphe, the once proud regiments now reduced to handfuls of bedraggled national guards staggering back from an all-nighter, either defending the wall or nursing a glass of absinthe at a local café.

And worst of all, fuelled by absinthe and despair, Paris had been declared a republic.

What would happen when the war came to an end was all too predictable, but, having already lost everything, would the mutineers care?

A shout rang near them, followed by shots. Jules drew Mary behind a *colonne Morris* and peered to the side.

A pack of guards were chasing a man down a side street. Fitter and younger, the youngster outran them.

Another shot, another shout. A shape staggered and collapsed over a stump, holding his chest. Clogs rang on the cobbles, away from them.

Instinct kicked in. They held back, waited to make sure the pack had gone, and hurried to the victim's side. Mary searched her pockets for a clean handkerchief while Jules carefully lowered the man to the ground.

Others arrived. Mary opened the injured man's jacket and pressed her handkerchief on the wound.

'Run to the American field hospital,' Mary said to Jules. 'Call for the ambulance wagon. Martial, knock on a door and ask for blankets.'

An elderly gentleman presented himself. 'I am a doctor,' he said in a shaky voice. 'Young man, let me look at your wound.' He pulled off his gloves and struggled down to his knees. 'He's shivering. Let's carry him into a house.'

'It's all right, sir.' Mary's voice did not waver. 'We are now waiting for the ambulance.'

'I am sorry, dear, but I am a doctor. I think that in the circumstances—'

Mary met his gaze, her hand still pressing on the wound. 'I'm a doctor too. I am not moving him, or he will bleed to death. In a moment, he will be taken to the American hospital, where I work.'

The wounded man's teeth were chattering.

'Here you are.' Martial spread a horse blanket over the victim. 'Let's try to move him onto that.'

'Shall we have a look at you, then, son?' the old gentleman insisted.

'Non. Ne me touchez-pas!' The victim waved towards Mary. *'Elle, l'Américaine . . .'*

The old doctor glanced down at Mary, his voice dripping with contempt. 'Well, good luck to you, mademoiselle.'

A team of horses clattered down the empty avenue. Two

men jumped out and expertly slid the groaning man onto a stretcher. Within minutes, they had him loaded onto the back.

The victim waved an arm towards Mary. 'Come and see me, right?' He managed a wink.

That night, huddled around a lamp, Martial, Arthur and Gontran were playing a fast game of *bouillote.*

'Seigneur!' Clad in pink velvet, Violette padded into the room looking like a china doll. 'Has someone died?'

Martial just glared at her.

There was a scratch at the door.

'Oh! Sorry, Bijou, I shut you out.' Violette picked up her Pomeranian and shook her ringlets. 'Jules.' She lifted her round nose. 'Could you explain to Madame Leboeuf that Bijou *has* to eat meat? She tells me it's too expensive and tries to feed him red beet instead. It is simply ridiculous.'

Jules replied in a tired voice, 'We are under siege, Violette. A million people are going hungry, and you worry about a *dog*. I, for one, am willing to keep it simply because we might be glad to eat it when all else has gone, but really—'

'Oh! You are horrid.' Violette pouted. 'I was going to invite you to the theatre with Léontine. Now, I don't think I will.'

'What's it in aid of this time?' Gontran guffawed. 'The Amazons of the Seine? New uniforms for our lady soldiers?'

Violette rolled her eyes. 'As you well know, the idea of women soldiers has been dropped. It was ridiculous anyway. It is a play by Molière, if you must know, in aid of war widows.'

'And you're having a new dress made for the occasion.'

Jules pushed his bottom lip forward in mock approval. 'How very patriotic of you.'

Violette gave him a hard stare, picked up Bijou in a dramatic show of spite and left the room.

'Why are you so hard on the poor girl?' Arthur's face was set. 'Just because the nuns have kept her in the dark doesn't mean she's stupid.'

'Her sense of entitlement is appalling. Some days, I wish I could take her with me to the Salpêtrière. She would soon change her tune.'

'Why don't you?' Arthur retorted. 'You need nurses.'

'She would have an attack of the vapours and mess up things even more.'

'She needs to grow up, that's all.' Arthur had a soft spot for Violette, who would never give a lowly civil servant a second glance, determined as she was to wed her dandy duke.

The following day, Gontran invited them all to the Gare d'Orléans to check on the construction of his aerostat.

The station had been transformed into a giant balloon factory. A smile of wonder spread over Martial's face as he stepped into the glass-covered space. '*Saperlipopette!* You really have to marvel at man's resourcefulness.' He scanned the huge space. 'Of all the mad ideas that have sprung up to get our mail out of Paris, this really tops it all.' While Gontran had gone over to one of the engineers, Martial lowered his voice and murmured, amidst the chatter and the hiss of gas, 'Do you really think Gontran will do it?'

Faced with the enormity, the ingenuity and the sheer scale of what lay before them, his friends failed to answer, awed by the courage required to undertake such a task.

Violette's eyes widened at the acres of silk. Silk was everywhere, flung across trestles, long thin patches sewn together by rows of seamstresses, silk stacked on pallets or shaped into striped aerostats that lay half-inflated on platforms, waiting, they were told, to be varnished.

'Just think,' Gontran returned and sidled up to her, 'this new industry is using up all the silk our Parisian belles are not able to wear, providing work for seamstresses and sailors! Isn't it wonderful?' In tailcoat and top hat, Gontran windmilled with excitement, hitting a sailor running past, a coil of rope over his shoulder. A gang of mariners sat on the ground, weaving a delicate net of ropes around an aerostat.

Gontran pointed to a deflated balloon bunched up in a corner. 'There it is! *Ville d'Orléans*, I believe it will be called.' Rubbing his hands, he canted his chin at another gang of mariners huddled around a brazier. 'These good fellows are putting the last touches to our nacelle.'

Jules's gaze went from the flimsy pile of osier to the billowing silk and returned to Martial with the message that, for all his buffoonery, Gontran may be a braver man than they were.

'Have you written your letters, gentlemen?' Gontran radiated the excitement of a child in a toy shop. 'I shall be leaving in three days' time.'

And so, three days later, Martial found himself in the dead of night with Jules, Mary, Arthur and Violette on the station concourse, watching the aerostat swell up in loud bursts.

Above them, the sky was clear, dotted with silver stars. Martial cast a discreet glance at Jules and Mary, standing very close to each other. Was it the cold night air, or had their relationship progressed?

'Where is Gontran hoping to land?' Violette asked.

'He's heading south.' Martial licked a finger and held it to the night breeze. 'The government has decamped to Bordeaux.' He held his finger up again. 'Hmm . . . basically, anywhere out of reach of the Prussians would be good.'

Violette stamped her feet to ward off the cold and watched the mail and ballast bags carried into the nacelle. Finally, several cages of sleepy pigeons were lowered inside.

Wrapped in a thick mink coat and hat, Gontran climbed in with an aeronaut called Rolier.

The little clan stood below, frozen and transfixed, their gaze on the flames pulsing heat into the silk. Slowly, the guide ropes and anchor were lifted. With a loud roar of gas, the balloon jerked upwards. Mary shivered and slipped her arm through Jules's.

Gontran waved to them and shouted something they did not understand. They watched them rise through the night air, listening for shots, relieved that nothing was heard but the *shoof shoof* of the gas.

'Ah zut,' Martial muttered as they headed back to the carriage, his nose in the air.

'Are they going in the right direction?' Violette held on to him as she stared into the darkness.

Biting his lower lip, he followed the tiny prick of flames now dancing above . . . Montmartre. It should have been floating south, somewhere over his hospital.

Violette checked their faces. 'Is it the wind?' Once the truth dawned on her, she asked, 'What countries lies north of France?'

When no one answered her question, Violette came to her senses. 'Oh no! They won't be landing in Prussia, will they?'

38

MADEMOISELLE MAMOUNA

Flore ran a cloth over the tin-covered bar while a troupe of blondes marched onto the makeshift stage in képis and frothy skirts.

She took stock. A year ago, she was in Noirac. A year ago, she was still clinging to the delusion that Ricar would slip into her father's clogs and carry on the family tradition of herding sheep and tending the sand vines.

If someone had told her then that she would work as a barmaid in a vaudeville theatre—in New York, of all places—would she even have *understood?*

God only knew where she would end up. The world was changing so fast.

Their 'theatre' was little more than a saloon tacked on to a wheelwright's business. Bill Moreton, her boss, repaired carriages. A few years ago, he had added a room big enough for several tables where his customers could wait while the work was being carried out. Over time, he had added a stage and a show inspired by English burlesque: a combination of ribald comedy, magic and song, oiled by cheap liquor.

Through the thick fog of cigar smoke, Flore grinned as

Minnie and her 'blondes' now filed onto the stage, legs twirling the can-can that was to make the name of the Wheel of Fortune, or so Minnie had promised Bill when she'd applied for the job.

Other theatres ran a rolling programme of touring troupes, but the Wheel had adopted a different format by offering a medley of resident acts. One of them was a duo called the McCann Brothers, whose barbed satire of political shenanigans reduced the audience to tears of laughter. For the McCanns, it was a case of 'where there's muck, there's brass'. Ruled as New York was by gangs, corrupt politicians and a posse of Bible-bashing philanthropists, the McCann Brothers claimed they would never run out of dirt.

The Wheel of Fortune's fame now rested on the shoulders of *Mademoiselle Mamouna, danseuse exotique* and the daring can-can she had brought all the way from *Paree*.

It had not taken Bill Moreton long to notice Flore's skill with money. Her English had improved. She was quick to calculate the price of a tray of drinks, always returned the exact change and had enough English to keep her acolytes, Clodagh and Deirdre, in check.

Safe behind the bar, Flore did not have to suffer the indignity of having her bottom pinched, although she did have to compromise. 'Hate to tell you this, darlin',' Bill had pointed to the high-necked blouse she'd worn on her first night and explained with an unambiguous gesture, 'but in your job, the size of your tips will be proportional to the size of your tits.'

The can-can girls marched off stage to a din of wolf whistles, followed by an old woman and her circus poodle whom Bill kept on simply because her act created a lull which allowed for refills.

The smoke thickened, the atmosphere grew rowdier, and

Deirdre and Clodagh worked the room ceaselessly, rushing around with trays of drinks and cigars.

The poodle had gone. Sensual, evocative, a plaintive accordion melody floated in, carrying a soupçon of the Orient. The public—mainly men—held their breath. The music grew louder. A drumbeat added to the suspense.

Just before leaving the Folies, Minnie had given Thérèse—Samira the snake charmer—part of her savings to teach her those luscious erotic moves. For a week and a half, she had refined them on the steamer, hidden between two lifeboats.

'Mamouna' burst onto the stage to a cacophony of whistles and shouts, and Flore started counting the proceeds for the night. A couple of Russians clung to the bar and watched, their humid blue eyes vague with longing and vodka.

Their gazes glued to flashes of flesh glimpsed through organza, men clustered around the stage. Flore grinned. The rotund gentleman in gaiters was here again, mouth open.

It wasn't at all what she'd had in mind when she'd escaped to the New World. Neither was the crumbling boarding-house where they lodged. A whole mile away from the Wheel, the house was not in the safest of districts, but how could she complain when Paris was aflame and people froze in gutters?

Martial had written, and, miracle of miracles, his letter had found her. Smuggled out by hot air balloon, Martial's letter told her how hard he found witnessing so many senseless deaths.

He described the revolutionary fervour burning through Paris. *Jules and I are doing our best to help—he patches up soldiers while I help feed the multitudes—but Paris is under threat from all sides. Winter has been cruel. Our government has forsaken our city, and within the walls a cancer is growing, fuelled by poverty and want. The working men's demands are simple: education for all, being treated with dignity and paid a living wage. Sadly, they are not heard, and I fear that their claims to turn Paris into a self-governing commune will soon lead to civil war, just as Minnie predicted.*

Martial wished he could picture her daily life. *Though I am comforted to know you are with Minnie, I cannot imagine where you are or what you do, so I rely on my memories. I see you carrying a tray of bread across the airial, warm from the oven. I hear you sing with your eyes closed on the charabanc to Sainte Elma. I remember your smile the day you once handed Hugo and me a ripe bunch of grapes.*

Yesu! Had he loved her then?

She jumped back to the present as Minnie appeared before her, holding out her coat. 'Home time. The girls are waiting outside. Bill says he'll lock up.'

Guarded by two brothers, the four girls headed for the Irish tenements, where frozen washing hung between blocks, ghostly in the moonlight. Clodagh and Deirdre peeled off, leaving Flore and Minnie to cover the last half mile in the dark.

'What a dump,' Minnie said as they approached their street. 'I really have to find us somewhere else. The walls of our room are so thin I can hear a fart next door. It's impossible to sleep when they all chatter like magpies. I'm done in.'

Their vinegar-faced landlady disapproved of the hours they kept, but it would be difficult to find anything cheaper near the Wheel. Wherever they lived, walking home at night would be dangerous, and if they moved, how would Martial find them?

Flore's fingers tightened on Minnie's arm. 'Listen.'

'Huh?' Minnie slowed down.

Behind them, the crunch of steps had slowed down too. Her heart beating wildly, Flore increased her speed, dragging Minnie along. The peeling frontage of their clapboard house was three lamplights away, though two of them were not working. The steps dragged, slightly unsteady.

Flore whipped around. A shadow slipped into an alleyway.

'Did you see him?' Flore searched the night.

'Stop it. You're creeping me out!' Minnie whispered as they climbed the steps.

Flore unlocked the door and relocked it quickly. She lifted the drape and looked out at the street. A shadow detached itself from the alley and staggered away.

39

PARIS IS STARVING

Four months into the siege, prey to one of the worst winters in living memory, Paris had run out of trees and food. Outside the wall, the Prussians had lined up their cannons. Something had to give.

Martial was in charge of supplies for the *cantine municipale*, the parish soup kitchen. The local priest who had hired Martial often expressed his relief at finding a man who would not garner the food for his own gain. While supplies were dwindling, the black market thrived. If you had money, it was still possible to procure what you wanted.

The poor were dying one by one, and in the communal cellars where food had been amassed in preparation for the siege, the last scraps were dwindling, musty and dry. It was time to surrender, but the Parisians were proud. Bellicose and armed, they wanted to show what they were capable of.

'May I borrow Bernard's services and the cart?' Martial asked Jules on a morning they were not due at the hospital. 'I am to fetch some supplies from the cellars of the opera. Would you like to come with us?'

'I would love to.' Jules motioned to the valet to help him

into his coat. 'I've always wanted to have a peep at that new opera.'

Bernard harnessed their last horse to the cart. Out of a team of four, the emaciated Gringolet was the only one to have survived. The other three had been requisitioned and slaughtered for food. Of the eighty thousand horses in Paris, very few were left. Hay had run out. Because Martial used the horse to transport supplies and take Jules to his hospital, Arthur, from his town hall, had made sure Gringolet's life would be spared.

'While I'm down in the cellars,' Martial said, 'you might be able to run upstairs and gawp at the ceiling.'

Jules took his gloves and hat from the valet. 'Yes. I'm sure a few *sous* should take care of it.'

Violette clattered down wearing her coat and hat, Bijou yapping around her ankles.

'Where are you two going? I told Bernard I had an appointment.'

'Sorry, Violette. Had we known, we would have warned the sisters of Saint Vincent de Paul that their supplies would be delayed.' Jules tucked his hat under his arm. 'And where is your appointment?'

'I ordered a dress, and I am due for my final fitting. It's Léontine's eighteenth birthday in a few days' time.'

'I see.' Jules's gaze was scathing. 'Where does the seamstress live?'

Violette waved a hand. 'Somewhere near Bastille. Bernard knows the address.'

'A dress . . . near Bastille.' Jules buttoned his coat. 'Really. Listen, the 11th arrondissement is not safe, you know that. *Bon sang*, Violette, this is not the time to try on dresses!'

The look Violette gave Jules would have withered a lesser man. 'Bernard will look after me.' She tightened her fur collar. 'I ordered it *months* ago, and anyway, I shall be trying it on *inside* Madame Couturier's shop.'

Did she just stamp her foot? She lifted her little round nose and glanced at Martial in an attempt to draw him into her camp. 'I am giving my seamstress work. Surely, that is a good thing?'

'Paris has changed, Violette,' Martial reasoned. 'Tempers are running high. Men are armed, and the poor are desperate.'

'*Viens*, Bijou.' Violette pivoted and stomped back up the stairs.

'Do you think she'll go?' Martial clambered into the cart and sat next to Jules.

'I wouldn't put it past her. She can twist poor Bernard around her little finger.' Jules ran a hand through his hair and donned the hat he had been holding. '*Bon Dieu*, how I wish I'd bundled her back to her mother's when I still could. That girl is a liability. Do you know the other day she scrambled up the wall with Léontine to watch cannons fire! If she gets herself killed, her parents will hold me responsible.' Jules concluded with a sarcastic grin, 'Her father is a very generous donor to our hospital.'

They trundled through deserted streets, meeting only hearses drawn by exhausted nags.

When they reached the new opera, Jules whistled at the impressive arcades, colonnades and domed roof.

'You've got to admire Garnier. According to what I read in the papers, he's been battling Haussmann all these years to be allowed space around his creation. Can't have been easy. Right in front of it was a hill called La Butte des Moulins.'

'Windmill hill? Here? But it's totally flat!'

'I know. God knows where they carted the soil away.'

'I find it pretentious.' Martial shrugged as the cart drew around to the back of the building.

'It's supposed to be. It's an opera!'

They stamped their feet while bolts were drawn. As soon as the door was open, Jules darted upstairs for a glance at the famed ceiling, while Martial and the coachman followed the employee down to the stores. Bernard in his great coat and Martial under his thick black cape dwarfed the bombastic little man whose round face boasted a splendid set of side-burns that rivalled even Bernard's facial fluff. Their steps were dulled by straw. Stacked up against a wall, little of it was left.

A gasp escaped them when they reached the central rotunda.

'See these columns and cupola?' The employee pointed to the ceiling. 'They hold the building together. There are four cupolas on top of each other. Such a clever design. Also,' he confided as proudly as if he had designed the opera himself, 'they had so much trouble keeping the water from seeping through that they contained it.' He tapped the floor with his heel. 'Right under us is an underground reservoir.' He opened his arms. 'Welcome, messieurs, to my kingdom.'

An eerie creak echoed when the little man opened a metal door.

'I'm afraid my treasure chamber is being depleted faster than we'd hoped.' Lantern aloft, he preceded them into the storeroom. It was nearly empty. A few sacks of flour, dried beans and potatoes were piled against the far wall. 'It seems we underestimated the amount of flour we would need. The cold is making the poor angry and desperate. I, for one, am praying for a ceasefire.'

Martial and Bernard exchanged a glance. They produced their affidavits and took just what they needed, unsure there would be any left when they returned next. Paris would not hold out much longer.

While Bernard and Martial stacked their meagre fare, Jules galloped down to them.

'Superbe, époustouflant!' Eyes sparkling, slightly out of breath, Jules beamed. 'Ah, the lush gold and colour upstairs. What a privilege to see it all!'

Inside the guard room, a bright fire crackled and a bottle of wine stood open.

'Paris may be tottering on the brink,' Jules hopped onto the cart and addressed the two men, 'but this fat little king will be comfortable for a while yet.'

'Assurément.' Bernard clicked his tongue twice and snapped the reins. 'Did you notice, messieurs, when the papers announced our armies' victory two weeks ago, how butter and cheese reappeared like magic?'

Jules pulled his cape tight against the biting wind. 'It may be that once the siege is over, we shall find catacombs stashed with pâtés, duck comfit and smoked hams.'

'Don't tease, monsieur, the slice of *pain ferry* I had this morning is but a distant memory.'

Made from a mixture of oats, wheat and rice at its best, or maize and straw at its worst, the rough bread sat on Martial's stomach with nefarious effects on his digestion.

Although Jules's household were better fed than most, the fare had become bland and repetitive. Everything had its price, of course, and according to Violette, Léontine de la Boissière had not yet had to give up her *petit pain blanc,* the fragrant bun she ate for breakfast.

However sick he was of eating stodge based on donkey fat, Martial was reminded how privileged they were on rue de la Bienfaisance. What he had seen in the cellars of the opera gnawed at him. How long could they hold on?

Back in their own parish, they clippety-clopped past a queue snaking outside the *cantine municipale.* People in rags huddled, blue with cold under thin blankets, human skeletons holding out bowls into which nuns ladled soup.

'Look at them.' There was a tremor in Jules's voice. 'They drink to keep warm. More and more of those poor wretches are found frozen in the gutter. I've never seen such a bitter cold.'

In their hospital, people were brought in suffering from the last stages of consumption, pneumonia and a particularly nasty variant of smallpox, which had spread from wounded soldiers who had not been vaccinated properly.

'Mon père, par ici!' One of the nuns called Martial to the back of the soup kitchen.

'Father, I know you have contacts in the *mairie*. I would just like to say . . . we allow them to take soup home, you know, for the old and the sick, but some of them have caught on and . . .' She opened her hands.

'I understand. I'll have a word with Arthur. He's been advocating ration tickets for ages.'

'It is long overdue.'

As soon as they got home, Jules went up to his room to catch up on sleep, leaving Martial to warm his hands by the range. Out of the corner of his eye, he noticed Violette cross the courtyard towards the stable.

Moments later, Gringolet trotted out, harnessed to the hansom.

He grabbed the cape he had just cast off and rushed out. If Violette was heading for Bastille, she was in danger. Deprived of food and wood, the eastern districts were powder kegs. Jules's coachman did not have the authority to refuse her.

Martial ran after the carriage and jumped in. They set off, skirting barricades, scaffolding and debris.

Along the empty streets, barefoot children huddled around rare sources of heat. Leaning over their rifles, bearded national guards in képis and red neckerchiefs cast them suspicious looks. Here and there, shopkeepers were barricading their stalls amidst shouts from housewives accusing them of withholding food to sell to the rich.

At last, Bernard drew up outside the arch of a paved courtyard where ragged children were playing listlessly. Gone were the songs, the arguments and the barking of dogs Martial had always associated with Paris. Today, the streets were silent. Dogs and sparrows had been eaten. Only the pigeons were spared.

'I'll just turn the cab around, Mademoiselle Violette,' Bernard called out. 'Go in quick as you can, and don't come out until you can see me.'

Through the glass front of Madame Couturier's workshop, Martial noticed a couple of girls busy sewing. From the size of the place, he guessed that only a few months ago it had been a profitable business.

Violette ran towards the glazed door. 'I'm not sure this is the place for a gentleman. I'm only trying it on and paying for the dress. I shan't be more than a minute. Perhaps you will wait for me in the coach?'

'No, wait!' Martial checked the courtyard. He tried the door, but it was locked from the inside. Annoyed, he kicked his heels and waited for Bernard to return.

A window opened above him. A housewife shook out a mat. Martial edged away from the wall. Conspicuous in his black cape and hat, he peeped through the glazed wall, silently urging Violette to hurry.

She stepped out from behind a screen in the yellow 'shepherdess dress' she had set her heart on for Léontine's masked ball, twirled in front of a mirror, clapped her hands with pleasure and handed Madame Couturier *the billet de nécessité,* which replaced money during the siege.

Martial sensed a presence behind him. A woman had

staggered into the courtyard, a bundle in her arms. Pale and haggard, she darted mad eyes around, headed for the work-room and knocked on the door. 'Look at what you did!' She dangled the naked corpse of a child in front of the glass. 'You refused to help me, and now my baby's dead!'

Eyes wild, Violette unlocked the door and ran past the woman to Martial, still in the yellow dress.

Madame Couturier stepped back, a hand on her chest.

The woman snarled at the two seamstresses. 'Why them? Why didn't you give *me* a job?'

'Mon Dieu, Annette. Annette, *je vous en prie.'* Madame Couturier pushed the woman back into the courtyard.

'My man was killed defending the city, and now my son has died. If you won't employ me, what am I going to live on?' She crept towards the door.

'Annette, please. I'm sorry, but how can I run my business when I don't get any orders?'

'I bet you had breakfast this morning! I bet your house is nice and warm.' The dead child clutched to her chest, the woman pushed her way inside and lunged for a pair of scissors.

Madame Couturier threw herself at her erstwhile employee. Helped by one of the girls, disarmed her and bundled her out. They feverishly locked the door.

'Wait!' Violette cried out. 'My clothes are still inside!'

The seamstresses drew the drapes. A stone hit the tall glass pane. Martial took Violette's hand and ran towards the street, but they were too late. Men in képis and red sashes were blocking the entrance to the courtyard. Having sniffed blood, the guards snarled, their mouths toothless and distorted. In her yellow shepherdess dress, Violette stood for everything they hated.

Martial lifted a hand. '*Citoyens,* there is no need for this. We came here with the best of intentions; now let us pass.'

A man spat at Martial's feet. 'Bloody priests, getting fat on our backs.'

The insult hit Martial like a punch. He opened his mouth to protest but thought better of it. The children surrounded them like a pack of dogs. From a window, a reedy voice echoed around the courtyard. 'We dance the *capucine*, there is no bread at home . . .'

Terrified, Violette clung to Martial, her nails digging into his hand. The children joined hands in a ring and danced ran around them singing, 'The neighbour has got bread, but it is not for us.' A shiver of terror ran through him. The song was a version of the original 'Carmagnole', the tune that had accompanied aristocrats to the guillotine.

What had he been thinking? Coming here was a terrible mistake. Eighty years after the Revolution and nothing had changed. Parisians were still hungry, still powerless, still furious.

Ears strained to the street, Martial breathed a sigh of relief at the sound of hoofs. Another stone hit the glass. An arm around Violette, he edged towards the arched exit.

'Leech! All priests are leeches!' A second window opened above them. 'You live off our sweat and keep us in chains with promises of eternal life!'

'There is no eternal life.' The mad woman dangled her dead child in front of Violette. 'Hell is here, right now!'

Violette screamed. She hid behind him. Shivering in her flimsy dress, her teeth were chattering.

Roused, the pack was closing in on them.

Bernard called out from the street, 'Mademoiselle Violette, *par ici*!' Catching Martial's eye, the coachman rubbed his thumb and forefinger together.

Martial dipped into his pocket. He hurled a handful of coins to a far corner of the courtyard. The urchins ran to it.

Bernard snapped the reins. Martial grabbed Violette's hand and dragged her to the carriage.

'Violette, *vite*!' Keeping his eyes on the mob spilling out towards them, Bernard lifted his whip. Taken aback at the casual address, the girl hesitated. Projectiles flew around them. Martial manhandled her into the carriage. Bernard brought down his whip. Stones bounced off the brougham. Eyes wild, the horse bolted down the narrow street, bumping into barricades, rubble and scaffolding.

Something was wrong. The reins were slack. Martial gripped the side, squeezed out and looked back. Bernard was slumped over the hood. His hat had fallen off. Blood dripped from a gash in his head.

Martial snatched the reins, pulled for all he was worth and pushed them into Violette's hand with orders to restrain the animal. He clambered around to the coachman.

Snorting, eyes wild, Gringolet fought the harness. With the help of a couple of passersby, Martial managed to transfer Bernard to the cabin. Hit on the head by the enraged mob, he was bleeding profusely.

'Look after him, Violette. Let's take him home. Jules will know what to do.'

Violette cowered away. 'But my dress . . .'

Martial gave her a withering look, struggled out of his cape and threw it at her. Hesitant, she used it to protect herself and cushion the coachman's head. Martial took the coachman's seat and galloped west along boulevard Haussmann.

By the time they reached rue de la Bienfaisance, Bernard had not regained consciousness.

Together with the groom, Martial carefully carried him to the stable, laid him down on what was left of the straw, covered him with a horse blanket and sent the groom in search of Jules.

'*Ma petite* Violette.' The coachman's eyes flickered. He stared at Violette in wonder. 'My beautiful girl.'

Disturbed, Violette lifted her gaze to Martial.

He was so startled that he forgot the cold. Violette's eyes were the same shape and periwinkle blue as Bernard's.

He had never noticed it before . . . but then, why would he? The man's face had always been hidden inside a thatch of straw-coloured hair and fuzzy sideburns.

He studied Violette's nose—yes, the bobble was there.

Reeling in shock, a string of images raced across Martial's mind. *Holidays in Normandy. He is ten. Uncle Hippolyte, Violette's father, hugs him and runs a hand over his bottom. Martial feels uneasy. That summer, during a game of hide and seek, he glimpses Uncle Hippolyte in a linen cupboard kissing a male servant. In Paris now, a younger Bernard, tall, athletic and freshly arrived from his native Normandy, pulls down the carriage step for his aunt. She bends her head like a swan and rests a hand on his shoulder with a smile.*

'Why does he say these things?' Violette whined, shivering inside Martial's cape. 'I don't like it when he speaks like that.'

Martial took the man's pulse. It was very faint. The gash on the man's head was worse than he had first realised, pink tissue now frothing at the edge of the wound. And where on earth was Jules?

Bernard gripped Martial's hand. 'Father, I promised her mother I'd never tell, but it's not right, is it? She'll never know me.'

'What is he saying?' Violette's lips twisted. 'Tell him to stop.'

'His intentions are pure. I swear on my honour.' Martial growled, 'Hold his hand. He hasn't got long.' Violette did not move. He raised his voice. 'This man gave his life for you.'

He crossed himself and intoned the prayers for the dying.

Violette hesitated. Martial narrowed his eyes. She took

the coachman's hand, knelt in the straw and whispered, 'Thank you for what you did, Bernard. I am sorry you got hurt, but you will be fine, I promise.' She gazed up at Martial. The look on his face told her otherwise.

She reeled back, still for a moment, and he knew that she understood what she had done and what she had to do.

Her voice wavering, she held the man's fingers in her own and spoke to him. 'Soon, we will see Paris free, Bernard. We'll go back to Normandy together, and I will tell everyone what a hero you are. I'll tell them how you saved my life. We'll go home very soon, back to our village, back to your family.' She pressed her lips to his fingers. 'And we will tell them . . .'

Bernard's hand went slack inside hers and the periwinkle eyes stared, lifeless, at his daughter.

Violette knelt over him and sobbed.

Jules rushed in and saw the blood pooling into the straw. 'What happened? Oh no! Bernard! Bernard, stay with us!' He crouched by his servant and placed two fingers on his neck. His shoulders slumped. He passed a hand over the coachman's eyes.

Bastien, the groom, squatted by his mentor, shaking with sobs. With a whimper, Violette scrambled up and ran to her room.

At first, she did not answer when Martial rapped on her door. He walked in and found her kneeling on her prie-dieu below a large cross on the wall. She had thrown a thick robe over the soiled dress.

She looked up at him, her face swollen with tears.

'I am sorry, Violette. I bear the blame,' Martial began. 'I should have listened to Jules and stopped you from going there. I knew how desperate people are in those parts.'

'Animals. They were animals. Did you see their eyes?' Violette left her prie-dieu for the long stool at the end of her tester bed, where she sat, hands tucked between her knees.

Martial hesitated, unsure of how to proceed.

'You will hate me for this, I know, but one day, God willing, you will thank me.' He went to close the door. They must not be overheard.

'Why did Bernard *say* these things? He was delirious, wasn't he?'

This was Martial's cue to lie, but she needed to know the truth.

'He wasn't.'

'W-what do you mean?'

'Bernard died protecting you because he . . . he was your natural father.'

'No!' Violette sprang up. 'No!' She strode across the room, twisting her fingers. 'Don't say that. It isn't true!' She buried her face into her hands and shuddered. 'It can't be true.'

'He was a good man. You do know that, don't you?'

Her face twisted as she spat, 'He was a coachman!'

'Violette, do you *truly* believe that God ordains whether we are rich or poor?'

'Of course I do. How could it be otherwise? You're a priest; you should know!' She pushed her hair from her face. 'What do I have in common with the harridans who attacked us this morning?' She stepped back. '*Mon Dieu*, Martial, how can you even *doubt* it?'

'Bernard gave his life for you. Is that not proof of the nobility of his soul?'

'I don't know!' She threw herself on her bed. 'Oh!' Her ringlets stuck out like snakes. 'Oh, poor, poor Papa. What if he finds out?'

'Oh, I wager he already knows.'

'Stop saying these things!' Eyes wild, Violette threw herself at him and thumped his chest with her fists. 'You are an evil, evil liar!'

'Don't shout. Someone will hear you.'

She stared at him open-mouthed, her face a Greek mask of tragedy.

'Who else knows? Does everyone know? Oh, if this is true, what a fool I've been, thinking I could hope to marry the Duc de Montmorency, when I am really just a . . .' She crumpled. 'A coachman's daughter.' She picked up her dog and cried vicious tears into its fur.

'No one knows. Listen, forget the duke. You should marry someone who loves you for who you are, not for your status.' Martial added in a soft voice, 'Two of our neighbours near Bordeaux are the emperor's natural sons. Their mother was a linen maid he met in prison before he took power.'

'Really?'

'Oh yes. They are well respected.' He pulled a chair and sat opposite her. 'Give it time. Today, your vision of the world has shifted, but soon you will see that courage and integrity are more important than some title inherited through sheer luck. Was Jesus not a carpenter?'

'Huh?' She put down Bijou. 'Why would Mama . . .' She rubbed her arms. 'I don't understand.'

'I remember Bernard when he came to your family. Tall, strong and so caring. Your father was often away on . . . business, I'm afraid.'

Martial went to check that the maid was not listening at the door. 'Violette, secrets have a habit of seeping out, but rest assured that if it does, it won't be from me.'

'Wait. Don't go just yet.' Violette went to the window, her back turned to him. She exhaled a long sigh and said in a voice so low he could hardly hear her. 'I held his hand. I think he smiled.'

It was only when Martial's body relaxed that he realised how tense had had been since the attack. 'What you did was beautiful. He died happy. Oh, Violette, he was so, so proud of you.'

She remained silent for a long time.

'I understand that it is a huge shock, but believe me, courage and integrity will see you through.'

Slowly, she turned to him. 'Martial,' she cleared her throat, 'tell me . . .'

'Yes?'

'Since you know my secrets, perhaps you will allow me to share yours.'

Martial lifted an eyebrow. 'I have secrets?'

Violette said with a shy grin, 'The girl you came here with before the war. Did you, do you have feelings for her?'

Martial's heart threatened to jump out of his chest.

Violette pointed to her mirrored wardrobe. 'Just look at yourself.'

Oh God, he looked a fright. His cassock was bloody and full of chaff, his hair plastered to his forehead and his cheeks on fire.

'If that secret gets out,' she murmured, 'it will be your own fault. You're as red as a beetroot.'

'Guilty as charged.'

'What will you do? Leave the priesthood? Will you have to go to prison?'

'I hope not,' Martial answered miserably. 'I just don't know what to do.'

'Courage and integrity, my boy,' she said in a gruff voice, 'will see you through.'

Chastened, he went to her and held out a hand. She took it in both hers.

That night, too upset to eat, Violette remained in her room, lost in prayer. The three men asked for a fire to be lit in the small boudoir, easier to heat than the formal dining room, and sat in silence around a bowl of lentils and donkey meat, which they ate in the light of candles made from horse suet. The scant reserves of gas were kept to fill aerostats. The lentils were followed by the usual rice pudding and jam, concocted with fake milk made out of a mixture of sugar, carbonate of soda, gelatine and horse oil.

Sickened by the coachman's death, another casualty of this nonsensical war, Martial felt wretched, wishing he had stood up to Violette that morning.

Jules was incensed. 'How am I going to explain to Violette's mother that her coachman was murdered for the sake of a dress? Not even by *Prussians*!' He banged the table. 'Bernard has been in our family's employ for nigh on twenty years. I loved that man. *Corne tonnerre!* I *told* her not to go!' His voice broke. 'Does that flibbertigibbet not realise there's a war on?'

'Perhaps you should follow Arthur's suggestion and take her with you to the hospital,' Martial said. 'I think you'll find her changed.'

Arthur nodded gravely.

'Oh God, that's all I need.' Jules hesitated. 'Oh, damn it all!' He threw his napkin on the table. 'All right. She can come with me, but the first swoon, the very first *hint* of the vapours and the damsel will find herself bundled up as ballast in one of those aerostats that take off every night.' He picked up his glass and drained the rest of his wine. 'And I hope a blizzard blows her to the North Pole.'

40
MINNIE HAS A PLAN

Flore stood by the shore. The bleating that came from meadows across the waves pierced her heart like a volley of arrows. Eyes closed, she inhaled the sea air and, for a few seconds, flew back to another shore, the shore where her roots lay buried deep in the sand.

Battered by sun and sea winds, the vines clung, resilient, to the dunes. Beyond, in the wild moor, squat cottages hid, safe inside their clump of oaks. Friends and neighbours sat around hearths, knitting or shelling corn. She was on her way home, ice cracking under her stilts. From the sheepfold rose the bleat of a newborn lamb.

'You okay?' Minnie pointed across the water. 'We could take a ferry to Brooklyn.'

Small boats were sailing up the East River, their multi-coloured sails flapping in the strong breeze.

Behind Minnie, the Manhattan skyline rose, clumps of five-storey buildings with not a ray of sunshine between them. A New World indeed. Whatever Flore had imagined when she left France, it was not this. Perhaps it was all she deserved.

'How about Staten Island?'

Flore shrugged.

'Don't know about you,' Minnie turned up her collar, 'but I've had enough fresh air. Why don't we find ourselves a nice ice cream parlour? Somewhere cosy, for ladies only.'

An icy wind lifted Flore's skirt and pulled at her hat. Across the water, a huge steamer belched past Staten Island.

Heaven only knew when Martial would join her. According to the news, French armies were getting thrashed and the siege looked set to continue well past Christmas.

'See that white *mousse*?' Flore pointed to the foam that topped the waves, frothed up by the wind. 'In French, we call them sheep.'

'We call them white horses.'

'To me, they look like sheep.'

'Yeah, well, they would.' Minnie rubbed her arms. 'You see sheep everywhere. So, have you had enough water for today?'

'Yes, thank you.' Flore was grateful to Minnie for accompanying her to the shore on Mondays, their free day. The ocean went some way to calming her bouts of homesickness, sometimes so strong they kicked her in the stomach and left her breathless.

If the weather was good, they would pick a spot and sit somewhere between the warehouses on the Hudson, walk along the East River or come here to Battery Park, where the waves were rougher. The wildness of the sea surrounding Manhattan somehow made up for the town being so controlled, so crowded.

'Let's see, you've seen St Patrick's Cathedral, you've been to Broadway, gone up the elevator at Stewart's and saw the Christmas windows on Fifth Avenue. What else is left to do? It gets draughty around the Croton Reservoir. We'll go there when it's warmer. Jeez, I sure miss Paris. I was doing real well with my ghoulish tour until the darned Prussians ruined it all,' Minnie said bitterly.

Right now, trapped under ice, abandoned by all, Paris was a prison for two million souls, though for Flore, only one mattered.

She missed Martial so much, it hurt. She missed the way he made her feel . . . wanted, special, like she mattered. She had taken him for granted, she knew that now, and she was paying the price.

Would Martial like New York? She was not sure. New York was greedy. Its appetite never satisfied, it chomped away at rivers and hills, straightened out any meandering road, gobbled up rustic farms and spewed up tenements. Marshes sank under the weight of hurriedly built constructions. In the centre of Manhattan, blocks loomed above a flow of pedestrians who marched like ants around the dark carapace of carriages. This year, a seven-storey monstrosity was being erected on Broadway. Seven storeys . . . God only knew where they would stop.

'Come on.' Minnie threaded her arm in Flore's and strode north, only slowing down once they had reached the commercial streets.

'There we are. Coffee inn. Perfect.' Minnie pointed to a gaily painted parlour. 'No liquor, no cigar smoke, no men to leer at us. We get leered at enough at the Wheel, don't we?'

'But you like being leered at!' Flore said candidly.

Minnie pushed the door open and chose a lace-covered table near the window.

After a glance at the menu, they ordered waffles, sarsaparilla soda for Flore and coffee for Minnie.

Through the steam that frosted the glass, the outside world looked mellow and safe. In a corner, two old ladies in crinolines were chatting in hushed German.

'Back at the Wheel, I noticed a certain gentleman seems

to like your dancing.' Flore wanted to know more about the portly admirer in white waistcoat and gaiters who rarely missed a show. Prodigal with tips, he had declared his interest last week by sending a bouquet of red roses to 'Mamouna' after the performance.

Minnie wrapped her fingers around her cup and deflected the topic with a question.

'How do you think Thérèse is doing in Paris, with the siege going on? Do you think she's had to eat her pythons?'

Flore shook her head. 'Pythons eat rats, she told me. They'll be easy to feed.'

'That's if there's any rats left. That's all they've got to eat now.'

Something, or rather someone on the other side of the glass caught Minnie's attention. Her mouth fell open.

Flore followed her gaze. A couple were crossing the road towards them. The man wore a dark coat, top hat and cream nankeen trousers. Blond, with thin sideburns and a trim moustache, he cut a fine figure.

Minnie's eyes widened.

The couple melted away among the multitude.

'Who was that? Do you know them?'

'Heck, if it wasn't him, it was his double.'

The waitress brought their waffles.

The sweet scent carried Flore back to the day Monsieur Godin had given Adeline a waffle iron of his own design and asked her to try it out. The world was a good place then. Unfortunately, she had been too confused to see it.

She poured maple syrup over her waffle and dipped a finger in it. Mmmm, nectar from heaven. Martial was bound to go crazy with all the new foods. After months of eating horse boiled in dishwater, the poor man would need fattening up.

'Who was it? Did you know him?'

Minnie shook herself. 'I did. He's the man who took me to Paris and dumped me there.'

Flore attacked a waffle. 'You never told me what happened, not really.'

'Bah, what's to tell? It's the old story of the country goose and the urban cad.'

'Hmpf, I know it well,' Flore said between mouthfuls. 'Back home, we have a song about it. My story is the one of the country goose and the soldier.'

'The way I look at it,' Minnie said philosophically, 'he's done me a favour. If he'd kept me as a mistress, I'd be alone again by now, languishing in some garret, waiting for the next man to pick me up, and then what? No. I've learned my lesson. I'll never depend on a man. Ever. I'm going to make it on my own.' She chuckled. 'In fact, I should have run out and shaken his hand.' She leaned forward and whispered, 'I have a plan.'

'Does it involve shaking your derrière and wearing a tiara?'

'Exactly. It involves Monsieur Spats.'

'Spats?'

'Gaiters. The man who sent me the roses.' Minnie's eyes sparkled. 'I think he has money, and I want to help him *invest* some of it.'

'But he's old. Don't you want to fall in love and marry someone nice?' Flore felt foolish as soon as she had spoken.

Minnie spooned cream onto her waffle. 'It never works, though, does it? Not for the likes of us. The best we can hope for is to meet a carpenter or a smith who doesn't drink, and I don't think they exist.' Minnie linked her fingers under her pointy chin. 'You see, girls dream about *love*, but for an ambitious man, marriage is an *investment*. If he wants to rise in life, he'll need to get a wife who'll help him up the ladder.' She sat back and made her point by tapping a finger on the table. 'He'll settle for the one that brings the best returns, and *then* he will search for the goose who will give him the most pleasure.'

It was exactly what Ricar had done, but how could Flore blame him? Crippled as he was, if he had married her, they would be scraping a living in a hovel on the outskirts of Bordeaux, no better than the wretches of the Lower East Side. All Ricar had to his name, as he had put it bluntly, were his shaft and his knife, and he had certainly made good use of the former. Adèle was pregnant.

Was Martial ambitious? He was, in his own way, but for him, it was different. He had money.

'Martial is not like that.'

'Martial's a dreamer. He's put you on a pedestal. You're lucky that he's so struck with you, but once you're together, you'll have to be the one with your feet on the ground while he goes around chasing clouds.'

'Is that how you see us?' Strange, so had Héloïse, all the way from the past.

'Definitely. He is not of this world.'

Flore's face fell. 'What if he never comes? That siege has been going on for *months*! They must be at their wit's end by now.' She heaved a long sigh. 'I wonder about those brave enough to escape in hot air balloons . . . so horribly dangerous. Imagine, they leave at night and never know where they will land. I read that the balloons are loaded with mail and pigeons that will bring messages back.'

Minnie grinned. 'Do you think he'll try and escape in a balloon?'

'No. Martial would never desert Paris.'

'Shame pigeons don't fly that far, huh?'

Flore smiled. Pigeons might not make it all the way to New York, but she'd just had an idea.

41
A MESSAGE ARRIVES BY PIGEON POST

'Monsieur Jules! Monsieur Jules! A message has arrived! By pigeon!' Bastien, the groom, ran into the courtyard holding a letter.

Martial strode out of the stable and caught a glimpse of his name, calligraphed next to his cousin's on the envelope. His heart leapt and fluttered for a hopeful moment. He tried to snatch the letter, but, encumbered as he was by cape, gloves and hat, Jules beat him to it.

How could a *letter* arrive here, Martial wondered, when the Germans had isolated Paris so thoroughly the city might as well be marooned in Siberia? Not only had the enemy cut the telegraph line, aerostats only ever went *out,* and very few pigeons ever flew back to their loft. Anyone caught sneaking out of the walls was detained and shot.

Postmen had been laid off, so how on earth had this letter made its way here?

Jules opened the letter and ran into the hall, shouting, 'Gontran is alive! He is sending us a message!'

Madame Leboeuf bustled out of the kitchen, wiping her hands on her apron. Bastien sat on the stairs at Jules's feet, his face glowing from the miracle he had carried into the house.

Violette's maid ran up past Martial and rapped urgently on her mistress's door.

Jules unfolded the paper and scanned his expectant audience. The chilly hall was still decorated with ivy as a nod to a Christmas that had been anything but merry.

'What happened, monsieur?' Bastien could not contain himself.

On the mezzanine, Violette's door opened. She tightened her robe, leaned over the banister and peered down at Jules. Her maid stood in the shadows.

Arthur came out of the kitchen in waistcoat and thick cotton shirt. To save on heating, he had been allowed to bring the *mairie*'s ledgers home.

The valet posted himself by the stairs.

'*Bon sang! C'est incroyable!* They landed in Norway!'

Martial choked. Violette squeaked.

'Sorry, sir, where is that?' the groom asked.

'A cold snowy country in the north, Bastien. A thousand kilometres off course. They were lucky.' Jules held out the letter and read, *'At one point, we dropped so close to the waves we were terrified they would engulf us. So, with no more ballast to discard, we had no choice but to cast a hundred kilo bag of mail overboard.'*

Martial's stomach lurched. Had the ballast contained his letter to Flore?

'Thankfully, a ship had seen us and picked up the bag. The wind blew us further north. Our clothes hard as leather with the cold, and our hair and faces covered in ice, we found ourselves above the clouds. The gas expanding in the heat of the morning sun threatened to burst our balloon. Poor Rolier had to climb up the ropes with frozen fingers to open the flap and let some of the gas out.

'Imagine our relief when we descended into a forest and landed in soft snow. We jumped out, vexed to see our aerostat whipped up by a gust, taking with it the last of our resources! Luck was on our side, and we found refuge and food in a hunter's cabin half-buried in snow. We were rescued the next day and marched into a village under a triumphal arch of boughs. France is well loved in those regions, and it is comforting to know that those brave Norwegians are praying for our victory.'

His breath coming in small puffs, Arthur interrupted Jules to explain: 'This letter, together with official communications and other messages, was assembled in an office in Tours, photographed, then the whole thing reduced to the size of a postage stamp, rolled up inside a goose feather and attached to a pigeon's tail.'

'You mean the pigeon did not carry it in its claws?'

Bastien's comment went some way to warm up the atmosphere.

'No, Bastien, it is much more interesting than that,' Arthur said charitably. 'As soon as the pigeon returned to its Paris loft, the quill was removed, the film unrolled, projected onto a screen and copied down onto paper by a clerk. Which is why,' he looked at every one in turn, 'it is not written in Monsieur Gontran's hand.'

Jules carried on reading. *'We had landed near Christiania. Eventually, we were taken to the English ambassador, who telegraphed the secret information we were carrying directly to Gambetta.'*

'Oh.' Jules frowned. 'A sentence seems to be missing here.'

'Hmm, must have written something that was censored.' Arthur did not seem surprised.

'After our odyssey,' Jules read on, *'I just wanted you to know that we are alive and well. I have never enjoyed myself so much. You should try it! Your friend, Gontran.'*

Violette was coming down the stairs. 'Hold on!' She held

out a hand. 'There is another page.' She pinched the letter from her cousin and blew between the sheets. 'Yes! Here it is. Now, let's see.' She met Martial's eyes with a grin and was about to read out the rest when all the restraint hammered into him by six years of seminary just gave way. With a growl, he snatched the paper and ran up to his room.

What were the chances, he marvelled as he pushed his door with a shoulder, of a message written in New York reaching him here, when so few pigeons ever made it through enemy lines? A realisation stopped him. What if it was from Hugo? Had he been wounded? Taken prisoner?

Wrapped in his eiderdown, Martial focussed on the letter, surprised to see that it was from Alfred Lecomte, the young accountant from the Godin factory.

Dear Martial, we hope this letter finds you in good health. We follow the scant news we receive from Paris with great interest. Flore telegraphed us to say that she was in New York with her American friend, that they work together in a theatre and that she is well. She asked us to tell you that she prays for you every day. You have remained in Paris to do your duty for France. We did not expect less of you, but news from the siege is not good and you are in our thoughts.

A whimper escaped him. He sank his face into his hands, overcome with relief. Flore still had feelings for him!

The Prussians arrived here a few weeks after you left, took over our factory and held Monsieur Godin hostage for three days before releasing him. They took all they could get their hands on to make weapons and all our supplies to feed their army. They found everything we had hidden in the cellars. It was devastating, but then again, we survived and never had to eat rats.

Perhaps you will not be surprised to learn that I have proposed to Adeline. She has agreed, and we hope to be married as soon as this war is over. Please join us in prayer for the fate of our native

Alsace and for Lorraine, which has never looked so bleak. What will we do if our families become German?

We hold you in our hearts,

Your friends, Alfred and Adeline

PS: Monsieur Godin sends his warmest regards.

A meteor shower exploded inside Martial's veins and lit up the world. Flore had not given up on him. Oh, how long would it be until he saw her again? He paced around his room, wanting to push away the walls. The temptation to fly away in an aerostat gnawed at him, but what would be the point when the Germans controlled the seas?

According to what he had seen inside the Opera cellars and Arthur's sober assessment, the city would not hold out much longer. They had run out of flour, eaten all the horses, and everywhere the starving poor were baying for Prussian blood, begging their leaders to let them out in a *'sortie torrentielle'*, keen to prove the stuff Parisians were made of.

Night and day, the Prussians shelled the walls and the arrondissements inside them. Jules's hospital had been destroyed and the wounded moved, ironically, to the Bal Bullier.

Why did I not kiss her that night? Martial's mind kept leaping back to their last day together in Paris. *She would be with me now.* And then he came to his senses. *How could I wish this nightmare on my beloved?*

He stood up, pulled the eiderdown tighter around his shoulders and rested his forehead on the ice-patterned glass. The courtyard was empty. The Bretons had been moved to barracks. Of late, national guards were brought into Jules's field hospital with wounds clearly inflicted by Chassepot rifles. French weapons. Stir-crazy battalions were let loose, drunk in the no-man's-land of the razed suburbs. Lacking in training, totally lost, the would-be soldiers charged around taking pot shots at anything that moved. More often than not, they shot each other.

Martial had enough. The one thing that carried him along was Flore, 'utopia made woman', as Jules called her.

He glanced at the letter with a sob of relief. Flore loved him, and she was waiting for him just at the other end of the rainbow.

42

DANGER LURKS IN THE STREET

It was Friday. The Wheel of Fortune was packed. Slumped against the bar, the Russian's leaden gaze was making Flore uncomfortable, glued as it was to her décolleté.

'Making it on your own' was all very well for Minnie. She had Mr Spats to protect her now. Flore wearily lined clean glasses up on the counter. The novelty of the New World was wearing thin.

Vlad was from Russia. It was all she knew. Russia, Ireland, Poland, Flore had heard of them, but where they were, she had no idea, and it bothered her. Once, as they passed a bookshop, Minnie had pointed to a patchwork of colours on a sheet of paper and told Flore that one of them was France. It looked nothing like Martial's hastily drawn sketch in Guise. She wanted to know more, but where would she start?

She filled the glasses with whisky, overcome with shame. *What would Martial want with a bar girl? What if he sees me for who I really am and comes to his senses—will I be stuck here forever?*

'Clodagh, five cents more, please.' Flore stopped the waitress on her way to a table.

'Ah, c'mon on, Flore, dat's all they gave me!'

Flore was getting used to both the girl's accent and her tricks. 'Go back and ask for five cents, or Bill will take it from your wages.'

She missed being called *Mademoiselle Flore*, she missed the respect with which employees were treated at the Godin factory.

Why did the Russian come here at all? she wondered. Slapstick left him cold, he hardly looked at the dancers, and his English was so poor the McCanns' political commentary couldn't mean much to him. Perhaps he was lonely.

Tonight, the shenanigans of the corrupt Mr Tweed of Tammany Hall were supplanted by news that starving Parisians, after four months of siege, had been eating their zoo animals.

Flore absently dried a beer glass, her mind travelling back to the Bois de Boulogne with Martial, gaping at Castor and Pollux. Having run out of hay to feed them, the young elephants had to be shot. When their keepers refused, soldiers had been brought in.

On stage, the duo's rendition of a French couple dining at a Paris restaurant had the room in stitches. Sharp in a tuxedo, hair parted in the middle, imperial moustache waxed to stiletto sharpness, Mac McCann was in his element.

'What takes your fancy, *ma chérie*?' He twiddled his moustache. 'Will you have *potage d'éléphant*? *Pour moi,* I must admit that the *ragout* de wolf in deer sauce appeals to my sense of equity.'

Rouged and plump, wearing one of Minnie's wigs, Mick replied in a high-pitched voice. '*Ooh la la,* so much choice! I 'esitate between the cat with its accompaniment of mouse mousse and the sauté de kangaroo, perhaps—or shall I have roast camel? What do you think, Henri?'

'Nah, I don't want you getting the 'ump.'

Men were slapping their thighs; women cackled and wiped their eyes.

Oblivious to the jokes, Vlad slouched against the bar, gazing at Flore like a lovesick donkey. Because discouraging customers was not something Bill took lightly, Flore held out the vodka bottle and, with a strained smile, refilled his glass.

Meanwhile, the gentleman in spats was casting impatient glances to the side of the stage.

Their set over, the comics took away their props to make way for the final act, while Clodagh and Deirdre went from table to table, encouraging patrons to order a last drink.

The first languorous notes of the accordion drew a gasp of anticipation from the room well before Mamouna's naked foot emerged from the curtain. Whatever Thérèse had taught her back in Paris, Minnie had made her own. Her fame was spreading fast. Straight out of a harem, eyes lined with kohl, lips reddened, she was unrecognisable. Thick dark hair cascading down her back, Mamouna sashayed and shimmied to cheers and whistles, creamy breasts billowing above a fringed bolero, the organza layers of her skirt revealing more than they hid.

Scanning the room for disapproving stares from the Bible brigade, Flore saw lust burning in men's eyes while the few women simply stared.

Monsieur Spats's mouth fell open as his dream girl rattled the beads on her hips and played with feather scarves the way Samira had played with her live boas. She leaned forward and shook her shoulders. Monsieur Spats's eyes popped out of their sockets. She rotated her hips. His Adam's apple bobbed. At the edge of the stage, she lifted her long skirt, slowly, temptingly, and when she ran the feather boa through her naked toes, Monsieur Spats promptly drew his jacket over his crotch.

The accordion wailed to the staccato beat of a single drum.

Slumped against the bar, Vlad was too drunk to care.

Minnie jumped off the stage and twirled around tables, gathering tips as she went. She sashayed, shimmied and shook around her admirer's table, leapt back up the two steps, onto the stage and out to thunderous applause.

How can she just do that? Flore too was mesmerised. It was as if Minnie became a different person.

The show over, people hung around for a while, chatted and finished their drinks. Flore counted the money and handed it to Bill, who locked it in a cast-iron safe.

It had been a good night.

Some time later, Minnie rushed in and whispered, 'Flore, come round the back!'

Flore made her way to the dingy space where the performers were changing, hit by the smell of bodies. Behind the curtain, Mick had taken off his blond wig but still wore his makeup.

'Listen.' Minnie had kept the thick black lines around her eyes and was reapplying rouge to her lips. 'I can't go home with you tonight. You'll have to find someone else to accompany you.'

Flore's throat tightened. 'Huh? Where are you going?'

'Remember I told you I had a plan?'

'A plan to get me killed! How can you just abandon me like that?'

'I'm not abandoning you. The girls will walk you home.'

Furious, Flore stormed back to the bar. Damn Minnie and her 'plan.' She had a pretty good idea of what that plan was about. Never depend on a man—ha!

'Ah, Flore. Good. You're still here.' Bill threw a thick fur coat over his shoulders. 'The girls have gone. Can you sort out the chairs?' He handed her a key. 'Sorry, got to rush.

Mother-in-law staying with us and all that.' He donned his top hat and left the building.

'Wait!' Flore called out to the empty room.

'Clodagh? Deirdre?'

The sound of trotting hoofs reached her from the end of the street. Her shoes rang on the bare planks as she hurried to the changing room in search of the McCann brothers. It was empty. Casting anxious glances into the dark corners, Flore hurriedly gathered the last few glasses, upturned all the chairs, turned off the gaslights, slipped on her coat and gloves and locked the small side door.

A biting wind hit her face. Winter had set in with a vengeance, and the mud that covered the pavements was now solid ice, ice that filled her chest as she pulled up her collar and set off for the mile-long trek home alone, comforting herself with the belief that perhaps miscreants would not be out in this weather. Would they?

She reluctantly left the wide gaslit avenue and rushed home, ears tuned to the night. Heavy steps crunched the ice behind her. She spun around but saw no one.

Quickening her pace, she skidded on the hardened mud. Her heart rate had doubled by now. Head down, she made for the dim pool of light at the end of the street and had nearly reached the boardinghouse when she heard a crunch coming from an alleyway. She swivelled, lost her balance, slipped on a frozen lump and went careering onto a railing. She cried out and picked herself up. A large shape sprang out. In the eerie glow of the streetlight, Flore recognised Vlad's face, congested with vodka and lust. He reached out and grabbed her.

She arched her back and twisted sideways, sickened by his breath. Vlad pawed at her breast and, mumbling in Russian, tried to kiss her. Flore hissed like a wildcat and wriggled out of his grip, but he drew her against him. She pushed him away. His hands were like steel. Whimpering in frustration, she tried to bite him. Only yards from home, she couldn't call out. If she did, Mrs Withers would be pitiless. A boiling rage erupting inside her, Flore threw her head back and slammed her forehead into Vlad's nose. At the same time, she lifted a knee and kicked him in the groin, moves Minnie had taught her in Paris.

The Russian howled and folded over. Flore stamped down on his foot, freed one arm, poked his eyes with two fingers and ran up the steps. Shivering, crying, she reached into her pocket and pulled out the wrong keys. A hand on the railing, Vlad crouched towards her. Flore cursed and tried again, feverishly trying to fit her key into the door. At last, the key turned and she stumbled into Mrs Withers's skeletal arms. Hair wound in *papillotes,* the woman's face was a picture of fury. Trapped between two evils, it took everything Flore had not to slap the woman.

Panting, aching, Flore touched her face. Her fingers were covered in blood. Vlad's blood.

Vacant, bloody and pale, the Russian hovered outside like a ghoul risen from the dead.

Mrs Withers locked the door and glared at her. 'You and your friend will have to find yourselves another place to stay. You have until the end of the week.'

'But he attacked me!' Flore objected in a raucous whisper.

'It would not have happened if you kept respectable hours. There are plenty of decent girls waiting for my rooms. I want you out.'

Flore gripped the banister and stomped up the stairs, cursing the woman, cursing her job and cursing Minnie for abandoning her. If they had to move, how would Martial's letters reach her? How would *he* find her when he came? And if he did not find her, what then?

43
PARIS IS ABLAZE

That terrible January had come to an end, and so had the supplies. Something was different that morning as Martial walked to the crossroad where rue de la Bienfaisance met avenue de Messine. A weak March sun glimmered in shards of frost. Without coal fires and the usual layer of manure, what was left of Paris sparkled, and in spite of the cold, an unaccustomed effervescence animated the square. People stopped to talk to each other. Paper boys ran about, hoarse and excited, shouting the news. 'The siege is over!'

The mood was a mixture of relief and anger. The French government may have capitulated, but Paris had been denied its righteous fight, and fight it would.

In Jules's *hôtel particulier,* hay was delivered just in time to revive poor Gringolet. Bastien, now promoted to coachman, had cried with joy, lifting handfuls of fragrant hay to his nose, offering them to the horse with words of endearment.

A few nights later, warmed by a roaring fire, the yellow salon was once again the hub where the survivors assembled at the end of each day under bright gaslight.

Since she had joined Jules's hospital as a children's nurse, Violette had matured. Under Mary's guidance, she did her best to apply her hygienic practices, regardless of the nuns' frowns of disapproval.

'Jules! Stop teasing me.' Violette pouted. 'How am I ever going to learn anything if every time I ask a question, you make fun of me? Is *proligarous* a swear word? If so, I'm sure that dreadful little man deserves it.'

Tickled by their banter, Martial lifted his head from the sketch he was drawing.

Sleeves rolled up, Jules was nursing a half-drunk cup of coffee, leaning against the window frame, following raindrops running down the panes. He faced his young cousin.

'*Polygamous* is said of a man who has several wives.'

'How can a man have several wives?' Violette asked, round-eyed.

'Are you discussing Monsieur Thiers?' Martial joined in their conversation.

'There, you see.' Violette looked crossly at Martial. 'You too know about him, yet no one had thought to inform me.'

'It's old news, Violette,' Jules said with a weary sigh. 'Our Président de la République started off with one mistress, Eurydice, the wife of a government official. Wanting to keep Eurydice near him, Thiers then married her daughter as soon as she turned fifteen, and, being a man of strong appetites, took her sister into his harem as well.' Ignoring Violette's shocked utterances, he carried on. 'King of the bourgeoisie, our little president has declared war on the Reds and sworn he would destroy them forever.'

The siege had etched weariness on Jules's long face. 'Which is why he has moved his government to Versailles, away from Paris.' The harsh sound of rain pelting the glass added to the sense of doom. 'As you can understand, the

Communards would lynch him if he so much as set foot in the capital.'

Martial was uneasy. On January 28, 1871, the Paris siege had been lifted and the Prussians marched into Paris. Bismarck had declared that Alsace and Lorraine were now part of Germany. France had been given hefty war reparations to pay.

The atmosphere in Paris was one of disbelief. Prussians camping on the Champs Elysées were a shocking sight for all those who had suffered for four months, all the while denied the chance to fight.

The government remained in Versailles, more terrified of Paris than of any Prussian.

The siege may be over, but for the working man—not that any men were working—nothing had changed. Workshops yet had to reopen, and since the national guards were not paid any more, half a million men were clamouring for work.

Abandoned by France, Paris had declared itself a 'commune,' a separate entity. The bellicose mood was reaching new heights, stirred up by placards, newspapers and anyone who had a voice in cafés and backroom clubs. The message was clear. France may have surrendered, but Paris would fight on.

'There wouldn't *be* any Reds if things had been dealt with fairly,' Martial remarked. 'To my mind, the best way to appease the situation would be to swap rifles for spades and pay the national guards to repair the bomb damage. There's enough damage to keep them busy for months!' It seemed obvious to him. 'Men are asking for jobs, for dignity, not charity.'

Every day, women and children suffering from malnutrition came to die in Jules and Martial's Bal Bullier field hospital. The *gardes nationaux* had kept their guns. They were trigger happy. Fights erupted at every street corner. Something was bound to give. The Breton contingent was barracked out in the suburbs to stop them from siding with the people.

It was clear to Martial that another revolution was brewing. *I am afraid Minnie was right,* he had written to Flore the previous night. *We are heading for civil war.*

Flore . . . Now that the mail was working again, one of her letters had trickled in at last, so loving, so filled with longing and adorable spelling mistakes, and he had made up his mind. America beckoned. Sadly, naval traffic had not yet resumed and he was still needed in Paris.

They did not have to wait long. A few days later, Arthur rushed in, his hair curled tight by the rain. He handed the maid his umbrella and shook off his wet coat. *'Oh la la, ça va chauffer!'* He called the maid back. 'Rosine, bring us some more coffee!' He handed her his wet gloves and went to the fire. 'The Versailles government has sent Paris an ultimatum.' The gravity of the situation reflected on his face, he looked at each of them in turn and allowed a moment of silence before dropping his bombshell. 'All rents that were frozen during the siege have to be paid. Including the six months of arrears.'

'What?' Jules's cup clattered down on his saucer. *'Nom de Dieu!* This *is* a provocation. Parisians have been out of work for months! They have no money. Thiers wants to destroy them!'

'There is worse.' Arthur slumped into a chair, his lips curled into a grimace. 'Our *mairie* has received notification to stop paying the Garde Nationale the *salaire de misère* that was keeping them alive.'

'That man is evil,' Martial growled. 'But he's not alone. Listen.' He picked up a paper and read out, *'Chancellor von Bismarck has released the eighty thousand French soldiers he was holding prisoner.*' He flung the paper down. 'Can you *believe* it? Those two have ganged up together. Bismarck is just as terrified of socialism as Thiers is! They will let those soldiers loose on Paris.

'Now the gates of Paris are open, the evil comes from our own government!' Martial sunk his face into his hand and said in a half-sob, 'All they had to do was to set up patrols and pay them to repair Paris. Instead, they're orchestrating a genocide.'

A few days later, Bastien was getting the hackney ready to take Martial and Jules to the hospital when Violette ran to them.

'Wait for me! Am I not going with you today?'

Jules placed both hands on her shoulders. 'Sorry. Paris is burning, Violette. It's best you stay safe. There's shooting in the streets. People get caught in crossfire. I should know, I'm treating shopkeepers and babies for shot wounds. It really is dangerous.'

Violette bit her lip. She had learned her lesson.

Martial now saw a different girl. Clad in a simple skirt and white blouse, her hair in a bun, gone was the spoiled china doll. As soon as the Paris gates had opened, the dandy duke and his friends had fled back to their estates. Free from the influence of Léontine, Violette had bonded with other nurses, and one by one, the prejudices absorbed at the convent were replaced by valuable life experience.

'Listen,' she whispered to Jules as he was about to climb into the carriage, 'there is a little boy, his name is Anatole . . .' She was speaking so low Martial could not catch everything. 'Will you? I promised him.'

'Je vais m'en occuper.' Jules patted her hand. 'I'll deal with it. Don't worry.'

'What was that about?' Martial asked once they were on the way.

'Anatole has a bad case of worms. Violette discovered them squirming like noodles at the bottom of his night pot. She wanted to know what could be done about them. He's very undernourished.'

'Who would have thought, huh? Our Violette coping with worms, scabies and diarrhoea without fainting.'

'Yes.' Jules gazed at the devastation around them. 'Bernard's death has deeply affected her. She blames herself, of course. I think she is trying to atone.'

'Hmm,' Martial mumbled. 'You might be right.' Jules would never know the truth.

'Listen, I didn't want to mention it around Violette,' Jules settled himself deep inside the hackney, 'but have you heard what happened in the Parc des Buttes-Chaumont the other day?'

'What in particular? So many horrors happen every day.'

'There was a demonstration. The army was told to shoot.' Jules ran a hand over his eyes. 'They shot into the crowd. Massacred everyone. Women, children, old people.' He let out a long breath, struggling to carry on. Martial scanned his cousin's face. It took a lot to upset Jules.

'They didn't know what to do with the bodies, so they threw them into the lake they have there.' Haunted, Jules struggled to find the words. 'Today, the decomposing bodies floated back up. They had to be fished out and a mass grave dug for them.' His eyes went to Martial, as if hoping he could wake him up from the nightmare. 'They called me over yesterday. Four hundred bodies, Martial. Four hundred . . .'

Martial didn't reply. The last tenuous thread that anchored him to God snapped.

Jules patted his leg. 'Time you went home, Martial. It's not safe for you here, not in that cassock anyway.'

'Not safe for anyone,' Martial replied. 'One denunciation and pfft! You're pushed against a wall and shot for a spy, no questions asked. A spy for the Reds or for the Prussians, it won't matter. Be careful what you say, Jules. I mean it. A word in the wrong ear . . .'

A stench of burning pervaded the air. They pulled their scarves over their noses.

Gringolet whinnied and stalled, ears flat against his head. Bastien shouted a command. The whip whistled above their heads.

Around them, Paris was burning. Every day, the army threw incendiary bombs at the rebels. In retaliation, the Communards torched every symbol of the monarchy, toppled statues and tore down ornate fences.

When they reached Pont de l'Alma, caught in a cloud of smoke, the horse sniffed the heat and, eyes wild, tried to turn back.

Bastien called out. 'Monsieur Jules, look to your left!'

Jules and Martial stared in horror. Upstream, the Palais des Tuileries was a wall of flames, the arcades along rue de Rivoli an inferno. Further back, the Louvre was still intact. On the Left Bank, smaller buildings glowed. A firebrand sizzled as it dropped on the carriage roof. Bastien jumped up and brushed it off with a curse. An eerie glow lit up the sky.

'Father . . . there is no hell . . . no afterlife,' a soldier had whispered to Martial as he was giving him the last rites. 'Hell's down here. I've seen it on the battlefield.' His words haunted Martial. God had abandoned men to their own devices, to their own vices.

The last scorched trees rose like charred fists. Bled dry, Paris howled with pain, cursing a heaven that God had deserted.

Jules heaved a long sigh. 'I'm tired, Martial. Tired to my bones, tired to the very bottom of my soul. It will take me a lifetime to forget what I've seen during these four months. I thought it would be over when the gates of Paris opened again. Now, I realise it's only just beginning.' His eyes bore into Martial. 'Go. Leave us. You've done your bit.' With a grimace, he barked, 'They shot Darboy. You do know that, don't you?'

Martial didn't answer. The Communards had shot the Archbishop of Paris and six priests. Nerves were frayed. A simple request from the Communards for secular education had escalated into an all-out war against the Catholic Church. Desperate for a scapegoat, the needy had already forgotten who had fed and clothed them throughout the siege.

'Is she waiting for you?'

After a long time, Martial murmured, 'Yes.'

'So you've made up your mind.'

Martial hesitated.

'Get out of that cassock. God is a dangerous commodity at the moment.'

'We'll discuss it tonight.'

'You've tried, Martial, God knows you have, but the Church is not where you'll find what you're looking for. Flore was right to leave. You both need a clean slate, and even if you discover that she isn't the right one for you, you can always—'

'I can't shake off the feeling that we're meant for each other,' Martial said with total candour. 'I have felt it from the first day. It is as if we're . . . predestined, somehow.'

'Give it a go. If you don't try, you'll spend the rest of your life wondering *what if*.'

'I will. I'll buy a ticket for the first steamer.'

'Do you speak German?' Creases appeared at the corner of Jules's eyes.

'Huh?'

'Now Alsace and Lorraine are under German jurisdiction, your steamer will be full of Alsatians running away from Bismarck. They don't speak French.'

'Then those poor souls will have to learn English,' Martial said. 'As I will.' They were approaching the boulevard Saint-Michel. 'I've forgotten the little I learned at school.' He pointed to the boulevard. 'Just tell Bastien to drop me by the bank. I need to change some of those *billets de nécessité.*'

'We'll wait for you.'

'No point. The queues will be dreadful. Now we're back to normal, everyone wants to exchange their *billets* for hard cash. I'll walk to the hospital from here.'

Martial patted the pocket in which he carried his money and passport securely wrapped in oiled-paper.

Jules tapped the roof. Bastien pulled the reins.

'I'll see you in about an hour,' Martial assured Jules with more confidence than he felt and headed for the boulevard Saint-Michel.

Inside the bank, lines of concerned customers waited to withdraw their money. After an hour's wait, Martial was only able to change a small amount. He returned the remaining vouchers to their envelope and lifted his scarf to his nose, though it did nothing to stop the acrid smell that pervaded the city.

Across the river, the fire was raging, and along the quays the booksellers' boxes were smouldering. The heat was so intense it had curled the advertising placards on the *colonnes Morris* that lined the boulevard.

Martial halted. On the other side of the river, inside the Tuileries Palace, beams collapsed in an explosion of glass and plaster. A blast of wind kindled the inferno, whipping a volley of sparks into the skies with a roar. What had Paris done, he wondered, to earn the fire and brimstone of Sodom and Gomorrah?

Martial's eyes widened in horror, hit by a terrible vision. Red, colossal and triumphant, Lucifer rose above the flames across the blazing skies. Struck with total clarity, Martial suddenly understood who was ruling the world.

He turned away, his feet dragging along the cobbles, the cassock nothing more than a magician's masquerade. He was tired, tired of what men did to men, tired of greed and power games. Jules was right. It was time to take stock.

A hansom cab galloped towards him. He lifted a hand. The horse snorted, a hoof just missing his shoe. The cab did not stop.

Worried now, Martial hurried up the boulevard. Apart from a few scavengers rummaging around abandoned houses, the streets were deserted.

Two ruffians detached themselves from a wall where they had been pasting calls to sedition. Their eyes, dull with absinthe, lank hair and torn clothes gave them away as members of the raggle-taggle army of dispossessed that clung to the Commune like leeches, underdogs who set houses on fire and killed gendarmes and nuns just because they could.

One of them rubbed his hands with a sneer. 'Let's go get us some priest!'

They dropped their pots and swaggered towards Martial.

He hesitated, wondering which way to run. He crossed the road, his vision blocked by an omnibus going the wrong way. The hospital was too far for him to reach by foot. Just across the river, the Right Bank was home territory. He spun on his heels.

The two men increased their pace. Martial darted towards the Alma bridge, assuming they would be too drunk to catch him. It soon became clear that, for ruffians, running was second nature. He tried to sprint. The cassock wrapped itself around his legs. By the time he reached the bridge, the drunks were closing in on him. One shot past and blocked his way, eyes burning with hatred. The other rushed forward and, confident he had got his prey, cackled, uncovering blackened teeth.

Panting, his hair over his face—a hot gust had blown his hat into the river—Martial faced his pursuers and took a step back. They came closer, so close he could smell them. He took another step and hit the parapet. Heart racing, his mouth dry, Martial wished he had listened to Jules.

It was too late.

Hunched forward, arms open, the ruffians taunted him. A blade flashed.

A hand on the rough stone, Martial cast a quick glance at the river below. Immune to the apocalypse, huge barges were gliding downstream.

A ruffian lunged out with his knife. Martial crossed himself, swung onto the parapet and stared down at the filthy water. Embers fizzed as they touched the surface.

His last thought was of Flore as she stood on the bridge that night, about to leap into the void. His heart thudding, he slipped down and held on to a ledge, the stone grazing his fingers.

The thug leaned over the wall with a howl of triumph and lifted his knife.

Martial let go.

44
FLORE MOVES HOUSE

Appalled by Flore's attack, the McCann brothers came to her rescue, and just after Christmas, she moved to the attic room of a comfortable brick house at the edge of Greenwich Village that belonged to a friend of theirs, a singer called Theodora.

In Paris, the siege had ended. The reports of street massacres in the press prevented Flore from sleeping, and still there was no news from Martial.

Without him, her future looked bleak, trapped as she was behind a bar, serving drunks, her dreams of becoming independent fast receding.

The move, however, was a huge improvement to her living conditions. The house was lovely, and Theodora, her new landlady, favoured velvet, deep armchairs, thick drapes and had a weakness for fringes and pompoms.

In her early fifties, slim, draped in paisley shawls, she glided over Turkish rugs, followed by her shadow, a silent maid called Betty, who had the darkest skin Flore had ever seen.

Once a beauty and a singer of some repute, Theodora's

portraits dotted around her house were testaments to a glorious past. Once the mistress of a prominent financier, she now lived in genteel poverty, a stark reminder of what awaited Minnie, who had—against her principles—fallen for the rich Abel de Jong, also known as Monsieur Spats.

Christmas at the Wheel had been busy. The ostentation with which the feast was celebrated in New York had baffled Flore. On Christmas Day on the airial, bells would peal loud and joyous over the moor to celebrate the birth of the Redeemer. Some large families might kill a goose, but never had she seen such lavish displays in shop windows and such bounty piled up on grocers' stalls. What was it about the new German fashion of decorating trees?

Minnie had moved in with Monsieur Spats, whose house was, she'd said, 'so lovely and warm you can run around in the buff even when it's snowing outside.'

Flore saw very little of Minnie. She spent what little free time she had studying English, keen to impress Martial when he eventually arrived. He already knew some English, having learned it at school, like all rich boys in Aquitaine.

Today, her free day, Flore was sitting in the parlour twirling a large sphere, the purpose of which escaped her. Outside, snowflakes stuck to the window, conjuring up a disturbing picture of Minnie running naked around a lavishly furnished mansion while outside the world froze, pursued by her admirer . . . wearing nothing but spats,

Theodora looked up from her embroidery. Heat crept to Flore's cheeks, but she had to ask. 'What is this?'

Theodora sat next to her and ran elegant fingers over the globe. 'This represents the world. Look, here is France, can you see it?'

Flore bit her lip. All she could see were blobs of colour.

'Blue represents the oceans and brown the continents. New York is here, on this side of America. When you came over by ship, you left France.' Theodora slowly trailed a finger across the blue. 'It took you a whole week and a half to cross this expanse of water. Now, if you were to cross America by train to get to, say, San Francisco, it would take you just under four days.'

'How about Russia?' Flore was beginning to understand.

Theodora tapped the top of the globe. 'Russia is a very big country, very cold too. Both extremities of the world are iced over. See the white? Actually, we've just purchased Alaska—here—from Russia. Alaska is nothing but snow, but as you can see, it will act as a buffer between our two countries.'

'Would Cochinchina be around the middle of the globe? I know it's hot there.' Sparks lit up inside Flore's mind as place names converted into shapes.

Theodora showed her Africa, where Betty's ancestors came from, and China. Finally, she pointed to Germany and explained how close it was to Alsace and why Chancellor Bismarck had wanted to acquire it.

'If you are interested in discovering these countries, there is a show called *Stereopticon,* where pictures are projected onto a very large screen. It's quite extraordinary.'

'Is it expensive?' Flore blushed again.

'Not really. Why don't we go together one day? I would like that.' Theodora's features softened. 'Your English is good, Flore. How are you getting on with writing our language?'

Flore shrugged. 'I tried to read the newspaper when I lived with Minnie, but it was difficult.' She added, 'I need to learn to write English if I'm to get anywhere, I know that.'

'Perhaps I can help.' Theodora's blue eyes creased into a smile. She went to a shelf and returned with a schoolbook. 'This is what I used to teach Betty. When she was a girl, slaves were forbidden to read and write, but she is bright and took to it like a duck to water.'

A knock on the door interrupted them. The sound of

Betty's steps and voices in the hall. Flore's heart missed a beat . . . and settled back into its lacklustre routine of beating only for herself. It couldn't possibly be—

'Well, well, what have we here?' Mick McCann waddled in, his cheeks reddened by the frost. 'Aha, I see you are educating yourself, dear girl.' He filled the room with his bubbling personality. 'Very wise. Very timely too. I just saw Minnie with the Tube. You might be promoted soon.'

Flore waited for explanations. She liked the comic duo, but their repartees always eluded her. She was glad when Theodora asked, 'Why do you call him the Tube?'

The parlour door let in Mac, handing Betty his snow-covered hat and gloves. Lanky, Mac's thick mousy hair and large moustache were a contrast to Mick's bald plumpness.

'He's Dutch, you see,' Mac said by way of an explanation.

'You are talking about Monsieur De Jong?' Flore ventured. Minnie's new beau—not that 'beau' fitted the man, who was neither handsome nor young—was of Dutch extraction.

'No, I don't see,' Theodora said.

'A tube is a hole in a cylinder . . .' Mac began.

'And De Jong is a silly Hollander!' Mick's stomach shook at his own joke.

Flore repressed a groan. The quip had, once again, totally bypassed her.

Minnie had explained to her that the McCanns were not brothers but a couple. Their life was an incessant string of puns and political satire that made Flore's head spin.

Mac rubbed his hands. 'We are the bearers of momentous news. We shall all be drinking champagne very soon.'

'How so?'

The answer to Theodora's question was delayed by the arrival of tea and cake.

Tea was a ritual, Flore had been told, an English fashion, a moment of elegance that punctuated the day. She was totally converted. At Theodora's, drinking tea made her feel classy.

Having forgotten the news he was to announce, Mac said to Flore, 'De Jong has patented a way to heat a whole house. He calls it 'central heating'.'

'Oh! I have heard of it.' Theodora rubbed her hands together. 'A wonderful idea.'

'Why the man needs central heating when he has a hot wench like Minnie escapes me.' Mick tittered. 'But she is set on making his fortune.'

'Do you not mean *he* is set on making *her* fortune?' Theodora questioned as she poured the tea.

'One would think so.' Mac's eyes twinkled. 'But on advice from Minnie, Bill Moreton has sold the Wheel of Fortune and bought a failing theatre on the corner of Union Square and Fourteenth Street with the help of De Jong's money.'

Mick rolled his eyes suggestively. 'With Minnie as an "arts adviser", the acts will be getting naughtier.'

Flore knitted her brow. 'Why do you say naughtier?'

'She's bringing the can-can to New York.'

'But we already dance the can-can at the Wheel!'

'Minnie's thinking of lines of girls twirling their legs just a *little higher* than they do in Moreton's barn, and décolletés that are just a *little lower*. There will be burlesque acts, copied from London, you know, farce, that sort of thing. She will carry on with her own exotic dancing, removing, it seems, one or two layers. Thank God the McCann Brothers are still on the menu.'

'We won't be removing anything,' Mac said primly.

'We'll always have something to ruminate about,' Mick stated with a philosophical sigh. 'Sadly, our own milch cow is facing slaughter. If Tweed goes udder, so do we.'

Theodora tittered at the pun. 'Cheer up, boys, New York

is full of villains. Just like our sidewalks, you two will never run out of muck.'

'Why do you say that?' Flore asked.

'City's run by quockerwodgers.' Mac's moustache drooped in disgust. 'Remodelling the law courts has cost us more than the Alaska purchase. But what can you do? As soon as anyone threatens to expose Mr Tweed, they're paid off to keep quiet.'

'We've exposed him so many times,' Mick sighed, 'but all we got were rotten tomatoes.'

'I remember the tomatoes,' Flore said, amazed to have followed a whole conversation. 'Clodagh and Deidre had never seen tomatoes before!'

She sipped her tea, wondering why Minnie had not shared news of the theatre purchase with her.

'When does Moreton plan to open the new theatre?' Theodora too was curious.

'At the end of the month, I think.' Mick could not hide his excitement. 'No more rowdy carousing around the saloon. Seats only, boxes and balconies. A proper theatre. A step up in the world and no mistake.'

No more bar? Flore hid her disappointment behind her cup. She did not particularly like working there, but she needed the money. A cold trickle of dread ran through her stomach. She still had not received any word from Martial. Now she had moved to Greenwich Village, how would he find her? What if he was wounded—or worse? Her throat closed up. What if both Jules and Martial had been caught in street massacres? How would she ever know?

45
MARTIAL BECOMES A TARGET

Martial's fingers slipped against the rough stone. He braced himself for the shock of cold water but was instead swallowed inside a tarpaulin that sucked him into its folds. The world went dark. He pulled at the canvas and looked up, his heart thumping against his ribs. In a few seconds, the barge onto which he had dropped would emerge on the other side of the bridge.

He dived into a pile of hay and pulled the cover over him, the sound of his own heart pumping inside his ears. Disoriented, breathless, Martial peered out just in time to catch sight of his attackers leaning over the parapet, looking the other way.

A burst of anger boiled in the pit of his stomach, scorching hatred for the two men, laughing, pointing at his cape, floating on the surface. Had the world gone mad? What falsehood had those wretches been fed to turn against the Church that had kept them alive for the past seven months?

Once his anger had abated, Martial remembered his own misgivings. How uncomfortable he had felt with the ambiguous role he had been expected to play, absolving the rich and promising the poor a glorious afterlife for bearing their cares without complaint.

He crawled out of the hay and leaned against the prow. A bitter wind scooped up clouds of smoke and slapped them down onto the river. Martial blew the acrid smoke from his nose.

The barge was sailing downstream with its cargo of hay, westward towards the last bridge. Soon they would be out of the walls. Who required so much hay in these parts?

Beyond the Pont d'Iéna were the Champs de Mars fields and, on the other bank, the dome of the Ecole Militaire. How far was he from Jules's house? Martial ran over the geography of the city in his mind.

Some days, when his bedroom window was open, a southern wind would carry the sounds of shooting and manoeuvres from the military school training ground across the river. The cavalry! This was where the hay was headed.

A plan formed inside his mind. While the hay was being unloaded, he would creep out of the barge, cross the bridge and, within half an hour, he would be home. A conservative area, the west was free from rebels.

The weight fell from his shoulders. It had been a close call. The barge had saved his life, for if the drop into the freezing water had not killed him, or his clothes not dragged him down, the thugs would have been waiting for him on the bank.

As they got closer, he peered out again and cursed under his breath. The parade grounds were crawling with soldiers in red-and-blue uniforms, while across the river cannons were being lined up along the Trocadéro Heights by a rabble of men wearing red armbands.

He would never get past them.

Brushing the worst of the hay from his hair and clothes, he clutched his way to the cabin. Inside, the bargeman was standing at the helm chatting to his wife, who sat behind him breastfeeding an infant.

Martial cleared his throat. 'Excuse me.'

The woman screamed.

The *marinier* looked him up and down. '*Bonjour, mon père.* Fell from the sky, did you?

'I did, actually.' Martial pushed his hands into his pockets and explained, 'I was set upon on the Pont de l'Alma, thrown into the water by ruffians and, well . . . I just came to thank you for saving my life.'

'Communards after you?' The captain pointed to the battery assembled on the hill. 'They're mad as wasps up there. You weren't hoping to get off here, were you?'

'I haven't had much time to think,' Martial admitted. 'I don't want to put you in any danger.'

The woman stared at him like a frightened doe.

'Hmm.' The captain gave the wheel a sharp turn. 'I'll be unloading in a minute, so you can't hide under the tarp.' He lifted his cap and scratched his head. 'Step down into the hold with the horse.'

'You carry a horse?'

'You might be moved by the Holy Spirit, but us mortals need traction of a different kind. The wife will show you.'

Martial followed the woman to the hold. She pointed to a narrow space, a few bales of straw piled between the hull and a huge cart horse.

'Marengo won't mind. Moreau will fetch you when we've cleared the toll.' She hurried away.

Martial sat on a bale, his head in his hands. By now, Jules must be going insane, wondering where he was. Perhaps he could escape as soon as the barge reached the Chatou locks; but every time he came up with a plan, Martial reached the same conclusion. He would never make it home. As long as he wore the cassock, his life was in danger. With President

Thiers pointing his guns at Paris, it had become 'them and us', and Martial was in the wrong camp.

He leaned against the hull with nothing to disturb him but the odd shout, the creaks of the winch and bumps against the stone quay. Next to him, Gringolet snorted and shuffled. An easterly wind carried roars and explosions in the distance.

A few hours later, Martial followed the mariner to the wheel room.

'I need to send a telegram to my friends, or they will assume the worst.' He pointed to his cassock. 'The mob has turned against the Church. Would you have some clothes I could hire from you for a couple of hours?'

Moreau looked at his wife, who nodded.

Once they had docked, wearing wide trousers and dark blue cap, Martial hurried away in search of a telegraph machine, relieved to find one in a suburb razed by the war, where the only sign of life was a Prussian encampment. He first cabled Jules, both at the hospital and at home, and told him where he was.

He also sent a brief message to Flore, addressed to her boardinghouse, care of Mrs Withers.

Money. He needed more money. In the small-town bank, he managed to exchange the last of his *billets de nécessité* under the distrustful gaze of the employee, unable to equate the rough clothes with Martial's educated southern accent.

'Could I have the balance of my account?' Unsure of Ricar's shenanigans, Martial was keen to check the state of his finances.

'*Je regrette, monsieur.*' The employee checked the *billets* again before exchanging them for cash. 'The war has disturbed our communications. I suggest you try a bigger bank, in Rouen or Le Havre.'

Martial grabbed the notes and stormed out.

How much money did he have at his disposal? What had really taken place that day in Guise? Had his father wanted a power of attorney, or was it one of Ricar's tricks? Martial stopped in his tracks. Clodomir Mercier! His lawyer would know. Yes, he would write to him at the earliest opportunity.

Moored downstream from the lock, Moreau and Marengo were waiting, the horse munching the long grass by the bank.

'Come up to the cabin and have dinner with us. The wife will want you to bless the babe. It will make her happy.'

'Yes, yes, of course. It's the least I can do.'

Baptisms, blessing babies was an aspect of the ministry Martial knew he would miss, being the vehicle for something greater than himself, the power to grant the important moments of people's lives—baptisms, marriage, funerals—a spiritual dimension. Yes, he would miss that.

The aroma of bacon and cabbage wafted around the wheel room. An orange setting sun seeped through the roof hatch of the barge and melted on the white tablecloth in liquid patches. A pan was bubbling on a small enamelled Godin range. The bed, Martial guessed, was probably tucked into the cupboard to the side. Ornaments on a shelf, a crib and the table covered in thick fabric gave the cabin a touching, cosy feel.

He caught himself envying the mariners. Caught in the daily trauma of the siege, he had forgotten how easy life could be. Every night, he woke up mauled by the guilt of having survived those whose souls he had consigned to God, good men, weighed down by their senseless death, their terror and their tears.

Would Flore still love him, Martial wondered, when she saw what he had become? A skeletal scarecrow who sobbed in his sleep? What kind of life had he to offer her?

'Cider?' Moreau lifted a flagon.

'Gladly.' Martial's throat was parched. He slid down the bench and admired the clear amber of the drink.

'My brother makes it.' Moreau filled two tankards to the top.

'Normandy is reputed for its apples. I come from Bordeaux. My family make wine.'

'Vintners, are they?'

After the smallest of hesitations, Martial replied with a nod. 'We make a rather good red wine, actually.'

Back in Paris, Martial had realised—through conversations with Jules and Gontran—that he did know rather a lot about wine, and not just the drinking of it. Now that he thought of it, did Flore's family not produce the delicious sacramental wine Father Anselme was so fond of?

From this snatch of conversation, a vocation was born. The die was cast. Martial would be a vintner. A smile splitting his face, he lifted his tankard to the mariner. *'A votre santé!'*

Madame Moreau ladled soup into their plates. She sat down and joined her hands when Martial said grace and rewarded him with a shy smile when he told her it was the best soup he had ever eaten.

The sheer relief at being alive washed over Martial in waves, punctured by the vision of a distressed Jules running around his hospital, searching for him. Paris was burning, and everywhere companies of soldiers were sent in with orders to shoot.

There was nothing to do but wait. The mariner lit petrol lamps and after a few rounds of cards, gave Martial a blanket and wished him good night. Down in the hold, Martial went to sleep, Marengo shuffling softly next to him.

Dawn was just seeping through the slats, when a terrible racket drew him from sleep.

A large carriage drawn by four horses galloped right up

to the barge and halted in an infernal racket, neighing salutes to Marengo, who nickered excitedly.

Through the slats, Martial recognised the silhouette of Bastien, jumping down from his seat, soon followed by Violette, who collapsed into Martial's arms.

'Martial! You're alive!'

'By the grace of God, I am, Violette. What are you . . .' Brushing the straw from his borrowed clothes, he glanced into the carriage.

Mary stepped down and held out her arms to an exhausted Jules. 'See, Jules, your cousin is fine. Careful how you go now.'

Jules stumbled towards Martial. 'I thought you were dead,' he sobbed. 'I should never have left you. I knew . . . I knew.' His shaking fingers dug into Martial's back.

'What happened?' Martial held Jules tight, surprised at how thin he had become.

On the barge, Moreau cleared his throat. 'Sorry, Father, but if I don't make the next lock by nine . . .'

Martial returned the clothes and waved as the mariner sailed downriver with a few more francs in his pockets and a tale to tell, of a priest who had fallen from Heaven right into his barge.

'Violette,' Martial pointed to the cassock that had nearly cost him his life, 'I need to change. Is there anything else I could . . .'

'Of course! The servants packed your trunk. We left Paris at first light. See? Here it is, tied it to the back of the carriage.'

Martial helped Bastien take down the trunk while Jules sat on the grass, his eyes glassy and damp.

'I'm afraid your disappearance was the last straw for him.' Mary took Martial aside. 'He needs to rest. Violette and I thought, a decision we came to as soon as we received your message, that it would be best for him to spend time at her parents' manor in Normandy.'

On the bank, Jules was sobbing, Violette kneeling near him.

'But the hospital, the nuns . . .'

'They have unleashed a revolution, Martial. The crowds are wild. You cannot return there. None of us can.' Mary wiped a quick tear from her cheek. 'The arches of rue de Rivoli are a pile of ashes. The rebels have destroyed the main ministries. Soldiers shoot indiscriminately. Women, children, their orders are simply to kill,' her voice wavered, 'to destroy the Communards to the last one, like rabid dogs.' A sob escaped her. 'After all they've been through.'

Martial removed his cassock. He held it for a moment, remembering his vows, his pledge to God, and realised that everything he had just survived had been in conflict with what he had once believed. He dropped the black cloth to the ground, as one would an old skin, and stepped into the clothes of a man in charge of his own fate.

Together with Mary, he helped Jules back into the carriage and galloped west, towards Rouen. By nightfall, they had reached Romilly and Violette's manor.

The steaming horses rode into the tidy front yard of a traditional building with exposed framework in pure Normandy style. His nose and throat filled with dust Martial jumped off and rubbed his back, sore from sitting on a folding seat. Roads in this part of the world were no better than tracks.

A plump blond woman in a floaty velvet housecoat ran out of the house, backlit by faint gaslight. Madame de Linières.

'Violette! Violette, *ma chérie, c'est toi?*'

'Maman!' Violette ran to her mother's arms.

Madame de Linières lifted Violette's chin, searching her face for signs of hardship. 'Oh, Violette, I've been so worried.'

Martial walked to them and kissed the lady's hand. 'Martial Boyer. I am a relative of Jules. Perhaps—'

'Yes, yes, Violette has told me.' The lady's gaze wandered past him to the carriage, to Bastien, intense . . . searching.

'The news from Paris is not good. The siege has weakened Jules. He is in need of rest. Could we stay with you for the night?'

'Of course.'

Violette tore herself from her mother's arms. 'I'll run in and tell the servants to prepare rooms, Maman.'

'Yes, dear, you do that.' Violette's mother replied absently, still searching the night.

Martial took Madame de Linières aside. 'Madame, I am sorry to be the bearer of bad news. Your coachman, Bernard, was caught in a crossfire.'

'Oh no!' Madame de Linières's eyes widened in horror. She tottered but did not take the hand that Martial offered to support her. With a shuddering breath, she straightened up and turned to her guests. 'Thank you for returning my daughter safe and sound. You are all welcome to stay for as long as you like.'

The following hour was taken up with servants carrying in luggage, warming beds, lighting fires and setting out cold dishes.

By the time the sounds of rushing feet and slamming doors had stopped, it was nearly midnight. Martial gave Jules's door a quiet knock and found him slumped inside in a deep armchair, staring at the flames.

'Mary, you must be exhausted. Will you stay with him tonight, or shall I?' Martial whispered.

'Poor Jules. He is not himself. I have seen this condition before, soldiers brought in from the battlefield, incapable of rational thought.' She got up and rubbed her hands. 'I will stay with him. If you could find us some chamomile tea, sweetened with honey?'

Carrying a candle, Martial went in search of chamomile, but the servants had retired for the night. He hesitated outside the salon, drawn by Violette's soft voice and her mother's sobs. He tiptoed away and, noticing a ray of light under a door, asked a servant for the calming beverage.

'I thought you had died.' Jules took the cup from Martial with an unsteady hand. 'It would have been my fault. I should have insisted, you see, I should—'

'Shh. I'm here. I'm alive, and so are you. We'll have many more days together, I promise.'

'Go, leave France. Go and find Flore. We'll see you off at Le Havre. Mary will stay here for a few days. I have convinced her that Paris is too dangerous.'

'I cabled my parents.' Mary removed Jules's shoes. 'They are relieved to know that I am safe, as you can imagine.' She shook her head. 'You can imagine what the American papers are making of this madness.'

'And the French papers of America.'

By now, Mrs Withers should have relayed his message to Flore.

'Violette will stay here.' Jules's smile turned into a grimace. 'She's had quite enough excitement for a while.'

'We all have.' Martial patted Jules's shoulder. 'It's over now.'

They settled Jules under a soft eiderdown. The pain in Mary's eyes told Martial that she knew the massacre wasn't over, that it would carry on, and that as long as a single Communard remained standing, no one was safe.

46

MINNIE'S CENTRALLY HEATED HOME

A heavy cloak of mist hung over the city. The Wheel of Fortune had closed. Moved to a better location, one Flore worried Martial might not find. Had he written to her?

Her skin crawling with goosebumps, Flore knocked on the door of her old boardinghouse. A shadow darkened the peephole, and as soon as the door cracked open, the smell of mutton and overcooked cabbage took her right back to the bad old days.

'Good afternoon, Mrs Withers.' Flore forced a smile. 'I've come to see if you've received any mail for me?'

'I 'aven't.' The woman went to close the door, but Flore stuck her foot in.

'If someone comes for me, will you tell him that I have moved to the address I gave you?'

Mrs Withers just shrugged.

'I work at the Wheel of Fortune. We've moved to the corner of Union Square.'

'I know where you work.' The woman grimaced. 'Should be ashamed of yourself.'

'Goodbye, Mrs Withers.' Flore turned away and hissed under her breath, *'Ratchasse.'*

She rode an omnibus that took her further north, to a compact white stucco mansion fronted with columns: Abel De Jong's centrally heated home. She had not seen Minnie for a while and had a few questions to ask her.

She dropped the heavy door knocker and listened as it reverberated around the hall.

A young maid in uniform opened the door with a smile of welcome. 'Miss Flore? Miss Minnie is expecting you.'

Flore followed the maid up the grand staircase and into a small boudoir, where Minnie was lying on a fur-lined daybed clad in a silk gown, her thick hair tumbling around her shoulders.

'Aw, Flore, it's so good to *see* you!' Minnie gave her two loud orange blossom-scented kisses.

'So much for never falling into the clutches of a man,' Flore remarked in French, unable to keep the bitterness from her voice.

'Ah, but you are wrong.' Minnie adjusted her robe. 'Abel has fallen into mine.'

Flore lowered herself onto an elegant chair, tickled to see that, upholstered in yellow silk, the boudoir was the exact copy of Jules's *salon* once glimpsed in Paris. The only difference was the soft warmth pervading the room and the fact that, back in Paris, the precious Violette, brought up by frigid nuns, would never have been caught lounging about half-naked on furs.

'It's not what you think, Florette.'

''Course not. It never is.'

'Aw, give me a bit of credit, will you?'

'Look at you and your grand mansion. You'll soon be the New York Païva.'

'Ha! I'm glad you said that.' Minnie shuffled up and rang a

bell. 'That is exactly what I am not. Anyway, that's beside the point.'

'What *is* the point, then?' Flore scrunched up her face. 'The Wheel closed down two weeks ago, the whole theatre is on the move, and though I'm grateful to have kept my bar job, you didn't discuss any of it with me. I thought we were friends.'

'We are friends, and I'm telling you now. I do have a plan, but it's kept me busy.'

The entrance of the maid, bearing tea and cinnamon pastries, went some way to soften Flore's mood.

Minnie grinned. She waited until the maid had gone and said in a conspiratorial tone, 'Abel loves me. He can't get enough of my Oriental dancing. He was worried he couldn't . . . you know.' Minnie's gesture implied a disfunction. 'My dancing has cured that—it's the boas, you see. They excite him, so as long as—'

'Boas?' Was Minnie proposing to dance with serpents?

'My feather boas. He's got a thing about feathers.'

Minnie's comment reminded Flore of a joke Mick had made, to the effect that the Dutchman was neither 'Jong nor Abel'.

'But you said you and men—'

'Yes, well, unlike you, I'm no nun. Women have needs too, in case you haven't noticed.'

Flore had noticed. Nights were torture, but slaking those needs had a price, which Minnie had often said was not worth paying.

'What if you get pregnant?'

Minnie's face fell. 'It won't happen.' She huddled to a corner of the daybed, suddenly vulnerable. 'I was once.' The pain that spilled from those words sent Flore right back to the convent, to Joseta's agony. 'He was the love of my life, the one I followed here all the way from Atlanta. He was ambitious, but I stood in his way. Me and a baby weren't exactly in his plans.' Minnie uttered a heartbreaking sigh. 'I wanted to keep it, Lord knows I did, but I'd have ended up on the street.' Her chin wobbled. 'I got butchered, but I survived. As for diseases, well, the way Abel was before . . . I've nothing to worry about.'

'Oh, Minnie!' Flore scuttled onto the bed and hugged her.

A sweet softness assailed her, melting the armour around her heart. Yesu, how long was it since she had held anyone? The memory of Nanette surged from the depth of her soul. Overcome with nostalgia, Flore crumpled into Minnie's arms.

'Darlin', what is the matter? What did I say?' Minnie caressed her hair. 'What's wrong?'

'I . . .' Flore mumbled, incoherent with grief. 'You haven't been talking to me all week, I've no news from Martial, and I —I miss my sister. Sometimes, I miss her so much I can hardly bear it, and I thought you were trying to get rid of me, and I would be here all alone in America. Oh God, I don't know what I thought.' The pain came at her in spurts, a black festering pus seeping from an abscess Minnie had unwittingly lanced.

She tenderly dried Flore's cheeks and held her at arm's length.

'Now, listen to me and listen to me good. Here's the plan. I won't be a dancing girl forever. La Païva may have three mansions, but she will die poor, and I'll tell you why. Her reason for living is to impress, to spend, to fill some gap that can't be filled. Mine is to run a theatre. Not a grand theatre with Alexander Dumas and stuff, but a place where people can forget how bad their life is for an hour or two.' Minnie glanced at the door and lowered her voice. 'Abel loves me. He buys me diamonds. I told him I love emeralds, to go with my green eyes, so he showers me with emeralds.

Of course, he wants me to wear them. So every time he buys me a jewel, I have the stone copied. I wear the copy and sell the real one, at a good price, mind—I know what these things are worth—and I invest the money in my theatre.'

Minnie sat back and contemplated her elegant boudoir.

'He knows I get a percentage as a "creative director", but he doesn't know how much. I decide on the casting and the acts.' She shuffled forwards and whispered, her eyes sparkling, 'Bill and I want to take burlesque to the next level.'

'Huh?' Flore blew her nose. What was Minnie talking about? '*Burlesque* means *bouffonerie, une farce, absurde et ridicule.* The McCanns are great buffoons, but where exactly do you think buffoonery is going take you? Even if you get Mick and Mac to dance the McCann can-can, it won't take New York by storm, will it?'

Minnie burst out laughing. 'The McCann can-can! Haha! I can just see them romping about, joining the real dancers. That is precious.' She sat up and patted Flore's knee. 'I'll take you up on it.'

'That's all burlesque is.'

Minnie put her arms behind her head and stared at Flore with an amused glance.

'Florette, nobody knows or cares what burlesque means. Like the can-can, like my dancing, it's exotic, it's different, and it's French, so people assume it's racy.'

'I heard about your can-can. If you're thinking of dancing in open bloomers—'

Minnie cracked up. 'Open bloomers! Ah, you are a funny one.' She shook her head. 'Listen, just before we left, the can-can was spreading around Paris like wildfire, so I decided I'd bring it to New York and push it past the Bible brigade. Thing is, I need financial backup. Actually,' she leaned close to Flore, 'I have a plan for you too.'

Flore crossed her arms. 'No. I'm not taking my clothes off, and I can't do the splits.'

'Shame, you'd make a mint.' Minnie sat up, suddenly serious. 'You've got a good head for figures.'

Flore touched her face. *'Ma figure?'* What did her head and her face have to do with anything?

'*Figures* means *numbers* in English. You're good at counting, right?'

Flore nodded, wondering where this was leading.

'Here's what I propose. You could be our accountant. You learned accountancy, didn't you, back when you were working with God, or whatever his name was?'

'Godin. Yes, I did, but he didn't approve of fraud. At the Wheel, Bill was paying graft to the local ringsters, and he gave money to the Bible brigade to "pray for our sins". He sold home-made whisky and never paid any tax. He tells me it's normal in New York, but it isn't normal for me, Minnie. It's wrong, and if you—'

Minnie brushed away Flore's concerns. 'Things have changed. The new Wheel is a respectable establishment. Listen, I thought Martial might like to invest some of his . . . income. We could go into business together.'

Distracted by the scent of the cinnamon pastries, Flore picked up the teapot.

'Why don't we have some of your delicious pastries, milady?' She poured them a cup, placed the fragrant pastries on gilt-edged saucers and met Minnie's gaze. 'I trust your business sense. I know your new theatre will do well, but from what I know of Martial, he is more interested in agriculture than culture . . . if he comes, that is.'

Minnie giggled at the use of *culture*. 'Of course he'll come. Wild horses couldn't keep him away. I'd stake my life on it.'

'Well then, when he comes, we'll ask him.' Flore's voice

wobbled. 'I can't understand why he hasn't written.' Her eyes filled with tears. 'On Minnie, what if he's—'

'Don't fret, *chouchou*. There will be a perfectly good explanation. There always is.'

The two women ate their pastries in companionable silence.

Flore unbuttoned her jacket and fanned herself. 'Phew. It's hot in here.'

47
MARTIAL MEETS GUY BROUSSARD

Martial peered into the distance, willing the skyline to reveal what hid behind the dense fog. It has been a week since Jules and Mary had waved him off on the steamer.

Violette had wanted to accompany them, but Martial had pointed out tactfully that Jules and Mary did not need a chaperone. As much as he had learned to appreciate Violette, the idea of spending hours on the folding seat inside the carriage with her filled him with horror.

Soon, Mary too would take the boat. Her life was in America, where she wanted to help other women study medicine. However, she had agreed to stay with her patient until he was better.

Suddenly, the salty mist lifted to reveal the circular Castle Garden Fort, the symbol of New York that greeted all newcomers. Martial stood by the railings, each breath of salted sea air filling him with a happiness such as he had never known. Soon, he would be with Flore.

'So a new life for you, huh?' Guy was a businessman from Bordeaux looking for opportunities in New York. Martial had spent most of the week with him and his young wife, a lively brunette.

They had been good company and, having avoided the siege, proved a welcome distraction. Martial had not revealed his full name to them. He had simply told them that he was from a family of vintners, heading for California to set up a vineyard.

Before he left, he had been in communication with Icaria, a French utopian settlement in Illinois famous for their wine. He hoped to make a halt there.

The ship blew its horn, and Martial's heart dissolved. After years of longing, months of waiting, hurting, dreaming and a brush with death, somewhere inside this mess of bricks and humanity, Flore was within reach at last, and tonight . . . tonight, she would be in his arms.

'Nearly there, Boyer.' Guy Broussard held out a hand. 'It was good to meet you. Shall we see you in New York, or are you heading out straightaway?'

His wife joined them, wrapped in furs. 'Do come and visit, Martial. We would love to see you again.'

'That is very kind of you. Yes, I imagine you will see me again. I look forward to it.'

The horn blew twice, final and authoritative. Sailors scurried around the deck, turning cranks, shouting orders. Bedraggled and smelly, the steerage passengers—Alsatians mostly—huddled on deck and prayed in German.

The Broussards took care to supervise the transfer of their considerable luggage.

His blood fizzing like champagne, Martial stepped out onto the gangway and into his new life. A life with Flore. An honest life, a life without lies.

48
THE WHEEL OF FORTUNE SPINS

Was the cab driver deaf? Martial repeated the address and drank in the strange city, amazed at the human circus, the skin colours, costumes, shawls, fur hats, Cossack boots, capes and leather coats worn by people bustling along the wide streets. Here and there, a grand mansion stood alone atop its own hillock, surrounded on all sides by muddy avenues. As they reached the centre, the architecture became more congruent, and the streets narrower as the cab crawled past wooden houses that had seen better days.

'Wait until I give you a sign.' Martial paid the driver outside a large ramshackle place. 'Maybe I go back with you.'

The man touched his cap.

His heart jumping inside his chest like a demented frog, Martial knocked on the door. A woman in a bonnet with a pinched face opened the door a fraction and squinted.

Martial lifted his hat.

'Madame, I am looking for Miss Flore Laborde. She gave me this address. Is she here?' Yesu, was his throat dry.

'She was 'ere, but she's left, I'm afraid.'

'Oh.' Martial swallowed hard. 'Where is she now?'

'She didn't say.' The woman sneered and went to close the door.

'Wait! She must have given you an address! I have come all the way from France to meet her.'

'I'm afraid you've wasted your journey.'

Martial swayed, steadied himself on the doorjamb and trudged back to the cab.

'Psst, mister!' A window opened above him. A hand motioned him to the side, away from the glare of the landlady scowling at him through the lace curtain.

'Are you looking for Flore and Minnie?'

Hope rushed into Martial's lungs. His breath eased up. The horse took a few steps. Martial signalled to wait.

'They work at a place called the Wheel of Fortune. The cabbie will know where it is.'

'Thank you, mademoiselle!' Martial clambered back into the cab and flopped onto the seat, weak with relief.

The bar smelled of spilled beer and cold tobacco. Flore set out the glasses. Ten minutes left to the interval. Absently, she put a hand to her lace collar, relieved that Bill had agreed to let her wear a less revealing dress. Her brush with Vlad had shaken him too.

Tall, heavily built, grey hair topping a rugged face framed with black sideburns, Bill Moreton had taken to wearing showy waistcoats, a floppy bow tie and, now he was a gentleman of leisure, he enjoyed a chat with his patrons during the interval. In his fifties, he had been delighted when Minnie had suggested the move, struggling as he was to run both the theatre and the wheelwright business.

He would have let the two Irish girls go, but Flore had offered to train them. They had responded well.

Business was good. The can-can was catching on. The McCann brothers always unearthed enough scandals to keep their banter 'fresh'—in both senses of the word—while Minnie's exotic dancing drew in the crowds from far and wide. Flore was relieved that no ringsters had yet come around to offer 'protection' from themselves. Perhaps Clodagh's and Deirdre's brothers had something to do with it.

The two girls were setting out glasses. From the laughter and gasps rising from the room, Flore knew that the interval was near.

In the old theatre, she had often worried about what Martial would think, discovering his ward dressed like a whore in a bar, but the recent events in France had changed everything. In the throes of a civil war, Paris was in shambles. According to the papers, Thiers had sworn to 'destroy socialism for a very long time', leaving the world aghast at the way he went about exterminating his own people.

There had been no letters. Flore had written to Jules and heard nothing. About to fall apart, all she could do was pray that Martial was alive somewhere . . . anywhere.

The bar soon filled with the smell of whisky, cigars and cheap perfume and the banter of customers retelling jokes. Clodagh and Deirdre by her side, Flore filled glasses, took orders and counted money. A bell rang. The mob scattered like a flock of starlings. The bar was quiet once again, glasses clinking in the backroom. Flore yawned. Sleep was eluding her, and food had lost all taste. Tomorrow, she would telegraph Jules again, make sure he had her new address. The lack of news was slowly killing her.

Martial's cab drew up outside the Wheel of Fortune, or so the cabbie said. All Martial could see was the sober black-and-white clapboard exterior of a coffin-maker whose Germanic name spread over the whole front of the building, proudly announcing Schlegelsteinberger —Undertakers.

'Well, I'll be damned.' The cabbie scratched his head. 'It was here last month.'

They scanned the street through the thinning mist, but this was the only building large enough to house both a bar and a wheelwright.

'I go and ask.' Martial jumped out and searched for a tell-tale notice. Surely, a theatre did not move without alerting its customers.

'Hallo.' A middle-aged carpenter in leather apron and Bismarck moustache came out. 'Are you looking for de Vheel?'

'Yes!' Martial cried out, the weight of the world slipping from his shoulders. 'Do you know where it is?'

'*Na ja,* they are not here anymore.'

Martial caught a glimpse of trestles where coffins were being varnished. To one side, a black hearse glimmered under a gaslight.

'They haf moved uptown. Hold on, I will gif you the address.' The man went to a table and scribbled a note. 'I cannot put the directions on my vall. It vould not look good for my business.'

'I understand. Thank you.' Martial gave the note to the cabbie, whose exaggerated sigh indicated that the fare had just doubled.

The theatre had moved but had kept the name, painted in garish letters over a tall narrow building.

Martial pushed the door open. An Oriental tune wrapped

itself around him and drew him up the stairs.

'I'm sorry, but you've missed half de show, sir,' a girl in white apron apologised.

His breath tightened. 'Is Flore here tonight?'

The girl raised an eyebrow. 'Sure. She's here every noight.' She added, 'Behoind the bar.'

Martial took several long breaths to quieten his heart and checked his appearance in a mirrored-door. He had lost weight, there were dark rings under his eyes, but he hoped Flore would like the neat moustache. He straightened the floppy bow tie, patted his coat and, dizzy with anticipation, followed the signs to the bar.

Flore handed Bill the night's takings and suggested he change the brand of whisky he favoured. It just wasn't selling. The new, more affluent crowd wanted something classier.

She stretched and rubbed her back. God, was she tired. How much longer could she go on like this?

At the edge of her vision, a man was hovering in the corridor. Resigned, Flore rested both hands on the bar. Another customer to entertain was the last thing she needed. She rubbed her face, and when she opened her hands, Martial was standing right in front of her.

She blinked and wondered if she was dreaming.

'I found you at last.' That voice.

The floor buckled under her feet.

'Flore? Flore, are you all right?' Martial ran around to her.

With a strangled cry, she threw herself into his arms. 'Martial! Yesu, I thought you were dead!' Laughing, crying, she kissed his cheeks, stroked his neck, ran her fingers over the rough cloth of his coat, pushed him away from her to have a better look and drew him close. 'You're so thin. Poor, poor darling, what have they done to you?'

She pushed him away again and said, her eyes full of reproach, 'I nearly *died* of worry. Why didn't you *write*?'

Martial wrapped his arms around her strong body and buried his face into her neck, inhaling great lungfuls of lavender and cold cigar smoke, surprised at how sturdy she was, how real.

The world swimming around him, he clung to the moment, the wonderful, magical moment he had been dreaming of forever.

'I wrote you, silly girl, of course I did. I even sent several telegrams.' His gaze lost in her large brown eyes, he understood what had happened. 'Your Gorgon of a landlady must have hidden them.'

Flore gabbled excitedly in Occitan. 'What? So the rumours that she was jilted right after her honeymoon must be true. Bitter old hex!' She gripped his sleeves, lest he should fly away. 'Oh. You're here. Here in New York at last!' She melted into him and gazed up in wonder. 'You came for me.'

'Amor . . .' Martial pressed his lips to hers. 'I thought the siege would never end.'

The way she dissolved into his kiss made everything possible—everything.

'Where are you taking me?' she whispered, breathless when at last they could bear to part.

He tilted his head. 'Wherever you want.'

'Away from here. Somewhere with big skies.'

'Ah. How about . . . San Francisco?'

Poking fun at her earlier self, Flore replied with a

mischievous grin, 'Cali-frounia, *hé*? It is not that far away. By train, it will only take only eighty-three hours.'

'With a few stops, perhaps, to visit a French utopian community?'

'Of course, and my cousin in Nevada.'

Martial drew her to him, overcome with bliss. Their souls, their bodies fused. As he kissed her, the contours of their limbs melted away; her warmth, her love spread into every cell and erased the horror of the past few months.

After a long moment, Martial took a few steps back, drunk with happiness.

Elegant, sober in a black and white dress against the gilded decor, Flore was more beautiful even than he remembered, and now at last, at long last, she was his.

A tune rose from the stage, slow and sensuous. Martial held out a hand. Graceful, Flore took it in hers and blushed when he placed his fingers on her waist. They took a few steps, then a few more. The music wrapped itself around them, seeped into their hearts and they waltzed, alone in the deserted café. Round and round they spun under the chandeliers, past the bar, the mahogany doors and along the brass balustrade. Faster and faster, lost in each other they danced into their new life, a beautiful life, reflected in the barroom mirrors to infinity.

Thank you for reading my book!
Before you go, do not forget to leave a review. This is huge for us humble authors and will ensure that Flore and Martial will waltz around the world of books for a very long time.

If you want to know more about the Vine Saga, subscribe to my newsletter and you will receive a 'hamper' with a prequel to the Sand-Vines, a recipe for my scrumptious pear and chocolate galette and links to 3 three songs from the Sand-Vines.
https://**www.michelecallard**.com/

NOTE FROM THE AUTHOR

The Sand Vines is a novel of historical fiction. Although I always strive for accuracy, I am, on the odd occasion, compelled to take some liberties with the dates for the sake of the story. Here are a few details if you want to know more.

The Folies Bergère were called the Folies Trévise at the time of our story and did not become the Folies Bergère until after the end of the Franco-Prussian War.

The boxing kangaroo did not hop onto the stage until 1897.

Mary Putnam was a real person. She studied in Paris, was part of the American Ambulance Service and shared her impressions of the siege with her parents in correspondence. A writer, educator and suffragist, she was a pioneer in women's health.

Icarian experiment in Texas. (Icaria & Icaria Speranza)

The Icarians were a French-based experiment established by Joseph Cabet in 1848 who established an egalitarian commune in Texas. The movement split several times due to functional disagreements. The last community of Icarians located near Corning, Iowa disbanded after 46 years and was one of the longest-lived non-religious communal-living experiments in the United States.

Monsieur Godin's foundry was taken over by the Prussians in 1870. He was incarcerated for three days. Started in 1856, the foundry was still owned by the workers in 1950 and eventually sold to Le Creuset. The building is now a *monument historique* and can be visited.

Empress Eugenie escaped on 4 September 1870 with Evans, her dentist, and chartered a yacht across the Channel at midnight. She spent most of the rest of her life in England.

Sainte Elma. Aliénor of Aquitaine's troubadours did invent saints to forge deeper bonds between the locals and their duchy, but Sainte Elma was not one of them. A lapsed Catholic, I may be, but I could not bring myself to disrespect the toes of a real saint.

OTHER BOOKS BY MICHÈLE CALLARD

The Bear And The Basque

The Wolf's Legacy

Born Under The Wrong Sun

Coming Soon, THE TEARS OF THE VINE,

Book 2 in The Vine Saga.

Published By Millefeuille Press

Printed in Great Britain
by Amazon

41378437R00233